a

whole

new

life

a whole new life

Betsy Thornton

THOMAS DUNNE BOOKS

ST. MARTIN'S MINOTAUR

NEW YORK

THOMAS DUNNE BOOKS.
An imprint of St. Martin's Press.

www.thomasdunnebooks.com
www.minotaurbooks.com

Library of Congress Cataloging-in-Publication Data

Thornton, Betsy.
    A whole new life / Betsy Thornton—1st ed.
        p.   cm.
    ISBN-13: 978-0-312-35759-7
    ISBN-10: 0-312-35759-1
    1. Women detectives—Arizona—Fiction.   I. Title.

PS3570.H6645 W47 2006
813'.54—dc22

                                                                2006040634

First Edition: November 2006

10   9   8   7   6   5   4   3   2   1

To E.J. and Tazzie

acknowledgments

I'd like to thank Tom Glass, once again for his weapons expertise, Hector Blaine for his help with the jail details and Deputy County Attorneys Gerry Till, Vince Festa, Doyle Johnston, and County Attorney Chris Roll for their advice on legal matters even when they didn't know they were giving it.

a

whole

new

life

prologue

THE MONSOONS COME to southern Arizona in July and August, dumping a good percentage of the rainfall for the year, often in quick violent thunderstorms that briefly turn the Cochise County high desert into a green oasis. The monsoons come from the south, from Mexico, flooding the washes and sweeping away cars whose drivers are foolish enough to cross the barriers put up to warn them.

One monsoon evening in late August, in the foothills of the Mule Mountains halfway between the newish, big, and booming town of Sierra Vista and the old, small, and arty town of Dudley, a woman walked out of a house. It was a nice house, not too big, built of cedar boards that had grayed enough to blend in with the surrounding landscape of mesquite, ocotillo, and desert willow. Red zinnias and yellow marigolds bloomed in metal-lined cedar boxes outside the front door.

Down the road a ways on one side was the Norton place, on the other, the Kleins', and beyond the Kleins' was the house being built by the man from Phoenix. The man from Phoenix rarely showed up, but he had a crew working there every day. They'd been there that morning, hammering, sawing, the cement mixer going full blast, until the drenching monsoon rains arrived at one thirty.

Now a light drizzle was falling, not enough to warrant an umbrella, more like a mist. The woman carried her purse and a bottle of spring water and wore loose black drawstring pants, a white T-shirt, and a wedding ring. She was in her forties, pretty, with long dark shiny hair held back with a pink terrycloth headband. It was early in the evening, but the dark clouds made it seem later. Somewhere thunder boomed and a long jagged streak of lightning lit up the sky.

The woman walked quickly to a blue Toyota Tercel and got in. She fastened her seat belt, then remembered: She hadn't taken her pill yet, her probiotics, special ones from some kind of soil organism, very popular now among the eternally fit. She took them twice a day, big white gelatin caps. She would tell anyone, whether she'd been asked or not, that she felt a million times better since she'd begun taking these very special probiotics.

She rummaged in her purse for the brightly labeled bottle, shook out a capsule, and swallowed it down with the spring water. Then she started the car. The clock on the dashboard lit up—almost seven. Damn. She was running so late, and being late made her anxious. Lots of things made her anxious—she needed to work on that. *So you're late,* she told herself, *so what? Calm down. You'll get there. Yoga breaths, yoga breaths.*

She pulled out of the driveway, turned right, and headed down the small road past the Kleins' and the skeleton of the new house. Her throat felt dry. At the end of the road where it met the highway, she stopped and gulped down some more of the spring water, then turned left. The highway started rising almost immediately into the mountains, and the rain came down harder. She turned on the wipers.

Clunk, swish, clunk, swish. Late, late. Her mouth was still dry. She finished off the water. *Calm down, calm down. Yoga breaths, yoga breaths.* She forced herself to slow down, the visibility badly obscured by the rain. Already the clock said seven twenty. Hours. This was going to take hours. A car came up suddenly from behind, its headlights hitting the rearview mirror and momentarily blinding her. Too close; she *hated* that. She accelerated just a little, but the car stayed right on her tail. It was so irritating; her skin felt hot, tingly. *Calm down.*

She knew the road by heart; at the beginning of the first straight stretch she slowed almost to a stop to let the car behind go by. Her face felt funny, kind of numb; her throat, too. The car passed, tires swishing like Velcro peeling off Velcro, then the red taillights faded into the dark. She accelerated again.

Her throat was so tight she could hardly swallow. Maybe getting a cold. She never got them, she was so healthy—she ought to be, she did everything right. A panic attack? *Relax.* Probably some kind of allergy; the pollen count would be incredibly high with all this rain.

The wipers hurried across the windshield, swish clunk, but her heart was going even faster. She tried to focus on the road as it steepened toward the tunnel that led into town, but now she couldn't even seem to *breathe.*

Something was really, definitely, terribly wrong. What she had to do, swish clunk, swish clunk, was get to town, *what was going on?* get help, the mountains so dark, the road slick, slick, slick: swish clunk, swish clunk, *hurry.* Suddenly she was six years old again, swinging on a wooden swing, her big brother on the one next to her, both of them going higher, higher—she reached for his hand—

Breathless, terrified at what was happening to her, she floored the accelerator, the car swerved, almost fishtailed, *God,* then she saw the red taillights of the car that had passed her going slow now on the final hill, too slow. She jammed on the brakes.

The blue Toyota Tercel hydroplaned, skimming the surface of the water, flying free, sailing off the road, over the mountainside, *hurry,* plunging down the steep bank, her purse flying against the windshield, the water bottle bouncing wildly. In a brief but seemingly eternal moment she reached for her brother's hand, missed; she'd done everything, *everything* wrong. She fell off the swing, then lost consciousness as the car hit the rocks below.

º   º   º

IT WAS AROUND nine when the man driving the gray Volvo turned off the rain-slick dark highway onto the smaller road that led to his house. He was in his late forties, with sandy hair thinning at the forehead, and he wore wire-rimmed glasses. He taught English out at the local college and had spent the past few hours in his office, getting things organized for the fall semester.

He passed the construction site of the house being built by the man from Phoenix, shadowy in the dark; passed the Kleins', lights on in their kitchen. He always read a poem to his first class, and earlier that day he'd driven all the way to Tucson, a three-hour round trip, just to get a copy of a certain poem. Probably could have found it online, but he'd wanted the book, tangible, real, though that wasn't what the poem celebrated.

> *So, with stiff walls about us, we*
> *Chose this more fragile boundary:*
> *Hills, where the light poplar, the firm oak,*
> *Loosen into a little smoke.*

Magical. In his office he'd marked those lines faintly in pencil, and now he couldn't get them out of his head. Would they get it, the class? Any of them? It was a junior college; they were working-class kids, which was fine with him, but they didn't have the background of kids from middle-class homes, and it was up to him to bridge that gap or it would widen even more, leaving them further and further behind in life.

Ah, even to see recognition dawning in the eyes of just one student was enough. He'd taught at an excellent college once, but he never would again: the vicious politics, the endless urgency to publish, and besides, there the students had all the answers. He could do so much more for these kids here—question them into understanding, get them to imagine whole new worlds they'd never dreamed of.

Okay, so he was a romantic. Keats was a romantic, too. What the hell was wrong with that?

As he pulled into the driveway, he noticed with relief that his wife's blue Toyota wasn't there. He sat in the car for a bit, at peace, letting the poem run through his mind. Finally he got out, breathing in the smell of the rain that still fell lightly, then passing the cedar boxes of red zinnias and yellow marigolds, picking up on the spicy scent of the marigolds. He unlocked the door and went inside.

Only one light on, a dim bulb in the lamp by the terra-cotta-colored wing chair, and the rest of the house was dark. He sat down in the wing chair and took off his wire-rimmed glasses, spotted with raindrops, and wiped them on his navy blue polo shirt. Then he was still, listening to the rain drip-dripping from the eaves, feeling the house settle around him, soft in its emptiness without his wife there, *the light poplar, the firm oak*—the phone rang, like some noisy intruder. Damn.

He got up, tripping on the edge of the rug in the semidark and banging his shin on the edge of the coffee table. Shit! He reached the phone on the third ring.

"Hello?" He rubbed his shin and made a face. "Oh. Hi, Anita. No, she's not here." His voice was extra polite. He didn't like Anita, and she didn't like him. Her voice was extra polite, too.

He said, "She's still at her yoga class."

Anita's voice shrilled at him. He held the phone away from his ear.

"No," he said. "Why should I be? They probably just went somewhere afterward for coffee or something. Sure, yeah. I'll do that. Soon as she gets home. Okay, okay. Yes. I'll write it down."

He hung up. Damn that pushy Anita. His peaceful mood was shot. He went into the kitchen, turning on lights. The refrigerator hummed to itself; somewhere outside, a cricket sang in counterpoint. Turquoise canisters that exactly matched the hand-painted tile on the counter stood in a neat line from large to small, containing nothing readily available to eat. He pulled open the door of the refrigerator, stared inside at vegetables that would have to be cooked, closed it, opened the back door, and stepped outside.

Ah. How good to be alone. He could smell the night, feel the solid presence of the mountains soaked with rain.

I am like the king of a rainy country.
Wealthy but helpless,
Young and ripe with death.

Who wrote that? Baudelaire! He had the poem somewhere in his office here at the house. It would be a great one to read to his students later on. He would find it, now. He went inside. Down the hallway to the front door was something strange. Lights, red and blue, flashing through the tall window by the front door onto the shiny floor.

What the hell? He went down the hall and peered out. A police car was in his driveway. And next to it another car. A sheriff's deputy was coming down the walk, followed by a woman with short dark hair. Coming to this house, his house. Almost immediately he heard knocking.

Annoyed, then all at once nervous, he stepped back, took a deep breath, turned the knob, and opened the door to a whole new life.

one

JACKSON WILLIAMS WAS sure right away that he knew how his wife had died. It was her tires. She never had them rotated. She never even looked at them. And just a week before her death he'd said to her, "Jenny, you need to do something about your front tires. The treads are pretty worn." But she hadn't. She'd driven over the Mule Mountain Pass on bare tires, in the rain, lost traction, swerved, gone over the edge, and crashed and died.

Now they were going to do an autopsy. Because he hadn't been able to get a straight answer from the medical examiner's office about when her body would be released, Ruth Norton, Jackson's neighbor and a good friend, had suggested a nondenominational memorial service, over in Dudley, followed by a reception at Ruth's house. Then there could be a quiet burial later when Jenny's body was released.

He'd gotten through the memorial service on automatic pilot, but after half an hour at the reception he'd felt he couldn't go on. So he'd slipped away, gone out back and up the rise where the mountain began at the end of Ruth's yard to a big rock, partially screened by a mesquite bush. There he sat now, polishing his wire-rimmed glasses and thinking about that autopsy.

It seemed so extreme. Couldn't they tell how Jenny had died without cutting her up? It seemed especially hard that it was *her* body they were cutting up; she had tended it so carefully, worked so hard at keeping it fit. And didn't they take out the organs when they did an autopsy? Took them out and weighed them: Jenny's liver, her pancreas, her kidneys, her little *heart.* Jackson swallowed, swallowed again. Something was caught in his throat, wouldn't go down.

He put the glasses back on, and Ruth's backyard below came into focus. The guests were milling around down there—some of his colleagues from the college, including Sid Hamblin, that envious ass, braying as usual; the Kleins, who were elderly neighbors; Jenny's friends from various exercise classes; her best friend, Anita, who had pointedly ignored him. There was Ruth, talking to Grace Dixon, Jenny's mom, under the apricot tree. Amazingly, he hadn't seen Grace in three years. Jenny had driven over to Green Valley, a retirement community near Tucson, to see her a couple of times a month, but she never took him along.

Ruth had looked nice at the memorial, elegant even, in some long dark gauzy dress that set off her reddish-brown curly hair with the streak of white that went back from her forehead. She never got dressed up except to substitute teach, and afterward she always changed into sweats and some old T-shirt the minute she got home.

His mind drifted. All those arguments he'd had with Jenny— arguments about what food to eat, how to decorate the house, arguments about what she called his lack of ambition, arguments about the time he spent away from home as well as about the times he was home but not doing what she wanted. He wished he'd kissed her, just once even, during those arguments, instead of always trying to have the last word.

An ant tickled across his hand and he shook it off. He'd kissed her when they took him to identify her body. Leaned down and kissed her forehead. Too late. It was like kissing some smooth, cool object, not like kissing a living person at all.

The voices grew louder from below. He heard laughter. Someone had brought wine. Maybe it would turn into an Irish wake. His own name drifted up, once, twice. Were they looking for him? He couldn't deal with them now. He shifted back on the rock, farther behind the mesquite bush. Coward. Then he heard a rustling behind him and turned his head, and there was Tyler, Ruth's eleven-year-old.

Tyler was okay. Tyler wasn't like the people below, Tyler was real. "Hey, sport," Jackson said.

"Hey." Tyler hunkered down beside him, stiff in dress khaki pants that were too big. He was a skinny kid still, though if he was anything like his two older brothers he would fill out in a couple of years. "What are you doing up here?"

"Best seat in the house." That sounded too flip. He cleared his throat. "Well . . . actually, it's hard for me to talk to people right now."

The skin at the corner of one of Tyler's eyes twitched, then twitched again. "Yeah," he said in a hushed voice. "And they're *laughing.*"

"People laugh for all kinds of reasons," said Jackson. "Like when they're nervous, for instance, or tired or angry or sometimes to keep from crying."

Tyler's eye twitched some more while he considered this. "I guess so," he said finally.

"What's this thing going on, by your eye?" asked Jackson.

Tyler shrugged. "Don't know." He looked a little peaked; the freckles on his nose stood out. "It's like there's a little bug under there that keeps jumping."

Tyler adored his two older brothers, Dan and Scott. Jackson tried to remember, how long had Dan been gone now? Over three years, he thought, but Scott had left only six weeks ago to spend time with his father before he went to college at U.C.L.A. Tyler must be lonely.

9

"When all this is over," said Jackson, "we'll play basketball again. *A lot*. I'm getting out of shape."

"*Cool,*" said Tyler.

THIS RECEPTION WILL *never be over,* thought Ruth Norton, coming out of her house with a glass of water for Jenny's mom, Grace Dixon. *Never, never.* Sid Hamblin, one of Jackson's colleagues from the college, was sitting on the outside stoop, blocking her way.

"Excuse me," she said.

"Sorry!" Sid jumped up, a big man in his forties with a black beard, wearing a black Hawaiian shirt printed with tiny green palm trees, his idea, apparently, of what one wore to a memorial service. He bowed and made a sweeping arc with his arm. "Ma*dame,*" he said.

She inched past him, trying not to make physical contact—he radiated a kind of jocularly aggressive sexuality that both annoyed her and made her nervous—went across the yard to Jenny's mom, handed her the water, then sat down beside her.

I am in purgatory, thought Ruth, sitting under the apricot tree with Mrs. Dixon. Someone had to look after her because Jackson was hopeless at that kind of thing and, in fact, had disappeared. Mrs. Dixon, an elderly widowed lady in poor health, had been driven here from Green Valley by a man who'd introduced himself as Henry, a gentleman friend. Jovial and outgoing, Henry was working the room, or rather, the yard.

Ruth wished she could go inside and take off her bra.

Mrs. Dixon sighed.

Ruth patted Mrs. Dixon's hand. "How are you doing? Okay?"

Behind pale blue tinted glasses, Mrs. Dixon looked at her without recognition. A white-haired old woman with some of Jenny's prettiness but faded, she was dressed in a black pantsuit with a silver and turquoise indian necklace. Her hands rested on a silver-headed wooden cane.

"It seems to me," said Mrs. Dixon, "they could have had better flowers for Jenny at the memorial than those weeds."

"Wildflowers," said Ruth gently. "Asters. Jenny loved to run. She would have seen them by the side of the road. They were kind of to evoke her memory."

And kind of to evoke Ruth's memory of her oldest son, Dan, moved out now for three years. Of her three children, Dan had always gotten along best with Jenny. He was a runner as well, and the two of them used to go for morning and evening runs together down the road to the highway and back, Jenny's hair pulled back in a ponytail, swinging, Dan loping along, almost a foot taller. Jenny had been different back then, giggly and fun—*looser*. The asters were to remind Ruth of that Jenny.

Ruth would have liked to explain, but none of this would mean anything to Mrs. Dixon.

Jenny's mom turned her head away from Ruth and stared at the long table where refreshments had been laid out. Flies buzzed around the plates of half-eaten food. Through Mrs. Dixon's eyes, Ruth saw what a bad job she'd done with it—*wasteful*, ordering platters of cold cuts from the Safeway even though so many people had brought casseroles, and not a salad in sight.

Mrs. Dixon sniffed and turned back toward Ruth to reach down for her purse. With a shock of guilt, Ruth saw she had tears in her eyes. For heaven's sake, how could she sit there feeling trapped, she, Ruth, of all people, with three boys who were all *alive*, all *healthy*? Mrs. Dixon had lost a *child*. No, *two*. She remembered that now—Jenny's brother was dead as well. All Grace Dixon's fretfulness and complaints were just to cover her pain. How could there be anything worse in this world than to lose a child? How could she bear it?

Where was Tyler?

She realized she hadn't seen him in a while. As Mrs. Dixon blew her nose, Ruth glanced around the yard, looked up the rise behind—and then she saw him, crouched by a big rock, talking to Jackson. She couldn't see all of Jackson, he was trying to hide behind some mesquite, but she recognized his pant leg. Tyler was safe. Thank goodness. Tyler and Jackson, both safe. She didn't begrudge them their escape, but she wished she could be up there with them. She turned back to Jenny's mom.

o   o   o

IT WAS TWO days after the memorial service. Eyes on the ground, under the load of his backpack, Tyler trudged down the road from the highway where the school bus had dropped him off, past the house being built by the man from Phoenix. The cement mixer was grinding away. Sometimes he would stop and watch, but today he didn't feel like it. He hated where he lived, out in the middle of nowhere at the edge of a mountain; just his house and two others. Not one single kid lived there but him.

Bees swarmed busily around the purple asters by the side of the road. What if they were *killer* bees? Killer bees were all over the state of Arizona. He heard it on the news every night. They attacked for no reason and stung you to death. He moved to the middle of the road, away from the bees.

As he passed the Kleins', old people, *boring,* he kicked at a convenient stone and it skittered away. At least there was Jackson. He rounded a little curve and then looked up, hoping Jackson would be home and might play basketball. His Volvo was there in front of the house along with a white Toyota and a sheriff's deputy's car. *A sheriff's deputy's car.*

Wow.

There was nobody in any of the cars. Tyler went to the gate and looked in. Past the cedar boxes of red zinnias and yellow marigolds, Jackson stood behind the screen door, looking out. Tyler waved, but Jackson shook his head, *no.* The little bug that lived by Tyler's eye jumped, jumped again. He trudged on. His mom's car wasn't in the driveway when he got to his house. She was substitute teaching, wouldn't be home probably till four thirty or so.

Tyler went inside to the kitchen, drank some milk from the half-gallon jug in the refrigerator, then made two peanut butter sandwiches. Now that his two brothers were gone from home, he played a lot more video games than he used to. He usually played Grand Theft Auto when he got home from school, unless Jackson was around and wanted to play basketball, but today he pulled up a chair to the window that had the best view of the front of Jackson's house.

Nothing was going on that he could see. Tyler finished the first sandwich and was starting on the second when a deputy in uniform came out of Jackson's house carrying a big box, followed by another uniform carrying Jackson's computer. Tyler watched as they put everything into the sheriff's deputy's car. One of them got in, and the other went back to the house. Then Jackson came out with a tall man who wasn't wearing a uniform. The tall man had a clipboard in his hand.

Tyler could see they were talking but couldn't hear what they were saying. The tall man gave the clipboard to Jackson, and Jackson looked at it for a while, then wrote on it. The deputy who'd gone back to the house came out again with another computer. Jenny's. They were taking both computers, and Jackson used his computer all the time. Why wasn't he stopping them?

THE NEXT EVENING Ruth, braless, in sweatpants and a faded red University of Arizona T-shirt that had belonged to Dan, walked over to Jackson's house carrying a bowl with what was left of the Million Dollar Chicken she'd made for dinner. Outside it was starting to cool down now, the sun low on the horizon, doves cooing in the cottonwoods. Jackson's gray Volvo was in the driveway. She went through the gate. Behind the screen, the front door was open.

"Jackson?" she called through the screen.

No answer. Through the mesh she could see the living room—the terra-cotta-colored wing chair, the beige couch, and the dark wood coffee table. Jackson must not have been spending time in the living room since Jenny's death: The tan and terra-cotta decorative pillows on the couch were placed in the same careful line that Jenny had fussed over so much when she was alive.

Ruth opened the screen door. "Jackson?" she called again. "It's me."

"Out back!"

Ruth walked through the living room to the kitchen with its hand-painted tiles. The outside door was open, and Jackson was sitting on the back stoop.

"What are you doing out there?" she asked him.

He didn't turn his head. "Listening to the doves."

Ruth smiled. "I brought you some Million Dollar Chicken," she said.

"Thanks."

"I'll put it in the fridge."

She opened the refrigerator door and placed the bowl inside, then came out to the stoop and sat down beside him. He was wearing jeans and his old short-sleeved blue plaid shirt with a rip in it that Jenny had always wanted him to get rid of. He looked so vulnerable. She touched him lightly on the shoulder.

"Ruth," he said, "when I went to identify her, they told me she was swerving all over the road, like she was drunk."

"Drunk." Ruth laughed. "*Jenny?*"

"Her tires were so bad. I should have just taken her car myself and gotten new ones. I feel so *guilty.*"

"Don't. It's not your fault. Jenny was a grown-up, responsible for her own tires."

"It's not just that. It's—" He stopped, shrugged.

"I know." Ruth sighed. "But that had nothing to do with her dying."

They sat in companionable silence. The cottonwoods rustled in a little breeze, and the doves cooed. Then Ruth said softly, "Tyler told me about the police coming. He said they took your computers and some other stuff."

"They had a search warrant."

"Why? For what?"

"I have no idea." Jackson rested his forehead on the palms of his hands. "There was a detective. I asked him, but he said it was just routine. Phil Jasper, he said his name was. One of the other cops had a camera. He went into the bedroom and took some pictures."

"The *bedroom*? Pictures of what?"

Jackson shook his head. "I couldn't see, from the living room."

"What else did they take?"

"A whole bunch of stuff. They had me read through this list, but nothing on it *meant* anything. Then I signed it. Even though Detective Jasper said it was just routine—to be honest, the whole thing scared me shitless." He paused. "The medicine cabinet. They took away half the stuff in the medicine cabinet. Old prescriptions, all Jenny's vitamins, that kind of thing."

"Jenny and her vitamins." Ruth sighed. "Maybe she was drunk on vitamins. Actually—" She paused. "There might be something to that. Hadn't she been taking some weird pills lately?"

"Probiotics."

"What's that?"

"Like the opposite of antibiotics. Don't ask me what's in them. She got them at the Co-op."

"Pennyroyal," said Ruth. "Remember a few years ago the Co-op was selling pennyroyal to bring on miscarriages and they found out it was really dangerous? Here's a thought. What if she was swerving because she was having a bad reaction to those whachamacallits—those probiotics?"

"God," said Jackson. "I never thought . . . that kind of stuff isn't regulated. Maybe in some people it builds up over time and poisons them. That would explain why they took everything in the medicine cabinet and why it's taking so long to release her body. Toxicology stuff. I think it's pretty complicated."

"Makes sense to me," said Ruth.

"Wow." Jackson whooshed out a sigh of relief. "That's what I love about you, Ruth, you always make me feel better."

"So stop worrying." Ruth took his hand and gave it a squeeze. "Everything will be okay, you'll see."

CREATIVE WRITING WAS Jackson's favorite class. It took place Tuesday and Thursday nights. At the first meeting he'd assigned them a topic for an in-class exercise, so he could get a feel for their writing right off the bat. No more than two paragraphs: What I Didn't Do on My Summer Vacation but if I Could Have I Would Have.

"Like *what*, Mr. Williams?"

"Like anything. Use your imagination," Jackson had said. "That's what this class is all about."

He'd been looking forward to this next class, after he'd sampled their work, but now, as some of them read their papers out loud, Jackson found himself distracted, thinking about the police coming. The search warrant. He'd felt sick, weak, when they left, but he'd gone over to Ruth's and played some basketball with Tyler, and that had helped. Then Ruth had come over, and he'd felt a whole lot better, but maybe, if he didn't hear from the police soon, he should call them, tell them about the probiotics.

Jackson wrenched his thoughts away from all that to focus on the students.

"I would have gone to the Tucson Mall," read Louisa, a beautiful, immaculate girl with long purple fingernails, "to the Gap. I would have tried on everything in the whole store that was pink. Pink camisole, pink shrunken polo shirt, pink khakis. Then I would have—"

Jackson glanced at the clock. "Oops." He raised his hand. "Hold it there, Louisa. I'm really sorry. We've run out of time. We'll finish up at the next class. Got some homework."

Groans.

"A character," he said. "Someone you know, maybe, or someone you make up. No more than two pages, double spaced." He stood and collected the writing samples.

"Oh," added Jackson as the class began to file out. "Carlos? Could I speak to you a minute?"

A gangly Hispanic kid with a shaved head and a wide humorous mouth stopped dead in his tracks and held up his arms defensively. "Hey, man, what'd I *do*?"

"Do?" said Jackson. "Do?" He held up Carlos's paper. He'd read it once, then twice, with rising exhilaration. "You wrote this."

What I didn't do on my summer vacation but if I could have I would have gone to the North Pole to see my dead nana. She lives there in an igloo under the Northern Lights with a sled pulled by tired penguins. When she was alive she made tamales wrapped in bitter words that froze my poor mother's heart. She was the Queen of Snow and Ice but if I could see her now, I would melt her in my arms and I would say, "Nana, sing and dance for me like you used to when I was a little boy before you were old."

"This is really good," said Jackson. "Alive."

Carlos smirked, ducking his head. "You think so, man?"

"I know so," said Jackson. "I'm looking forward to what you do next."

"Thanks, Mr. Williams. Thanks a lot." He paused, dancing on his feet. "Thought you'd give me a hard time."

"Why's that?"

"'Cause I wrote about the North Pole. This teacher I had in high school, he always said, you know, write about what you know."

"I think you did." Jackson paused. "What's your background? You do much writing in high school?"

"Naw." Carlos looked bemused. "The smart kids did that. My nana? She hardly spoke English. My mom didn't finish high school. I'm just a dumb Mexican."

"What does that mean? A dumb Mexican?"

"Aw, man, you know. What'd they ever write, Mexicans?"

"Are you kidding me? There are some fine Mexican writers. I'll lend you a couple of books."

"Hey, that'd be cool. Thanks." Carlos cocked his head. "You got kids, Mr. Williams?"

Stunned, for a moment Jackson didn't answer. "Yes," he said finally. "A daughter."

"She go to Buena High School?"

"No. She's back east, with her mother."

"Bet she misses you," said Carlos. "Bet you're a good dad."

Uncomfortable, Jackson involuntarily looked at his watch.

"Well, later, man," said Carlos.

"Later," said Jackson. "I'll bring you those books, next class," he called after him.

Jackson sat at his desk for a few minutes after Carlos left. A good dad. His daughter was twenty-one, and he hadn't seen her since she was three. It would have been easier to lie to Carlos, but that would have felt like a betrayal, both of his daughter and of Carlos. *Tired penguins.* If Carlos made good on his early promise, maybe he could get him published somewhere, some little magazine. He had a friend, Casey, in Chicago, a professor with a lot of connections to the literary scene. They e-mailed each other all the time. *My computer,* he thought. *When will I get it back?*

Suddenly anxious, he stood, gathered up his things, switched off the light, and left the classroom. The hall was dim, just the night-light. As he went through the door to the outside he saw Harry, the campus cop, standing in the parking lot, talking to another man whose face he couldn't see. They both looked over at him, and then the man moved away from Harry and walked toward Jackson down the pavement.

There was something familiar about him: a man Jackson's age, with blunt features in a ruddy face and a buzz cut, wearing jeans and a red pocket tee. Then Jackson realized who he was—the man who'd come to his door with the search warrant. Detective Jasper.

A prick of fire stung Jackson's chest, spread. What was Jasper doing here, at the college? Come to update him on the investigation? The detective came closer. He had a piece of paper in his hand.

"Detective Jasper," Jackson said. "This is a surprise. I was thinking about calling you." His voice sounded strange in his ears, false.

The detective's face reddened to a deeper shade. "Yeah? What about?"

"I was wondering when I'd get my computer back."

"Not for a while." Detective Jasper shifted his weight on the balls of his feet and looked at Jackson almost apologetically. He cleared his throat. "I'm here to serve you."

"Serve me?" he said blankly.

Like a waiter. No, a cop—to protect and to serve. Serve what? It was hard to think. The prick of fire was spreading all over Jackson's chest; his chest was burning up.

"Jackson Williams." The detective thrust the piece of paper at him, his voice suddenly formal. "I'm here to serve you with a warrant for your arrest, for the murder of your wife, Jenny Williams."

No. No. How could that be? *The murder of your wife, Jenny Williams?* Had he actually said that? Didn't you have to have evidence to accuse someone of a crime? Out of the corner of his eye, Jackson saw Harry looking at them—the campus cop whose daughter he had taught freshman English a couple of years ago, a daughter who had still lived at home with her mother and her *father*—then Harry turned and faded away into the dark.

What kind of evidence could they possibly have? How strange the parking lot looked under the dim lights, as if he'd never seen it before, but there was his car, his gray Volvo, ready to take him home; he wished he were there right now. He would be soon, because surely Detective Jasper would realize in a moment that he had made a mistake.

"You have the right to remain silent," the detective went on. "Anything you say can and will be used against you in a court of law. You have the right to an attorney—"

t w o

THIN HIGH CLOUDS streaked the morning sky. When she heard the cars pull in at Jackson's, Ruth put one of Dan's old sweaters on over her sweats and stumbled out the door. After Jackson's call from the jail last night asking her to see about his car and to go and hire a lawyer for him—he'd been adamant about which one, Stuart Ross, over in Dudley—she hadn't fallen asleep till some time after 4:00 A.M., and even though she'd showered an extra long time she was still a little groggy.

Sid Hamblin, smug, bearded, excessively large, was standing beside Jackson's Volvo wearing an ancient tweed jacket, jeans, and desert boots. He'd been the only one she'd been able to rouse at the college. Behind the Volvo was a tomato red Volkswagen bug, one of the new ones, with someone—Ruth couldn't see who it was—sitting behind the wheel.

"Thank you so much," she said to Sid.

"Thank God for Hide-a-Keys, huh?" he said. He slid the key to the

Volvo into a little black plastic box. "You want this back where I found it?"

"No, I'll take it," said Ruth.

She reached for the box, but Sid held it just a little too far away, wiggling it, teasing her. Ruth shivered in annoyance.

He smiled mockingly. "So how the hell did Jackson manage to go and leave his car in the college parking lot?"

"He went off with someone," said Ruth. There was no way she was going to tell him who—let him find out for himself. There would no doubt be something in the *Sierra Vista Review* this afternoon; he'd know soon enough.

"Please," she said. "I have a lot to do today. Could you just give me the key?"

He held the box aloft. "So where is Jackson now, that you couldn't just drive him over to get his car?"

The Volkswagen honked impatiently.

"It's complicated," said Ruth. "I don't feel like explaining right now. If you could just let me have the key—"

The Volkswagen honked again.

"Coming!" Sid shouted. He shoved the little black box at her and turned away.

Her grogginess replaced with an adrenaline rush from her confrontation with Sid—such a tiresome, immature person—Ruth hurried back home and went into her bedroom. What to wear to see the lawyer? She'd recognized his name as soon as Jackson said it. Stuart Ross. He'd won a big murder case over in Tucson several years ago, defending a homeless man accused of killing a city councilman. It had been on the news for days. Ruth didn't know a single person who'd been on the news for days. Why on earth, she wondered, had he moved to Dudley?

In the mirror, *oh, no,* she saw that during the time she'd been dealing with Sid her hair had dried with a cowlick on top. She changed into a pair of black pants, black went with everything, white weskit blouse, a spot up by the shoulder, double damn, and she wanted to look especially presentable. She pulled a red jacket from the back of the closet, found an old tortoiseshell headband to take care of the cowlick, dabbed on lipstick. Shoes, what shoes?

Her face felt flushed; beads of sweat were forming on her forehead. It wasn't even hot. The sooner she saw the lawyer and got him to straighten out this terrible mistake, the sooner Jackson would be out of jail. Out by this afternoon, she hoped, at the latest. She could invite Jackson to dinner tonight, make something special. What if Stuart Ross was really busy, a famous lawyer like that; what if he refused to take the case? She would have to be very persuasive, convince him. There was a time when she'd been good at dealing with people, *grown-ups,* but it seemed so long ago.

MARA HARVEY'S MOM had told her once that the first minute after a plane took off was the most likely time for it to crash. A month past her twenty-first birthday, Mara closed her eyes and gripped the armrest tightly, feeling the plane bump along fast, faster, then leave the ground and go sailing into the sky. In a way it was exhilarating, except nothing was holding it up now. She said a little prayer for world peace and began to count: one thousand one, one thousand two.

Mara wore tiny black sunglasses, three silver hoops in each ear, a rose tattoo where a vaccination scar might be, and her mother was dead. One thousand twelve. One thousand thirteen, one thousand fourteen, one thousand fifteen. *How could she be dead?* she thought for the millionth time. *How could she? Don't cry.* The man sitting next to her would see. She'd noticed how he'd glanced at her midriff, the line of skin that showed between her short pink T-shirt from H&M and her low-rider J. Crew khakis. It was the *style;* everyone dressed like that. He was a creep. One thousand thirty.

Her father wouldn't be creepy. God, what if he was? No, he was an English professor. And a poet—her mom had told her a long time ago he was a poet. All Mara remembered was a game, popping up from behind a chair in a kitchen and being swung high into the air by a man with long sandy hair who was laughing and saying, *Got you now!*

Her mom had liked him: She'd said, "I loved him, but I liked him, too. He was fun. He noticed things no one else did and got all excited about them."

"But, mom, why—"

"You can't live on poetry," she'd said abruptly and wouldn't talk about it anymore.

One thousand forty-five.

Her mother wouldn't be playing tennis, or going to her book club, or to the doctor, or to the hospital where they filled her full of poisons that made her sicker. She was dead; she'd died two years ago, and Mara didn't think about it as much as she used to, but when she did it was still like it just happened. Mara liked to think sometimes that her mother, without the distractions of her tennis games and her book club and her doctor, was hovering round her like a guardian angel, and that was why the plane hadn't crashed shortly after takeoff.

One thousand sixty.

Mara opened her eyes and looked out through the cloudy scratched porthole. Far below were tiny houses, ant cars on the roads, and, to her left, the silver ocean, glittering.

OVER IN DUDLEY, Stuart Ross, attorney at law, was thinking about how he probably wouldn't ever bother with marriage again, not that it didn't have its advantages. For one thing, you never had to go out on dates. He had a date tomorrow night with a waitress from the Quarter Moon Café. The café stayed open late, and he stopped by sometimes; they'd gotten into a couple of conversations, and he'd asked her out.

Her name was Dakota, and she was somewhere in her thirties, so not *too* young. She wasn't really a waitress, she'd pointed out, because her artwork hung all over the walls of the café: delicate princesses in pencil and soft gouache, asleep in desert landscapes or dead in transparent coffins under crescent moons. A little creepy, sure, but he hadn't asked her out for her artwork. Dakota waitressed in these low-cut ethnically embroidered tops that showed off her well-rounded breasts. Dating had its advantages, too. For one thing, it wasn't marriage.

He'd been married twice, first to an okay person really, but she was far away, remarried long ago, and he never saw his kid. Kid? Grown up now. His second marriage had been to an alcoholic woman, which made sense considering at the time he'd been supporting himself by picking up legal work in bars. It was amazing how many times he'd shown up in court half drunk and no one had noticed. Until everybody did.

A month of rehab, then years of A.A.

That was all behind him now.

The Dylan CD of *Blood on the Tracks* playing softly, Stuart sipped rich, well-sugared coffee from the Dudley Coffee Company and leaned back in the chair in his office on Main Street, just a short walk from the courthouse. He had a good view of the tourists ambling past the Western Art Gallery across the street, the jewelry stores, and the three antique shops.

Stuart hadn't had a drink for six years. He only went to A.A. once a month now and never ever had even the slightest urge to drink. When he first moved here from Tucson, he'd taken a job as a deputy public defender with the county, but he'd struck out on his own after a while and was now fully self-employed. Some private clients, but mostly contract work from the county for indigent defendants. All that was left now of his former renegade status was his empathy for the down-and-outs he usually represented, mostly substance abusers of some kind, and, of course, his ponytail.

He'd just come back from visiting a client at the jail, a kid charged with possession with intent to sell, a weak case that looked like it would go to diversion. That meant if the kid just kept his fucking nose clean for a year he'd end up free and clear with no felony record. So even if he never saw his own kid—he wasn't *proud* of that—maybe at least he was helping somebody else's.

He wasn't rich, but he wasn't poor, either; in fact, he was doing A-OK. And outside it was a nice fall day, sun-filled and a little breezy. Stewart relaxed, savoring the feeling of well-being while it lasted, because something bad could happen any minute. Truth be told, he was in a codependent relationship—rehab jargon—with his job, his moods rising and falling with the fates of his clients. A client he'd fought hard for could, at this very moment, be violating probation; the prosecutor could call and rescind the offer of diversion for the kid in jail . . .

Blocking these negative thoughts, Stuart burped loudly. Too much caffeine. Outside a woman strode determinedly down the narrow sidewalk toward his office, going out into the street to get by a clot of aging tourists in bright L.L. Bean and Eddie Bauer polo shirts and shorts displaying thin legs that were veined and knobby kneed. The woman looked employed, nice red jacket, black pants, and shoes with heels too high for walking comfortably. Somewhere in her forties, middle-aged. *Like me*, Stewart thought sadly, and belched again.

He opened the top drawer of the desk and popped three Tums Ultra, losing sight of the woman. Then almost immediately the bell in the outer office tinkled. Ellie, his office manager secretary, chosen for her good looks and air of impenetrable rectitude, was out on another extended coffee-cum-shopping break.

"Hello?" someone, a woman, called out.

Stuart crunched the Tums hurriedly, swallowed, wiped his lips with the back of his hand, and went out to the reception area. It was the woman in the red jacket. Bad lipstick, too pink or something; lines that softened rather than hardened her face; thick reddish-brown curly hair, a streak of white going back from the hairline, held in place with some sort of plastic headband. An odd smell filled the air, musty, medicinal, somehow familiar.

"Well, hi there," he said, in his Ben Matlock voice. Taller than she was by half a foot, he looked down at her.

Up close he could see that the jacket was from another era, shoulder pads like a football player's. Thrift store, maybe. Suddenly he realized what that smell was—mothballs.

"Are you Stuart Ross?" she asked.

"I sure am." Still Matlock.

"My name's Ruth Norton." She took a breath. "I'm here to see about hiring you, on behalf of my neighbor. He—"

"Hold on. It's better if we talk it over in my office." Stuart gestured at the coffeepot Ellie set up each morning, fronted by tiny foam cups and full of a dark burned liquid he never drank. "Coffee?"

"No, thank you."

"Good choice." Stuart smiled down magnanimously as he escorted her into his office.

She sat in the straight-backed, unforgiving client chair. Stuart closed the door and turned off the Dylan CD.

"*Blood on the Tracks.*" Ruth's voice cracked a little.

"A Dylan fan?"

"I'm more Joni Mitchell. But mostly all I've listened to for years is heavy metal."

Stuart raised his eyebrows. "Heavy metal?"

"I have three boys." She sniffed. With the door closed, the smell of mothballs was almost overpowering.

Stuart's nose twitched.

"I'm sorry," she said. "I need to get rid of this jacket. It—it—" She sneezed, stood, and slid it off her shoulders. Without it, she was instantly better-looking. "It *smells.*"

Stuart stood up gallantly. "Here." He removed the jacket from the back of the chair. "I'll put it on the coat-hanging thingie outside."

As he did so, he thought, *Three boys.* Drug case, maybe; a frazzled mom dragging out her old work clothes to see a lawyer, one of her kids busted for dealing something—he hoped for her sake just marijuana and not cocaine or methamphetamine. Except she'd said "neighbor," so maybe not a drug case after all.

"Here's how it works," said Stuart, getting down to business, when he got back to his chair. "First thing we discuss is a retainer, which varies depending on the nature of the case—"

"What happened is—" Ruth cut in.

He held up his hand. "Wait. I don't want any details. You haven't hired me yet, so there's no confidentiality. They could haul me into court as a witness."

"But how can you know if you'll take the case or not, if I don't tell you anything?" she said.

"We'll get to that. A retainer covers my expenses, and if it's not used up you get a portion back." Stuart's mellow lawyer voice swelled; he'd made this speech a million times, but he still kind of enjoyed it. "It's sort of a deposit, to show good faith, like when—"

"Could you listen just a minute?" Ruth exploded suddenly, startling Stuart into silence. "I'm sorry, but this is very stressful. I couldn't sleep last night worrying. Can't we cut to the chase? When they arrested Jackson—"

"Jackson?"

"Jackson Williams, my neighbor. They told him he'd been indicted. What does that mean exactly?"

"He's been formally charged."

Ruth shuddered. "I'm authorized up to ten thousand, okay? This damn headband. It's giving me a headache." She ripped it off her head and snapped it in two, right in front of him, then dropped the pieces onto the red industrial-grade carpet. *"There."*

Menopausal, thought Stuart. Maybe she would take off her shoes, throw them next—hopefully not at him.

"Jackson teaches English at Cochise College, the branch in Sierra Vista," Ruth went on. "He's a *good man.* He's charged with first degree murder—for killing his wife, Jenny." Her voice rose. "Mr. Ross, it's completely untrue, and I'm begging, *begging* you to take this case."

First degree murder. Momentarily stunned, Stuart heard the tinkle of the front door opening, hopefully Ellie returning. "Well, then"—he cleared his throat—"we'll go with the full ten thousand." He paused. "For starters."

"So you'll take the case?"

"Yes. I'll go see him at the jail today, make it official."

A teacher, he thought. That was an edge right there. Depending on circumstances, maybe not a plea; a trial, way way down the road, of course. *Easy there, Stuart,* he told himself, but years, years had gone by since he'd had a first degree murder case. He could almost taste it, him in his three-piece suit, arguing to a full jury at the pinnacle of the criminal justice system, the awesomeness of it, the majesty.

He opened the desk drawer for a cigarette, but he hadn't smoked for months, *years,* and there weren't any. A plea bargain lay on the desk in front of him; he shuffled it in a businesslike way.

"He needs to get out of jail, *right away,*" said Ruth urgently. "Can you do it by this afternoon?"

"Depends on his conditions of release."

"What does that *mean*?"

Stuart held up a finger and picked up the phone with his other hand. He punched in numbers. "Stuart Ross here. What's the bond on Jackson Williams?" He waited, staring down at a shard of tortoise-shell headband on the floor. *Get rid of her,* he thought, *as soon as possible.* "No kidding. Jesus Christ." He hung up and said to Ruth, "Five hundred thousand dollars."

Ruth blinked, then her eyes widened in shock.

"But," Stuart went on, "he'd only have to come up with ten percent. That's fifty thousand. He got it?"

"I—I don't see how."

"Then he won't be getting out this afternoon," Stuart said briskly. He glanced at Ruth's crestfallen face. "It's an absurd amount. I'll work on getting it lowered. Best thing for you to do now is go home."

ON MARA'S TWENTY-FIRST birthday, the man she knew as Dad handed her an envelope with her name on it in her mother's handwriting. She'd taken it up to her room, where a different, earlier Mara lived, a Mara-in-high-school with a mom and a dad. She'd dropped out of college to be with her mom, and now she didn't know exactly where grown-up Mara lived or what her plans were.

Biting her lip, Mara had turned the envelope over and over, and then she'd carefully slid a paper knife under the flap. When it was open, Mara touched her tongue to the flap where her mother had to have licked to seal it. *Stupid.*

Inside was a piece of paper with her real father's name and his address, a rural route address, which the note said was near Dudley, Arizona. "Ooh," said her best friend, Stacy, when Mara told her about it, "are you going to write him?"

Write him? All she'd done was write, answering all those sympathy cards, till her hand had felt paralyzed. Her whole being had felt paralyzed since her mother's death. She needed a jump start to get back into a life. Seeing her real father might do that, and she couldn't afford to take the chance he would say no to a meeting, so she'd gone online and Googled him, found the name of the college where he worked, and called the English department. "I used to be a student of his," she'd told the secretary, "and I want to send him a card." She read off the address. "Is it still current?" The woman told her it was.

Mara walked though the arrival gate in the Tucson airport and ducked into a restroom before she reached security. She shrugged off her backpack, took a makeup bag out of her purse, removed her sunglasses, and applied more blush and some lip gloss. She bent down and brushed her short streaked blond hair backward to give it body, then combed it in place with her fingers.

Mara was only four when her mom married Roy Harvey. Her real father had moved out west when she was three, and before he left, her mom had made him sign a paper giving up all parental rights so Roy could legally adopt her. Her real father—had he been upset, giving her up? Laughing, sandy-haired. *Got you now!* Did he ever think about her, wonder what she was like now, what she was doing?

A poet. Even though he hadn't been told she was coming and in fact hadn't seen her in eighteen years, she had this fantasy of someone superintuitive who, like destiny, would be waiting right here in the airport to meet her.

She put her sunglasses back on and left the restroom. Past security, groups of people in shorts and tank tops waited for the arriving passengers. Relatives, friends, *moms*. She scanned them from behind her sunglasses. There was no actual reason why he would be there, and he didn't even know what she looked like. She didn't know what he looked like, either, except his hair, but she thought she might recognize him anyway. Maybe he'd be holding a sign up with her name on it. Men of all ages glanced at Mara, who was unaware of them specifically but buoyed up by the attention. None of them held a sign.

She lingered, pretending to look through her purse, till the crowd dispersed. Then she bit her lip, wanting to cry. *Mara, you are a stupid idiot,* she told herself. *Shape up. Why would he be here? He doesn't even know you're coming.*

SIERRA VISTA IS the biggest town in Cochise County, but the courthouse is in Dudley, left over from the days before Sierra Vista even existed, when Dudley was the county seat and not just a tourist town. Ruth lived between the two, a little closer to Dudley, but she spent more time in Sierra Vista, where there were bigger grocery stores and a Wal-Mart and a Target. Dudley was quainter, more charming, and now that Scottie and Dan were both gone, Ruth tried to come to Dudley more, as part of some vague plan for a new life.

Not this kind of new life, though. More or less dismissed by the lawyer, Ruth strode down Main Street, carrying her smelly jacket, dodging tourists. Her feet hurt in the uncomfortable shoes. *Fifty thousand dollars for Jackson to get out of jail.* Good God. Jackson didn't have that kind of money. Ten thousand dollars for the lawyer's retainer had been a stretch; she didn't know the details of his financial situation, but she knew that much.

Ruth would have been happy to help, but all she had was two thousand three hundred and forty-two dollars in a savings account, down from almost four thousand due to the lack of substitute teaching jobs over the summer. If she didn't get called in to substitute soon it would be even less.

That lawyer—she couldn't believe she'd broken her headband right in front of him. It was just that he was so pompous and superior, she'd had to do something to get his attention. A ponytail. Who did he think he was kidding? She felt sad about the jacket; it had always worked for her back when she and her ex-husband, Owen, had run a business in Southern California. *Aha,* Owen used to say whenever she wore it, *you've got on your power jacket.* Now it was tainted. She would probably never wear it again.

Ahead of her was the Convention Center, a pale green Art Deco structure converted from the old Phelps Dodge company store, and to her left the Mining Museum and what everyone called the Grassy Park, where they set up booths from time to time and held arts and crafts festivals. She'd dragged Tyler to one this summer.

At the corner by the post office was the guy with the long gray beard, dressed in an orange satin robe and a pointed cap, who was, though Ruth had no way of knowing this, an occasional client of Stuart Ross. He was almost always there, tinkling a bell at the people who passed. The Magician, they called him. He supposedly lived in a cave in the hills above Dudley. Half the residents wanted to get rid of him, but the other half, led by an aging activist called Ken Dooley, thought he was colorful and wanted to keep him. Ken Dooley wrote letters about various causes to the local paper every week, and in a recent one he had defended the Magician, calling him the Fool on the Hill.

The Magician tinkled his bell at her now, muttering to himself. As she passed him she smelled sweat and patchouli oil. *Poor man,* she thought, *mentally ill.* She usually tried to smile at him nicely—*you're okay*— but today she was too upset.

She reached her old metallic green Honda Civic, opened the trunk, and threw in the red jacket. The car seat was hot. She opened the window, turned on the air-conditioning, and waited for the air to cool. The heat made her dizzy. As she started the Honda and backed out, it hit her full force: Jackson was in jail. *Dear God,* she prayed, though she hadn't gone to church in many years, *please get him out as soon as possible.*

ONCE MARA GOT off the freeway, at Benson, she pulled the rented white Toyota into a Circle K and looked again at the map she'd printed out from Mapquest. The route looked pretty straightforward, not like there were even choices. She got out of the car. It was amazingly hot. She considered pulling a pair of shorts out of her backpack and changing in the car, then decided not to.

Inside the Circle K, she bought a large diet Coke. She felt lonely. "If I just follow the road and don't turn off, it should get me to Dudley, right?" she asked the clerk, as much to make some human contact as anything else.

The clerk was young and chubby, with hair that was strangely frizzy, as if it had been burned. She looked past Mara's shoulder with great disdain. For a second Mara thought she wasn't going to answer.

"Yes," she said coldly, and dropped the change into Mara's outstretched hand so carelessly that Mara had to bend over and pick up three pennies.

Jeez, Mara thought as she left the store, *what did I do?* A black pickup truck with a shot muffler pulled in noisily next to her Toyota. The driver, a man in a cowboy hat, leaned out the window as she was opening the door.

"Hey there," he said. "How'd you get to be so damn good-lookin'?"

Mara got in hastily. Thank God she hadn't changed into shorts. Wasn't anyone around here normal? Music, she needed to have music. She dug around in the backpack and found her iPod and earphones. She scrolled down to a playlist, not really looking at it. Dashboard Confessional came on.

Places You Have Come to Fear the Most.

Mara mourned with the music, driving through a landscape as different from New York as the moon, all red dirt and scrubby-looking plants, dark blue mountains in the distance; then through a town, where giant trees shaded a little artificial lake with trailers huddled around it. Trailers everywhere—what if her father lived in a trailer? Well, she didn't care; she wasn't a *snob.*

Then another little town, Tombstone. She'd seen the movie, but the movie *Tombstone* didn't have all those little tourist stores on the outskirts. Mara briefly considered stopping to buy all her friends funny western gifts, like that paperweight a kid had brought to school in the fifth grade, a scorpion encased in a bubble of plastic.

Stacy, she thought. It would be so cool to call Stacy from Tombstone. She took off the earphones, found her cell, and punched it on. It chimed immediately. *Amazing.*

"Stace?" she said eagerly.

"It's Brian."

"Brian." Her voice deflated. "We said we weren't going to do this. Remember?"

"I just wanted to make sure you were okay."

"Like I'm some helpless little kid? I'm fine. Good-bye."

She punched off the phone. *Jesus Christ, Brian, get a clue.*

She didn't feel like calling Stacy anymore. Or listening to Dashboard Confessional. Emo. The lead singer sounded just like Brian, all wimpy and sorry for himself. She scrolled down to another playlist, then changed her mind. Brian walked around all day with *his* iPod playing, like a zombie, missing everything, not even there. She tossed the iPod onto the passenger seat.

On the other side of Tombstone, she drove a long straight stretch, and then the road went up into mountains and finally through a tunnel. She took the first turn after the tunnel; the sign said Tombstone Canyon. Tombstone after tombstone; it was creepy.

The canyon was leafy green, though, with funny-cute wooden houses built up on the hills on either side. Down a couple of miles at another Circle K, she lucked out and found a policeman parked there, young and dark and very nice. She showed him the address.

He laughed. "That's back the way you came," he said. "Halfway to Sierra Vista." He drew her a detailed map on the back of the computer printout.

FROM DUDLEY, RUTH drove all the way over to Sierra Vista for groceries. When she finally got home, work was going full blast at the construction site down the street. Muscular tanned men wearing red and blue bandannas and tank tops swarmed around the half-finished structure, a cement mixer grinding busily away. The elderly Kleins, who lived closest to it, had walked down to Ruth's one night to complain about the noise. But what could anyone do?

Inside her house, Ruth kicked off her uncomfortable shoes and put away the groceries: makings for chili, two half gallons of milk that Tyler would consume in two days, rice, salad stuff, potatoes, and a bar of fancy Swiss chocolate, half of which she ate standing up by the sink.

The house had been a pitiful shack when she and Owen had bought it that summer twelve years ago as a spur-of-the-moment investment, liking its isolated mountain setting. Then they'd flown in from L.A. with Dan and Scott on long weekends to work on the remodel, gutting the kitchen and bathroom, adding rooms. Owen had a genius for remodeling and decorating. When he was done, the kitchen, with its black ceramic tiles and stainless steel fixtures, looked like it came from a magazine.

They'd only just finished and had gotten back to L.A late at night when Owen had blurted out his confession. "I'm in love," he'd said, "with Tony." Tony? "Who the hell is she?" Ruth had said blankly, in shock, not really taking it in. "He's not a she," Owen had said.

The next morning, Ruth, eyes swollen from crying and pregnant with Tyler, had hustled Scott and Dan into the old Dodge van, piled with as much stuff as would fit, and driven all the way here without stopping. A place that was nowhere. The people, nobodies: *normal*.

Looking back, she was ashamed at her thinking. By now she'd long forgiven Owen. How could he help who he was? And he'd tried for so long.

All these years later, the black ceramic tiles always looked smudged, the stainless steel embossed with water marks that even steel wool, when she'd tried it a couple of times, wouldn't remove. The refrigerator was covered with children's drawings, announcements of sporting events and concerts, snapshots, and to-do lists from three years ago. Tyler had left his bowl on the table as usual, instead of rinsing it in the sink; there were little dried-up Cheerios stuck to the bottom.

One bowl instead of three. Dan liked Grape-Nuts; Scott, Cocoa Puffs. Ruth felt a pang. Her two big boys, gone, out in the world. And now Jackson in jail. *Fifty thousand dollars to get him out.* At least his lawyer had said he would get the bond lowered. So maybe Jackson could be out by tomorrow.

She put Tyler's bowl in the sink, filled it with water, and thought about sweeping the kitchen floor and mopping it. Instead she stared out the window at the backyard, where the cat that belonged to Mrs. Klein was stalking a hummingbird at the feeder hanging from the apricot tree. She opened the window to the hum of cicadas.

"Sssst—kitty, kitty. *Stop that!*"

Beyond the tree were the bones of a shed, half built by Jim, an elementary school teacher and former—what? "Boyfriend" sounded too, well, *young.* Gentleman caller? She had liked having him around all right, though more for the safety than any excitement, but the boys had hated him, called him Dumbo behind his back, because of his ears. Of course, it was wrong to judge people by appearance, but the more time she'd spent with Jim, the more she'd noticed his ears.

"It's not like your life is full of a lot of options, Ruth," he'd said in a snit when she broke it off.

God, it was hot. So hot. Her face flushed, and little beads of sweat gathered under her hair, on her forehead, trickled down between her breasts. Her body felt weak, her energy seeping out in the sweat. She sat down heavily in a kitchen chair. It wasn't any hotter than usual. What was wrong with her? The prelude to a heart attack? From the stress of dealing with that lawyer?

Then she remembered, a few nights ago, she'd woken up in a drenching sweat, suffocating under the covers. This morning, too, getting dressed.

No, oh *no.* Ruth stood up with a start. A *hot flash.* Wasn't she too young? *That's it for you, girl, you've had it.* Jim had been right, no more options. She hurried through the living room to the bathroom, youth draining away with every step, and looked in the mirror. She looked the same. She pulled the bathroom curtain aside for better light and froze.

Down the road a white Toyota was parked at Jackson's house, and a woman stood beside it. She couldn't see her clearly, but she was blond, maybe in her thirties, and pretty. You didn't dress the way she was dressed, in tight low-riding pants and a top that showed your midriff, if you weren't pretty and young, or at least young enough.

As Ruth watched, the young woman opened the gate to Jackson's house. Who was she? Lost, needing directions? Ruth left the bathroom, pulled on her old Reeboks, and went out the door and down the road. In the distance the cement mixer was still grinding busily.

"Hello?" she called as she reached the driveway. The woman, younger than she'd thought, twenties, not thirties, wearing tiny sunglasses, was knocking on the door of the aged wood-frame house. "No one's home."

"Oh." The young woman's shoulders slumped. "I saw the car." She nodded toward Jackson's old gray Volvo.

"Like I said, no one's home." Ruth paused. "Who are you looking for?"

"Jackson Williams." Her voice rose worriedly. "He lives here, doesn't he?"

"Yes." Curious, Ruth opened the gate and came into the yard. The flowers needed some tending to. She bent and deadheaded a couple of marigolds in the flower box. She tossed the corpses into the yard. "I'm Ruth Norton. I live next door. Are you one of his students?"

"No." The young woman smiled tentatively. "Do you know him very well?"

"Friends for years," said Ruth.

The young woman took off her sunglasses, and Ruth could see now she was really young, barely into her twenties if that. "I'm Mara." Her voice lilted up at the end of the word, hopefully.

"*Mara?*" Ruth knew the name from Jackson, but surely this wasn't— it couldn't be, how old would she be now? "Mara?" she said again. "Jackson's *daughter*?"

"He talked about me?"

"*Yes,*" said Ruth. "He always hoped he'd see you again one day."

Mara's face lit up.

A lizard with a blue throat did push-ups on the gray siding of Jackson's house as Ruth's heart broke for Jackson, his daughter finally coming to see him and he was sitting in the county jail accused of murdering his wife. This was terrible. What in the world was she going to tell the poor girl?

"Look," she said, "he won't be home today." She hesitated. The key to Jackson's house was under a rock by the door, but she didn't feel right about just letting Mara in. "Where did you come from?"

"New York."

"Ah. Well . . . it's hot out here. Why don't you come back to my house. There's iced tea, and we can talk." She paused. "All the way from New York. They don't feed you on planes anymore, do they. You must be hungry."

three

STUART SAT ON an orange plastic stackable chair at a wooden table in the windowless law library at the Cochise County jail. Heavy brown law books lined one wall, and the other three walls were cinder block painted pale green. He had to get the contract signed to make it official so he could call over to the county attorney's office and ask the prosecutor assigned to the case for the disclosure file.

The door opened; a man came in. The regulation orange-and-white-striped jumpsuit, white T-shirt, white socks, and neon orange plastic flip-flops that he wore robbed him of much of his identity, but he appeared to be in his forties and wore wire-rimmed glasses. The guard behind him stepped back outside and closed the door.

Stuart got up quickly. "Jackson Williams? Stuart Ross." His hand shot out, and Jackson took it.

Jackson's hand was cold as ice. "Thanks for coming, Mr. Ross."

"Stuart. Stuart's fine."

Stuart sat down again, and Jackson sat, too, across from him at the table. Behind the wire-rims, his eyes were green; straight nose, high fore-head, sandy brown hair thinning at the hairline. An English professor.

"Listen—" Jackson began.

"Wait." Stuart held up his hand. "I'm going with the full ten thousand that you authorized as a retainer. That covers hiring an investigator, among other things. You need to sign this contract." He reached down, pulled it out of his briefcase, and shoved it across. "That way I'm officially retained, so whatever you tell me is protected by client confidentiality."

Jackson signed and pushed the contract back over to Stuart. "I have no idea what this is all about. I mean, it's . . . it's crazy, *Kafkaesque*. Detective Jasper arrested me right after my class last night over at the college. He read me my rights, then brought me over here. He wouldn't tell me anything."

"What about you?" said Stuart alertly. "Did you tell Detective Jasper anything?"

"No. I said I wouldn't talk to him or anybody else until I had a lawyer."

"Good thinking," said Stuart fervently. "It was precisely the right thing to do."

"I'd already thought of you," Jackson said, "because of that big murder case you won in Tucson. The homeless man?"

"Robert Buehler," said Stuart casually, as if it were just another case and not the apex of his career. "Sure."

"Anyway"—Jackson sat up straight—"they let me call you, but you weren't home, so then I called my neighbor Ruth and asked her to go see you."

Stuart nodded.

"Mr. Ross, *Stuart*," Jackson said imploringly, "I need you to get me out of here *right away*. I'm a working man. I have a job to get back to. I have *classes*. There are kids waiting to be taught. This whole thing is a waste of everyone's time, and I can't do anything about it because I'm hog-tied, sitting here in jail. There's a big misunderstanding here. I didn't kill my wife."

"And you'll plead not guilty at the arraignment. Let's leave it at that," Stuart said. He was feeling a little rushed. He had a court appearance later on, and he'd told the guard to break in after half an hour. He leaned down and took a legal pad out of his briefcase. "I don't have the disclosure yet, so I can't fill you in on any details. You understand about disclosure?"

In spite of himself, Jackson gave a little smile. "Like in *My Cousin Vinny*. All the information that goes to the prosecutor gets disclosed to the defense."

"Right," said Stuart. "I thought we might chat a bit and you could give me kind of a general idea of what went down. We'll get into specifics after I've read through the disclosure."

"All right." Behind the glasses, Jackson's eyes clouded, and he blinked as if to clear his vision. "Jenny was driving over the Mule Mountain Pass, in the rain, and her car went over the edge. She was"— he took a breath—"*dead* before anyone got to her. The police told me the man in the car in front said she was swerving all over the road, like she was drunk. I know she wasn't drunk, she never drank. At first I thought it must have been a blowout or she hydroplaned—her treads were pretty thin."

That was it? There was nothing there. Stuart waited for him to say more. "And?" Stuart said after a while.

"Well, they don't arrest someone for murder because his wife's car has a blowout or it hydroplanes."

"No, they don't." Stuart leaned back in his chair and looked at Jackson. Another little silence grew; he let it go on for a while, then said, "I'm your lawyer, okay? You can be straight with me. Why do *you* think they arrested you?"

"I don't *know*. I don't even know why she was swerving on the road like she was. But, well"—Jackson shrugged—"I have a theory about that. She was taking these pills—probiotics."

"What the hell is that?"

"Like *anti*biotics, but *pro*." Jackson's voice was exasperated. "Some sort of herb and mineral mixture they sell at the Co-op that's supposed to cure everything. You know the kind of thing I mean, totally unregulated. She'd been taking them about a month. She might have been having an allergic reaction, or maybe the stuff builds up over time and affects the nervous system or something."

"That's a thought," Stuart said—but just a thought: There had to be a lot more to it than that or Jackson wouldn't have been indicted. "Look, I haven't seen the autopsy report yet. Everything's just speculation till then."

Hopefully the county attorney's office would send over the disclosure by late this afternoon and he could go over it thoroughly. *Shit, date with Dakota, mustn't forget that date with Dakota, tomorrow night.*

He leaned across the table. "I'll have a lot more questions for you later after I've read through the disclosure, and I'll be able to answer some of yours. I have one more for now, then we'll wrap it up for today. You and Jenny? Good marriage?"

"No," said Jackson.

What? Stuart stared at Jackson, taken aback. "How so?"

Jackson's face flushed. "It was my fault."

"Really." Stuart regarded his client with something approaching wonder. Could it be he was dealing with an honest man? "You fought a lot? Any, um, domestic violence convictions? That kind of thing?"

"No, it wasn't, you know, *overt* like that. We argued quietly, always very polite." He sighed. "And Jenny tried. She really tried so hard to make everything nice, like she was running a marathon of perfection or something, and the more she tried, the more . . . *tired* I got." His eyes met Stuart's. "I was exhausted."

For a second Stuart drifted back to the last plodding days of his first marriage. They reminded him of that cover on a Despair comic book, a couple in front of a TV. *Want to see if there's anything good on? Why bother?* He glanced at his watch again to stave off these thoughts and then looked across at Jackson with fellow feeling. "Marriage is a hard road," he said.

The guard was at the window in the door.

Stuart rose. "Unfortunately, our time's about up. I'll go over the dis-

41

closure and get back to you soon, and we won't be so rushed," he promised.

"But *wait.*" Jackson's hand went out toward Stuart. "What about getting me released?"

"At present there's a five-hundred-thousand-dollar bond."

Jackson nodded. "So they said, but—"

Stuart interrupted. "You'll need ten percent. You got fifty thousand?"

"Nowhere near, but"—his eyes were urgent—"surely you can get it lowered."

"Probably. It's a ridiculous amount for an employed professional like you. I'll file a motion to modify the conditions of your release, try for release on your own recognizance. If that doesn't work, at least we'll get the bond reduced way down. What's the most you can lay your hands on?"

"At this point I'll do anything, put up the house," said Jackson fervently. He shrugged. "Ten thousand?"

"That's ten percent of a hundred thousand. I should be able to get it down to that with no problem."

"*When?*"

"As soon after the arraignment as possible. Look, I know it's tough. Another thing." Stuart eyeballed Jackson to get his attention, because he found it paid to be as vehement as possible about this. "Don't talk to *anyone but me* about this case. No friendly cellmate, no sympathetic visitor from the outside, not that woman who you got to hire me, either. Ruth." Suddenly Stuart was struck by a thought. "How close a friend is she, anyway?"

"Ruth? We've been neighbors for years. We're good friends."

The guard came in. Stuart shook Jackson's hand and put a paternal hand on his shoulder. "Hang in there," he said.

STUART WALKED THROUGH the bleak lobby and out of the jail, hyped up with the rush of thoughts about the case, as he headed for his black pickup with the bumper sticker that said I AM NOT THE ENEMY. Thinking about the case, trying to separate the facts from the emotional elements. Facts? What facts? Why the hell had Jackson even been arrested, much less indicted? Oh, well. Clients often left out the important stuff, that first meeting. They didn't understand your role as a lawyer; they wanted you to *like* them.

Poor guy. Crummy marriage. Still, how many men killed their wives out of simple boredom? There were divorce courts for that. Of course there might be money involved, and then all bets would be off. Check it all out. Get George Maynard for his investigator; he was the best.

While Stuart had been inside, clouds had gathered over the mountains behind the complex of tan brick buildings that housed not only the jail but the sheriff's office and Justice Court One. He stood by the pickup sniffing the air. There was a hurricane brewing somewhere down in Mexico. Maybe it would rain.

He looked at his watch. Ten minutes to get to Division One over at the courthouse. An hour there, then back to his office, no, pick up the disclosure file, don't wait for them to send it over, then office, leave early, take it home with him. *Mustn't forget the date with Dakota tomorrow.*

TYLER LUNGED AND grabbed the ball from Mara. He bounced it down the cement drive away from the hoop, stood on his toes, aimed. The ball whooshed through the net.

"Three-pointer! Jason Terry scores again!" Tyler pranced, holding his arms aloft, his eleven-year-old elbows like little knobs. "And the crowd goes wild!"

Mara flopped down on the grass by the driveway. "Good shot," she said without rancor, kicking off her shoes and pulling the hair up off the nape of her neck to dry the sweat. Ruth had told her this most incredibly awful thing—her father had been arrested for killing his wife! Ruth said it was all a big mix-up, but before she could tell her more Tyler had come home from school, and now here she was playing basketball, but Ruth had said right off that her father was a really nice person, and they were sure to find out soon it was all a mistake.

Tyler flopped down beside her, using his ratty white T-shirt to wipe his face. The skin twitched once, twice, at the corner of one eye. He lay prone on his back on the cement, his Michael Jordan sneakers frayed and enormous. "You play pretty good," he said.

"I know, I know. For a girl."

"I didn't say that." His voice was hurt.

"Who's Jason Terry?"

"He played for the U. of A. The U. of A. always has one of the best basketball teams in the country. How come you've never seen your dad?"

"He's not my dad," said Mara carefully. "I've got a dad back in New York. He's my father."

"Where's your mom?"

"My mom died of cancer."

"Oh," said Tyler, skin twitching again. He closed his eyes tight to control it.

Mara noticed the twitch and, in some visceral way she couldn't have explained, felt a sudden kinship with Tyler. With his eyes closed, she could see his long eyelashes. He had beautiful skin, like a girl's.

"I have a dad." Tyler looked at the afterimage of the sky on his tightly closed eyelids. "He doesn't live with us."

"Oh," said Mara.

Tyler opened his eyes and, amazed at himself, said it: "Because he's gay."

He looked over at Mara to see her reaction. He talked about his dad a lot, but he hardly ever told anyone his dad was gay. He guessed he told Mara because she had all those earrings and a tattoo and was from New York.

"No kidding." Mara leaned her head back casually and looked up at the sky. There were some big clouds hovering over the mountains now. "Cool."

Tyler brightened. "Yeah. He lives in L.A. with his partner, Tony. They have this really great house with a swimming pool and everything. Me and Scott and Dan go see him every summer." His voice faltered. "I mean, we *did*."

"Scott and Dan?"

"They're my brothers. I'm the youngest, Scott's next—he goes to U.C.L.A.—and Dan's the oldest. He's twenty-two. He lives in Seattle with his girlfriend." He stole another glance at Mara. She looked even better than she had when his mother had introduced them; sweat had washed off all that makeup gunk. "You're going to stay with us, right?"

"Um-hum. For now, anyway."

"Take Dan's room. It's the best. Scott's is still full of his junk." He paused. The skin twitched again at one corner of his eye. "Mom didn't marry Dad when he was gay. He got gay later."

RUTH SAT IN her car parked at the mailbox out by the highway and unfolded the *Sierra Vista Review* to the front page. LOCAL ACTIVIST AC-CUSES BORDER PATROL OF HARASSMENT was the lead story.

In a letter to a Dudley weekly, Ken Dooley, fifty-three, stated that the border patrol had come on his land several times without permission to look for illegals and twice had threatened him. Dooley went on to say that as a proud citizen of the United States of America he owned a gun and was not afraid to use it against intruders. He added . . .

Ken Dooley, the local activist, who'd written the letter to the *Dudley Weekly* defending the Magician. Thanks to him, Jackson wasn't the lead story on the front page. Maybe there was nothing in the paper about Jackson at all. Then she saw it, bottom right. COCHISE COLLEGE PROFES-SOR CHARGED IN WIFE'S MURDER. Her stomach lurched.

The article was short, ending on the same page. She scanned it. Jack-son Williams, popular professor, was arrested last night, charged with the murder of his wife, Jenny, after an autopsy revealed traces of a lethal poison in her system. *A lethal poison.* Ruth felt a little nauseous. They didn't say what it was, didn't mention the probiotics. But surely, even unregulated items didn't contain any lethal poison. She read on. Blah, blah, blah. Just a recounting of the night Jenny died, nothing new, nothing to tell her why, why, *why,* they had arrested Jackson. Ruth rested her head on the steering wheel.

Everything was in the hands of that lawyer. She shoved the paper under the passenger seat and drove back down the road. Mara and Tyler were playing basketball. She parked at Jackson's, got out, and found the key under the rock by the planter. At some point Mara might want to see her father's house, and Ruth wanted to check it out first, maybe tidy up a little.

She opened the door and pocketed the key. The living room looked just as it always had when Jenny, an anxious housekeeper, was alive. Jenny used to complain that Jackson never helped with the housework, but he'd obviously been straightening up on a regular basis since her death. It was spooky, as if Jenny had come back from the dead to put things in order. Ruth fled to the kitchen.

Jackson had left a bag of sugar out. Tiny ants formed a long line from the counter down the cabinet and over to the door. Ruth stowed the sugar in the refrigerator and wiped away the ants with a moistened sponge. Then, to get her bearings, she sat down on a wooden chair at the farmer's table Jenny had refinished three years ago in a frenzy of activity after her miscarriage.

Mara had come to visit, something Jackson had always wanted, and now it was spoiled. Hopefully Jackson would be out tomorrow. It was so strange sitting here in Jenny's kitchen. Jenny had ground her coffee beans here at this table, before she'd stopped drinking anything but spring water. Ruth could almost smell those beans now, deeply, almost overwhelmingly fragrant.

She could see Jenny clearly, too: little, only five-three but perfectly proportioned, wearing sweats because she always seemed to have just come back from working out somewhere. They'd never really been close. Ruth always felt a little clunky with Jenny and her determined chin, her pert little nose, her eyebrows like soft wings over her brown inquisitive eyes. Inquisitive? More like relentless. Ruth had learned to field her questions, ever since that day . . . why think of that *now.* That was over two years ago. But she couldn't stop.

"I've been meaning to ask you this for so long," Jenny had said, the two of them cozy in this kitchen, drinking coffee.

"What?"

"Well, you know how the boys go see their father and his partner every summer?"

"Yes."

"You don't mind?"

"Mind?" Ruth laughed. She loved Owen as much as she ever had, once she'd gotten over the initial shock. "Why would I mind? I get a break and they have a great time. Owen's always been an excellent father, and he pays far more than he's required to for child support."

"Umm." Jenny nodded, eyes distracted. She leaned across the table. "But don't you *worry*?"

"Worry?"

"For heaven's sake." Jenny folded her hands at the table as if in prayer. "*You* know. A gay man and his partner." She lowered her voice almost to a whisper. "M-O-L-E-S-T-A-T-I-O-N."

It took a second for Ruth to decipher the spelling, and when she did, she felt a sudden pain, exactly as if someone had thrust a sharp knife deep into her abdomen.

"Of *course not*." Ruth's voice was thick with hurt. "What? If Owen were straight and I had daughters, does that mean he'd—" Tears came to her eyes. "If you knew him you'd never—" She stopped, overcome.

The kitchen hummed with tension. Clearly Jenny must hate her. She wanted to just get up, go, but she couldn't move.

"Ruth, oh *God*." Jenny stretched her hand tentatively toward Ruth, then withdrew it. "I didn't mean—I—" She fell silent as if collecting her thoughts. They sat, the two of them, paralyzed by good manners.

"Look," said Jenny finally, "My brother—I never tell people this, so please, please, don't say anything ever to Jackson, but, well, he was molested by a homosexual. When he was ten."

"Where's your brother now?" Ruth asked.

Jenny blinked as if startled, then bowed her head, hunching her shoulders like a battered child. "Dead."

Wait, thought Ruth, *wait a minute here, how did she get to be the victim while I'm the bad guy now?* "I think," she said, her voice like ice, "that *pedophiles* molest children, not *homosexuals.*"

"You never *know.*" Jenny's voice rose. "Children don't tell. They think it's all their fault." She looked a little demented. "It's so—so *irresponsible* to take chances. You've got three boys, and you should be more careful to protect them."

"How dare you," said Ruth. She stood up, looming over Jenny, wanting to—to *strangle* her. "How dare you accuse me of not taking good care of my boys." She began to shake. "I live for them."

Jenny had never even apolo—

Forget it.

Ruth came to in the present. She was actually shaking, just as she had that day with Jenny. It amazed her how this little incident still had the power to upset her. She'd never told anyone about it, just carried it around with her the way she might carry a bullet lodged in her flesh too close to a vital organ to remove.

Outside something rumbled, like a truck shifting gears. Thunder. Rain. Maybe it would rain tonight. They needed it. The desert always needed it.

A SPRINKLE OF rain fell on the tin roof of Stuart's little wooden house in Dudley and on the two chinaberry trees growing in the front yard. Inside Stuart lay stretched on his secondhand beige couch reading through the disclosure file on Jackson Williams. Newspapers were stacked everywhere, on the floor and on the enormous coffee table. On top of the coffee-table stack was the page from the *Arizona Star* with the *New York Times* Sunday crossword puzzle, stained with coffee and mostly completed. The TV was on, the evening news on Channel Four, but the sound was off, anchorwoman mouthing earnestly.

Xerox of Jenny Williams's driver's license. Pretty, dark haired, pert. Five foot three, one hundred and four pounds. Not an organ donor. A request for bloodwork on blood drawn from the defendant. That was odd. No reason for it that Stuart could see at this point.

What exactly had killed Jenny Williams? He skimmed the autopsy report. Respiratory failure and cardiac arrest, brought on by a lethal dose of aconite. Aconite. What the hell was that? Aha. Jackson had mentioned something about probiotic buildup—maybe aconite was one of the ingredients. If it was, then case closed and a possible lawsuit for wrongful arrest.

Check it out, sure, but he didn't think so. Detective Jasper, the primary on the case, was more workmanlike than inspired, but he wasn't stupid.

Stuart skimmed the evidence sheet. One of the items seized by the police during the search of the house was an amber plastic bottle of the prescription medicine variety from the Wal-Mart pharmacy in Sierra Vista, dated two years ago, labeled Jackson Williams, ampicillin capsules, but containing not ampicillin capsules but traces of aconite, the same deadly substance found in Jenny Williams's body.

So much for the probiotic buildup.

Was Jackson that stupid, to poison his wife, then leave the evidence right there in his own house instead of disposing of it? They'd photographed the amber plastic bottle from two angles before they'd collected it from under a bed. Under a bed? Stuart squinted at the less-than-stellar-quality photographs. The bottle was barely visible, shrouded in the folds of what Stuart thought was called a bed skirt. The defendant had meant to dispose of it, the prosecution could argue, but when he went to get it, it was gone. Frantic, maybe he even looked under the bed, but he didn't see it.

Nonsense, the defense would say; anyone could have planted it there to frame my client. What *was* aconite? Where did it come from? Was it readily available?

Nothing else on the evidence sheet seemed especially damning. A book, *Herbal Remedies,* probably something to do with that probiotic stuff. Right now he was still skimming, getting the gist of things. He turned pages of depositions. Man in the car behind who witnessed the accident; colleague of Jackson's from the college, Sid Hamblin, saying it was common knowledge the only reason Jenny and Jackson didn't divorce was because the house was in her name and Jackson never had a dime. *Common knowledge.* Stuart snorted. The most egregious form of hearsay.

But *was* the house in Jenny's name?

And here, Anita Selby, worked for a real estate agent, thought you should know, just had to blah, blah, blah, best friend of Jenny Williams, blah, blah, remembered a conversation, *more hearsay,* Jenny was pretty upset—exception to hearsay, *excited utterance?* he would have to fight that one—Jenny said to Anita, whoever the hell Anita was, gossipy busybody, Jenny said, really upset, two days before she died, *I'm thinking about leaving my husband. Anita, he'll kill me.*

It was raining harder outside now, the tin roof amplifying the sound. Stuart sat back, suddenly tired, letting the deposition fall to the floor. Enemies. He needed some good solid enemies of Jenny Williams. Lots of investigating to do. George Maynard. He reached for the phone and punched in George's number. George was the best as long as he stayed off the sauce.

MOST OF THE people who'd been at the A.A. meeting were gone when George Maynard stacked the last chair in the room at the Sierra Vista Methodist church where it had taken place. "See ya," he said to the quartet who were cleaning up the coffee fixings. He opened the door and stepped outside into the dark. It was raining and had been for a while. The tires of the cars on the road past the parking lot slick-slicked on the asphalt. He didn't mind the rain, though it made the sidewalk a little treacherous for a man in cowboy boots.

The air smelled fresh, newly washed, filling him with energy, making him want to be doing something significant, important, not like that piddley-ass feuding-neighbor civil case he'd just finished up for the attorney in Sierra Vista. It paid the same as anything else, but without the satisfaction. He'd almost reached his car, a yellow 'fifty-six Cadillac

Coupe de Ville, when he noticed the woman standing by her car a few feet away. Tight sexy clothes, blond hair straggly with the rain.

"It's so *wet*," she called to him gaily.

Then why didn't she get in her car? She'd been waiting for him, he'd bet on it. Kind of been giving him the eye at the meeting. Celine, was that her name? One week sober and shaky, *bad news*. She came a little closer. How to be kind and still get rid of her? His cell phone chimed. Ah. Rescue.

"Oops—got a call," he said. He opened his door, ducked inside, closed the door, and punched on the cell. "George Maynard here."

"Stuart Ross. Got a big case for you. Are you free?"

"Yep. What kind of case?"

"Stop by my office tomorrow, say ten thirty, and we'll talk about it."

"Not even a hint?"

"First degree murder," said Stuart.

George smiled.

I'M INNOCENT, THOUGHT Jackson. *How could this be happening to me?* It was after lights-out, and he was lying on the thin mattress on the slab suspended from the wall of his cell, the muscles in his arms and legs and back twitching from the state of alertness he'd felt obliged to maintain all day long.

His classes, what would happen to them? Sid Hamblin—Sid Hamblin would take over his creative writing class, he knew it. When Sid had offered one himself, no one had signed up, because Sid was notorious for using his classes as an audience—he took up half the hour talking about his personal experiences and imagined or inflated triumphs.

The release hearing. Did they let you out immediately afterward? Or did you have to wait? Ruth would have to pick him up. God, it could be a *week*. He had to get out of here. He had to save Carlos and the rest of the class from Sid Hamblin's rambling accounts of how he drove across the country when he was twenty-one.

The more he thought about the probiotic buildup, the more convinced he was that it was what had killed Jenny. Some people liked Jenny and some people didn't, but who could have hated her enough to poison her? Once they found out that was the cause, maybe he could get out even sooner.

Almost everything he had ever done had been innocent or at least without serious malice and, he saw now, stupid. He was an intelligent stupid man. He had married Jenny. But how could he have avoided that? The first time he saw her, six years ago, he'd was skiing with a friend at Mount Lemmon. He didn't ski well, and he'd been floundering at the bottom of a slope when this amazing butterfly-like creature had floated down a hill and alighted right in front of him.

He hadn't known many athletic women. She was so graceful, so sure of herself in her own body. A *mystery*. It had seemed like destiny, inevitable, but he should have left her there on the slope, a beautiful image. Instead he'd pursued the puzzle he saw as Jenny; God help him, he'd married her, and the more the puzzle of Jenny had unraveled, the less of Jenny there seemed to be.

Now, with Jenny dead, he could remember those first three years, when everything had been okay, better than okay. Jenny so graceful when he was a klutz, he so well read when she was poorly educated; they'd seemed to complete each other. Then at some point completion had turned to opposition, and after that it had been a long slide downhill. Why was it that in real life, unlike in poetry, everything was so often less, thought Jackson as he lay on a mattress on a slab in a cell, than it appeared on the surface?

four

THE MAGICIAN WALKED slowly down Main Street. It had rained all night on the town of Dudley and on the mountains surrounding it and on the mountain pass that led into it where Jenny Williams had lost her life. The rain had shrouded the mountains in white mists and filled the washes on the flats and the drainage ditches in town and made the wild fennel that grew in the ditches doubly aromatic.

Now it was morning, seven o'clock, and cloudy, but the rain had stopped, though it still dripped intermittently from the gutters and eaves of the wooden houses and turned the brick buildings on Main Street a rich deep red.

In his ancient black sneakers, the Magician walked—no, hobbled, because his bones were aching—down Main Street, past the galleries containing art meant to be hung in tidy middle-class living rooms. His long gray beard was sodden, and the damp intensified the stale, un-washed smell of his orange satin robe so much that even the Magician, usually oblivious, was aware of it. The tip of his cap pointed downward, and his shoulder ached from the weight of his leather bag.

He was carrying a rock, quite a beautiful one he'd found by his cave, streaked with quartz, turquoise, and malachite. Malachite, malachite, malachite. *Three times.* Nothing got through when you thought three times. My rock, my rock, my rock.

How his bones ached, and the small of his back, too. All the shops were still closed, but he stopped outside a restaurant, just a cubbyhole really, the Cornucopia, and looked at the pictures on the menu posted in the window. An orange, a banana, a pineapple, something green and fuzzy. His mouth watered. Kiwi, kiwi, kiwi.

Then out of the corner of his eye the Magician saw a police car, cruising slowly down by the Convention Center and headed his way. *Aha.* Malachite, malachite, malachite. He backed away from the restaurant, stepping off the damp sidewalk and into the narrow street. My rock, my rock, my rock.

The police car was coming closer. It made the gentle curve by the post office, passed over the striped crosswalk. The Magician raised his arm; the rock flew out of his hand and hit the window of the Cornucopia restaurant. Glass tinkled like wind chimes. The police car skidded to a stop, and Officer William Blackwood jumped out, hand on his gun holster.

"What the hell is going on here!"

The Magician raised his arms high over his head, as if invoking spirits from the four corners of the heavens. "It flew, Officer," he said. "It flew, it flew, my rock flew like a bird."

A bird, a bird, a bird.

AT 9:00 A.M., Stuart walked into his office, the Jackson Williams disclosure file under his arm. "See if you can run down Victor Robles," he said to Ellie. "He's the prosecutor on this homicide case."

"He already called. About ten minutes ago." She looked up from her desk, dark bangs flirting with her eyelashes. "He said welcome aboard."

"I'll call him right now."

"No. You don't have time. You've got an initial appearance at nine thirty over in J.P. Court. Your pro bono." She touched the corner of her mouth with a long red fingernail. "The Magician threw a rock through the window of the Cornucopia restaurant." She paused and added pointedly, "Ken Dooley's already called."

"Aw, shit," said Stuart disgustedly. "Don't tell me I have to deal with Ken, too."

The guy was a pain in the ass. What was with him, anyway? He'd appeared out of nowhere four months ago, and his rabble-rousing letters had quickly become a fixture in the *Dudley Weekly*. He needed to get a life.

Stuart went into his office and put the file down on his desk. He was all fired up to work on the case this morning, but what could you do. He came back out and took a tie from the pocket of the jacket he kept ready on the coat-hanging thingie. He put on the tie: orange and green swirls that didn't really work with his blue-and-white-striped shirt. Then he shrugged on the jacket and picked up his briefcase.

"It's the rain," he said to Ellie. "That cave must get pretty damp."

Ellie giggled. "And this woman's called you twice," she said. "Ruth Norton?"

Stuart frowned. The headband snapper. He was working for Jackson, not her. He needed to have George Maynard talk to her at some point since she might have useful information as a friend and neighbor, but she was way down the list from, say, Anita Selby the dear, dear friend. He hoped she wouldn't be one of those tangential people who called and called. "And?"

"She says it's important."

"If she calls again, tell her I'm in court and I'm really busy. Get her number and tell her I'll try to get back to her. George Maynard's supposed to be here at ten thirty. If I'm not back by then, get him to wait."

STUART PULLED INTO the last remaining parking spot in front of the J.P. court at the county complex on the outskirts of Dudley and got out, carrying his briefcase. Led by Ken Dooley, a line of picketers walked slowly up and down in front of steps leading up to the building. Ken wore dark sunglasses, a faded Hawaiian shirt, jeans, and sandals, his graying hair a boyish tangle of curls. The rest of the picketers were mostly women. *Ken's harem,* thought Stuart. Wearing a mélange of colorful third world clothing, they carried signs held aloft. ONE PERSON'S HOMELESS IS ANOTHER'S HOLY MAN! KEEP THE MAGIC IN OLD DUDLEY!! FREE THE MAGICIAN!!!

It wasn't that they were stupid. Under the Thai batiks, the Indian beaded blouses, were intelligent, often highly educated people, watchdogs for civil liberties. Stuart was glad to have them around, but in this case, they needed to understand that all the Magician, otherwise known as Ikan Danz, wanted right now was a nice dry jail cell.

"That's his lawyer," someone said.

"Hey, Stuart, you with us or against us?"

"I'm for the Magician," Stuart said, heading for the steps.

"Counselor Ross!" Ken detached himself from the group and loped over.

The air filled with a whiff of patchouli oil. Stuart stepped back, holding his briefcase protectively to his chest. The sun winked off Dooley's dark glasses; Stuart couldn't see his eyes.

"Got to get to court," Stuart said hurriedly.

"Just hold on a sec," Ken said. "I have someone here who wants to talk to you. It's worth your while." He turned and beckoned. "Come on, Frieda."

A woman with long dangly silver earrings walked over, wearing a dress embroidered by Guatemalan peasants. She was thin as a stork, her black hair streaked with gray and pulled back into a long braid.

"Mr. Ross?" she said. "I kind of look after the Magician." Her face was earnest, a helper, a do-gooder. "This isn't right. He's a free spirit. He doesn't belong behind bars."

"One man's prison is another man's palace," said Stuart.

"That's pretty glib, don't you think?" Frieda chided.

"Best I could come up with." Stuart moved to one side. He saw now that she was more intelligent than he'd thought, but he didn't want to get caught up in a dialogue out here.

"Wait!" She blocked his way, holding up an envelope. "I've raised the money to pay for the window he broke. Two hundred dollars."

"Wonderful. I'll tell that to the judge."

"Don't you want to take it?" she said.

"Give it to the owner of the Cornucopia for restitution. Got to go." Stuart turned, dodged Ken, and ran up the steps.

Inside it was calm. The cloudy light shone off the beige linoleum. The big clock on the wall said nine twenty-five. Two women were sitting on the long green vinyl couch in the lobby. One of them, red eyed, clutching a Kleenex, was an otherwise healthy-looking blonde in jeans and a leather vest. The other, Stuart knew: Chloe Newcombe, the victim advocate from the county attorney's office.

"Chloe," he said.

Chloe touched the shoulder of the other woman, murmuring a reassurance, then got up and came over. She was dark haired, wearing a black jacket, tan pants, and little heels.

Stuart cocked his head sardonically. "Slow day at the county attorney's?"

She bridled. "What's *that* supposed to mean?"

Stuart kept a straight face, but he always liked to see Chloe, liked to spar with her. Hell, he liked to spar with everybody when he had the time, but lots of people wouldn't engage. "Misdemeanor, criminal damage," he said. "No *statutory* victim here"—he looked around the lobby, eyes skimming off the blonde—"that *I* can see."

"She is a victim, you asshole. She's been traumatized. He broke her window. She's going to lose some business, and she was just getting by as it was. How would you like *your* window broken?"

Stuart raised his eyebrows and tsked-tsked. "Is that a threat?"

"Besides," Chloe went on, ignoring his remark, "there's restitution. Who's going to pay for it, the penniless holy man?"

"The women outside are going to pay for it. They've raised two hundred dollars. Tell her that, okay?" He paused, struck by a thought and also wanting to brag. "The Jackson Williams case? I got it."

Chloe's eyes widened. "Wow."

"Did you do the death notification to Jackson, by any chance?"

"None of your business."

"You did. I bet you did. You may fool everyone else, but you can't fool me, Chloe. How did he take it? Pretty *traumatized*, I bet. A *victim*. Hey, you know, you'd be a good witness—"

"Don't even try," said Chloe between her teeth. "We have confidentiality. If you depose me, Stuart, I'll kill you. I—"

"Counselor Ross?" The bailiff was at the door to the courtroom. He gestured with his head. "Got your client inside."

Refreshed by the encounter with Chloe, Stuart strode into the court.

Greatly diminished without his robes and pointed cap, the Magician a.k.a. Ikan Danz sat at the defense table, dressed in an orange-and-white-striped jumpsuit. Of indeterminate age, with his matted graying beard and pouchy eyes he looked like one of those winos who hang out on big-city streets near bars endlessly muttering to themselves.

"Kiwi, kiwi, kiwi."

Stuart sat down at the table next to him, standard reassuring hand going out. Touch, touch, touch; part of the job. Of course the guy was nuts, but was there a diagnosis? Couldn't find one in the file. "It's okay," he said.

"What, what, what."

"A week," said Stuart. "I think I can get you a week."

The Magician's rheumy eyes cleared. He smiled, revealing surprisingly white teeth. "That'd be *good*," he said.

UNDER HIS BLACK watch cap, Eminem sneered his beady-eyed stare from the black-and-white poster over Dan's bed as Mara dressed: khakis and a violet-colored shrunken rugby shirt. For a second she stared back at Marshall Mathers, mimicking his attitude, matching him sneer for sneer. Then she went into the kitchen.

Ruth stood by the sink, wearing silver beads and one of those long tunic tops everyone wore a few years ago, burgundy, and black pants, like she was going out to do something vaguely important. She had pretty hair, dark reddish brown, so thick and curly, with that cool streak of white. Was it natural? Looking at Ruth, she thought it probably was.

"You look nice," Mara said.

"Why, thank you." Ruth smiled self-consciously. "Tyler's long gone to school. Have some breakfast."

Mara spotted a box of Cheerios on the counter and picked it up. "I'll have some of these if that's okay," she said.

"Milk's in the fridge, bowls and spoons in the drainer," said Ruth.

Mara got a small yellow bowl, opened the refrigerator, and took out the milk. The kitchen was messy, cluttered with bits and pieces of Ruth's and Tyler's lives, a room where no one needed to stand on ceremony. The way the kitchen in Mara's mother's house had been, when she was alive. Now it was so empty. Most nights Mara and her dad just went out to eat.

"Tyler's got this little twitch," she said without thinking. "How come?"

Ruth sighed. "I don't know. It started after Jenny's accident."

Mara stood still, holding the milk carton. "You keep saying accident. How—how did she die exactly?"

"I told you, her car went over the side of the mountain, at the top of the pass going into Dudley."

"But"—Mara poured milk into the yellow bowl— "it doesn't make sense."

"I know it doesn't." Ruth sighed again. "I was hoping Jackson would call last night to tell me what happened with the lawyer, but he didn't. Look, it's complicated. When they did the autopsy, they found some kind of poison in Jenny's system. It was in the paper."

"Poison?" Mara picked up her spoon, realized she actually didn't want breakfast, and set it down. "So they think my father poisoned her,

and he's in jail," she said matter-of-factly. "Well, I mean, do you think maybe he did?"

"Of course not," said Ruth in a shocked voice. "I think it was these homeopathetic pills she was taking. Probiotics. They'll have to analyze them, I guess, to confirm it." She paused. "Jackson couldn't do something like that. Trust me. He's—oh—helpful, *kind*—just, I don't know, a very nice person."

"What about Jenny? Was *she* nice?"

"I've known—knew—Jenny for years, from being neighbors. Talking-over-the-fence kind of thing, except"—Ruth gave a forced little laugh—"there's no fence."

"Oh," said Mara.

"Anyway," said Ruth, rallying, "I've been trying to reach Stuart Ross—that's his lawyer—to find out what's going on."

"Is he a good lawyer?" Mara asked anxiously. "This is kind of in the sticks." She flushed. "I mean—"

"He came here from Tucson. He won a big murder case there. He's kind of arrogant—but I guess that's how they all are. I've called him three times, and he hasn't called back. I've got some shopping to do, then I'm thinking I'll go park myself in his office. You'll be okay here on your own?"

"Sure." Mara stretched and yawned to hide her disappointment that Ruth hadn't asked her to come along. "Is it okay if I take a shower?"

"Of course." Ruth stood, picked up her purse from the back of a chair, and extracted her car keys. "I'll get going, then."

"Do you think my father will be released soon, then? Like maybe today?"

"I hope so."

Ruth left the kitchen, and when Mara heard the front door close, she dumped her Cheerios in the garbage bag under the sink. Ruth hadn't answered her question when she asked if Jenny was nice. *Ruth hadn't liked Jenny.* That was interesting. Why not?

Mara left the kitchen and went down the hall and into Tyler's room. Jeans and T-shirts littered the floor, and he'd made his bed by pulling the red quilted spread up over everything without smoothing the lumps. Through the window she could see the back of her father's house: a wooden stoop leading to a door, and a little plot with two shriveled tomato plants. She sat down at Tyler's computer, under a big poster of a basketball player, and logged on to her e-mail account.

Hi, Stace, she wrote after deleting two e-mails from Brian without reading them, *I'm here in Arizona and I still haven't met my father. You're not going to believe this but HE'S IN JAIL FOR KILLING HIS WIFE. Don't worry, he didn't do it, but if you run into Dad DON'T SAY A WORD!!! Anyway he'll be getting out today so—*

She paused. Ruth hadn't sounded, well, totally sure about her father being released today. She deleted "today" and turned the "so" into "soon." Then she read over the e-mail and deleted the whole thing. She trusted Stacy, but she knew it would get out. *Hi, Stace,* she wrote, *I'll be seeing my father soon. It's hard to get to a computer here, so don't worry if you don't hear from me for a while.*

She hit Send and immediately felt lonely.

What if her father wasn't released right away? Could she go see him in jail? Were they allowed to have visitors? Yes, they were; she'd seen it in a thousand movies and TV shows, the wife or the girlfriend or the daughter of a prisoner falsely accused, sitting in front of a thick glass window visiting. Lots of times, at the end of the visit, the wife or the girlfriend or the daughter would put her hand up on the thick glass, and the innocent prisoner put his hand up, too, in the same place.

Two hands reaching, but not touching.

"MAN, THIS FEELS good," George Maynard said happily as he closed the file, tilted way back in the client chair, and swung his feet in their dusty tan cowboy boots up on the corner of Stuart's desk. "A first degree murder case." He raised his bushy gray eyebrows. "That friend of Jenny's—Anita Selby? One who quoted her as saying—what was it?— *he'll kill me?* They can use that? It's not that hearsay bullshit?"

"I'm not sure," Stuart said. "Might be excited utterance."

"I'll start with her, see if she's maybe holding a grudge against the husband. It'll give me an idea of Jenny's life, too."

"Good a place as any." Stuart tried not to look at the scuffed bottoms of George's boots digging into the finish of his secondhand but nevertheless cherrywood desk. George was a former cop out of Sierra Vista, in his late forties, big nosed, with a full head of gray hair, combining hard-edged energy and a laid-back attitude that had deceived more than one suspect.

"Not drinking now, are you, George?" Stuart asked casually.

"Nope. Been sober six months and three days. Got me a sponsor and all that good stuff." George's brown eyes twinkled. "I'm dancing."

"Dancing?"

George nodded. "Dancing my way across Cochise County. Takes the need to drink right out of me. In fact, they got a pretty good band, Friday nights, right outside Dudley at the Branding Iron. You ought to try it sometime. Not a bad way to meet the ladies."

"Sounds good." Stuart couldn't remember the last time he'd danced; maybe it had been five years ago with beautiful Erica, who'd given him the shaft. He paused. "Heard about you and Sandy. I'm sorry."

"Yeah. But what can you do? I put her through hell for years with my drinking." George shrugged nonchalantly, but his eyes veered away. "Another thing." He rubbed his hands together. "Got any idea how come they wanted bloodwork?"

"Nope. Wondered that myself," Stuart said.

"Well, I guess that's it for now. Stay in touch, okay?" George swung his legs down from the desk and stood up. "Have Ellie make me a copy of everything. I'll stop by and pick it up later."

He walked out of Stuart's office to the reception area, leaving behind a residue of free-floating energy and a whiff of tobacco.

"You be good now, Ellie," Stuart heard him say.

Ellie giggled like a little girl. "You, *too*, Mr. Maynard."

The dancing detective. Ellie never giggled like that around him. Stuart didn't know if George had ever actually cheated on Sandy, but there'd always been plenty of women who would have liked him to.

How did he do it, Stuart wondered as he opened a paper bag and took out a sandwich he'd gotten at the Dudley Coffee Company, early lunch. The sandwich had looked good when he'd pointed to it sitting under the glass bell, but now, when he bit into it, it tasted flat. He suspected it was tofu.

His phone rang.

"Stuart Ross here."

"Stuart, hey—Victor Robles."

The prosecutor in the Jackson Williams case, a good man; Stuart could work with him. "Well, what do you know," he said, imagining Victor, gray haired with a youthful face, sitting in his deceptively chaotic office. "Victor. My favorite prosecutor."

"So you got the Williams case." He laughed. "It'll be good to see you keeping busy for a change. Marilu said you came by and picked up the disclosure."

"Yep. Very interesting." Stuart chuckled; he and Victor, just two good guys having a good time. "I see you've gotten a statement from the infamous Anita Selby."

"Infamous?"

"She will be. I've got George Maynard on it." He paused. "So what's up?"

"I got some more disclosure, results on some bloodwork."

"Ah-a," Stuart said. "Noticed the request for bloodwork in the file. Couldn't figure out why."

"Guess you'll know soon enough, huh?"

"I'll send Ellie over to pick it up."

Stuart hung up. *Bloodwork, bloodwork.* Why? Still not a clue. Meanwhile, he needed to file a motion to modify conditions of release and get Jackson out of jail, and he had a plea bargain to do in court for one of his druggie kids at one thirty, then he had to run over to the Justice Court in Sierra Vista. No time to see Jackson today to go over the disclosure with him. It would be good to get Victor's new disclosure stuff now, mull over it on the lunch hour.

Don't forget, date with Dakota tonight.

Stuart got up and went into the outer office to ask Ellie to run over to the county attorney's, but she'd gone to lunch. Damn. He went back to his desk and opened the disclosure file on Jackson to reread the part about the bloodwork before he ran over to the county attorney's to pick up the file himself.

The front-door bell tinkled. *Son of a bitch.*

He went out, and there was that woman. The headband snapper.

RUTH HAD FOUND a parking space in the alley behind the post office and pulled down the rearview mirror to check her hair and, though she normally didn't use it, spritzed on a little hairspray, from a tiny bottle that had been rolling around on the car floor for months, a free gift from her hairstylist.

Why had she bothered? The lawyer with his ponytail was glaring at her, wearing the ugliest tie she'd ever seen.

"Look," he said, "this is a bad time. It's always a good idea to make an appointment," he added pointedly.

Ruth bridled. "And how do I do that? Your secretary, who seems completely bored, if not brain dead, says she has to check with you, and you're never here. I need to know when Jackson's getting out."

"I'm about to start on the release motion right now."

"About to?" Ruth's voice was aghast. "You haven't even started? You have ten thousand dollars of Jackson's money and that's the best you can do?"

"A retainer," the lawyer said in exasperation. "If it's not spent on the case, he gets it back. Anyway, the judge isn't going to consider a release motion till after the arraignment. That's not for a couple of days."

"A couple of *days?*" Ruth felt tired. She wanted to sit down, but then he would just loom over her.

"Longer," said the lawyer. "They'll set a date for the release hearing at the arraignment. It's the best anyone could do. Maybe you should go home and study up on our criminal justice system."

"Justice?" Ruth's eyes flashed. "Where's the justice in the criminal justice system if they've gone and arrested Jackson for no reason at all? What kind of case could they possibly have? I *assume* you're looking into it. Did Jackson tell you about the probiotics Jenny was taking?"

"Sorry." He held his arms wide, palms up. *So theatrical.* "I'm not at liberty to discuss what I talk about with a client."

"This release hearing," said Ruth. "Can I go to it?"

The lawyer looked at her thoughtfully for a second, then looked away as if she had been found wanting. "It's an open hearing, but I think it would be better for Jackson if you didn't."

Ruth whooshed out a breath. "They'll have the hearing, and then he'll be out. You promise?"

"It's out of my control. But yes, I don't see why not. He's a solid citizen, employed, no record and unlikely to flee. Probably a slam dunk, okay?"

Ruth backed away toward the door. "You have to let me know as soon as it happens. I'll need to pick him up. Your secretary has my number."

"Right. Sure. Fine." The lawyer looked weary standing there, defeated.

She put her hand on the knob and pushed the door open. It tinkled. "Another thing," she said.

"What?"

"At the hearing? I hope to God," she said between her teeth, "you don't plan to stand in front of a judge wearing that truly hideous tasteless tie."

RUTH LEFT THE lawyer's office, dodging tourists, passing the Western Art Gallery, then the Cornucopia restaurant, whose plate glass window had been replaced with brown cardboard, the menu written on the cardboard with red Magic Marker. It had been cloudy when she'd gone into the law office, but now the clouds had parted a bit and sun shone through. With Mara here, it was even more of a setback that Jackson wouldn't be getting out right away.

She was low on funds and needed to be subbing, but she hoped the schools wouldn't call the day Jackson was released, because if you ever said no, they didn't call as much. Still, Jackson was more important. The lawyer had said slam dunk. The charges were so absurd, she was sure that once he was out it would basically be over.

Only yesterday she'd walked this same way, coming back from that same office in humiliation. Today the Magician and his bell were gone from the corner by the post office. She turned at the corner, passing the iron bench where two old men sat, hanging out, on her way to where her car was parked in the little alley behind the post office.

Her face flushed. *No, not another hot flash. Ignore it.* At least it hadn't happened in the lawyer's office. It had gone well in the lawyer's office. She hadn't let him intimidate her at all.

As she approached her car, smiling, a rusty red pickup pulled in noisily beside it, radio blaring—Randy Travis, "Have a Nice Rest of Your Life." Ruth wasn't a country music fan unless you counted Lucinda Williams, but as Randy Travis's nasal voice drifted lazily up to the windows of the dusty library housed above the post office, it tinged the rain-damp alleyway with gentle sarcasm and filled her with exhilaration.

It had been a while since she'd felt so good. She'd been spending her life as a mom, protecting people, guarding her words, for so long she'd forgotten how it was to be anything else. Since Dan and then Scott had left home, she'd been in a kind of mourning for her boys, but years before that, with Owen's confession, a part of herself had been lost. Now, with that lawyer, it felt as though she'd rediscovered that part, the person she used to be, who wasn't afraid to say anything.

five

"He's a slum landlord, a complete cheap fucking bastard," said Dakota, tugging her gauzy white peasant blouse up a little higher on her round unfettered breasts, "and, *and* the worst part is the jerk blames *me*. For what? Living in his crummy house? The toilet overflows just about every fucking day, and how long, *how long* does he take to fix it? Three fucking weeks. In those three weeks, you know what happens? The fucking plumbing backs up even more and all this gunk comes out of the drain hole in the bathtub. Gross fucking black *gunk*, like you wouldn't believe. Well, you can imagine how much mold there is in that bathroom, probably by now the whole house—"

Stuart drifted, staring past Dakota at one of the many color photographs of the faraway French wine country that dotted the powdery brick walls of Chez Ramon. It helped to have interested parties at a release hearing, but that Ruth Norton woman, you never knew how she might act—barging into his office and accusing him of not doing his job.

"Well? Do you? Are you even *listening*?"

He started. Dakota had apparently asked him a question. "Sorry. I just spaced out for a second." He leaned across the table toward her solicitously. "Do I what?"

"Do you know that mold can actually kill you? I mean, it's super toxic. Especially for someone like me." She paused and coughed delicately, then took a sip of wine, her second glass. "I'm hyperallergic. They've done a lot of studies on mold now, and you wouldn't believe what they found out. It destroys your whole fucking *immune* system. That's why—"

If that Ruth Norton only knew, Stuart thought, tuning out Dakota again, *how much time I've spent on my druggie kids. Gotten them into the halfway house, hired them to work for me while they're there. I open my house to them, make big pots of spaghetti. Actually, I haven't done that in a while; maybe I should—*

"—a good case?"

Mentally, Stuart jumped at the word "case," flicking one hand as though a fly had lighted on it. Dakota was staring at him, She was pretty in the candlelight, the way her curly black hair was kind of messy and punk, but now her look had become vaguely hostile. He sensed he was once again screwing up a date.

"A good case? of course." He squared his shoulders. "Definitely."

"I knew it, I knew you'd say that! I'll sue the pants off that fucking bastard! My God, the pain and suffering alone! He looks like a bum, but everyone knows he's rich. Look at all the houses he owns. I can't pay you up front, but you can take it on a contingency basis. *You'll clean up.*"

"Whoa, whoa, whoa, whoa." A touch of veal piccata burned in Stuart's throat. "I'm a *criminal* lawyer. You want civil." He paused. "I can give you some names."

"But don't you learn how to do everything in law school?"

"To a degree, but then you specialize, you—"

Dakota cut in. "Does this mean you're not going to take my case?" Her black eyes flashed. "Why the hell not?"

"I can't. Actually, I'm really overloaded right now."

She blinked in disbelief. "You *jerk*. You're giving me the runaround, aren't you?"

"I—"

"And you know what else? I've poured my heart out to you and you haven't even been listening."

"I—"

"They're really true, those lawyer jokes. You lawyers are all alike, aren't you, just insensitive, money-grubbing *freaks*. That's *it*. I'm outta here." Dakota stood up, face tragic, tugging at the front of the peasant blouse. "I—I refuse to put up with any more of this—this gross insensitivity."

Stuart watched her go, stalking past the couples getting along just fine at the other tables, past the hostess in her black fishnet stockings and out the door. *How can she say I'm money-grubbing,* he argued automatically to the jury, *when I just turned down a case where I could really clean up?* He signaled to the waiter for the check and looked at his watch.

Eight fifteen. Early. And he hadn't had a chance yet to look at that new disclosure with the bloodwork; thanks to Ruth Norton, he hadn't gotten over to the county attorney's till nearly five. He'd go home, unplug the phone, stretch out on his couch with the file, and read it through, every word. What luck, the whole unbooked evening ahead of him.

JACKSON SAT ON a gray metal bench at one of the two gray metal tables, bolted to the floor like everything in the pod, staving off dread and pretending to read a tattered paperback copy of *One Hundred Years of Solitude,* a book he had read once before in his early twenties. In reality he was studying his surroundings, the inside of a jail.

The fluorescent lights were intense, glaring off the beige linoleum, the shiny pale green cinder-block walls, the glass window where the guards could look down and see what everyone was doing; Jackson the murderer and nine other inmates of the pod, racially balanced to avoid confrontations: five Anglos, five Hispanics.

At the end of Jackson's table, three inmates stared at the TV, limited to two undisturbing channels, twitching and batting at each other's arms as the animal channel explained how jellyfish mated.

"Go, jelly man, give it to her!"

"Hey, Jackson!"

Jackson looked up and saw Leroy from across the room, playing cards with three other inmates. Leroy grinned at him. His head was shaved, and he was missing several teeth.

"How come you're always reading, man?" Leroy said.

Jackson looked at him with interest. How had he lost his teeth? A fight? Or bad dentistry? And what was he in jail for? There was a fascinating story there, he was sure. " 'Cause I'm not playing cards," he said.

Leroy guffawed. "College professor," he explained to the other three guys.

For a moment all three looked at Jackson with awe. *"Cheez,"* one of them said. Then they went back to their cards.

In a way, thought Jackson, it was like a class. You walked in that first day and you didn't know who anyone was, but you made assumptions. Then they began to sort themselves out, and you found out that half the time your assumptions were wrong. Carlos. Look at Carlos with that wonderful paragraph. *Tamales wrapped in bitter words.* This was interesting, but he needed to get out, if only to see what Carlos wrote next.

He would get released, he was sure. Then he could straighten out everything. His lawyer was coming tomorrow with the disclosure, and then he would finally know what was going on.

Across from him the Mexican kid they called Paco stuck his thumb in his cheek and made little popping noises at regular intervals. He looked about fifteen, but he had to be older to be in here. He didn't speak any English.

"Gin, baby, gin!!"

"Mothafucka!"

The new guy, the old man with a gray beard they called the Magician, sat on the floor in lotus position. Jackson thought he was a mistake, because one of the guards had told him how it worked: racial balance, plus the nutcases got a pod to themselves. Putting a nutcase in with the regular inmates could be like a match to a powder keg. But so far so good. The Magician's eyes were closed, and his head rolled round and round as he muttered to himself.

"Hey, Leroy, man, you *palmed* that card!"

"Jelly *roll!*"

What if I don't get out? Jackson thought suddenly, and the dread he had been staving off rose to confront him. Suddenly he was tired. So tired. His back ached for his reading chair at home; his stomach gurgled around a leaden mass of thick half-cooked macaroni, fatty ground beef, and watery tomato sauce.

The Magician stood up and began to walk along the edge of the pod, stately and careful like a drunk on the way to the next bar. His mouth moved as he muttered to himself.

"Go, man, go *jellyfish*!!"

"*Chingatumadre!!*"

Someone whistled, shrill and painfully piercing.

The muscles in Jackson's neck seized up, sending rays of pain clear to the top of his head.

The Magician kept moving along the edge of the pod, coming closer, still muttering. Jackson could hear him now.

"Kiwi, kiwi, kiwi."

Totally nuts, poor guy.

Paco put his thumb in his cheek. Pop.

The Magician was only a couple of feet away now. Jackson stood up, keeping his place in the book with one finger; he thought he would go lie in his cell. The Magician was so close, Jackson could see the tangled knots in his long gray beard, little pits on his red nose. He looked straight at Jackson.

"Kiwi, kiwi, kiwi."

Embarrassed for the guy, Jackson wanted to look away, but he couldn't. The Magician had grabbed him by the eyeballs, like in those staring competitions you play as a kid. The Magician raised one skinny arm high and plopped it down on Jackson's shoulder.

As if restored by the touch, suddenly the Magician's eyes, like blue marbles in their pouches of flesh, turned remarkably clear. Sentient. Then he spoke, so softly only Jackson could hear.

"Jenny," he said. "Jenny, Jenny."

"FAVORITE *SIMPSONS* SHOW," Mara said to Tyler.

He giggled. "Kamp Krusty."

Ruth and Mara had gone to Sierra Vista that afternoon to return the rental car. Since Jackson wouldn't be getting out right away, Ruth decided Mara could just as well drive the Volvo. Then they'd cooked dinner together, and now Mara, Ruth, and Tyler sat in the living room on two growing-boy-battered old couches draped with colorful Mexican blankets, a Scrabble board on the low table between them.

"I have to admit," said Mara, "that's a good one."

Ruth put her K tile on the triple letter space next to the A in ELATE on the board, then put an A tile in front of the T. "Why, I do believe that's *thirty-four* points," she said. "And I'm out."

"Oh, *Mom*!!" said Tyler in disgust.

"Ka's not a word," said Mara.

"Oh?" Ruth smiled smugly. She'd been in a good mood all evening, singing out loud as she and Mara fixed the chili. Some country song, "Have a Nice Rest of Your Life." "You want to challenge?"

Mara glanced at Tyler. He had his hand over his mouth and was shaking his head back and forth. "No," she said.

"Smart move," said Ruth. "Not that it matters. I win, by ten points, plus whatever you guys have got. And now"—she stood up and stretched, smiling—"I think I'll go to bed and read. You guys can put the Scrabble stuff away."

"Ruth?" Mara said, a little anxiously.

"Yes?"

"I want to talk to you about something."

Smile gone, Ruth sat down next to her on the couch, looking concerned. "What?"

"I was thinking, when Jackson gets released the lawyer's going to call you to pick him up?"

"That's right."

Mara took a deep breath. "Let me do it."

"Pick up Jackson?" Her brow furrowed. "I don't know. He won't even know who you are." Seeing the stricken look on Mara's face, she added hurriedly, "I mean, just at first. I don't think—"

"I'll be driving the Volvo. I'll introduce myself. He'll be so surprised. *Please.* Please, please, please, I'm begging you. I really want to."

"He'll have just gotten out of jail."

"All the better," cried Mara. "Don't you see? It's my way of saying, *Even if you were in jail, I know you didn't do anything.*"

"Oh, why not," said Ruth, giving up. "Then if they call me to sub, I can go." She stood up. "Night-night." She left the room, humming.

Mara folded the board so all the tiles slid to the center, then poured them into the pouch and put everything into the Scrabble box. Tyler watched her.

"I want to go with you when you pick up Jackson," he said.

"You can't. You have school."

"What if I'm out when the lawyer calls?"

"I won't be at the house." She lowered her voice. "I'm going to the release hearing. I'll sit in the back. Jackson won't know who I am, but that way I'll recognize him when I pick him up."

"*Cool,*" said Tyler.

"That's me," said Mara. "The very coolest of the cool." She put on an Eminem sneer. "Super, ultra, mega cool, baby. And don't you forget it."

Tyler giggled. Mara glanced down the hall that led to Ruth's bedroom. "Come on, let's go in the kitchen," she said.

At the kitchen table in the semidark, Mara leaned toward Tyler conspiratorially. "Tell me about Jenny," she whispered. "Did you like her?"

"Dan liked her." One corner of Tyler's eye twitched, almost imperceptibly. "They used to run together all the time. She was different when she first moved here."

"What about you?" Mara studied Tyler's face in the dim light. His pupils were big as an owl's. "You didn't like her, did you?" She smiled at him reassuringly. "It's okay. You can tell me, I'm the cool one, remember?"

Tyler giggled again. "Well . . . she was kind of a drama queen."

Mara looked at Tyler suspiciously. "A drama queen? Where'd you get that expression?"

"Scottie called her that. And then later, Mom did, too."

"Do you even know what it means?"

"Like everything she did was really important, even if it wasn't. She lied, too. Scottie told me one time he'd caught her in a couple of lies. After you talked to her for a while"—Tyler flopped his head down on the table—"you just felt tired."

"What about Jackson?" Mara bit her lip. "Did *he* like Jenny?"

Tyler rolled his eyes. "He was stuck with her. I guess he had to." He glanced at the door to the living room, then scooted his chair close to Mara. "I know something," he whispered. "But you can't tell Mom."

"Why not?"

"She might go all funny."

"Right," said Mara. "I won't tell, unless you give me permission."

Tyler got up, closed the door to the living room, then came back and sat down. "There's this guy," he whispered. "He used to come to their house, when Jackson wasn't there."

"You mean, to see Jenny?"

Tyler nodded.

"So. Maybe he was a friend."

"Jenny had girlfriends, not *guys*. Besides, he was kind of sneaky, like he didn't want anyone to see him. He went in the back door—the only place you can see it is from my bedroom window."

"Humm," said Mara.

"And," said Tyler, "the last time I saw him go in was the same day Jenny died."

Mara looked at him in astonishment. "The day Jenny *died*?"

Tyler scooted his chair even closer. "I know who he is," he whispered. "*Randy.*"

"Randy who?"

"Dunno. *But you can't tell Mom.* Not yet."

"When can I?"

"When Jackson gets out. The guy might figure out I told and come after me. Mom can't protect me like Jackson would. He works right down the road at that house they're building. That's how I know his name. I heard one of the other guys talking to him."

STUART STRETCHED OUT on his couch. Aaah. He leaned over and took the lid off the coffee-to-go he'd bought at the Dudley Coffee Company on his way home. The aromatic fumes of Hawaiian Kona Dark Roast drifted up. Aaah. The red disclosure file along with the additional disclosure in plain manila lay on top of the stack of newspapers whose corners he had squared in the event—what had he been thinking?—that Dakota ended up coming home with him.

He just didn't have a way with women lately. They all seemed to be mad at him, not fake mad like Chloe, the victim advocate, when they were sparring, but really mad, like Dakota. And that Ruth Norton. What had he ever done to her except agree to represent her neighbor when she'd asked him to? So what was her problem?

Stuart picked up the new file and opened it. Results of some bloodwork. Blood given voluntarily by the defendant. He scanned through the jargon, looking for the point, and found near the bottom of the last page: *Physical examination of the blood given by the defendant rules him out as the donor of the sperm found in Jenny Williams's vagina.* Holy shit. Jenny had had sex the day she died, and not with her husband.

Well. Well, well, well. While Jackson sat at home, nursing his ennui, it looked like Jenny had found a way out of *her* boredom. A lover. Shit. Was this good? On one hand, it was—it brought in another suspect—

but on the other hand, it gave Jackson a motive. Nothing like a little in-fidelity to rouse murderous passions.

OVER IN SIERRA Vista, TV blaring from the living room of the one-bedroom apartment he'd moved into after his break with Sandy, George Maynard threw the remains of the Kentucky Colonel's fried chicken dinner, original, that he'd picked up on his way home from the A.A. meeting, into the trash can next to the sink. Then he went to the living room, opened the desk in the corner, and got a notebook and a ballpoint pen. He sat down on the ugly purple couch, muted the sound on the television, lit up a Marlboro, and read through the interview with Anita Selby for the third time. He'd practically memorized it al-ready, just wanted to be sure to catch any discrepancies when he talked to her.

Bam, bam.

Someone at the door. George got up, went to the front window, and drew back the curtain. Outside under the streetlight, parked behind the Coupe de Ville, was an old Volkswagen bug covered with silver stars in a field of midnight blue. Damn, it was her—that woman he'd danced with at the Branding Iron two Friday nights running, and the second Friday she'd come home with him. How had that happened? He hadn't even been drunk.

Bam, bam, louder this time.

George went back, closed the file, rested the cigarette in the ashtray, strode across the room, and opened the door. She stood outside, her dark curly hair tousled, wearing a gauzy white blouse that made the most of her breasts. George's eyes veered dutifully away from her breasts to her face. Her eyes were starry bright and pink-rimmed as if she'd been crying.

"Hello, Dakota," he said.

"Hi." She threw her head back dramatically, combing her fingers through her hair. "I am *so* stressed out. I just had the date from hell. *Un-believable.*" She paused. "Aren't you going to ask me in?"

"Look, this isn't a good time. I'm working." He improvised slightly. "Deadline I have to meet."

"Well, I drove all the way here from Dudley. You can damn well take a little break." She slipped past him into the apartment.

"God damn it, Dakota, I—"

Her lip trembled.

"Okay, okay. Calm down."

"This guy, he was just awful. He didn't listen to a word I said. All he wanted was—" She rolled her eyes meaningfully. "He was a lawyer, too. You'd think they would have better—" She stopped, and sniffed. "You've been *smoking.*"

George went to the ashtray and snubbed out the cigarette. "What lawyer is that?" he asked.

"The one on Main Street. Stuart Ross."

"Oh, man." He sat down heavily on the couch. "I'm working for him."

"What does that have to do with anything?" Dakota walked past the counter to the kitchen and gave a little scream. "Oh, my God, Kentucky Fried Chicken, do you have any idea how much poison is in that stuff?"

"Then I'll die happy," said George.

"Anyway," Dakota went on, "you don't have to worry, Stuart's out of my life. Forever. I plan to never see him again for as long as I live." She opened the fridge. "Don't you have any bottled water?"

"No," said George. He paused, struck by a thought. "Jenny Williams. You know her, by any chance?"

"I might have heard the name. Why?"

"You read the Sierra Vista paper?"

"That redneck Republican rag? No way. Just the *Dudley Weekly.* Ken Dooley's letters, mostly."

"Ken Dooley? Guy that hates the Border Patrol?"

"Who doesn't hate the Border Patrol?" said Dakota with a sneer in her voice. "You've read Ken's letters?"

"Never. They had an article about Dooley in the Sierra Vista paper. Let's get back to Jenny Williams—the woman whose car went over the edge at the Mule Mountain Pass a few weeks ago?"

"Actually"—Dakota came out of the kitchen and began to roam the living room, stopping at the CD player—"speaking of Ken, I think he said something about that."

"You mean, in a letter?"

"No." Dakota lowered her voice. "In private."

"No kidding." George perked up. "So what did he say?"

She scanned the rows of CDs. "All you have is this ancient country-western stuff," she said in disgust. "Randy Travis, Dwight Yoakum, George *S-T-R-A-I-G-H-T*."

"George Strait," said George, "the Frank Sinatra of country music."

"So?"

"I got the Eagles."

"Desperado, why don't you—" Dakota began to sing in a high, thin voice, then stopped. "Hey, that's *you.* A desperado. A fucking cowboy teddy bear desperado." She rolled her head around. "God. I am so fucking *tense.* I need a massage."

"What did Ken Dooley say about Jenny Williams?"

"I guess he knew her."

"How?"

"Who the hell knows? God, do you have to be a cop *all the time?*"

"Yep."

She walked over to the couch and sat down. "That's why you're so tense. You're a tense person, and I bet you don't even realize it. Totally out of tune with your body." She reached over, put her hand on his neck, and rubbed. "I *knew* it. Your neck muscles are like *iron.* You know what you need?"

"What?"

"A full-body massage," Dakota said firmly, moving in. "All the muscle groups."

"Oh, man," said George. He closed his eyes as her hands moved down his body. "Hey!" he protested. "That's not a muscle."

Dakota giggled. "Feels pretty tense, though."

"God damn it, Dakota."

She giggled again.

Wasn't there a time, George thought dimly, with a certain nostalgia, eons and eons ago in a world of senior proms and backseats of cars, when you never knew but you hoped—when you were always ready but you couldn't be sure—a time, eons and eons ago, when sex was an accomplishment? A victory?

six

IN THE COOL mist of the early morning, Jenny Williams ran fast, fast, down the aster-lined road from the highway. She wore a pink sweat-band, a gray sweatshirt, and gray athletic shorts, and her tanned legs were strong, well muscled. Her ponytail swung from side to side. Ruth could almost hear Jenny panting as she breathed in and out, in and out, could almost hear the thud of her running shoes as they hit the asphalt.

When Jenny reached her house, she would always stop, hands on her knees, head down for a moment, then she would reach up, pull off the sweatband, and free her hair from the ponytail. As Ruth stared down the road, Jenny faded into a blur of purple asters—she would never reach her house again. Ruth took a deep breath, a little trembly. She looked at her watch. Time to get Tyler up for school. She went back inside and closed the door.

o o o

It was air-conditioning cool in the law library at the jail, but tiny beads of sweat collected on Jackson's forehead as he read the results of the autopsy. He looked up at his lawyer.

Stuart sat across from him wearing a navy jacket with metal buttons, staring at the green cinder-block wall, not exactly twiddling his thumbs but looking as though he could be.

"Aconite?" Jackson said. "A lethal poison? Homeopathic remedies often have very small amounts of poison in them. I hope—"

"*Herbal Remedies,*" Stuart cut in. "They seized a book with that name."

"It was Jenny's," said Jackson. "I was about to say, I hope they analyzed the probiotics."

"Uh, you might want to keep reading," Stuart said.

Jackson went back to the red disclosure file. He read everything once except the part about the amber bottle under the bed containing traces of aconite. That he read twice. Then he looked up at Stuart.

"This is a mistake," he said. "There *were* ampicillin capsules in that bottle, just like the label says. I remember taking most of them. It was a couple of years ago when I got that ear infection. You can call my doctor and confirm it."

Stuart threw up his hands. "You're missing the point. Who cares what the label says?"

"But how can it be aconite?" Suddenly his throat was incredibly dry. "It has to be a mistake," he croaked. "I don't even know what aconite is!"

"I'll tell you what it is," said Stuart. "It's what killed Jenny. My guess is someone spiked those probiotics."

"If I didn't know the truth," Jackson said, "and I read this—I would actually think I'd done it." He stopped as the realization rushed over him. Jenny had been *murdered.* He'd never known anyone who was murdered; it was completely out of the realm of his experience, and now it had happened to his own wife. "I didn't do it, I swear." His windpipe felt obstructed. "And if I did, why the hell would I leave the stuff under the bed?"

"Exactly the point I would make," said Stuart.

"It's so obvious. Somebody's trying to frame me." *I've been framed.* Jackson shuddered. Hanging there in the empty air, the words sounded absurd, meaningless, the kind of thing some cartoon criminal might say. Except they were true. Who? Who would do something like that?

"I hear you," Stuart said. "I'll be checking out the aconite, who might have access to that kind of substance, and also who had access to your house."

Denial, Jackson thought. Being so sure about the probiotic stuff, that was all just a form of denial. He should have known they wouldn't have arrested him if the probiotics had been what had killed Jenny. But this—this was far worse than he could ever have imagined. *Who?*

"—doors?"

"What?" Jackson blinked. "Sorry. *I can't think.* I need to digest everything. What's the worst that can happen with this? I mean, what if I were convicted?" He swallowed. "Are we talking about the *death penalty* here?"

"No, no," said Stuart soothingly. "It's not the kind of thing that gets charged as a capital crime. There's a bunch of criteria that have to be met for the death penalty—torture, extreme cruelty, more than one victim, that kind of thing. The most you could get is natural life."

"Whoop dee doo, natural life." Jackson giggled involuntarily.

"Focus, okay?" Stuart said. "Even worst-case scenario, at trial, there's a good chance you'll get no more than twenty years."

Jackson took a deep breath.

"We were talking about who had access to your house," Stuart went on. "The way I see it, I could make a case for someone spiking Jenny's pills with the aconite, then planting the rest in that bottle and putting it under your bed. You lock your doors?"

"Yes. But we always hid a spare key under a rock in the planter by the door."

"Is that common knowledge?"

"I don't know. I suppose so. Anyway, it's an obvious place to look. *God*." He clenched his fists. "Who would hate Jenny that much? And that bottle under the bed—Who could hate *me* that much?"

"Well," Stuart cleared his throat, "we got a couple of people don't exactly like you, right here in the disclosure file. Anita Selby? Sid Hamblin?"

"Anita hates me, for sure."

"Why is that?"

"God knows. We used to get along okay, then she kind of turned on me." Jackson paused. "You know what? Anita called that night, just before they came to tell me about Jenny."

"Yeah?"

"*She* knew about the key. Maybe—No. She wouldn't kill *Jenny* just to torture me. She was her best friend. As for Sid, well, he's the biggest gossip at the college. He'd say anything about anyone if he thought it would get people's attention."

"Is it true, what he said?" Stuart asked. "The house is in Jenny's name?"

"No. It's in both our names. *See?*" Jackson added disgustedly. "Sid didn't know what he was talking about."

"Okay, Sid's irrelevant. I don't care about Sid right now. Jenny's death makes the house yours?"

"Yes."

"But if you had divorced, you could have lost the house in a settlement. The prosecution could argue that killing Jenny was a way to make sure you got the house."

Jackson's face reddened. "That's ridiculous."

"Calm down. Just covering all the bases. Enough of that, let's move along. I—"

"Wait," said Jackson. "There's something I wanted to tell you. Last night in the pod something really weird happened. There's this crazy man, they call him the Magician?"

"I know him." Stuart looked annoyed. "He's in *your* pod?"

"Yes." Jackson leaned across the table. "He acts like he's completely nuts, but he came up to me, put his hand on my shoulder, and said, 'Jenny, Jenny, Jenny,' *clear as a bell*."

Stuart shrugged. "Probably heard some of the other inmates talking about your case. He's what they call chronically mentally ill. He'll babble along and then out of the blue he has these moments of lucidity, but they don't *mean* anything. Look, we're running out of time, and I want to get to this." He reached into his briefcase and handed another file to Jackson. "A little more disclosure. Results of some bloodwork." He paused. "What it says is, Jenny had sex with someone the day she died."

"*What?*" Jackson left the folder lying where it was. "But we didn't—" Then he caught on. "*No.* Are they *sure*? Who with?"

"You tell me."

"I don't know. Jenny had a lover?" he said wonderingly. "I had no idea. Who the hell—" He gazed past Stuart's shoulder at the law books lined up on the wall, big brown books full of dry and useless information.

"The investigator's working on it," Stuart said.

"*Shit.* Then that's it. It had to be the *boyfriend*. Maybe she wanted to break it off. Or maybe he's married and she threatened to tell." He clutched his head, trying to imagine this new Jenny. He'd had no clue she even existed. "God damn it. I could find out, if I weren't stuck in this damn jail. *You will get me out of here, won't you?*"

Stuart nodded. "Seventy-thirty your favor I can get you out on your own recognizance. And if not, at least we'll have some bargaining power. I should be able to get the bond reduced to a hundred thousand with no problem."

GEORGE MAYNARD WAS parking his yellow Coupe de Ville in front of the Sierra Realty Company, a tidy little stucco building with a red tile roof in a newish upscale complex on the outskirts of Sierra Vista, when his cell phone chimed.

"George? Stuart here. You talked to Anita Selby yet?"

"Just about to. What's up?"

"Got some new disclosure." Stuart paused. "The bloodwork. Jenny

Williams had sexual relations the day she died. And not with her husband."

"Hot dog." George perked up considerably. "Then who?"

"I have no idea. Jackson doesn't, either, but maybe Anita does."

"Gotcha."

George punched off his cell, shrugged on his tan corduroy jacket, and slipped on a bolo tie with a silver and turquoise clasp, which he always kept at the ready in the glove compartment. *Sam Elliot*, he thought, favorite movie star of cowboy rednecks everywhere. *I'll play it Sam Elliot*. He smoothed the front of the jacket, patted the pocket with the little voice-activated tape recorder, and got out.

Behind the plate glass window of the realty company were listings of houses and acreage for sale in the area along with a big photograph of a woman with a tiny nose, Anita Selby, Realtor of the Month.

Sam Elliot opened the door and sauntered into the cool, no, downright chilly office. Six desks, three on each side, stretched to the back. They were crowded with homey paraphernalia—family photographs, flowers in tiny vases, fuzzy animals—but only two were occupied: one by a blond man in a plaid jacket; the other, the second desk on the left, by the Realtor of the Month, in her forties, big gold earrings gleaming, white hair either premature or the color stripped out.

"Miz Selby?" he said, advancing closer.

She got up right away, a little hustler, smiling a big warm smile for the man she thought, or at least hoped, was a buyer. She wore a bright red pantsuit and was way too thin. She came toward him, hand outstretched.

He took it and squeezed tight. She held on a couple of seconds longer than necessary. Little bony fingers.

"You must be the man who called about the Hereford property," she said brightly. "Mr. Jenkins?"

"No, ma'am." He looked down at her. "Name's George, George Maynard." He glanced at the man in the plaid jacket, obviously listening, and lowered his voice. "I'm an investigator for the attorney Stuart Ross."

She frowned, perplexed. "Ross . . . Stuart Ross . . . that lawyer in Dudley? Why—?"

"He's the attorney for Jackson Williams."

She looked shocked. "I don't have to—" She stopped, looking up at George. Her eyelashes fluttered, almost imperceptibly. "Do I?"

George smiled apologetically. "You kind of do. Sooner or later. There's a little place nearby we could have some lunch, talk."

"DAD?" SAID MARA, standing in Ruth's kitchen at the red wall phone while Ruth sat politely in the living room, leafing through a *Sunset* magazine she'd already read. She could hear Mara quite clearly. "Sorry about calling collect. My cell ran down."

Ruth stared down at a wooden deck that could be assembled in only one day with ordinary household tools.

"*Fine,*" said Mara. "How's Bully Boy?" She paused. "It's raining? Poor Bully. He loves his walks. It's hot here."

Ruth turned the page.

"No. I haven't even met him yet. Can you believe it? He's at a conference."

Why, why, thought Ruth, *do they never tell you?* They start off telling you, they come home from school and tell you every little detail, then it gets to be less and less, and one day they stop completely. Look at Dan and Scott; everything was always fine these days, all the time, when they called home.

"I know. I know I should have," Mara said. "But I'm twenty-one, Dad. I waitressed all summer, I saved the money. If I screw up, it's my own responsibility."

And now Tyler was getting that way, too.

Oh, stop worrying. Trying not to, Ruth turned another page and stared down at a recipe for shrimp and crab jambalaya. Ever since she'd stepped outside this morning and had her little vision of Jenny, she'd felt disoriented, not herself. *Jackson will be home soon,* she thought. *We'll have a party. I know his daughter now, which makes it even better.* So what was with this sense of dread, as if some terrible news, some disaster, lay just around the corner? *What are you worrying about? What?*

From the kitchen, she heard Mara saying her good-byes. Ruth closed the magazine and jammed on a perky smile.

GEORGE AND ANITA sat on red vinyl seats in the last booth at the back of the Lone Star Café and ordered from enormous menus with little cowboy boots designating the restaurant's specialties.

Anita glanced at George, then touched her perfect hair. Her gold earrings gleamed. "I'm feeling kind of nervous," she said. "I mean, you're not taping this, are you?"

"Taping this?" George raised his eyebrows. "Sure, I'm taping this, got a little microphone right here in my carnation."

"What carnation?"

George looked down at his lapel. "Oops, no carnation."

Anita laughed, self-conscious and a little giddy. She touched her perfect hair again. "So we're just going to talk and that's it?"

"You might be asked to give a deposition to the defense later, but there's a good chance we'll just talk and I'll be on my way. Look at it like this, everyone's entitled to a defense, right?"

Anita looked doubtful. "I guess so."

They paused as the waitress set down a burger and fries for George and a salad, ranch dressing on the side, for Anita. She took her fork and wiped it on her napkin.

George picked up his double burger, oozing bacon and cheese. "You and Jenny were pretty tight, huh?"

"She was my best friend." Anita poured two drops of dressing from the little cup onto her salad, then disconsolately speared a cherry tomato. "We met when she first got here, oh, five years or so ago. Jenny sold real estate for a while, too. I miss her so much."

She sighed and gave him a look, up from under her eyelashes, flirtatious in its helplessness. Coming on to him a little bit. Divorced, George would bet on it.

"We were on the phone almost every day," she went on, "and Fridays, I'd meet her after work at the Outback Bar and Grill."

"Sure," said George. "That place over in the foothills. Been there a few times myself, though not lately."

"It's nice there," said Anita a little defensively. "Everyone's friendly. We'd have a couple of drinks, you know, yak it up."

"I bet." George chuckled. "Couple of attractive women out on the town, leave hubby at home and have a blast, huh?"

For a second Anita looked uncertain. She touched her hair again. "I mean, you couldn't expect her to spend every second with her husband," she said. "She had to have her own life, too."

George held out his hands, palms up. "'*Course* she did."

"Let me backtrack a little," said Anita. "Jenny liked the atmosphere at the Outback, but she didn't really drink. I mean, she quit three years ago, when she got pregnant."

George paused, surprised, in the act of biting into his burger. "Pregnant?"

"She miscarried. It was so sad. The doctor said she should just forget about having children. But you know what? Jackson would never talk about it. *Never.* Jenny said it was like he was just *gone*. And after that, when her brother, Kevin, died, she told me Jackson wouldn't talk about that either."

"Her brother? Must have been pretty young. What'd he die from?"

"I'm not sure. I mean, I never met him, but"—Anita lowered her voice—"I think it was *drugs*."

George tsked-tsked and changed the subject. "You didn't like Jackson much, did you?"

"*I hated him.*" Anita's voice was unnaturally loud. An old man sitting at the counter looked over. Her face reddened. "I mean," she said, "because of the way he treated Jenny."

"No kidding," George said. "You ever see him hit her, be violent?"

"No, not *that*, but it's almost as bad to be ignored. Jenny was always *anxious* around him, like whatever she did wasn't going to be good enough. Finally she gave up, she just *wanted out*. She told me that. It's all in my statement. Didn't you read it?"

"Sure, but why don't you run through it again for me."

Anita rolled her eyes up. "The day before she died, Jenny called me and said she needed to talk. We went out to lunch, but then we just chatted, she didn't bring up anything special, and afterward we went and sat in the park—over by the old high school?"

George nodded understandingly. "Yes."

"That was when she told me. She said, 'I'm going to leave Jackson. I'm going to tell him tonight.' And then she started crying. 'Anita,' she said, 'I'm so scared. *He'll kill me.*'"

Word for word, thought George, the way she had told it in her statement. Word for word, nothing added the way it might be if you were really remembering. "Whew." He raised his eyebrows. "So, did she tell him she was going to leave him?"

"Of course she did." Anita stared at George as if he were crazy. "She had to have. That's what this is all about."

"Called you and told you after she broke the news, huh?"

"She didn't have to. It's obvious. Even before they found out she was poisoned, I knew she'd told Jackson and he'd killed her just like she said he would."

"I used to be a drinker," said George. "You know? Out in the bars till late, and when I was leaving, I'd always say to people—this was back when I was married"—he smiled—"'Gotta go, my wife's gonna kill me.'"

"*No,*" said Anita emphatically. She sat back in the booth a little farther away from George. "It wasn't *casual* like that. Anyway, when you look at the whole picture it doesn't even matter if she actually said it or not."

"Wait." George scratched his head. "You mean she didn't say it right out?"

"Weren't you listening? It was basically the gist of the whole conversation."

"The gist? So she didn't actually say he'd kill her?"

Anita looked exasperated. She picked up her diet Coke. "She *did* say that."

"She'd put up with him for a long time. Why'd she suddenly decide to leave, I wonder?"

"It wasn't sudden. It all accumulated till she'd finally had it." Anita tilted the foam cup up and crunched ice.

"Or maybe he'd had it. Gave her an ultimatum."

"Who? *Jackson?*"

"No. What's-his-name. The boyfriend."

"*What* boyfriend?"

"That miscarriage," George persisted, a shot in the dark. "Maybe the baby wasn't Jackson's. Maybe that's why he wouldn't talk about it."

Anita's gray eyes hardened. She spit her ice back into the cup and set it down.

"You bastard." She stood up, reaching into her purse, eyes like opaque marbles. "You think I was born yesterday? You butter me up, then move in for the kill! You're trying to smear her reputation! Isn't that what defense lawyers do? Blame the victim?" Anita's voice was like steel. "I've *cooperated,* but this is as far as I go. I'm talking to my lawyer!" She flung a twenty onto the table and stalked out.

George sat alone in the booth. Toughened up pretty good at the end, but there were other ways of finding out who Jenny Jackson's boyfriend was. What he did have made it clear Anita hated Jackson, which should make a dent in her credibility. He was sure she was lying, the way she told the story so precisely the same, lying to get even with Jackson. Any reason for that other than Jackson's treatment of Jenny?

WHEN TYLER GOT home from school, Jackson's Volvo was parked in front of the house, but his mom's car was gone and the house was empty. His mom and Mara must have gone somewhere together. The Safeway probably; they ate a lot more food now that Mara was here. Having Mara around was almost as good as having his brothers back, and in some ways better, but he wished he hadn't told her about seeing the man go into Jackson's house, because now, along with his eye twitching, he had a stomachache.

Mara got along so well with his mom; they talked and talked. What if she just blurted it out accidentally sometime before Jackson got home? Then his mom would get upset like she always did when she was worried and throw all these questions at him. Tyler opened the refrigerator. Out of milk; not much else there. He found an apple and ate half before throwing it in the trash, burying it deep so his mom wouldn't find it and get mad at him for wasting food.

Then he roamed the house, going from room to room, ending up in his bedroom. He looked out the window at Jackson's backyard. He could see the stoop where Jackson liked to sit in the evening. Sometimes he would look out his bedroom window and see Jackson sitting there and Jackson would wave at him. But that was when it was still evening, not as dark.

If someone was in Jackson's backyard in the dark and looked over at Tyler's bedroom window, they wouldn't be able to see in, would they? Tyler told himself it was probably okay, but his stomach ached, like someone had kicked him there hard. He wished Jackson were home right now, so he could talk to him. At least he hadn't told Mara *everything*.

"HELLO?"

When he heard her voice, so sweet, so familiar, Jackson's knees almost buckled under him. He turned his back to the guard down the hall and cupped his hand over the receiver. "Ruth," he said, "it's me, Jackson."

"Oh," she said. "Oh, my goodness. How *are* you?"

"Okay, but listen, I can't talk long. I talked to my lawyer. It wasn't the probiotics. It was something called aconite. They found traces of it in a bottle under the bed."

"*What?*"

"Someone must have planted it."

"*Who?*"

"I don't know. But I just found out Jenny was having an affair with someone. I don't know who. Ruth, before she died, can you try to remember everyone who went to the house when I wasn't there?"

"I don't—I can't—I'm still taking it in."

The guard was coming toward him down the hall.

"I have to go," said Jackson. "If you think of anything, tell my lawyer."

STUNNED, RUTH SAT on the beat-up couch in the living room still holding the phone. In a matter of minutes everything she had assumed about Jenny's death had shifted from faulty probiotics to deliberately planted poison and a mysterious lover. How creepy, how awful that Jenny had been having an affair. Why couldn't she just ask for a divorce? From Tyler's room Ruth could hear Mara and Tyler, giggling, goading each other on, playing some game on the computer probably. *Keep them out of this,* she thought. Children, innocent.

She could hardly remember the days before Jenny died, much less remember who had gone to Jackson's house. She'd been innocent, too. Like she'd been with her ex-husband, while he was falling in love with another man. An innocent, faithful dupe. But it wasn't the time to replay *that* movie.

She focused back to the present. The only person she could think of off-hand that she'd seen going to Jackson's was Jenny's friend Anita Selby, and she had nothing to do with anything.

AFTER HE TALKED to Ruth, Jackson didn't go sit in the pod but lay back on the cot in his cell, staring up at the ceiling. His stomach rumbled from the canned lima beans they'd served at dinner. He wished it were lights-out. They were so bright, and other than a little crack on the right-hand corner of the ceiling, which was blurred because he wasn't wearing his glasses, there was nothing to see. Sensory deprivation.

Natural life. That meant *as long as you lived,* there would be no hope of ever getting out. But Stuart had said twenty years, hadn't he? He'd get out in his sixties.

Jackson closed his eyes against the ceiling, with its meaningless crack in the right-hand corner. He fell asleep then and dreamed a nervous dream of Jenny, in her workout clothes, jogging toward him, while he waited at the house where they lived. She was trying to tell him something, her mouth was moving, but he couldn't hear. "What?" he said, and saw with horror as she came close how fat she'd become; mounds of fat on her arms, her legs, her chin and cheeks, even her round brown eyes swollen with it. *She'd had a lover, and he hadn't even known it.*

She looked at him balefully. "Guess I'm important *now,*" she said.

Jackson opened his eyes with a start, staring straight up, seeing only the ceiling with its meaningless crack. He closed his eyes again, the insides of his eyelids burning red from the constant light.

seven

"C-R-two-zero-zero-zero-five-zero-six-seven-one. State versus Jackson Williams!"

Mara gave a little gasp. Sitting near the back of the crowded courtroom, behind what looked like an entire extended family of Mexican nationals, she craned her neck to see better. Eight prisoners, some in orange and some in red jumpsuits, were slouched in the jury box in various states of extreme boredom.

Ruth had been called to sub that morning, so it had been easy for Mara to jump into Jackson's Volvo and drive over to Dudley. She'd thought she might recognize her father right away, but in the jumpsuits the prisoners all looked alike.

One of them rose; it must be Jackson, since they'd called his name. He had wire-rimmed glasses, sandy hair. It was horrible: He was shuffling toward the podium where a lawyer waited, shuffling because he had chains on his ankles. His hands, too. Mara sat rigid with embarrassment for him. How terrible, *cruel.* The lawyer at the podium must be Mr. Ross—a ponytail?—waiting for her father.

"Motion to modify conditions of release. You may proceed, Mr. Ross," said the black-robed judge from his box, a small man with a gray mustache, seated high above everyone else.

"Your Honor." Mr. Ross rested a fatherly hand on Jackson's orange shoulder. "As you can see in the motion, my client is an excellent candidate for release. A highly respected member of the community, a *teacher,* Your Honor, in a time when the rest of the world is merely chasing the dollar. And needless to say, no priors whatsoever. All he wants is that his good name be restored to him. He owns his home and has no *reason* to flee. I'm asking that he be released on his own recognizance."

"Thank you, Mr. Ross." The judge's voice was weary. "Prosecution? Miss O'Connor? Are there victims present?"

A woman rose from a table up front. Mara had noticed her earlier in the hall. She had a blond pageboy and wore a black suit over a red tee and carried herself with a businesslike confidence.

"No, Your Honor," she said, "but I do have a letter from Mrs. Grace Dixon, the victim's elderly mother, and one from Mrs. Dixon's doctor." She waved sheets of paper aloft.

"Judge!" Mr. Ross seemed to be barely suppressing outrage. "Defense hasn't seen any letters."

"They were faxed to the victim advocate, Miss Newcombe," Miss O'Connor said to the judge. "She just got them an hour ago. I made copies for the defense"—she walked over and handed them to Stuart—"and Your Honor, if I may approach, copies for the court."

Mara watched as Miss O'Connor gave the judge copies of the letters. In the moments of silence as he read them, Mara contemplated Miss O'Connor; she was just about as cool as you could get. She had everything under control, and look how mad she'd made Mr. Ross.

The judge set the letters down. "Let it be duly noted that the court has read the letters from the victim's mother and her mother's doctor. You may proceed, Miss O'Connor."

"Well, Your Honor, the state absolutely opposes this motion. The defendant is facing possible life imprisonment, so obviously he has every reason to flee. The victim's mother lives in Tucson and is elderly, ill, and housebound, or she would be here today. As you can see from her letter, Mr. Williams has put her in a state of terror for her life."

"*Your Honor!!*" protested Mr. Ross.

Miss O'Connor paused. The set of her shoulders expressed saintly patience under extreme duress.

"Mr. Ross, that's enough," said the judge. "You've had your say. Proceed, Miss O'Connor."

"It's already affected her health," Miss O'Connor went on. "The defendant's release could damage it even further. Her doctor's letter reinforces this. Were he to be released, there's no telling the toll it would take."

"Your *Honor*," said Mr. Ross, "this is outright slander. No one has threatened Mrs. Dixon in any way, and besides, my client is presumed—"

The judge cut in. "I *said* that's enough, Counselor. I'm ruling on the motion." He banged his gavel. "Motion to modify conditions of release is granted."

Mara's heart fluttered.

"Bond is reduced to two hundred and fifty thousand dollars."

Two hundred and fifty thousand dollars? Was that good? Mara had never been in a courtroom in her life. There was no one to ask. No one Mara knew in the entire courtroom and no one who knew her. But the lawyer's shoulders were slumped, his arm around her father as Jackson shuffled, grim faced, back to the jury box. Her father sat down and put his head in his hands.

It wasn't good. What was going on? The lawyer could tell her. She'd just wait outside the courtroom till he came out. Mara stood up. A good-looking Hispanic kid in a black T-shirt with a Vin Diesel shaved head, a few seats down from her, stood up, too. He smiled and let her go by first.

o　　o　　o

ELDERLY MOTHER IN *a state of terror for her life, indeed,* Stuart fumed. Prejudicial hogwash. Damn that bleeding heart Judge Harrison. From what Jackson had said, there was no way he was going to be able to come up with enough money to post this bond. But even though he hated to lose, Stuart couldn't help feeling a traitorous twinge of relief, knowing his client would be safe in jail instead of outside, screwing things up.

Stuart walked at full speed out of the courtroom, just ahead of a Mexican kid with a shaved head. He had to be in Justice Court in fifteen minutes, needed to pick up a file at his office on the way. He dodged a pretty blond teenager coming toward him just outside the door; a girl-friend, probably, of one of his druggie clients.

"Mr. Ross—"

"Sorry. Not now," he said without stopping.

"Wait!" she called. "Is Jackson Williams going to be released?"

Who was she? One of Jackson's students? "No," he said over his shoulder.

"Why *not*?"

"Call my office. I'm running late."

WHAT WAS THE point of calling his office? He wasn't even there. Mara stood disconsolate in the big marble lobby of the courthouse.

"Hey, you here for Mr. Williams, too?"

She looked up. There was the Mexican kid who'd let her go out before him. "What?" she said.

"You left when they were done with his case," he said, "and I saw you trying to talk to his lawyer. Those lawyers. No time for anyone." He gave her a smile, so cockeyed that she smiled back involuntarily.

"How do you know Jackson?" she asked.

"He's my teacher. He's supposed to be really good, but just my luck I only had him a couple classes and then they arrested him and took him away."

"Oh!" said Mara. "I'm Mara, I'm his daughter."

"No shit." He looked at her with interest. "He mentioned he had a daughter back east. *Cool.* I'm Carlos."

"He was supposed to be *released.*"

"Guess his lawyer screwed up." Carlos shook his head sadly. "You'll have to go see him in jail. My brother did some jail time, pretty depressing. Here, give your dad my card, tell him I said hello."

Mara took his card. It said CARLOS ACUNA, KING OF THE UNIVERSE. So juvenile and arrogant, but it made her smile.

He smiled back. "Don't take it too serious," he said. "I'm kind of a liar. Just ask your dad."

STUART LEFT THE courthouse, leaped into his truck, drove to his office, parked illegally, and ran in to get the file he needed for Justice Court.

Ellie handed it to him. "I called over to the jail," she said. "They transferred the Magician into the nut pod."

"Good. Call Ruth Norton, okay, and tell her Jackson's not getting released."

"Okay," Ellie said. "And Ken Dooley was here, asking about—"

"Tell him I died," said Stuart.

"And, Mr. Ross?" She looked upset. "I need to talk to you."

"Not *now*, Ellie, for Christ's sake."

"Soon!" she called as he went out the door.

On the way to Justice Court, Stuart thought about Jackson's case. George had told him about the interview with Anita. Story too pat, and she hated Jackson. Not credible, according to George. But would a jury see her that way? See if George could dig up some dirt, maybe a little slippery real estate deal, a dissatisfied buyer, a jealous coworker. Nothing from Anita about the boyfriend, but George had some kind of lead there, would get back to him.

Stuart was liking the boyfriend better every day. Sure, the prosecution would say that gave Jackson a good reason to murder his wife, but the burden of proof lay with them. The more players, the more it confused the jury. Maybe the boyfriend would turn out to be a sleazeball—or better yet, as Jackson had surmised, married and Jenny had threatened to tell his wife if he wouldn't tell her himself and leave her for Jenny.

And if we had some ice cream, we could have some pie and ice cream, if we had some pie.

Got to find that boyfriend.

He parked at the Justice Court, ran up the steps, and pushed open the door. The bailiff was standing just inside.

"Sorry, Counselor, everything's been continued."

"What?"

"Judge went home with the flu."

What next? Stopped in his headlong rush, Stuart's body caught up to his brain. *Was that a chest pain?* No, probably just indigestion—that funny-tasting cheese Danish he'd had for breakfast. Suddenly his energy was gone and he was filled with a Sisyphean weariness. He turned on his heel and trudged back out the door and down the steps. He got into his truck and drove slowly back to the office, circling the parking areas several times before he found a place far, far away.

Damn tourists, taking up all the spaces, boosting the economy, raising the rents. His had gone up twice in less than two years. He thought of a bumper sticker he'd seen a few days ago: IF IT'S CALLED TOURIST SEASON, WHY CAN'T WE SHOOT THEM?

He trudged past the post office and the Cornucopia restaurant, which had a brand-new window and was packed, doing a thriving business in spite of all that whining from the owner. He reached his office. Through the big window he could see Ellie at her desk, reading—what was she doing reading, *on his time*?

He pushed open the door. The irritating little bell tinkled.

Ellie looked up. "Mr. Ross? Can we talk now?"

Stuart whooshed out a sigh and sat down. "What about?"

"I have to quit."

Stuart stared at her blankly. "You what?"

Ellie looked like she might cry. "I have to quit working for you."

"When?" Stuart asked flatly.

Ellie bit her lip. "Tomorrow."

"*Tomorrow.*" Energized with disbelief, Stuart stood up abruptly. God, she actually flinched as if he were going to hit her. He sat back down. "Ellie," he said quietly, reasonably. "You can't quit tomorrow. Whatever happened to two weeks' notice?"

"My mom needs me." Her voice was plaintive. "My grandmother had a stroke up in Phoenix. She's in the hospital, and we have to go up there and help her."

"Help her?" Stuart threw up his arms. "She's in the *hospital,* Ellie. That's what they do in hospitals, they help people. You can't wait, maybe a week? What does she need *you* for?"

"To hold her hand. It's *lonely* in hospitals."

"Your mom can still go. You can join her later."

"My mom's *scared* to go to Phoenix by herself. There's all that *traffic.*" Ellie began to cry, great shuddering sobs. "Oh, Mr. Ross," she blubbered. "Why do you always have to *argue* so much?"

Mara had just finished cleaning Ruth's kitchen when she heard the sound of the school bus out on the highway. She went into the living room to the window and watched until Tyler came into view, meandering down the road, swinging his backpack, kicking at stones. She went out to meet him. He looked different.

She giggled. "What's that on your hair?" It stood straight up over his forehead in little spikes like a hedgehog's.

Tyler ducked his head and brushed at his hair, his face red. "Wax. This kid at school had some."

"Let me see. *C'mon.* Look at me."

Tyler raised his head.

"It's cool," Mara pronounced. "It really is. I *like* it. Listen, Jackson didn't get released."

"Oh, man!" Tyler's face twisted up as if he might cry. He threw down his backpack on the driveway. "How *come*?"

"His lawyer sucks."

"But I *miss* him," said Tyler. "And I wanted to tell him about Randy."

"Speaking of Randy, when you walked past the construction site," said Mara, "did you see him?"

"No. Just a couple other guys. He hasn't been around for a while."

He walked past Mara into the house. Mara picked up the backpack and followed him to the kitchen.

"Wow," he said. "What happened in here? It looks so *clean*."

"Paper towels," said Mara. "You wipe everything with paper towels. My mom taught me that. You're absolutely positive he wasn't over there?"

"Absotively, posilutely." He opened the refrigerator, took a long drink of milk from the plastic jug, and wiped his mouth on his sleeve.

"Listen," said Mara decisively, "we're going to fix this Randy thing right now. I'm going to go talk to those other guys, see what I can find out. At least get his last name."

"*No*," said Tyler. "What if they *tell*?"

"I won't say who I am." She paused. "Wait!"

Mara left the kitchen and came back a few minutes later, wearing her sunglasses, a baseball cap pulled down low across her forehead, and Dan's red University of Arizona sweatshirt.

Tyler giggled.

"I could sure use a beer right now," she said in a deep voice.

Tyler giggled some more, falling painlessly off his chair onto the floor.

"I'll go out the back and around to the road," Mara said, "so they can't see where I'm coming from."

He scrambled up and followed her out to the back door. "Be careful," he called after her, his voice quavering a little.

Mara went around to the other side of Jackson's house and out to the road, past the Kleins', to the half-finished house belonging to the man from Phoenix. Two sunburned men in red bandannas, muscular arms gleaming, were loading bits of wood into a dusty, battered brown pickup truck. She stopped a few feet away.

"Hello?" she said gruffly.

One of them kept on loading the truck as if she hadn't even spoken, but the other one grinned at her, teeth white against his sunburned face. "That is some getup," he said.

He looked like a pirate, *dangerous*. Maybe this wasn't the greatest idea.

"Thanks," said Mara, trying for casual and forgetting the deep voice.

"Didja hear that?" said the man to the other one. "It's a *girl*."

"I'm looking for Randy," said Mara. "Randy, Randy, um—" Her voice squeaked. "I can't remember his last name."

"You must mean Randy Gates," said the pirate man. "He quit a couple, three weeks ago."

The other man got in the truck, but the pirate man came closer, so close Mara could see the coarse black hairs on his arms, smell his sweat, dusky and sweet. He reached out suddenly and flicked at the bill of the baseball cap, and the cap fell off.

Mara backed away, heart beating a little fast.

"What do you want with old Randy anyway?" he asked.

"Nothing," she blurted out.

"I bet." He grinned again, slow and sure, as if he knew exactly why she was there. "There's nothing Randy can do for you that I can't."

"*Earl.* Let's go, let's go, let's go," said the other man impatiently from the driver's seat of the truck. "*C'mon.*"

"Think about it," the pirate said to Mara. He turned away and got in the truck. He leaned out the window. "You know where to find me," he said. "I'm here every day."

His partner gunned the engine loudly and backed up the truck.

Mara watched as it careened down the road to the highway, going too fast of course, macho pigs. The encounter had left her feeling smaller, diminished. What did he mean, *There's nothing Randy can do for you that I can't?* She didn't even want to think about it. She leaned down and picked up the baseball cap. Then it struck her, something the man had said. Mara took off, loping down the road. Tyler was waiting by the front door, eyes big.

"Did it work?" he asked.

"Yes," said Mara, not meeting his look. "His name's Randy *Gates*. Listen to me." She hustled Tyler inside the house. "He quit a couple, three weeks ago. That's what the man said. Around the time Jenny was killed. We *have* to tell your mom."

RUTH PULLED INTO the driveway and got wearily out of the car. It was late, getting dark already. She'd stopped at the Safeway on the way home and there had been long lines at every checkout. God, she hated subbing; it wasn't like you got to know the kids. And it had been eighth grade, the worst. They'd all switched places so the seating chart the regular teacher had left was no help at all. And the lesson plans were indecipherable. And, *and* she had had cafeteria duty, which had left her only fifteen minutes for lunch.

Considering what they paid, was it even worth it? Her middle was rigidly compressed by her tummy-control pantie-hose and her feet, in red flats, fashionable ten years ago, ached. Owen paid generous child support, but it had shrunk when first Dan, then Scott left home. Once Tyler was in high school she should start thinking about a real job.

But Jackson should be out. Mara would have brought him home. They could sit down together and discuss everything he'd told her over the phone. There weren't any lights on at his house, so he must be *here*. Ruth walked to the back of her car and opened the trunk to get the groceries, summoning up energy to welcome Jackson home.

Tyler came running out. "Mom! You don't have to do that. I'll take care of it." What was that on his hair? She was too tired to ask.

"You're home!" said Mara at the door. "How was your day?"

"Where's Jackson?" Ruth asked.

"Come into the living room," said Mara, "and sit down." Ruth came in. "Would you like some tea, coffee, fruit juice, soda, water?" asked Mara brightly.

"Water." Ruth sank to the couch. "Where's Jackson?" she said again.

"Water it is," said Mara efficiently. "By the way," she said over her shoulder as she went to the kitchen, "I'm making dinner."

Ruth rested her hand on her forehead, too tired to ease out of her pantie-hose, as Tyler staggered by, carrying two trips of groceries in one. The last time Tyler had volunteered to bring in the groceries was when he accidentally broke the kitchen window with a baseball bat.

Mara came back, carrying a glass of water. She handed it to Ruth. "Jackson didn't get released," she said.

"No!" cried Ruth. "His lawyer said it was a sure thing." She sat up straight on the couch. "Why *not*?"

"I think it was because Jenny's mom had her doctor write a letter saying she might die if he got out."

"*What?*" said Ruth, appalled. "That mean old bi—How could she?"

She stood up, energized by shock, and went into the kitchen. Tyler was putting away the groceries. Ruth walked to the counter, crumpled the empty plastic bags, and put them in the trash can, which was, oddly, stuffed with paper towels. "How could she?" she said again.

"Tyler and I need to tell you something," Mara said.

Ruth stared suspiciously at Mara. "What?" The phone rang. "Get it in the other room, Tyler, would you?" she said absently. "Tell them to call back." She paused. "What?" she said to Mara again.

"Wait till Tyler gets here," said Mara.

"Mom!"

Ruth felt her ears ringing. Her face flushed suddenly, sweat prickling the back of her neck. Oh, God, not another hot flash. "*What*, Tyler?"

He came in the kitchen, carrying the phone, his voice hushed. "It's *Jackson.*"

Ruth grabbed the phone. "I'm going to tell him about you now," she said to Mara.

LIGHTS OUT, BUT Jackson tossed and turned. *Hi, this is Mara. Hi, this is Mara. Hi, this is Mara.* Her voice rang in his head.

"Mara," he'd said, stunned, shamed that he would be talking to her for the first time in eighteen years from the county jail. "How is Maggie?"

"My mother died," Mara had said. "Last year. Of cancer." Then the guard had said time was up. "I'll come visit," she'd said. *I'll come visit.*

Maggie dead? Maggie, who had taught him to dance, *you klutz, funny.* So light on her feet even when she was pregnant.

So many times he'd imagined what Mara might be like. Little Mara. The name had been his choice. Maggie had wanted to call her Stephanie. Such a stern name, with a hint of crutches. He would have gone with naming her after Maggie, kind of Yeatsian, but she hadn't wanted that.

Maggie hadn't wanted a lot of things she used to want before the baby came. Things like freedom and spontaneity. He knew now that those things were meaningless, really. Maggie said he didn't care about the baby, but he did, more ferociously than he ever could have imagined. He just couldn't see why the baby couldn't join in with them in the life they already had. He'd been so immature, such an asshole.

Well, how much better had he been with Jenny? Things had been all right once—until the miscarriage. It might have brought them closer together, but instead he'd withdrawn and Jenny had thrown herself into the self-improvement schemes that dominated her life from then on. Maybe they should have talked about it more, but he'd been unable to, had willed himself not to think of it, never thought of it if he could help it, but hearing Mara's voice brought it all back. The blood.

All he could think of was the blood in the bathroom, all over the toilet seat, the toilet water deep red with it. He took her to the emergency room at the Sierra Vista Hospital. The fetus had already passed, they said.

Late at night, maybe 2:00 or 3:00 A.M., Jackson groaned in his jail cell, filled with primeval horror. Jenny had flushed the toilet. All that blood going down the drain, all that blood and the fetus; it could have been another Mara, *flushed down the toilet.*

eight

THE DOOR TO the office of the English Department out at Cochise College was half open. Inside was a big dark-haired bearded man in a denim shirt and buckskin vest. He was tilted back in his chair, feet on the desk, reading through a sheaf of papers. George tap-tapped on the doorjamb, and the man looked up.

"Sid Hamblin?" said George.

The man took his feet down and tilted forward heavily. "That's me. Come on in."

"I'm George Maynard, investigator for Stuart Ross—an attorney over in Dudley?" George came in, reached in his shirt pocket, took out a card, and passed it over.

"*Sure,*" Sid said heartily. "Office right there on Main Street. I live in Dudley—114-C Moon Canyon—moved there when I got divorced a couple of years ago. I know why you're here. Sit down, sit down."

George sat on an old oak chair. The office was small and extremely cluttered. Shelves filled one wall, jammed with books and journals, more of them on the desk. Behind Sid was a psychedelic poster of the Grateful Dead at Fillmore West and next to that a window. Outside in the parking lot George could see his yellow 'fifty-six Cadillac, two male students with backpacks hovering around it like wasps around a big piece of fruit.

"Hell of a thing, divorce," George said.

"But it sure beats murder, huh?"

"Let's talk about that," said George. "Jenny's murder."

Sid smiled and stroked his beard. "Uh, no offense, but this is a bad time. I'm a busy man. Only reason you caught me free was because a student didn't show up for a conference. You'd have been better off coming to my house to talk about poor Jenny."

"But here I am," said George.

"Speaking of Jenny." Sid opened a drawer in his desk and took out a brightly colored plastic bottle. "Probiotics. Jenny turned me on to them. You should try 'em. They really give you a boost. Jenny was a wonderful woman, by the way. Used to see her at those departmental get-togethers—a bright light in an otherwise dreary scene."

"Where else did you see her?"

"Sad to say, that's about it." Sid reached down and brought up a bottle of water. He opened the pill bottle, shook one out, and swallowed it with the water. Against his dark beard his mouth was red and wet.

"Let's talk about Jackson," said George. "You seemed pretty anxious to let the police know the lousy state of his marriage. Some kind of rivalry going on there?"

"No rivalry, not at all. I'm not into these ego trips—more of a live-and-let-live kind of guy. Except when it comes to people murdering their spouses. That kind of gets to me." He looked at his watch. "Uh-oh, time's up. Got a class." He rose from his desk—a big man; he seemed to fill the room. "Young minds are waiting."

George stood, too. From somewhere a bell rang.

At the door Sid said, "Wish I could have helped you out more."

Students jammed the hallway outside.

"Mr. Hamblin!" A young woman, overdressed in a short red skirt and spikey mules, stopped dead. "I missed your last class," she said plaintively. "Could you tell me the assignment?"

"Forget the assignment," said Sid.

The young woman looked lost, confused. Sid chuckled. George stepped to one side to avoid a couple more students.

"Hey, guy!" Sid called loudly to someone down the hall. "Who's the man?" He made his index finger into a gun and sighted along the barrel. "Noam Chomsky!"

Gnome Chompski, thought George, *whoever that was. Gnome Chompski and the seven dwarfs.*

THE PHONE RANG in the office of Stuart Ross, attorney at law. In the middle of composing a response to a motion to revoke probation for one Jeremy Seagal, CR200300437, Stuart clenched his head, tugging at his hair with both hands. Not again. It could just fucking ring. The machine picked up after eight rings, but no one left a message.

Well, good.

Stuart went back to the motion, but he'd lost his train of thought. God damn Ellie and God damn her mother, and her grandmother, too. *Wow,* he thought, *I'm turning into a heartless monster.* The phone rang again.

Stuart jerked involuntarily, knocking over his cup of Kona Dark to-go from the Dudley Coffee Company. He stood up hurriedly to escape the stream of liquid seeping over the edge of his desk toward his khakis. Wasn't he supposed to be in court in twenty minutes? No? No, it was okay. That was yesterday.

Stuart went out of his office, through what had once been Ellie's domain, to the small restroom for paper towels. Even though Ellie had been gone hardly any time at all, little piles of documents seemed to have swelled into mountains overnight. In the bathroom there were no, God damn it, *no* paper towels. He grabbed a fistful of toilet paper and started back through the reception room, knocking a stack of papers off Ellie's desk on the way. He knelt to pick them up.

The bell tinkled.

Stuart looked up, and there at the door was that headband-snapper woman. *Damn.*

The phone rang.

It rang some more as Stuart, crouched and vulnerable on the floor, armed only with toilet paper, stared up at Ruth. She looked a little spiffier than he remembered her looking, not so thrift store. Actually passably attractive for a middle-aged woman. He straightened up, dropping the toilet paper.

"Aren't you going to answer your phone?" she said.

"What?"

Ruth came over to the desk and picked up. "Mr. Ross's office." She paused, glancing at Stuart. "Dakota?"

Aw, shit. Stuart groaned, shaking his head back and forth warningly.

"I'm so sorry, Dakota," said Ruth, her voice melodious, "Mr. Ross is in a meeting right now. I can—No? No, I'm sure he's not avoiding you. He's very, very busy. All right. Fine." She hung up. "No message," she said to Stuart.

"In a meeting," said Stuart gratefully. "How'd you know to say that? And it sounded so true."

"My ex-husband and I ran a very successful business in L.A. I know all about office management." Ruth looked around. "This place is a pigsty. No wonder Jackson didn't get released."

"I resent that," said Stuart hotly. "He didn't get released because one, we got assigned a lousy judge and two, Jenny's elderly mother opposed it. This victim's rights stuff has played hell with the criminal justice system. And my secretary quit." His voice turned whiney. "She didn't even give notice."

Ruth knelt and picked up the papers, put them back on Ellie's desk, then walked around the desk and sat in Ellie's chair.

"It's hell," said Stuart. "I don't even know anymore where I have to be or when."

"Why don't you look at your calendar? It's right here." She held it up.

"I—I didn't know."

"You have a one o'clock this afternoon in Division Five and a four o'clock in Division Two."

"Shit," said Stuart. "That's *right.*"

"And"—Ruth shot him a meaningful look—"it looks like Jackson at two thirty." Her expression changed. "Oh, dear."

"I didn't forget *that,*" said Stuart defensively.

"I told him about Mara last night."

"Who's Mara?"

"*God,*" said Ruth. "Jackson's daughter."

"Ah. Didn't know he had one."

"Well, he does." Ruth straightened some papers on the desk and picked up a stack of catalogs. "Junk," she said, dropping them into the wastebasket. She picked up a stack of *People* magazines. "More junk." She threw them away, too. "Sit down. You're making me nervous."

"You're"—Stuart's voice was hopeful—"you're not a legal secretary, are you?"

"No, I'm not."

Not a legal secretary. Stuart sat down. The toilet paper was on the floor where he'd dropped it, but he felt too stressed to pick it up, go into his office, and mop up the coffee. It would just have to dry on its own.

"There's something I have to tell you," Ruth said.

"What?" Stuart's voice was weary.

"My son Tyler told me this last night. He should have told someone sooner, but"—she shrugged—"he's eleven. He was home alone the day Jenny was killed. They're building a house near us, and Tyler knows some of the construction workers because he stops and watches them work sometimes—on his way home from the school bus." She paused.

"And?" said Stuart.

"He saw one of them go into Jenny's house by the back door when Jackson wasn't home—it was around noon, the day she was killed. He saw him go in other times, too, when Jackson was gone."

"You're kidding me." *Jesus Christ.* Jenny was banging this construction worker? "Maybe she hired him to do some work on the side," Stuart said, keeping his voice neutral. "I don't suppose you got his name?"

"Yes, we did get his name." She paused significantly. "Randy Gates."

Randy Gates. He'd never been a client, but Stuart had sure seen the guy in court, plenty of times, seen him graduate from marijuana to methamphetamines. Randy Gates, habitual criminal. Stuart's face was as blank as an unwritten letter. *Never let them know what you're thinking.* "Interesting," he said.

"Interesting?" said Ruth. "A lot more than that. I'm thinking he might have been Jenny's lover. He might have planted that poison. And"—Ruth's voice was triumphant—"he quit the job *right after Jenny was killed.*"

MARA TURNED THE key and pulled open the door to Jackson's house. She stepped inside but left the door open a couple of inches behind her. It smelled dusty inside, close, like her long-dead grandmother's old house on Long Island Sound smelled when she went with her father, her *dad,* to open it up for the summer. For a second Mara teetered on the edge of remembering summers there before her mom got sick; picnics and sand everywhere.

She took a deep breath and tiptoed down a short hall to the living room.

Dust motes danced in the sunlight that streamed through curtains not quite drawn. The room was oppressively neat. Mara kept her hands to her sides, as if to touch anything would be a violation—of what, she didn't know, but it didn't look like a room where you might fling your coat on a chair or couch, hang out, play Scrabble.

She walked carefully through the room to a hall and found a kitchen. Turquoise canisters and matching kitchen towels, a farmer's table. She opened the refrigerator. A fast-food cardboard container, rigid tan fries spilling out. Something brown and liquefied in a plastic bag in the vegetable keeper. In the freezer, frozen peas, a box of organic tofu burgers, yuck, and a carton of Ben & Jerry's New York Super Fudge Chunk.

What did he *eat?*

Mara went to the back door and looked out. From here she could see Ruth's backyard, the mountain, and a big cottonwood tree. Beside the door was a hook, with a medal on a beaded chain hanging from it. Ooh, St. Christopher. Patron saint of travelers. She was a traveler. Mara took it off the hook and put it around her neck for luck. She could return it later.

Mara left the kitchen, went down the hall and opened a door to a room empty except for an exercise machine, closed it, then found a bedroom with a king-sized bed and a TV, closed that door hurriedly and went to the end of the hall, opened still another door, and there was her father. His presence anyway, in the rows of books in the built-in bookcase, a desk with a computer monitor and keyboard but no hard drive, stacks of papers and more books, one of them open, facedown. Photographs hung on the wall. Ooh.

She went closer for a look. A man in wire-rimmed glasses, with a mustache and an earring, grinned at her rakishly from a place of mountains and a stream—Jackson; but in that place of freedom, he looked nothing like the chained man in the courtroom. Next to that a photograph from the same place, but a woman. Mara stepped back a pace. *Jenny.*

She made herself look. Jenny, little nose, dark hair, shining eyes, in a tank top that showed off buff and burnished arms, legs strong in hiking shorts. Alive and well and happy; she looked younger in the picture than Mara's mom had been when she died. Now she was dead, too; that was what this was all about, Jenny being dead. Everything was jumbled in Mara's head and not like anything she had imagined when she thought of the sandy-haired man who tossed her in the air. *Got you now!*

Mara opened drawers at random—here were his pencils, pens, old photographs, printer cartridges, envelopes, paper clips—shut them. Old photographs. She opened that drawer again, riffled through photographs not suitable for framing, blurred or red-eyed or damaged. Mara looked down at a photograph of herself: tanned, white haired, and laughing, wearing only underpants, taken at a beach when she was two.

Her mother had had one just like it, except this one had been torn into four pieces, then Scotch-taped together.

Why was it torn? Had Jackson done it, then had a change of heart and taped it together? Hated her, then loved her again? No, probably it was *Jenny*. The Jenny Ruth didn't like; Tyler, either. But why would Jenny hate her so much she'd torn up her picture when she'd never even met her?

On the desk was the book, open, facedown, poems by Louise Bogan, whom Mara had never heard of. She picked it up. A poem, the last verse marked faintly with pencil.

> *Come, let us counsel some cold stranger*
> *How we sought safety, but loved danger*
> *So, with stiff walls about us, we*
> *Chose this more fragile boundary:*
> *Hills, where the light poplars, the firm oak,*
> *Loosen into a little smoke.*

"Hello? Anybody home?"

Mara jumped guiltily. A man's voice. Coming from the front of the house. She picked up the book, put the taped photograph in to mark the poem, then hurried down the hall. The door she'd left ajar was now wide open, and a man stood in the opening.

"Wow. You sure clean up good," he said.

He was blocking the light so she couldn't see him very well, but he sounded familiar. "What?" she said blankly.

He walked into the hall, smiling, white teeth glinting. "Saw you go in earlier," he said. "Never introduced myself the other day. Name's Earl Kershaw. Thought I'd stop by, seeing as how you know Randy and all."

The man from the construction site. The flirty pretend-friendly one who looked like a pirate. What was he doing here? Standing in the hall, blocking her way out. Should she make a run for the back door? Ruth, wouldn't she be home soon? She'd said around two, but it was already later than that. Tyler?

He came a step closer. "Randy and I go way back," he said. "Told ya, didn't I—there's nothing you can get from Randy that you can't get from me."

Turn. Run, run to the back door. But Mara felt paralyzed. "Like what?" she said coldly, trying to keep her voice from shaking.

"Like maybe"—he reached behind to his back pocket, pulled out a Baggie, and dangled it in front of her—"a little weed?"

"*Marijuana?*" said Mara.

"Sure. Randy told me, he sold to the woman who lived here. The one who was . . . uh . . . Who're you? Her kid?"

"Not exactly," said Mara. "*Jenny* smoked marijuana?"

"Regular customer, according to Randy," said Earl. "How 'bout you? Got a sample right here. Want to try some?"

"RUTH NORTON'S BACK at my office," said Stuart in the law library of the county jail.

Jackson's eyes lit up. "She is?"

"My secretary quit. Ruth's helping me tidy up. Sounds like you've been talking to her about your case. Thought I told you that was a no-no."

"I thought she could help," said Jackson defensively. "And I told her to tell you everything."

"Well, as it turns out, she did tell me something. Ever heard the name Randy Gates?"

"Randy Gates?" Jackson looked at Stuart, his face blank. "Who's that?"

"Jenny never mentioned him?"

"Maybe she did," said Jackson. "One of those many times when I wasn't listening. Unless he was her—" He was still trying to take it in, believe it, that Jenny had had a lover. He didn't recall her as someone who would do something like that. He felt his mind start to drift, last night's bad dreams still with him. He sat up straight and tried to look alert.

"Boyfriend," Stuart finished for him. "Maybe. Ruth's son saw him going to the house a few times."

"*Tyler?*" said Jackson, alert for real now. "I'd like to keep him out of this as much as possible. He's just a kid, you know?"

"Do my best," said Stuart hurriedly. "Depends on how it all plays out."

"This Randy Gates—what kind of person is he?"

"A loser," Stuart said. "A drug dealer, for one. She hang out with drug dealers?"

"Are you *kidding*?" said Jackson. "She was so healthy, everything organic. A drug dealer? I can't imagine—" Well, of course he couldn't imagine. He'd given up imagining Jenny altogether at some point soon after the miscarriage. "I didn't really know what she did," he said. "I didn't know who she saw. I went off to work and she did things, all kinds of things, I guess, but mostly yoga and jogging and reading books about how to be perfect. She used to try to tell me about what she did, but I never listened."

And the less he listened, the more dramatic Jenny became. Soon everything was a drama, white hot and demanding his immediate attention. Sometimes he thought she even made things up, just to get his attention.

But he'd been too busy. Too busy noticing, for instance, the way light came through half-open curtains and formed triangles, or hearing fat black grackles in the cottonwoods squabbling raucously, or remembering that line from a Roethke poem about the child on top of a greenhouse, and elms plunging and tossing like horses.

A child, like Tyler. Now Tyler might be dragged into this. Why *hadn't* he paid more attention?

"I guess I had other things on my mind," he said.

RUTH LEFT STUART'S office before he got back from his late-afternoon court date. She pulled the door to behind her so that it locked. Presumably he would have a key, though you couldn't assume much with someone so disorganized. Well, it was better now; Stuart had kind of explained how things worked, and they'd gone over the billing before he'd gone to court, and she'd even managed to type up a motion on the computer and lay it neatly on his desk.

Now she drove home into a sun that was blinding, thinking she'd told Mara she would be home no later than two and it was nearly five. She felt uneasy, nerves jangling, why? Stuart, for one; he carried around an infectious sense of pointless urgency, probably headed for a heart attack one of these days. Then there was the coffee; she'd drunk almost half a pot at the office, so she was doubly hyped up from all that caffeine.

Ruth turned off onto her road and passed the construction site; no men working there now, all gone home. *That* was why she was uneasy. In the excitement of finding out about Randy, she hadn't given it much thought till now. *Mara had gone and asked the men about Randy.* Stuart had told her he had an investigator working the case; he could have done it. Who knew what kind of men they were? What kind of man this Randy was?

Children. Ruth had never regretted having children, but she'd done it so blithely, without a thought of how hard it would be. All that worry—it never stopped. She had visualized her children dying from unknown causes in their cribs, necks broken in falls from high places, carotid arteries sliced through by broken windows, arms lopped off by passing cars, bullied to suicide by vicious classmates, diagnosed with early terminal cancers, hit by trucks, killed in car accidents, blown up with bombs, drowned in flash floods, murdered by careless gunmen, smashed to smithereens in plane crashes.

But Mara was a grown-up—well, twenty-one, and not even her child. *You don't have to be the mom all the time. She's fine. Don't worry.*

She passed the Kleins' and Jackson's and pulled into her own driveway. Tyler came barreling out the door.

"Mom!!"

She didn't see Mara. Ruth felt distinctly unwell. She picked up a book she'd brought home with her and got out of her car. "Where's Mara?"

"Mom, listen to this!!"

"Tyler. *Where is Mara?*"

"Here. I'm right here."

Ruth looked over to see her standing at the door. *Thank God.* Her knees felt weak. She headed toward her.

"Mom," said Tyler excitedly, as she reached the house. He and Mara followed her into the living room. "This friend of Randy's came to Jackson's when Mara was there!"

Mara rolled her eyes.

Ruth blinked. "A friend of Randy's came to Jackson's?"

"Earl," said Mara. "Earl something."

Ruth sank onto the couch and put the book on the coffee table. "What did *Earl* want?"

"He tried to sell her some *dope*!!"

"Dope?"

"I told her she should call the cops, but she won't."

"I'm not calling the cops," said Mara, her voice wearily worldly. "It was only marijuana."

Only marijuana. Ruth had smoked it herself years ago and more recently had found a Baggie of it under Scott's mattress. Wasn't it a lot stronger than it used to be? Laced, probably, with who knew what. She tried to suppress fears that Mara might be on the road to a heroin habit.

"Earl told me Jenny smoked marijuana all the time," Mara said.

"Oh, she *did not*," said Ruth, aghast. "If you'd known Jenny, you'd have known he was lying. He *saw* her smoking it?"

"No, but he said she was a regular customer of Randy's."

Ruth shook her head. "I don't think so."

Mara sat down next to Ruth and picked up the book from the coffee table. "What's this?" she asked, changing the subject.

Ruth brightened. "*Arizona Rules of the Court,*" she said. "It has all these standard legal procedures in it. I'm going to study it." Ruth sat up straight. "I have a job—working for Jackson's lawyer."

nine

RUTH AND MARA cooked dinner together, chatting excitedly about Ruth's new job, while Tyler set the table. Stuart had meant to call George to clue him in about Randy Gates but instead fell asleep on his couch after eating inferior Chinese takeout: kung pao shrimp, with possibly moldy peanuts, that would later wake him in the night with serious heartburn, thinking, *Gotta get George on that Randy Gates guy.*

In his new pod with the nutcases, the Magician sat on a bolted-down chair at a bolted-down table, next to an emaciated young black man who hadn't moved an inch in an hour. The Magician moved his hand slowly, slowly, until it just touched the young man's arm. "Jenny," he whispered. "Jenny, Jenny."

JACKSON SAT IN his pod, under the fluorescent lights, reading the same sentence in *One Hundred Years of Solitude* over and over. What difference did it make? But it was better than lying in his cell thinking and thinking; squirrel-cage, monkey-mind thinking.

"Hey, Professor! Maybe you could help me out!"

Jackson looked up. One of Leroy's friends, a bulky man called Ringo, thirtyish, with an acne-scarred face, was standing in front of him holding a sheet of paper.

"With what?" Jackson asked.

"I wrote this letter to the judge—for my sentencing?" He shrugged. "About how sorry I am I did it and all."

"Let's see." Jackson took the paper and scanned it.

"Maybe you could fix the spelling?" Ringo fidgeted, looking worried. "I'm not too good a speller, man, you know?"

"No," said Jackson, shaking his head decisively. "Keep the spelling errors. They don't matter. In fact, they make everything more authentic."

Ringo's brow wrinkled. "Come again?"

"Real," said Jackson. "Honest. It's *feeling* you want to convey, if you want the judge to think you're truly sorry. It should sound colloqu— natural, like the way you talk. See, this line here is very good, but then the next one kind of cancels it out." His voice rose, happily, fervently. "Why don't you try . . ."

GEORGE PUSHED OPEN the door of the Outback Bar and Grill, and the first thing that hit him was the sweet smell of alcohol. Ahhh . . . scores of days and nights and years full of warm and instant camaraderie; hilarious jokes, long-winded stories, teams that won and teams that lost, *you're my brother, man, I love ya.* And here now, tonight, Johnny Cash on the jukebox—"Ring of Fire"—wow, if that didn't take him back a long, long way.

George stepped back outside and used his cell phone to call Stan, his sponsor.

"Hiya. George here," he said when Stan answered. "I need help."

"Where are you, George?"

"In front of a bar."

"Go home, George."

"Can't. It's part of an investigation. I started in and had a moment of weakness is all. Johnny Cash was on the jukebox, and all of a sudden it was déjà vu all over again."

"How's this for déjà vu, George? Remember that time you woke up in your car at the Circle K parking lot at eight in the morning and those little kids were staring at you through the car window? Shouting, 'A wino! A wino!'? Remember how Sandy cried when you got home, worried out of her mind you'd been killed in a car wreck? Then, when she saw your condition, sort of sorry you hadn't been?"

There was a long silence.

"Yeah," George said finally.

"You okay?" asked Stan.

"Yeah. I am. I can handle it now. Thanks."

George ended the call and went back into the bar.

The jukebox was silent now, the place dim, brighter behind the bar from the neon beer signs reflected in miniature on the rows of bottles. A weeknight, the place nearly empty; no one at the tables along the wall, two guys and a woman at the bar near the middle, another guy at the far end. George sat down at the near end.

Elbows on the bar, the female bartender was talking companionably to the threesome. She was maybe late thirties, blond with a snub nose, wearing a red miniblouse. She saw George and came down the bar. Several gold chains of varying lengths descended into her cleavage.

"Hi there." Big warm smile that made it to the eyes. He liked that. She kind of reminded him of Ellen Barkin when Al Pacino had the hots for her in *Sea of Love*. "What can I get you?"

"Ginger ale," said George.

"Ginger ale it is," she said, not missing a beat. Despite the cleavage, her voice was faintly masculine, no nonsense; look but don't touch.

She left, and George stared at the deer's head—stag's, actually, with those antlers—mounted on the wall behind the bar, its glass eyes full of nothing. As a kid, he used to hunt with his dad up in the White Mountains. He'd fight with his last breath for the right to bear arms, but he'd seen so much death these last years, the stag's eyes kind of made him sick.

The bartender came back, put down a little white paper napkin, a glass with ice, a stirrer, and a can of ginger ale. She poured some of it into the glass. "That'll be two dollars."

He gave her three. "Name's George Maynard." He reached in his coat pocket, pulled out a card, and pushed it across to her. "You're—?"

She looked at the card, raised her eyebrows, then wiped her hands on the towel tucked in her belt, reached over, and shook his hand, a good firm grip. "Mickey," she said. "Mickey Dings."

"You been working here long?"

"Forever." She grinned. "Feels like it, anyway."

"Well, Mickey, maybe you wouldn't mind if I ask you a few questions?"

"What about?"

"A customer—Friday-night regular. Jenny Williams? You knew her?"

"Yes." She flinched. "Little *Jenny*. It makes me sick. Imagine her husband doing that." She wrinkled her snub nose in disgust. "It's so fucking lame, I can't believe it."

"What have we got here?" George smiled to take out any sting. "The judge and jury?"

"Looks pretty cut-and-dried to me, from what I read in the paper." She raised her eyebrows. "What? You're saying it's not?"

"We'll see. Tell me about Jenny."

"Well, okay, she came in most Fridays, with that Anita Selby. You know how it goes, come with a friend, if you don't score you can still have a good time."

"Jenny was looking to score?"

Mickey shook her head. "Not Jenny. Anita. She wasn't totally blatant about it, but it was pretty obvious. Jenny was a good choice to come with 'cause usually she'd stay out of Anita's way."

"What do you mean, stay out of her way?"

Mickey smiled. "Anita could get huffy as in B-I-T-C-H-Y if you moved into her territory, or what she thought was hers. I know; I saw it happen two or three times. Once with Jenny even."

"With Jenny? I thought they were best friends."

"Oh, they made up since then. This was three or four months ago I'm talking about. Anita shows up with some guy Jenny knew, and Jenny starts talking to him, kind of flirtatious. Pretty soon, he's not paying attention to Anita anymore. She got all pissed off and stormed out. They kind of laughed about it, like *What's with her?* But I think something was going on there—'cause they left together."

"Oh?"

"Jenny and Anita didn't show up together the next week, but after that they did, dear friends, same as usual."

"Some guy," said George. "You got a name?"

Mickey shook her head. "He never came back. A big guy, late forties maybe, beard. Talked a lot. I think, yeah"—she snapped her fingers—"He worked out at the college, like Jenny's husband. That's how she knew him."

Big guy, beard . . . *Sid Hamblin,* thought George. Sid, who said he only saw Jenny at departmental get-togethers. Fucking liar.

ARIZONA RULES OF *the Court* slid off the pillow where Ruth had propped it to read and landed with a thud on the floor. She woke with a start, reached for the light switch, and fumbled it off. Tired from the day, she fell back asleep almost at once, sinking into a dream, something about a Rule 32. She had no idea what a Rule 32 was, but she had to type up a motion for one because Owen needed it *right away.* She had no idea either why she and her ex-husband had set up a new business in a place that looked like Stuart Ross's office, but somehow it seemed reasonable.

"Where's the book?" she asked Owen. "The *Rules of the Court?*"

Owen smiled. He was so handsome; he'd always been the most handsome man she ever met, and he hadn't aged a day since she'd last seen him eleven years ago. "You don't need the book anymore," he said. "It was all a big mistake. I'm not gay after all."

"Not gay?" said Ruth in wonderment. How could that be? And she was filled with happiness, joy even—she would be safe now, back in her old life. Safe, safe, safe.

Then she woke, opening her eyes to pitch-black. The room, the house, was silent, her two oldest boys gone, Jackson gone, too, so the silence stretched beyond the house. Somewhere Mara and Tyler breathed in, breathed out in sleep, but she couldn't hear them. *Jenny,* she thought. If Jenny had to be dead, why couldn't her car have exploded when it went over the side of the mountain, burned her body to ashes like a funeral pyre instead of leaving it intact and even now, still unburied, tainting the silence?

t e n

Two pounds heavier from a steady diet of white bread, bologna, and pasta, the Magician in his ancient black sneakers stepped out into the sunlight, his pointy cap tilted downward, his leather bag over his shoulder. The bag tinkled when he moved; they'd given him back his bell. Due to the vigilant efforts of his fans in Old Dudley and the crowded conditions at the jail, he'd gotten early release. He blinked, screwing up his eyes.

"Free at last," chirped the woman who'd met him in the lobby, saying too brightly, "I'm Mirabelle Hadley from SEABHS." *See bus.* She wore a purple pantsuit and was overweight and looked very clean. "Oh, my, isn't it a beautiful day! Look at that sunshine!"

The Magician blinked again and wiped his watery eyes on the sleeve of his orange robe. The bell tinkled. "See bus, see bus, see bus," he said.

"SEABHS," said the woman in the same artificial chirpy voice. "Southeastern Arizona Behavioral Health Services. That's where I work.

Ken Dooley called me about giving you a ride back to town." Her eyelids fluttered. "Such a caring man. A good friend."

She came closer, took his arm a little gingerly, steered him over to a red car, opened the passenger door, and stood aside for him to get in. She smelled like some kind of sweet metal.

"Robot, robot, robot," said the Magician, standing his ground.

She smiled as if he'd said something very witty, but he sensed something else, behind the smile. Pain. *See bus, see bus, see bus,* he thought, to block it.

"Go on," she said encouragingly. "Get in. We'll have you in town in no time."

He got in the car, tinkle, tinkle, tinkle. The woman closed the door after him. His cap hit the roof, so he took it off. The woman came around to the driver's side and got in, too. She sniffed a couple of times, then pushed some buttons, and all the windows in the car slid silently open. She started the car and backed out.

As they drove toward town, the wind coming through all the open windows tugged at the Magician's hair and long beard, tickling his face, making his nose itch, but he could no longer smell the metallic woman.

"Ken Dooley told me to talk to your friend Frieda," she warbled. "Among others. My goodness, you have a lot of friends. You're a very lucky man." She glanced over at him. "Let me ask you something, sir."

The Magician said nothing, preoccupied with balancing his cap on top of his leather bag.

"I don't know your history," she said, "but you must have meds. Are you taking them regularly?"

The cap slid toward the floor, but the Magician caught it in time. "His story, his story, his story," he said.

"Yes," said the woman. "Well. It's shocking they didn't see to your meds in jail. Always trying to save money."

They had reached the far end of Main Street. The Magician sat up straighter, sniffing the air. He could smell dog shit, patchouli oil, and the alcohol that drifted down from the bars on the Gulch.

"It's odd," said the woman. "I can't get a handle on what your diagnosis would be. You're not like any . . . I should have looked at your file. I was thinking, we could backtrack a bit here. I could run you over to the doctor. Doctor Cleveland. He's *very* nice. He could update you a bit on the meds."

"Stop. Stop. Stop." The Magician put his hand on the door handle.

The woman slowed, but before she had a chance to stop the Magician had pushed the door open. She braked and pulled to the curb in front of Va Va Voom, a store that sold retro and vintage clothing and objects.

"Sir," she began, but the Magician stepped out of the car.

One foot, two foot, onto the sidewalk. Tinkle, tinkle, tinkle. One foot, two foot, he put on his pointy cap. Displayed in the window of Va Va Voom was a charcoal gray skirt appliquéd with a fuzzy pink poodle, a pair of Mouseketeer ears, and a toy robot from the fifties. Robot, robot, robot. Tinkle, tinkle, tinkle. One foot, two foot, free again.

GEORGE YAWNED AS he turned down Moon Canyon, headed for Sid Hamblin's house. Dakota had been parked in front of his apartment building when he got home from the Outback Bar and Grill, and one thing had led to another. He had to tell her to stop showing up like that.

He was driving the clunker, an ugly gray 'eighty-five Oldsmobile; it was what he drove anytime he went to talk to a suspect who would be looking for the Caddy. That morning when he'd called over to the college, they'd told him Sid was out for the day. *With any luck he'll be home,* thought George, and yawned again.

The clunker belched clouds of gray smoke as he drove up the steep hill at the end of Moon Canyon. The road had turned to dirt a little way back, and the Olds wasn't much good on hills, but then the Caddy wasn't either, for that matter.

Halfway up, George parked and got out. It was hot, but he wore his tan corduroy jacket to conceal the Colt Commander pistol in his shoulder holster. Better safe than sorry. Sid struck him as someone who could fly off the handle and get physical if crossed. Actually, so did Anita.

The mesquite grew thick on the rocky hillside; the air was electric with cicadas. For a second George contemplated Anita, with her perfect makeup, looking to score—but later for that. Above him was Sid's house, an A-frame of gray aged wood with a big deck, architecturally at odds with the rest of Old Dudley. A black Ford Explorer was parked a little way down the driveway to the house. Um-hum. Sid had looked like the kind of guy who would drive a big bully vehicle like that to look down on people from.

Over the blur of cicadas, his cell phone chimed. Damn.

"George Maynard here."

"George? Stuart. Listen, the little kid that lives next door to Jackson's saw someone going in to see Jenny the day she was killed. Saw him some other times, too, but never when Jackson was home."

"As in maybe that's the guy that was making it with Jenny?" said George. He glanced up at Sid's house.

"Maybe. Guess who."

"Sid Hamblin."

"Sid Hamblin? What does he have to do with anything? No, it was Randy Gates. You remember Randy."

"The druggie?" George said in surprise.

"Yep. He was working construction down the street from Jackson's, but he quit when—" Stuart's voice faded out.

"I'm losing you," said George.

"Check it out, okay?" Stuart shouted. "See if you can locate blah, blah, blah, blur—"

"What?" said George.

But Stuart was gone. Damn cells. Especially in Dudley. The hills blocked them. Randy Gates, that little shit, Jenny seemed too classy a lady for the likes of him. He didn't fit in. Maybe important. George knew from experience that things that didn't fit in were important.

Right now, though, he was standing in plain sight of Sid's house and had been there long enough for Sid to look out a window and see him, element of surprise gone. Might as well have driven the Caddy.

George trudged the rest of the way, up steps that led to a small porch on the side of the house. A potted fern that had died of thirst long ago shed crinkly leaves on the wood railing. He knocked on the varnished oak door, listened, knocked again. A terra-cotta sun hung by the side of the door, and next to that was a window, slatted white blind down. George peered in, trying to see through the slats.

"No one's home," someone said. "Just called him on my cell."

George turned.

A man with curly gray hair and sunglasses stood a few yards below. He was wearing a long cream-colored collarless shirt that George wouldn't be caught dead in and sandals with tire bottoms, and he carried what looked like a goddamn *purse.*

"Yeah?" said George. "I just used *my* cell, and they don't work too good around here."

"You have to get to know the blind spots," said the man.

George gestured with his head toward the Ford Explorer. "That his?"

"It is." The man shrugged. "He probably walked downtown."

"So even though he's not home you came up here anyway?"

"I wanted to drop this off." He brandished a newspaper. "Here." He tossed it up, and George caught it: the Dudley local weekly; he'd never read it. He set it by the door.

"Thought he'd get a kick out of my latest," said the man.

"Your latest?"

"Letter. I'm Ken Dooley," the man explained importantly, as if that meant something.

Well, it did. Ken Dooley was that guy who'd threatened the Border Patrol, and Dakota had mentioned him in reference to something Ken had said about Jenny. *He and Sid were friends?* "Hey," said George, "you must have known Jenny Williams."

"Jenny Williams." Ken took off his sunglasses and polished them with the hem of his shirt. His eyes were blank as a newborn baby's. "I met her a couple of times."

"Here at Sid's?"

"Can't remember where," said Ken glibly. "If I see Sid, I'll tell him you stopped by. Who'd you say you were?"

"Harry," said George, reaching. "Harry Potter."

Ken laughed. Haw. Haw. "Bet you get razzed about that, big time."

George looked at his watch and suppressed a yawn. "Got to run," he said. "Sales rep meeting in twenty minutes."

THE MAGICIAN PASSED the last house on Brewery Gulch and climbed slowly up the dirt path that led to his cave, panting a little. He'd gotten out of shape from being in jail, though his bones didn't ache as bad as they had when he'd gone in. He had his bell in his hand, and in the leather bag five dollars and forty-two cents he'd made from tourists by ringing his bell all the way up the gulch. Robot, robot, robot.

He smelled creosote and prickly dust and jasmine. Jasmine, jasmine, jasmine. The path turned around a stand of mesquite, and then he saw the balloons. Red balloons, their strings moored under rocks on each side of the cave entrance. Jasmine. Frieda had been here. Frieda, Frieda, Frieda. He reached the balloons. They were a little deflated, slack, as if their air had slowly leaked out while they waited for him. He removed the rocks from the strings of the round red balls of air and freed them. They bobbled and moved away, but only a few inches, like faithful pets.

He stooped and went into the cave. There were three gallon jugs of water, his sleeping bag, and on top of it a paper sack. He looked inside. Dried apricots, currants, walnuts, pecans. Frieda, Frieda, Frieda. He opened his leather bag and took out three bologna sandwiches and put them in the paper sack.

Then he lay down on the sleeping bag and went to sleep.

o   o   o

"WHAT'D YOU FIND out about Randy Gates?" Ruth eyeballed Stuart significantly from behind her desk in his office. "It has to be important. I mean, Jenny would never smoke marijuana. She was one of those my-body-is-a-temple kind of people."

"My investigator's on overload right now, but he'll be working on it." Stuart finished off a cheese Danish, then leaned over and grabbed a tissue. He wiped his fingers. "What's on for the day?"

"Court appearance at ten in Division One," said Ruth, "then another at eleven thirty over in Justice Court. Files are on your desk for this morning, and I'll pull the ones for this afternoon."

Stuart groaned. "Busy day." He went into his office for the files.

"You could eat a little healthier," called Ruth. "All that sweet stuff raises your blood sugar too fast, then it plummets. What are you doing Saturday night?"

"Nothing."

"Then come to dinner at my house. I'll have Million Dollar Chicken, and you can meet Mara and Tyler."

"Sure," said Stuart, coming out with the files. "Why not."

"Your tie's crooked," Ruth called after him as he went out the door.

Alone in the office, Ruth thought she might look at Jackson's file and go over it, but even though she went through all the filing cabinets and even, surreptitiously, Stuart's desk, she couldn't find it anywhere.

Mara was going to visit Jackson in jail tomorrow. Today she was going to spend her time at Jackson's house, with the doors locked, she *promised,* apparently planning to read every book that he owned. Ruth sighed worriedly, then turned back to her desk and went to work.

Billing. That was the key, not the legal stuff. Billing could make or break you. She worked for an hour, then sat back in her chair and looked out the window.

All she'd done since she'd moved to Arizona basically was substitute teach, working with other people's kids so she could be home with her own when they got out of school. Now here she was in a grown-up's place where she could look out at the people going by on the street instead of being trapped inside an institution, and hardly any of them were kids, or if they were she could just enjoy them, didn't have to monitor them and worry. She could think frivolous thoughts whenever she wanted to—maybe even buy some new clothes.

Ruth felt as though without even knowing it she'd been living in a dark closet, and now a door had opened and she could see the vibrant world outside and be part of it again.

The bell tinkled, a door *did* open, and a man walked in. He had curly graying hair and tinted wire-rims and wore jeans and a loose white Indian kurta.

"Hello there," he said. "I was just walking by, and I saw you sitting at Ellie's desk."

"It's mine now," said Ruth, with a touch of pride. "I'm Mr. Ross's new office manager. Ellie quit."

"She did? Gee. And you're—"

"Ruth Norton."

"Ken Dooley." He smiled modestly. "Maybe you've read some of my letters in the paper."

Ruth brightened. "Yes, I have. My goodness. You were in the Sierra Vista paper, too. Is the Border Patrol still giving you trouble?"

"Sure, but I don't mind," said Ken. "I'm fighting the good fight. Trouble is my business." He ran his fingers through his hair boyishly. "Guess my friend Stuart doesn't mind a little trouble, either. Heard he got the Jackson Williams case. I was thinking about it just the other day. Who's the investigator Stuart's got on it? Guy with the bushy eyebrows, fiftyish—forgot his name."

"Me, too," said Ruth, "if Stuart ever told me. I haven't met him yet. You were thinking about the case?"

"Yeah. Wondering if it was something I might want to look into."

"Oh." Ruth flushed with excitement. "That would be so wonderful, if you could help. Jackson is definitely innocent. There's no doubt in my mind at all."

"*Really?*" His eyes met hers. "Why don't you tell me all about it."

"I can't," said Ruth. "But I can make an appointment for you to talk to Mr. Ross."

"That would be dandy," said Ken Dooley, "but not now. I'm up to my ears." He shrugged. "Maybe later. I'll call."

GEORGE DROVE BACK to Sierra Vista and called Stuart from his apartment.

"Stuart Ross, attorney at law."

"Ellie?"

"No, Ellie quit. This is Ruth, I just started working here."

"Ellie quit? Damn. Well, hello, Ruth. This is Stuart's investigator, George Maynard."

"George Maynard. Oh, good. Someone asked me your name and I didn't know it. Now I do."

"Stuart around?"

"No. He's really busy today. I can have him call you."

"That's okay, I'll call him at home this evening. When he's not out there in the stratosphere."

Ruth laughed. "I know just what you mean."

George hung up. He tried to place who she was; he knew some legal secretaries, but no one called Ruth. Randy Gates—Stuart had asked him to locate Randy Gates. He yawned, took off his shoulder holster, picked up the phone again, and spent the next half hour or so smoking too many cigarettes and calling around to friends in law enforcement, to get a lead on Randy's whereabouts. Couple of possibilities, which he wrote down.

Then something else occurred to him, and he called back Matt Hooper, best cop he knew in Sierra Vista. "Anita Selby," he said. "Got anything on her?"

"Anita Selby? The real estate lady?" Matt laughed. "You're kidding me."

"I'm not."

"Woman of the Year here in Sierra Vista," said Matt. "Two years ago. I was there when she got a plaque from the mayor."

So the only thing Anita had ever done to get the attention of law enforcement was get an award. Well, he planned to talk to her again, spring Randy's name on her. Randy was a lowlife, and Stuart couldn't see a connection to Jenny Williams, but that was all the more reason to check it out—you couldn't get locked into a theory. For all he knew Jenny had been a big-time dealer, hiding behind respectability. Just thinking this made him tired.

He stretched out on the couch and propped his sole pillow under his head. Damn Dakota. He needed to focus on this case instead of doing calisthenics every night. Weren't there any women out there anymore who enjoyed quiet nights at home, just talking, maybe a little television after dinner? Thinking this, he fell asleep.

GEORGE WOKE SUDDENLY. *What? Where?* He rubbed his left arm, still asleep from being wedged under the sofa cushion. The light coming through the front window was dim—dusk—he'd slept for hours. Shit. Sid Hamblin. *His A.A. meeting*—forget that, Sid had priority. He groaned, got up and strapped on his shoulder holster, put in the Colt Commander, jacket over everything, then staggered outside to the Olds.

He picked up a Whopper with cheese at McD's on the way out of town and ate while he drove, window down, cool air blowing in. By the time he got to Dudley, he was wide awake. It was dark now, half moon low in the sky. He wanted to smoke, but he'd forgotten his cigarettes. He drove slowly up Moon Canyon and parked a ways down, before the dirt road started, where he couldn't be seen from the A-frame, then got out and walked.

Lights streamed from the wooden houses along the canyon, where people were sitting on their porches, voices easy in the evening cool. From inside, televisions murmured. When the road turned to dirt, George saw the Ford Explorer and, even better, a light coming from a back window of the A-frame. He hiked up the dirt road, stumbling on rocks and potholes in the dark, reached the steps, and went up to the door, panting a little from too many cigarettes.

The newspaper Ken Dooley had tossed to him was still where George had put it by the door. Guess old Ken wasn't *that* important.

George knocked, knocked again. The slatted blind was still down, darkness behind the chinks. He went around to the deck. Double French doors, uncurtained. The moon gave a little more light here, enough to see, dimly, inside but the light he'd seen on in the back didn't reach here. He could make out a living room, a big leather couch. He went closer. The French doors were not only not locked but slightly ajar.

"Hey, Sid," he called. "George Maynard here."

Silence.

He'd spent years as a cop knocking on doors, and something here didn't feel right. George pulled the gun from the shoulder holster and stepped inside without touching the doors. A light coming from a hall at the back of the room gave some visibility, but not much. "George Maynard here, Sid," he said again. "Thought we could talk."

He skirted the big leather couch and banged his knee on an end table as he headed for the hall. At the end of the hall was an open door where the light was coming from, and through the door George could see a computer, intricate pipes busily forming and re-forming on the screen saver.

Suddenly he felt a presence: eerie but familiar, not human.

"Sid?"

No answer. Something cracked underfoot. He looked down. Pale green disks the size of big buttons were scattered on the floor. *What the*—then he saw the empty bottle. Tums Ultra.

"Sid?" he called again, but he knew what that presence was. He took a deep breath and went through the open door into the room.

Sid Hamblin was lying on the floor a few feet to the side of the computer desk, facedown, one arm out like a swimmer heading for the shore. He was wearing only a pair of boxer shorts, gray with red hearts, and his flesh was greenish white as though he'd spent his life under a rock. *Jesus Christ.*

An image, lasting only a second but precise as a digital picture, flashed into George's mind. A woman, forty-five years old, strangled on a bed, her nightgown pulled up, exposing her privates. His first homicide. Instinctively, against all his training, he'd reached over, pulled the nightgown down.

George got to Sid fast, thinking *heart attack*—CPR—no sign of blood or trauma. He squatted down, checked the pulse points, then saw the purple bruising on the white flesh of the outstretched arm, the legs where they touched the floor. *Lividity.* The guy was dead, and had been for a while.

Probably already dead when George had knocked on his door that morning and chatted with Ken Dooley.

He took another deep breath, thinking of the Tums Ultra scattered in the hall. Heart attacks sometimes masqueraded as indigestion. Type-A kind of guy, sure, but what came to George's mind was poison, just like Jenny Williams. And Jackson in jail, so maybe off the hook. Something nudged at the corner of his mind, something related to Jenny Williams that Sid had said, but he couldn't get hold of it.

On the screen saver, the intricate pipes were still obsessively forming and re-forming. George reached over and jiggled the mouse with the sleeve of his corduroy jacket. The screen cleared; rows of cards. Free Cell. Those last moments before he died, the guy had been playing Free Cell.

Now it was time to call the cops. Dudley P.D. *Oh, man.* George groaned. Stick around, make sure they did it right. He wished he'd brought his cigarettes.

STUART WAS LYING on his couch virtuously watching the Discovery Channel when his phone rang.

"Stuart Ross, attorney at law," he said unthinkingly.

"George here. Sid Hamblin's dead."

Stuart sat up on the couch *"What?"*

"Yeah. I found him, couple hours ago. Couldn't rouse anyone at his place this morning, so I went back up there tonight, walked right in, doors weren't locked. He was lying on the floor by his computer, dead as dead can be."

"No *shit*. How?"

"Dunno for sure. I called Dudley P.D., then hung around to make sure they did the scene the way they should. They're calling it an apparent heart attack."

"Heart attack." Stuart felt a twinge of anxiety. "How old was he, anyway?"

" 'Bout your age. Reason I went to see him was he lied to me the first time I talked to him out at the college. He might have been having a thing with Jenny Williams."

"*What?* And you didn't tell me?"

"You were big on Randy Gates. Besides, the damn cell was fading."

"I'm still big on Randy Gates. You know he's got a couple of assaults, in with the drug stuff. Randy was at Jackson's the day Jenny died. He could have planted the aconite under the bed then."

"If he did, I'm betting he was someone else's pawn. Don't worry, he's next on my list. I already got a few leads as to his whereabouts." George laughed. "The more I think about Randy, the more unlikely it seems, him and Jenny, a health nut, for God's sake. She— *Bingo, I got it.*"

"Got what?"

"What I was trying to remember. Sid was taking the same stuff she was. Those probiotics. In fact, he took some right in front of me, in his office. Said she turned him on to them."

"Son of a bitch," said Stuart. "Someone spiked his pills, too? Hot dog. That would get Jackson off the hook." He paused. "Uh, maybe."

"Yeah, maybe. If Sid bought the pills after Jackson got arrested. Wait for the autopsy. Could have been a heart attack. If not, keep your fingers crossed and hope for the best. For all we know he choked on a Tums; they were all over the floor."

"I'll try to get a rush on it." Stuart gave a hollow chuckle. "Throw out those magic words, *serial killer*."

o o o

THE MAGICIAN WOKE in the night. The sound that woke him was mingled with whatever he'd been dreaming, so he didn't know if it was near or faraway, anymore than he knew if it was eight o'clock at night or three in the morning, but he knew his sounds. Bug sounds, bird sounds, animal sounds. Dog, cat, skunk, rabbit, javelina. Once a mountain lion. Mountain lion, lion, lion. Rain sounds and wind sounds, the sound a rock made as it settled deeper into the earth.

This sound had not been bug or bird or animal. Not rain or wind or rock. Then he heard it again. Not close yet, but coming. *Human.* Robot, robot, robot.

Dressed except for his old black sneakers, he rolled off the sleeping bag and pulled them on fast, no time to tie, grabbed his leather bag, stooped his way out from the cave, and peered down the hill.

The path up wound around. He saw the shape at the curve. Human coming. *And he knew who it was.* Someone who'd figured things out—that they didn't add up. Robot, robot, robot. He hurried as quietly as he could up the rise behind the cave. Human getting closer. He began to run, tripped on a rock, grazed his ankle, rubbed it, smelling the copper penny of his own blood. Bleeding, bleeding, bleeding. The shoelaces on one shoe caught on a mesquite bush branch, and he tugged his foot free, leaving the shoe behind.

He smelled mesquite. Smelled stale earth dust, smelled, faintly, skunk. Smelled human. Closer, closer. Robot, robot, robot. Jail had weakened him. The bag was heavy, full of treasures weighing him down. He tossed it away and ran, tripped, fell down again.

eleven

GEORGE PARKED THE Caddy in front of a trailer up on blocks in Lot Nine of the Shady Rest Trailer Park and got out. The trailer had a mini white picket fence and neat graveled yard, with a big ocotillo plant in the middle. Next to the ocotillo was a hand-painted sign that said DUN ROAMIN. He walked past that trailer, and two more, to Lot Six.

It was 9:00 A.M. At eight, Sandy had called him; her mom had sent her money to buy a new washing machine, and she'd asked if he would mind meeting her at the mall in the afternoon to go to Sears with her to help pick one out. She had a theory that you didn't get as good a deal on major appliances if you weren't with a man.

The trailer in Lot Six had a rusty wire fence surrounding a dirt yard full of weeds surrounding a beat-up old couch that looked as if it had been rained on more than once. By the door were a tricycle and a yellow plastic toy truck, missing its wheels.

"Dylan!" a woman's voice cried from inside. "*Please.* Didn't you hear Mommy say no?"

A child wailed.

George opened the gate and walked inside. Hairy seeds from the weeds grabbed at his legs and stuck to the denim of his dressiest pair of jeans. He pulled a few of them off.

"Hello?" he called to give warning.

Inside the trailer was a sudden silence.

He went up the cinder blocks that served as steps to the door and knocked. The door was half ajar. "Anybody home? Brianne?"

A slender woman in her early twenties, in jeans and a black top that showed her midriff, came to the door. The last time he'd seen her was six years ago, when he was still a police detective and she was being held in juvie on marijuana possession charges. She'd been blond then, and now her hair was spiked and hennaed a deep mahogany, but with her even features and pale lucent green eyes, she was still beautiful, beautiful enough, George thought, to be on TV or in the movies.

Which in her case was a curse: scared away the nice guys and brought on the losers.

"Brianne," he said. "Looking good."

"Detective Maynard," she said dubiously. She closed her eyes. "Please, God, I don't need this." She opened her eyes again. "What are you doing here?"

"Private investigating." George handed her his card. "I'm not a cop anymore," he said. "I'm off the force."

"Mommy!"

She turned her head. "Dylan, hush. Mommy's busy." She looked down at the card.

"You got a kid now, huh?" said George. "Randy's?"

"Yes." Her mouth turned down. "For what *that's* worth. We're not married or anything. I'm, like, a single mom." She paused. "Do I have to talk to you? What about?"

"Brianne," said George, "this is not about you. Hear me out. You got a meth lab in the backyard, I don't even care. I mean, I do, in a way, for your sake and the kid's, 'cause you're a whole lot better than those losers you used to hang out with. *Smart.* I always figured sooner or later, you'd find your way."

There was a silence.

"The yard's a mess," said Brianne after a moment. "This guy was supposed to haul away that couch, but he never showed. I don't have time to do everything. I work nights and leave Dylan with my mom, so I'm too tired to do much in the daytime, just clean inside a little." She sighed. "Okay, sure, whatever. Come on in."

George came in, to a living room, fairly neat, dominated by a twenty-seven-inch TV and little doilies. They were everywhere, on the backs and arms of the couch and an old recliner, on an end table, and on the head of the child sitting on the couch.

"Dylan," said Brianne, "what are you doing?"

"Me pretty," he said. He giggled wildly and flung the doily at her. He was maybe three, his cheeks pink, his hair a tangle of black curls.

"You certainly are." Brianne smiled. "Pretty as pretty can be. Why don't you go to your room now, okay, honey? So Mommy can talk to this man."

"Okay, honey," Dylan mimicked, giggling again. He got up and retreated behind the recliner, where he sat on the floor.

Brianne ignored him and fell onto the couch. "Sit down," she said to George.

He sat on a dilapidated upholstered green chair, springs shot. "Cute kid," he said.

She nodded. "He looks just like Randy in his baby pictures. Randy's the best-looking guy. That's what always got to me. That and how goddamn charming he can be. He treats you like you're the most special person in the world, you know? And then you turn around and he's doing it to someone else."

"He paying child support, I hope?" George asked.

"Yes. No. I mean, he *was.* He had a construction job, oh, up till pretty recently. Then he just went and quit." She shrugged. "Or got fired. Whatever."

"Asshole," said George with feeling. "What's wrong with these guys, anyway? Way past thirty and still no sense of responsibility at all. He got other kids, too?"

"Not as far as I know." She twirled a spike of hair. "He better not, 'cause he never even wants to see Dylan that much. I don't care about him anymore, except for the child support. I mean, you can only take so much and then the love is gone."

"So you don't see him anymore?"

Her eyes shifted away. "Not really."

"Where's he hanging out now?"

She stared at him for a minute. "Shit," she said in disgust. "I just caught on. And I thought you were all concerned about *me*." She rolled her eyes. "God, how dumb can you get? You cops are all the same. This is about Randy, isn't it? What the hell's he done now?"

"Aw, Brianne, he didn't do anything far as I know. I just need to talk to him like I'm talking to you."

"Well, I have no idea where he is. None. He mails me the child support, or he *did*, with no return address. I haven't seen him in months."

George didn't believe her for a second. "You think you owe him anything? Why, Brianne?" He leaned toward her. "What's he ever done for you?"

"What's anyone ever done for me?" said Brianne. She looked at her watch and stood up. "Dylan, time to go to Grandma's." She turned to George. "No one's ever done anything for me except my mom, including you."

To Jackson's left was a Mexican man, and beyond the plate glass window were three members of the Mexican's family; a boy, a girl, and presumably a wife. The wife had the phone to her ear, and the Mexican man was shouting at her in Spanish.

To Jackson's right, a straggly-haired blond Anglo talked to a sobbing woman on the other side of the plate glass.

Suspended in a time eighteen years ago, when he had lived in a scruffy apartment in the East Village in New York City, waking to a child jumping on the bed, Maggie beside him, Jackson waited for Maggie's daughter, *his* daughter, to come into the visiting room. She was late; he'd thought maybe she wasn't coming after all—too ashamed, or scared.

Then the guard had shown up. "Williams. You got a visitor."

A breathless young woman appeared beyond the glass in front of him. She wore a lilac-colored T-shirt and tiny sunglasses. She was tall and blond and beautiful. His daughter. Pride swelled inside him, unearned pride, but he couldn't help it.

She removed her sunglasses and picked up the phone. Jackson hurriedly picked up his own.

"I got lost," she said, still a little breathless. She put her hand over her free ear, to block out the sound of the man shouting and the woman sobbing. "Can you hear me?"

"*Yes.*" He paused. "You look like your mother. Beautiful."

"Thank you," said Mara. "Everyone always says that. I mean"—she flushed—"that I look like her."

"It's true."

"She died. She had cancer." Beyond the glass, Mara's eyes filled with tears. She glanced at the people around her and blinked them away. "Sorry."

"For what?" said Jackson. Maggie, beautiful Maggie, younger than he was, had died of cancer, was dead. He already knew, of course, but Mara telling him again now brought it closer to home. He felt dizzy as if he might drop the phone and fall off his chair onto the floor. "You have every right."

"It just isn't *fair*. It's—it's—" Mara took out a Kleenex from somewhere, and blew her nose. She blinked away tears again. "Anyway," she said matter-of-factly. "Ruth and Tyler say hello."

Jackson felt relieved. Even though he'd spoken to Ruth on the phone, somehow he'd imagined that pretty soon she and Tyler would forget him entirely. With Mara there, maybe they would remember him a little longer. "Give them both a hug for me," he said. "Your mother—" he began, but Mara got teary eyed again.

142

"Not *here*," she said.

He looked at her, trying to think what to say, how to help her with her mother's death, the space around them filled with a woman's sobs and the voices of children speaking in Spanish. If he were only out, they could go somewhere and talk.

"Carlos says hi, too," Mara said.

"Carlos?" said Jackson, astounded. "My student? You met him? Where?"

"At the release hearing. He says you're a really good teacher. Listen, I know you like poetry." She looked at him obliquely from under her eyelashes. "I thought since I don't know you yet, I would read you a poem."

She opened a book that Jackson couldn't see. "I hope you can hear over this racket," she said, and began to read. *"Come, let us tell the weeds in ditches—"*

The Louise Bogan poem, the one he'd read his class that first session, lifetimes ago. Stabbed in the heart, Jackson closed his eyes. He knew the poem so well, all the noise around him seemed to stop, leaving him in a bell jar of silence. He listened to it all the way through. It was magical in a way, but in another way the worst thing she could have done, because it made him see things so clearly.

He was living in a sterilized world, everything neutral colored and fluorescent, and he would be here forever, hardly ever get to see his daughter. Even now, the guards were hustling the visitors to go. He began to cry.

"Oh, my goodness," said Mara. "I didn't mean to upset you."

He put down the phone and lowered his head so she couldn't see until he got himself under control. Then he raised his head. "Thank you for the poem."

A guard came up to Mara. *"Wait,"* she said to him fiercely.

"Better do what he says," Jackson said warningly. "Please come back again."

"Oh, I will." Mara hung up the phone and stood up. Then she leaned down and picked up the phone again. "Don't worry," she said. "Everything will be all right. We'll get you out of here." She put her free hand on the glass and spread it wide. "I promise."

GEORGE STOOD IN the bright, even light of the appliance center at Sears looking down into the maw of a washing machine, thinking of what Brianne had said. *You cops are all alike.*

"It's a front loader," said Sandy. She'd had her hair cut newly short and frosted since he'd last seen her and was wearing a jogging suit, red trimmed with white. Because she had to dress up a bit for work— secretary for an elementary school principal—she used to wear mostly jeans and a sweatshirt on weekends, but now she looked so shiny and plastic it was as though she were wrapped in cellophane.

Good God, thought George, *she's turning into someone like Anita Selby.*

"Can I help you folks?" A very young man materialized from nowhere, crisp white shirt and red tie. He looked as clean and spiffy as an altar boy.

"Maybe," said Sandy. She glanced at George. "Front loaders cost more, but they're definitely the best."

"That's right, sir," said the young man. "You can't go wrong with a front loader. Less water, less electricity, won't tear up your clothes. It'll save you big bucks in the end."

George tried to focus on front loaders, but he kept thinking about Anita. A cold person really, under that phony smile. Poison, a woman's crime, people said. Had Jenny been carrying on with Sid and lied to Anita about it, then Anita found out? So she'd—

"*George?*" Sandy was staring at him impatiently. "Well, what do you think?"

He glanced at the price displayed on a big yellow sticker. "It's a lot of money."

"You spend money to save money," said Sandy.

"Your missus is right," said the young man.

Sandy smiled at the young man, maybe a little too brightly. Maybe not. After the divorce she'd gotten her teeth professionally whitened, and she smiled a lot more than she used to.

"This the best deal you got on a front loader?" George asked.

"This one's on sale, this week only," said the young man. He lowered his voice. "Between you and me, it's the best deal in the whole store."

"What I meant," George said to him, "was maybe you got one with a ding in it somewhere. You know? 'Cause this is more than we want to pay."

Sandy opened her mouth, but George gave her a look.

"Worth every penny," said the young man.

George looked at his watch. "Maybe we should shop around a little more," he said.

"Tell you what," the young man said, "now that I think of it, we do have one that's similar, with a little scratch on the side. We close the deal now and I'll give you two hundred dollars off."

"What do you think?" George asked Sandy. "Can you live with a little scratch?"

Sandy nodded. "I'll take it," she said.

Her eyes were shining, full of elation at getting a good deal, even though as far as George could see a front-loading washing machine wouldn't make any difference to anyone in the world except Sandy, and not even her after a while when she got used to it.

An image, unwanted, rose up in front of him: Sid Hamblin lying on the floor in his boxer shorts, gray printed with red hearts—the kind of thing women gave men for Valentine's Day. He imagined Sid opening the present. *Thanks, honey!* He hadn't even looked at Sid's face, busy checking the pulse points, being a professional. *You cops are all alike.* He focused back on Sandy.

"Happy now?" he asked her as the salesman wrote up the sales slip.

"Yes," said Sandy. "Thank you."

She smiled at him, a woman with extremely white teeth and newly frosted hair in a red and white jogging suit. George looked into her blue eyes and saw, reflected back, not himself but an accommodating stranger.

THAT EVENING STUART came to dinner at Ruth's and afterward they all sat in the living room and played scrabble: Mara, Tyler, Stuart, and Ruth. "Sid Hamblin certainly looked like the kind of person who would have a heart attack," said Ruth. "Overblown." She sighed. "I didn't like him much, and now I feel bad about it."

"Save your guilt," said Stuart, "for something that matters." No reason, he thought, to get her all riled up and freaked out by telling her about his suspicions concerning Sid's death unless they were confirmed.

"Sid Hamblin? That fat guy at Jenny's memorial?" Tyler asked.

"Stocky," said Ruth.

"How come you didn't like him?"

"Tyler, hush for a moment."

Stuart lined up his Scrabble tiles on the little wooden holder. A, E, I, I, I, U, U. He scowled. And he was in third place, in front of Tyler and behind Mara, who was second, and Ruth. He scowled some more. It was only a game, but he couldn't help wanting to win. It was in his blood.

Mara placed some of her tiles, using an I that was already there, to make JIVING, hitting the double word space with the G. "That's thirty-four," she said.

"Very good," said Ruth. "You're catching up to me." She wrote it down.

"Think I'll pass," said Stuart with a gambler's rakish air. "Taking all new tiles." He put his old tiles aside, pulled new ones out of the bag, and lined them up. I, N, A, B, T, T, E.

Ruth put down GLAZES, hitting the double letter space with her own G, plus the double word space, plus picking up INTONE with the S. "My goodness, that's *forty-three*," she said. She glanced at Stuart, but he refused to meet her eyes.

"Ma!" said Tyler. "No fair, you always, always win."

"Bad sport, bad sport," Mara taunted. "She hasn't won yet."

"It's not winning that's important," said Ruth, automatic as a schoolmarm. "It's how you play."

"Easy for *her* to say," Stuart said to Tyler.

146

It was Tyler's turn. He always took forever. He squinted at his tiles, moving them around. Stuart looked at the board, then stared down at his own lined-up letters.

"I have an idea," Mara said to Stuart. "About what you could do to get Jackson released."

"Yeah?" Stuart looked at Mara warily. They hadn't talked much about Jackson over dinner. It had been a good dinner, too, something called Million Dollar Chicken, made with salsa and honey, served over couscous. Ruth said it took only half an hour to make, and she'd given him the recipe. Everything had been relaxed, even fun. Now here was the price tag. "What?"

"You could talk to Jenny's mother, make her understand he couldn't have done it. Then maybe she'd write a new letter saying it was okay for him to be released."

"No way I can do that," said Stuart. "As Jackson's attorney, I'm not allowed. And she's been talking to the prosecution, obviously, so she's convinced he killed her daughter. Of course she wouldn't want him released."

"Her name is Grace," Ruth said to no one in particular. "Grace Dixon."

"Grace Dixon," said Mara. "You *know* her?"

"I sat with her after the funeral." Ruth sighed. "What an ordeal."

"She doesn't like Jackson?" said Mara.

"I don't know what she likes," said Ruth.

"*I* could talk to her," Mara said to Stuart. "Where does she live?"

"Some retirement community outside of Tucson. But you can't." He stared down at his tiles; he had something there, but he couldn't figure out just what. He moved the A to the front of the line. "It would be the same as me talking to her."

"That sucks." Mara stamped her foot on the floor. "I have to do *something*. I promised Jackson. He's *suffering*."

Tyler giggled wildly and put down SHIT, using the T in INTONES, the H landing on the double letter. "Twelve," he said.

"Your turn," Ruth said to Stuart.

Stuart moved his tiles around, arranging. He looked at the board. *Aha.*

"There must be something I can do," Mara persisted.

"Tell you what," Stuart said distractedly. "You might be able to talk to Jenny's mother through the victim advocate, over at the county attorney's office. I'll give you her name."

Stuart glanced at Ruth as he put down his tiles: ABETTING on the triple word space, hitting the G in GLAZES. "Used up all my letters," he said triumphantly. "Eighty-three points."

"TYLER!" SAID RUTH, after Stuart left. "Trash under the sink is full. You need to take it outside."

"Aw, Ma." Tyler groaned theatrically. "I have a tummy ache."

"I can do it," said Mara.

"No," said Ruth. "It's one of his chores."

Tyler walked slowly into the kitchen, pretending he couldn't bend his arms and legs. It was hard taking the trash bag out of the container under the sink without bending his elbows, but he managed to do it.

"There are chicken bones in there," called Ruth. "Make sure you close it tight, so animals don't get into it."

Cheating, Tyler bent his arms and tightened the tie. Then he walked stiff-legged out the back door and around to the side of the house to the big garbage can. He opened the can, threw in the bag, and clamped on the lid. Stars studded the sky; a cricket chirped.

He'd had a stomachache for so long, he was almost used to it, but it was better than thinking. If he thought too hard about not thinking about what he was trying not to think about, he would think about it, and then he would *have* to tell. Standing under the stars, Tyler struck a pose and did a series of rapid karate chops, swish, swish, swish, then kicked out with one foot. Hah. Got 'em in the balls.

twelve

GEORGE PARKED THE oil-belching Olds in the little strip mall across from Sierra Realty. He'd rather have driven the Caddy, but Anita had already seen it, even commented on it, when they'd left the real estate office together. It was a workday morning, early, and the parking spaces in front of the realty office were full of cars, including Anita Selby's, a red Honda Accord. He knew the Accord was Anita's because fifteen minutes ago he'd watched her pull in and get out, this time wearing a navy blue pantsuit, *serious.*

He took the lid off the foam cup and sipped. Then he put it down, opened the window a bit, and lit up a cigarette. He didn't think asking Anita to lunch would fly after that last time, and he didn't want to walk into an office full of people, all staring, while Anita hissed at him and threatened to call her lawyer. What he needed was an unguarded moment.

Three cigarettes later, no, damn it, four, Anita sashayed out of the office and got into the Accord. He started up the Olds and followed, three or four cars behind, as she drove south out of town, past the big mall and the new developments, out into open country, going toward the foothills. Then the cars thinned out, and he drove slower so he would still be pretty far behind, just a harmless old codger in his crummy Oldsmobile.

Coming up on Jack Rabbit Road, her right blinker flashed. George slowed even more; there wasn't much up Jack Rabbit Road except three or four high-end-of-the-dollar houses, so he wasn't afraid of losing her. By the time he made the turn onto Jack Rabbit, the red Honda Accord had vanished. The road ascended, hilly, curving, sides thick with live oak and bird of paradise, no sign of her car—then there it was, just a curve away, red through the live oak, in front of a house, blurred by the brush, but wood and adobe, *big,* another car there, too.

He pulled over to the side where the live oak was even thicker, opened his window, and heard voices.

". . . *love* it," Anita was saying. "Big fireplace in the family room, oak floors throughout."

"It didn't say *anywhere* there wasn't a *pool,*" whined a woman's voice. "It didn't, did it, Freddy?"

"No, dear."

"We're really set on having . . ." The voice faded away.

Showing a house. This could take years. It was heating up outside. George kept the engine running for the air-conditioning but left the window down. For a while, he drifted, smoking carefully—fire alert level high—flicking his ash into the foam cup, where it hissed out in the coffee left at the bottom. Then he heard voices again. A little sooner than he'd expected.

". . . have to dredge out the *mountain* to put one in," the woman whined. "There's just no *way.*"

Car doors slammed. Engines started up. George realized, too late, he should have turned his car around before he parked. A Jeep Cherokee drove by, tires spitting dust, the Honda Accord just behind. Oh, well, just let her go by; she wouldn't recognize him in the Olds. The Honda passed him, too, then braked, pulled over, stopped.

Anita Selby got out, slamming the door behind her hard. She marched over, a little awkward in pointy-toed heels not intended for hiking.

"What the hell do you think you're doing!" she shouted. "*Stalking me!* I'll put a restraining order on you, God damn it. I mean it."

"Easy, easy," said George soothingly. "A couple more questions is all."

"*More?*" She stamped her foot, but she looked tired, defeated, her perfect hair mussed, lipstick almost gone. "This is ridiculous. I told you everything I know."

"I can see why you're pissed," said George, "and I don't blame you one bit. Show people this beautiful house and all they care about is a damn pool."

"*Assholes,*" said Anita vehemently. "You, too." But she didn't look quite as angry. "Wasting your time digging up dirt on Jenny, stalking me, when there are people you *should* be talking to, people a lot more involved than I was."

"Like Randy Gates?"

Her face froze. "Who?"

"Why don't you get inside," said George. "Air-conditioning's on. Take a load off while you tell me all about those other people."

TAPED TO THE open door of the office of Victor Robles, the deputy county attorney prosecuting the Jackson Williams case, were several cartoons about lawyers and a quote from James Burke about slime rising to the top. They had been there all the years Stuart had known Victor. Stuart tapped on the doorjamb, and Victor looked up from between two columns of red disclosure files on his desk.

"Stuart. Hey." He stood up, extended his hand, and shook Stuart's. "Good to see you." He had gray hair and a youthful face. "Come on in and close the door."

Stuart did and sat down on the only other chair in the room. Out the window on his left was a view of the parking lot, and on one wall, next to Victor's law degree from the University of Arizona, was a sole act of rebellion; a large poster of Bart Simpson.

"So, how's it going, Victor?" Stuart asked. "Your oldest still in law school?"

"He's taking off a year," said Victor. He made a face. "He decided maybe he wants to make movies instead."

"Practical," said Stuart.

"You know how it is with kids."

"Sure," said Stuart, though he didn't. Not with kids like Victor's, good kids, who never got in trouble. He settled back in the chair. "Jackson Williams. Some case, huh? A real can of worms."

"A can of worms?" said Victor neutrally. "I don't know about that."

"You heard about Sid Hamblin?"

"Yeah, about an hour ago. I was out of town this weekend." Victor steepled his fingers. "Jesus Christ. A heart attack. How old was he, anyway?"

"Our age."

There was a little silence. Victor tilted back in his chair and studied the ceiling.

"My investigator found him," Stuart said.

Victor tilted forward. "George Maynard?"

"Yep," said Stuart. "Best there is."

"When he's sober."

"He's sober," said Stuart firmly. "Been going to A.A. six months now." He paused. "They sure saved *my* life once upon a time."

"*You* saved your life," said Victor, clearly never having given up anything to a Higher Power. "I really respect that in you, Stuart."

"Thanks."

There was a little pause.

"Anyway," said Victor, "George was probably wasting his time, talking to Sid. His statement wasn't admissible, so his death is neither here nor there as far as Jackson Williams goes."

"You think not?" Stuart said. Might as well put his cards on the table. "What if the cause of death turns out to be the same as Jenny Williams? Sid was taking that probiotics stuff, too."

"No shit. Jeez." Victor picked up a pen, put it down. Then he shrugged. "But so what? Aconite is not an ingredient of probiotics. For all I know half the college is taking it. It's not relevant. That book they seized, *Herbal Remedies*?"

"Yeah? It was listed in the evidence inventory, but I haven't seen it yet."

"Oops, sorry," said Victor. "Guess my secretary forgot to include a copy of the relevant part in the disclosure file. Anyway, it was sitting there right in Jackson's house, and it's got a couple of pages devoted to aconite. *Aconitum napellus,* monkshood. Talks about fatal dosages and everything."

Shit, but outwardly Stuart's expression didn't change.

"Is that damning or what?" said Victor smugly. "Not only that, you can buy *Aconitum napellus* right off the Internet if you know what you're looking for. Haven't got the report back from the computer guys yet."

Stuart shrugged dismissively. "I'm not worried. I got a feeling about Sid. I think he was poisoned, too, and my guy's been sitting in jail, out of the picture. I asked Dudley P.D. to put a rush on the autopsy. If the cause of death turns out to be the same as Jenny Williams, then case dismissed, Jackson goes free."

"Unless Sid bought those pills before Jackson got arrested. They work in the same damn place, for God's sake. Plenty of opportunity," said Victor. "Then you're hoist on your own petard."

Stuart already knew this, had spent a couple of sleepless nights over it, but a good offense was the best defense and all that. "In my opinion," he said, "the case sucks. There's more. I have a witness who saw someone going in the back door of Jenny's house the day she died. Guess who? Randy Gates."

"No. *Randy Gates?*" Victor looked appalled. "You're kidding me. She's way out of his league."

"I didn't say they were engaged."

Victor laughed. "You think it was Randy who had sex with her and that looks good for your client?" He leaned across the desk confidingly. "Between you and me, if my wife was screwing around with Randy Gates, I'd consider poisoning her myself."

"Randy's a damn good suspect whether they had sex or not," said Stuart, treading water. "Sleazy guy with a history of violence. He was at the house, could have planted the aconite."

"Not Randy." Victor shook his head. "Thinks with his dick. Too dumb to do anything that complicated."

"So he's working for somebody else. Whatever. Someone had sex with Jenny, and if it wasn't Randy, all the better. It brings in even more suspects. Reasonable doubt."

"It's a toss-up," said Victor.

"That's your headache, isn't it?" Stuart tried to look smug. "Toss-ups are fine by me. Toss-ups are what reasonable doubt is all about." He looked at his watch. "Got to run." He stood up. "Good talking to you, Victor."

Victor smiled, no, *beamed,* as if he'd just gotten a ten-thousand-dollar raise and his kid had decided to go back to law school. "I'll reinforce the rush on the autopsy," he called after Stuart as he went out the door.

Stuart walked out of the office, past the legal secretaries, and down the long hall to the reception area and the door. Damn. Outside he felt as though he'd just played three fast games of touch football in a row. He hadn't paid much attention to the fact that they'd seized that *Herbal Remedies* book. Jesus Christ, a book about aconite right there in Jackson's house. If Sid had been poisoned like Jenny, unless they could prove Sid had bought the pills after Jackson was arrested, then Jackson was screwed—all that Randy Gates stuff, everything, was just a smoke screen for a jury.

And Victor didn't even know that Sid might have been having a thing with Jenny Williams. Hadn't had time yet to think about that perfect motive and put two and two together and try for a match with the sperm in Jenny's vagina. Two homicides. *Aw, man.* Next thing he knew he could be begging Victor for a plea to save Jackson from the death penalty.

What the hell, wait for the autopsy report. Proceed normally until then and hope for the best.

"I've never heard of Randy Gates in my entire life." Anita fanned the air and grimaced. "Ugh. It stinks of cigarettes in here." She wound down her window. "Who is he, anyway?" she asked lightly, her voice a little too casual.

"Drug dealer."

"A drug dealer. Great. More slander." She slouched in her seat. "Jenny *never* did drugs. She didn't even drink alcohol."

"Just reporting what I know," George said. "He was seen at her house the day she died. Other times, too. If you got an explanation, I'd like to hear it."

Anita sighed wearily and put one hand on the dashboard as if to check out her manicure. A good one, pale polish, French tips. Sandy had had French tips once, which was the only reason George knew what they were. "Probably," she said, "she was buying drugs for Jackson."

"Jackson," repeated George. "Good one. Throw the slander right back in my face." He paused. "How about this? How about if she was buying dope for Sid Hamblin."

Anita froze, the hand on the dashboard stiffening to a claw. "Sid's *dead,*" she said wonderingly. "I read it in the paper yesterday. A heart attack."

"High blood pressure probably," George said. "They haven't done the autopsy yet. Gee, I hope the stuff Jenny was getting for him from Randy was marijuana and not methamphetamine. You rev up a bad heart with meth and there's no telling . . ."

"Oh, God." Anita fanned the air some more.

"Probably was just marijuana," said George. "You can go all night, I hear, on meth, and who wants that kind of action when you're out of your twenties."

"Whatever that means," said Anita flatly.

"I figure Jenny was buying it just to keep things interesting in the sack. She was sleeping with Sid, wasn't she?" He paused. "Must have pissed you off when you found out."

"I do not believe this," said Anita through her teeth. "I really don't. As if I cared. Okay. Here's something for *you* that you're not going to want to hear."

"And why not?"

"Because it's about Jackson, and you don't want to hear anything about Jackson because you're *working* for him. Poor little innocent Jackson."

"What about Jackson? I'll listen to whatever you want to tell me."

"Jackson and Ruth Norton."

"Who the hell is Ruth Norton?"

"His neighbor. Jenny used to complain how she could never get him to fix anything in the house but if something needed fixing next door he'd be over there in a shot. He spent *all his time* next door, even when Jenny was home."

"And—?"

"God." Anita looked at him in disgust. "How obtuse can you get? They were having an *affair*. Jenny told me, *crying*, Ruth Norton and Jackson were having this blatant affair right under her nose."

IN THE COUNTY attorney's building, a woman with short dark hair came out of the office of the victim witness program into the reception area where Mara was sitting in one of the chairs. The woman was dressed all in black except for her red shoes: black pants, black top, and a black choker necklace with red Chinese letters on a pendant.

Mara stood up. "Chloe Newcombe?"

"Yes." Chloe smiled.

"I'm Mara Harvey." Nervously Mara slid the St. Christopher medal she'd taken from Jackson's house back and forth on its chain.

"Mara Harvey." Chloe frowned, looking puzzled. "I'm really sorry, it doesn't ring a bell. Did we meet in court?"

"No. Actually we've never met. I'm here about Ja—Jenny Williams."

"Ohmygod," said Chloe, making it all one word. "*Jenny Williams.* I know the case, of course. It's so sad." She looked distressed, as if she really thought it *was* sad and wasn't just doing her job. "Are you a relative?"

"I'm Jackson Williams's daughter," Mara said reluctantly, because she had to say it sometime, and now Chloe would ask her to leave.

"*Jackson's* daughter." She stared at Mara. "But not Jenny's, I take it. Wait. Oh, shit." Suddenly, in front of Mara's eyes, she became an actual person. "Stuart. That *dog.*"

"I—" began Mara, blushing, but Chloe interrupted.

"Come on," she said, gesturing for Mara to follow. "Let's go outside."

Mara went with Chloe out the back door and through the parking lot to a picnic table under a chinaberry tree. It was mild outside, still Indian summer. The ground around the table was littered with yellow leaves and cigarette butts.

"Smoking area," said Chloe, sitting down on one bench. "I don't mind the butts, if you don't."

"No," said Mara. "It's okay."

"I know why you're here," said Chloe. "I could kill Stuart. This is just so typical. He sent you to ask me to beg Jenny's mom to change her mind about opposing the release, didn't he?"

Mara bit her lip. "I'm sorry," she said. "Only he didn't send me, it was my idea."

"Or so he made you think," said Chloe. She paused. "Well, I can't help you. I'm here for the victims as an advocate, and I can't coerce them into doing what they don't want to do. Jenny's mother is old and tired, and now she's lost her only daughter. She needs some peace."

"But he didn't do it," said Mara anxiously.

"He's your *father.*" Chloe looked astonished, as if realizing this for the first time. "My God, this must be really hard on you. Damn that Stuart. I hate this. Are you close to your father? Of course, you must be."

"I hadn't seen him since I was three," said Mara, "until Saturday."

"Oh. Then I don't feel so bad." Chloe looked down at the ground for a moment, then raised her eyes. "You grew up, just you and your mom?"

"No. I have a dad. He adopted me."

"And he's okay? You love him?"

Mara blinked, thinking of her dad, all alone at home except for the dog. Thought of him sitting in his old leather chair, reading some book about American history. He had loved her mother as much as she did, and she'd left him there all alone. But it was worse when she was there; it doubled the sorrow. "Yes," she said. "Yes, I do love him."

"Well, then, *he's* your father," said Chloe. "It's not biology, it's time spent together that counts." She stood up. "Look, I have to go. This conversation we had is between you and me. I wish I could help, but I just can't." She moved away. "And give Stuart a swift kick in the rear for me, okay?"

Mara gave a little giggle. "Okay."

She watched Chloe walk across the parking lot. At the door, Chloe turned back. "I wish you the best," she said. "Take care."

Mara sat on the bench for a few minutes, smelling the leaves and stale tobacco smoke, trying not to think of her dad. She was here for Jackson. She'd promised she would get him out. She had the key to Jackson's house, which had been Jenny's house, too, so Jenny's mother's address was bound to be there somewhere.

STOPPING BY FOR a quick twenty-minute update before heading over for a hearing in Division Two, Stuart squared his shoulders and looked at Jackson across the table in the law library at the jail. "Sid Hamblin?"

"What about him?"

"He's dead."

"*Dead.*" As far as Stuart could tell, Jackson looked genuinely shocked. "How?"

"Apparent heart attack."

"*Apparent?*"

"They always say that until it's confirmed by an autopsy." No point in going into things until they had the facts. There was always the chance Sid actually *had* died of a heart attack. "He have a history of heart problems?"

"Not that I know of. But he could have had problems without symptoms. I guess a lot of men don't have any symptoms, then one day they just fall over dead."

"Yeah?" For a second Stuart seriously contemplated making an appointment to see a cardiologist, then dismissed it. Where would he find the time?

"Whew." Jackson leaned back in his chair and blew out a long breath. "I'm still taking it in."

"On a lighter note," said Stuart, "I've hired Ruth as my office manager."

"You have?" Jackson's face lit up the way it always did when Stuart mentioned Ruth. "That's really great. You can discuss my case with her anytime. You have my permission."

"Listen to me," Stuart hurried on. "They seized your hard drive in the search. There's something I need to know. Is there anything incriminating on it?"

"Like what?"

Stuart threw up his hands. "I don't know. Searches on the Internet for various poisons?"

"No! Of course not!"

"Late-night diatribes in a chat room or e-mails about how much you hate your wife? Like I said, I don't know. You tell me."

"Chat rooms. I've never gone into a chat room," said Jackson. "As for e-mails, I delete them."

"Look, I don't know exactly how it works, I'm just a lawyer, but I'm pretty sure they can retrieve deleted e-mails."

Something flickered in Jackson's eyes. He looked down at the table and back up. "Casey," he said reluctantly.

Stuart pounced. "What? Who's Casey?"

"He's a professor at the University of Chicago,'" said Jackson. "A friend from the old days."

"And?"

Jackson shrugged, his eyes veiled. "It's hard to explain. Let me think about it."

The guard came into the room. "Time's up, Counselor," he said.

Stuart rose. "You think about it," he said to Jackson. "Think hard. I don't want any surprises."

IT WAS LATE afternoon when George cruised slowly by the Santa Rita Apartments, a low-rent complex off Fry Boulevard. Sun glinted off the turning leaves of the young trees planted along the sidewalk. In the parking lot at the end of the complex, an ancient white Toyota Corolla was jacked up, and a young woman stood beside it looking down at a pair of legs that extended from underneath.

George pulled over to the curb. The young woman had short black hair streaked with blond and was painfully thin. The sleeves of her red sweatshirt were pulled down over her hands, and she was walking in place on the asphalt, shivering, though it wasn't especially cold. George wound down the window.

"Hey, Rosie!"

She looked over, and her mouth formed an O. "Hi, Detective Maynard," she said flatly. "Long time no see, thank God." She pushed up a sleeve and scratched at her arm.

When she did that, George looked away for a moment. Down the street, in the fall back-to-school light, a couple of kids were skateboarding, hopping the curb. He looked back. "So how's it going, Rosie?"

"What do you *want*?" She scratched at her thin arm some more. Scratch, scratch, scratch. George could see the red marks left by her nails.

"Nathan around?" he asked.

Her eyes veered down to the legs under the car. "No way. I have no idea where he is." Her voice rose. "I haven't seen Nathan in years, Detective Maynard. Not in years and years and years and years. Not in infinity."

"You can come out now, Nathan," George said loudly to the legs. "I'm not a cop anymore."

After a moment, the legs scooted forward, then the arms, and then the rest of Nathan, a muscular young man with black hair and grease on his nose. He stood up and brushed at his faded jeans.

"Don't believe him," Rosie said to Nathan warningly as she scratched away. "They tell you all kinds of lies to get what they want. And you didn't do anything, so why is he here? That's what I'd like to know, if he's not a cop. If you talk to him you'll stop fixing my car, and you have to fix my car or I'll be stuck in this stupid place forever and ever."

"Shut *up,* Rosie," Nathan said. He walked over to George's car. There was black grease in the pores of his face. "She's right, I haven't done anything."

"Neither has Randy Gates," said George, "but I'd like to talk to him."

"Randy." Rosie snorted, twisting her body around.

Nathan looked past George's car, eyes as far away as the mountains outside of town, then back at George. "He moved away." His voice was bland.

"You sure?"

"Yeah. Texas, I think. Or was it Florida?"

"Alaska!" shouted Rosie. She began to dance around on the sidewalk. "Hawaii! Puerto Rico!"

"If I could talk to him," George said to Nathan, plowing ahead even though he knew it was no use, "there might be something in it for him."

"Sorry." He was already backing off, eyes guarded. "Can't help you."

Rosie danced up close, her movements manic as she trailed her hand along the side of George's car. She rubbed at a spot on the window with her sleeve.

"No harm in trying," George called to Nathan as he receded down the sidewalk. "If you run into him, maybe you could give me a call."

"Oh, we will, we will, we will," said Rosie.

Nathan slid back underneath the car. George could hear the clunk-chink of the kids' skateboards down the street as they hit the curb.

"Here's my card." He handed it to Rosie. He could see little red spots all over her face as she took it. He remembered how pretty she was the first time she got into trouble. "Aw, Rosie," he said sadly. "You ought to know better than methamphetamine. Speed kills."

"Speed kills." She stared at him, muscles in her face twitching. Then she laughed. "That is so, so sixties." In her eyes, though, he saw a scared little girl.

He reached his hand out to that little girl, caught her wrist. "It's okay," he said soothingly. "Calm down. It's *okay*."

For a second she did calm down, as if for that second she believed what he said, that it *was* okay. "At Patsy O'Reilly's," she whispered. "That trailer park across from the café in Huachuca City. Lot Twelve." Then she was gone, whirling away. "Fuck you, too, George Maynard!" she shouted.

"Yo! Jackson!" called Leroy.

Jackson looked over, on his way back to his cell after talking to Stuart. Leroy was sitting on the bunk in his own cell with a game of solitaire laid out.

"What?" said Jackson.

"Hey, man, you're a hero."

"Oh?" said Jackson suspiciously. Leroy had a way of getting close, then turning on you. "Why?"

Leroy grinned. "Ringworm got *probation*."

Jackson raised his eyebrows. "No kidding."

"Yeah, man, I was in court. The judge gave this long speech, where he said he was gonna send Ringo to D.O.C. but then he changed his mind when he read Ringo's letter—that one you helped him with. Said it was one of the best letters he'd ever read, that it showed true remorse. So he put him back on probation."

"That's great," said Jackson dubiously.

Leroy grinned again. "Two weeks. I give him two weeks tops before he bashes his old lady again, breaks another one of her ribs, and he's back in here." He paused. "Or maybe he'll just poison her, man, you know what I mean?"

o   o   o

GEORGE THOUGHT WHAT he should do next was drive immediately to the trailer park in Huachuca City in case Rosie was telling him the truth—but he couldn't do it. *You cops are all alike.* He had to be psyched for it, and he was tired. Too tired to deal with Randy Gates.

The neighbor, thought George, to keep his mind on the case, so he wouldn't think too hard about Rosie. Anita said Jackson was having an affair with the neighbor. Ruth somebody. Norton. Anita was a loose cannon, and to his mind a possible suspect, but that didn't mean some of what she said might not be true. Maybe look into this Ruth Norton pretty soon. If it was true, not so good for the case, but no one had to know, rules of disclosure didn't apply the same way for the defense. And if the prosecution did find out, at least the defense would be prepared.

I didn't think this way when I was a cop.

Ruth. Wasn't that Stuart's new secretary's name? Aw, so what. Anyway, Stuart would have to be pretty desperate to hire someone who was connected to a homicide he was working on.

George drove down Fry Boulevard, then turned onto Ninety-two away from town, headed for his apartment. It was getting toward sunset, and because he was tired, he decided to skip the A.A. meeting. Maybe he'd call the pizza parlor near his place and order a meat lover's pizza ahead of time to pick up. He punched on his cell to do just that but, damn, the cell had run down.

He thought of Dakota then: He didn't love her and she didn't love him; what the hell was the point? Why was he seeing her? *Tell her it's over, next time she shows up.* His mind veered to Brianne, who just might make it, and then, in spite of himself, he thought of Rosie, who almost certainly would not.

The mountains were purple now, in the late afternoon light that slanted through the trees, a little mist gathering in the leaves that were beginning to turn yellow. The mountains, the mist in the trees, the trees themselves tore at his heart. It was all so damn beautiful and for what?

In the purple light, it seemed to George that the trees were actually bleeding, bleeding into the ground. Everything was dying.

Up ahead, on his right, the red and blue neon glowing in the twilight, was the Qwik Stop liquor store, one vehicle, an old rusted-out pickup in its parking lot. *A beer would be nice,* he thought. *Or maybe a six-pack.* He slowed as he approached and pulled in, just like that, hardly even noticing.

t h i r t e e n

THE MORNING SKY was overcast, the sun diffused, leaving no shadows. Without the interplay of light and dark, everything seemed uglier, Frieda thought as she climbed the winding rocky path that led to the cave. Her long skirt of woven Guatemalan fabric kept catching on the creosote bushes, threatening to trip her up, and the string bag she'd bought last year at the Co-op to replace paper bags and save the trees was heavy and dug into her bony shoulder. She took it off and sat down to rest on a big flat rock.

Below, she could see where the shabby wooden houses at the end of the gulch thinned out. The poorest people lived here. A Hispanic-looking woman was hanging out clothes on a line strung between two ailanthus trees in one of the backyards, and in another a little mixed-breed mutt was frantically digging in the dirt. The dog's chain was way too short. How could people be so cruel? She should report it, but there wasn't anything like a Humane Society around here.

You couldn't do everything, she thought, no matter how much pain you felt at not being able to. But if everyone did something, it could make all the difference. Ken was always saying that. Ken had shown up one day not so long ago and inspired them all. Lots of people didn't like Ken, and she could understand why—he irritated them on purpose, just to get them to react—but often he said profound things, and the most profound was *Choose something to care about. Just one thing can be all it takes to change a life.*

She'd chosen the Magician, and in her string bag was more food— fruit and nuts—and a surprise, a bright yellow yo-yo. It was silly, but maybe he'd like it. He really wasn't as out of it as people thought. They'd actually had conversations, and sometimes he said things that were really smart, smarter than the things most people said, if you knew how to listen.

Frieda stood up resolutely, slung the string bag back onto her shoulder, and started climbing again toward the cave. Just one more turn of the path and there it was. The rocks she'd placed on the strings of the red balloons when she left them there the day the Magician was released were gone, but the balloons were still there, a little way up the hill, strings tangled on some mesquite bushes.

She went to the mouth of the cave and looked in, but there was no sign of the Magician. Probably already downtown, though she hadn't seen him when she'd passed his usual spot at the post office. She'd leave the stuff inside like she had before, away from the wild animals. She stooped and went in, wrinkling her nose against the musty smell, and the first thing she saw on top of the sleeping bag was his pointy cap. He never went downtown without wearing it, so he must be around. Maybe peeing or shitting somewhere in the bushes? Frieda smothered a giggle. How embarrassing.

She took everything out of the string bag and put it in the paper one she'd left the last time. It was empty, and the Baggies of fruits and nuts were arranged in a neat line on a shelflike formation that jutted out from the wall. He'd hardly eaten anything. Then she went back outside.

She wanted to say hi before she left. "Hello!" she called. "Mr. Magician, are you there?"

Maybe he was taking a hike. He did that sometimes, walked over the mountains the long way into town. But not without his cap. She climbed the little rise by the cave to see better but saw nothing except rocks and bushes and dried-up weeds growing in the red dirt. Overhead big black crows careened and swooped. She went a little ways farther up the rise and saw something brown caught on a mesquite bush.

It looked like—Frieda gathered her skirt up and ran up the slope—his leather bag. It *was* his leather bag, upside down, hanging from a branch. *What?* Frieda felt disconnected, numb. Then she began noticing other things, three pennies and a torn ten-dollar bill on the ground, a dirty white handkerchief in the grass a little ways away.

"Mr. Magician!" she called anxiously. "Hello!"

She walked farther up the slope and found a red and green braided yarn bracelet, a white card that said STUART ROSS, ATTORNEY AT LAW, a paperback book, *Stranger in a Strange Land*—she'd given him that—and then, farther up still, his gold metal bell. There she stopped.

"Hello!" she called again. She could keep going to the top of the rise and down again, but suddenly she was terrified at what she might find. "Mr. Magician!" Her voice caught in her throat. *"Please answer!"*

MARA HAD WAITED till the next day to search Jackson's house, so she could do it while Tyler was still at school. There were a lot of men working at the house being built down the street. From the side window in the living room of Jackson's, she could see the pirate man, Earl, having a smoke with another guy. He probably wouldn't come back here, but just in case, she locked the front door.

Then she looked around. Jackson had an office with a desk. Did Jenny have a desk somewhere? Not in the living room. The bedroom? Mara entered reluctantly. The sun streamed in, oblique through slatted blinds. It was neat but dusty, a large room with a king-sized bed covered with a velvet patchwork crazy quilt in jewel tones. An oak bedside table, a wrought-iron lamp with a red fringed shade, and a braided rug—all matching—were on each side of the bed. Ah, there, a desk with a black leather chair.

Mara sat on the chair, kicked off with one foot, and spun around in a little circle. Spinning, she could feel Jenny's eyes on her even though she had never met her, even though Jenny was dead. Because people's spirits did stick around—her mother's did, Mara knew that. Jackson had loved her mother. But Jackson hadn't loved Jenny. Mara had figured that out from things Ruth and Tyler had said. Jenny's disappointed spirit was probably roaming about seeking resolution.

"It's not *my* fault," said Mara out loud.

She opened the top desk drawer. It was all paper clips and pens, envelopes, Post-its. Where was Grace Dixon? She pulled open the side drawer and found files, neatly labeled from AEROBICS to ZEN; no Grace Dixon under the *D*'s, but in the middle a file labeled MOM—full of letters. Mara pulled one out at random.

Printed on a label adorned with a roadrunner in the upper left-hand corner was an address: Grace Dixon, 212 E. La Cholla Way, Green Valley, AZ. She glanced at some other envelopes to make sure, but they all had the same Green Valley address. She'd thought Jenny's mom lived in Tucson. Green Valley, where was that? She could check it out—go to Mapquest on Tyler's computer. She opened the top drawer again and copied the address onto a Post-it. Then she sat and stared at the envelope with a letter inside. It was postmarked two years ago. She shouldn't read it.

Dear Jenny,

I see no reason why I should pay for your training to be an aerobics instructor. I don't know why you quit your real estate job. Surely that was more lucrative than teaching people to bounce around like idiots would be. The next time you need financial assistance, I hope you don't think it's all right to come to me. I realize Jackson is an ineffectual person, with no real earning power, but it was your choice to marry him, so now you must live with the consequences.

Bitch! Mara stopped reading.

ORGANIZED BY KEN Dooley, a raggle-taggle band of middle-aged women, young people with tattoos and multiple piercings, and three dogs wandered the hills above the Magician's cave. A breeze had come up; the sky was still overcast, a pearly gray, and the careening crows stood out against it like black punctuation marks. Ken, in a leather jacket and a bright Peruvian knit cap, strode up a hill with one of the young men.

Frieda stood watching from the top of one of the higher hills, her long skirt and her hair, where it had come loose from the braid, blowing in the wind. Looking down at them, for a moment she felt strong, powerful. A witch. A witch of the mountains, searching for the Magician.

One of the dogs barked. Another answered. Someone shouted from across the way. Ken and the young man descended from their hill. Suddenly Frieda's energy peaked and she felt herself beginning to fade. They'd been here for an hour already and found nothing but more odds and ends from the Magician's bag.

He could have lost it, Frieda thought, and someone found it, hung it on the branch. He could be out in the mountains now or downtown, looking for it. Ken Dooley called out. Someone shouted again. Frieda looked in the direction of the shout and saw Josh, one of the younger men, waving his arms, beckoning to her. She came down from her hill toward him.

"What?" she asked when she got there.

Josh had a goatee and a pierced eyebrow. He pointed to the ground at an old dirty black sneaker.

Her eyes met Josh's. "His *shoe*," she said. "He only has one pair. What will he do without it?" She bent down. The white laces were spattered with brown paint.

"Don't touch it!" Ken was behind her.

Frieda straightened up. "His shoe," she said again, numb. "It's got paint all over it."

"Frieda," said Ken gently. He put his hand on her arm. "I don't think it's paint."

Of course she knew that, just didn't want to think it. *"Blood,"* she whispered. "It's blood, isn't it."

"Heavy-duty voodoo," said Ken.

Frieda's mouth trembled. "What should we do?" She shuddered. "Do you think—I mean, should we go to the *police*?"

"The police." Ken's mouth turned down in disgust. "What are they going to do? They don't *care*. We need representation, and he has a lawyer. Here's what I think you should do, Frieda."

RUTH WAS SITTING at her desk doing some billing and humming her favorite heavy metal song ever, "Sweet Child of Mine," to herself. She'd emptied the coffeepot, washed it out, and made a fresh pot with the coffee she'd bought at the Safeway on her way to work—store brand gourmet, maybe not the very best, but better than the awful stuff Stuart had. After all, she'd be offering it to clients; in the end it didn't pay to look cheap just to save a little money.

She'd almost finished the billing—only two more statements to go—when the bell tinkled. She looked up and saw a thin middle-aged woman in a long ethnicky skirt and dangly silver earrings. The woman looked familiar, but Ruth wasn't sure why. Her face was plain, without a speck of makeup, her hair pulled back in a braid, strands of it loose and wild in the front, as if she had been walking in the wind.

Ruth smiled at the woman. "Hi. How can I help you?"

"I need to see Mr. Ross, *right away*." The woman's voice was breathless, but she spoke with middle-class authority as if she knew her rights and was here to collect on them. "It's *urgent*," she added.

"Mr. Ross won't be back for a while," said Ruth apologetically. "Maybe I can help?"

"My name's Frieda. I—"

"*Frieda,*" Ruth cut in. "Now I know why you look familiar. You had a booth at the crafts fair in Grassy Park this summer. I went with my son. You sell herbal oils and stuff like that." As soon as she said it, she was sorry. What if the woman started on some long speech, then—

But Frieda went on as if Ruth hadn't spoken. "Mr. Ross and I met over at Justice Court last week. I was one of the people protesting the Magician being arrested."

"The Magician," Ruth cut in, surprised. "You mean, with the hat and the bell? That man?"

"Yes. Hasn't Mr. Ross ever talked about him? He's his client."

Ruth stared at Frieda in disbelief. "He is?"

"Yes." Suddenly Frieda gave an exhausted little moan and looked as though she might cry. Then she did.

"Oh, *dear,*" said Ruth. She grabbed a box of Kleenex, another thing she had brought from home, and sat on the chair next to Frieda. She pulled a tissue out of the box. "Here, have one of these."

Frieda took it and blew her nose. There was a little silence.

"Coffee?" offered Ruth.

Frieda shuddered. "I don't drink coffee."

"No," said Ruth. "Of course not. Are you okay?"

"Yes." She closed her eyes. "*No.*"

"Look," said Ruth kindly, "why don't you tell me all about it. Maybe I can do *something.*"

WHERE THE HELL was George? Stuart's head throbbed and his throat was raw as he drove back from Justice Court over in Sierra Vista after a tough case: assault, with a victim who wanted vengeance and a woman judge big on victim's rights. He hadn't really been up to it. His client had gotten six months real jail time, almost unprecedented for a simple misdemeanor when the jails were crowded enough as it was. Not that the scumbag hadn't deserved it. Still, as usual, Stuart hated to lose.

All the way back from Sierra Vista, he'd been calling George and getting nothing but a recording.

Now he stood in his office with a sore throat, a headache, and two women: Ruth and Frieda, that woman he'd spoken to outside of Justice Court in Dudley the day the Magician was arrested. She was sobbing, nearly incoherent. He struggled to make sense of what she was saying, something about the Magician being missing, his leather bag, blood. *Blood?* Damn. A harmless old guy. Vulnerable as all get-out.

"So what are you going to do?" wailed Frieda.

Stuart felt a little dizzy. He went over to Ruth's desk to prop himself up. "I'm just a lawyer," he said, "not God. Have you reported this to the police?"

Frieda shook her head. "Ken said they wouldn't do anything."

"Ken can go to hell." Stuart picked up the phone on Ruth's desk and punched in numbers.

"Dudley P.D."

"Hi. Stuart Ross here. Who you got there now?"

"Officer Brill and Sergeant Nelson."

"Tell Sergeant Nelson to hang around," Stuart said. "I'm sending someone over there to talk to him right now. A woman named Frieda." He hung up. "It's all set," he said to Frieda. "Sergeant Nelson, Jack Nelson, that's who you need to ask for. If you really want to help the Magician, get over there now."

"That was excellent," Ruth said to Stuart approvingly after Frieda left.

"Thank you." He was exhausted; the phone call had taken the last of his reserves. He clutched the edge of the desk and closed his eyes.

"That poor, poor man," said Ruth. "I remember passing him by the post office just the other—" She stopped. "What's wrong? You look awful."

"I don't feel so good." Stuart staggered back and sat down heavily on the chair by the window. "And I'm worried."

"What about? The Magician?"

"Sure. Among other things. George Maynard, my investigator. I can't locate him, I've been trying all day."

"Oh," said Ruth. "Well, I'm sure he'll turn up."

"My *head.*" Stuart groaned. "If it's not too demeaning, could you maybe bring me a cup of coffee?"

"Coffee?" said Ruth.

"Yes. Coffee."

"When you don't feel good?" Ruth came closer. "Actually—" She reached out and put a practiced hand on his forehead.

Stuart closed his eyes again. He felt delirious, but her hand was cool, so soothing. For a split second he fell into a false memory from his childhood, some black-and-white movie on TV, World War One and he was a wounded veteran, lying between cool white sheets in an army hospital somewhere in England and she was—

"It feels like you've got a fever," she said. "You should go home and go to bed."

Greer Garson.

"It's only two thirty," Stuart whined.

"So what. I've been holding down the fort all day, I can keep doing it. Besides," she added sternly, "what good are you if you're sick? It's not fair to your clients."

"Okay. Okay." Stuart rose.

"Stay in bed," Ruth called after him as he lurched out the door, "and drink plenty of fluids!"

"Hey, Jackson!"

Jackson looked up from the statement one of the inmates had given him to go over. It involved a sick mother and a pregnant fiancée. "Yeah?"

Leroy smiled falsely, displaying the black holes in his teeth. He walked over and sat down.

"Whassup?" Jackson asked. *If I spend much more time here,* he thought, *even my closest friends won't be able to tell me from the other inmates.*

Leroy whooshed out a breath. Jackson caught a whiff of bowels that hadn't moved in days. "Remember that old guy that was in here one night? The looney tunes with the beard?" Leroy snapped his fingers. "What'd they call him?"

Jackson stared at Leroy. "The Magician?"

"Yeah. The Magician. Didn't you and him know each other?"

Jenny, Jenny, Jenny. "Not exactly."

"Hey, I *saw,* man. He said something to you."

It was none of Leroy's business. "It was nothing," Jackson said. "What about him?"

"Somebody offed him, man."

Jackson's stomach lurched and he tasted faintly mildewed bologna. "What do you mean, somebody offed him?"

Leroy shrugged. "He's gone, man. Heard there was blood all over the place."

"*What?*" said Jackson. "*Who told you that?*"

Leroy shrugged again, suddenly losing interest, as if now that he had managed to get Jackson's full attention, the challenge was gone. He stood up. "Hey, Paco, *chingatumadre,* hombre."

The Magician was dead? *Jenny, Jenny, Jenny.* Jackson had bought Stuart's explanation about the Magician picking up on things, but now he wasn't so sure. The guy hadn't seemed that crazy. Maybe he'd actually known something about Jenny's death. Maybe someone had killed him because of what he knew. Maybe that Randy Gates.

His mind whirled. Who on earth had Jenny been screwing around with? *He should call Stuart.*

But Stuart had been so edgy the last time he was here, as if he were hiding something. Then there was that e-mail to Casey. Jackson had written it in a low period, hadn't meant it at all, not really. If they retrieved that, how the hell was he going to explain it to Stuart? And how was Stuart going to explain it to a jury? Call Ruth. Ruth was working for Stuart now; she could tackle him. Mara. Another thing to tell Ruth. Mara in the middle of this mess now. Tell Ruth to keep her safe.

o   o   o

JUST WHEN YOU figured you were through the hardest part, thought George, safe, you weren't safe at all. He saw now that it had been there the whole time, that *need*, waiting for him. Six-pack on the seat beside him, he'd gone way over the speed limit getting to his sponsor's house—luckily no cops around. He and Stan had stood and popped the tops, poured all the beer out onto the driveway.

He'd spent the night on Stan's couch, then the next day he'd taken off—gone to five different A.A. meetings, thinking about the case and not thinking about it as he drove. Tomorrow, talk to Ruth Norton. Stupid to wait. Give her priority over Randy Gates. He drove to Willcox, the Junction, Douglas, Elfrida—must have gone to every A.A. meeting in the whole damn county.

Now Dakota was banging on his door, locked against just that eventuality. He went into the bedroom and closed the door, but he could still hear the banging. What the hell, if he could handle the booze he could sure as hell handle a little door banging. The cigarettes—handling them, now, that was something else. He lit up and sat on the bed, smoking and staring at the blank wall until, finally, she went away.

fourteen

CARRYING TWO BAGS of groceries, Ruth walked down a cement path, treacherous with fallen hard, pale brown chinaberries, to Stuart's house. A television was on inside, loud, a jumbled burr of voices. She went up the porch steps and knocked on the door. Did someone say "come in"? She wasn't sure with the noise from the TV. She tried the door, and it wasn't locked. She opened it partway.

"Stuart? Hello?" she called over the television. "It's Ruth!"

"*Come in!*"

She opened the door all the way and came in.

"What you don't know about your drinking water," said a man's voice, "can kill you. More when we come back."

Music swelled. Stuart lay on a beige couch, bleary eyed, covered up to his chin with an old blue sleeping bag. Ruth looked around. All the furniture was old and beat up, and newspapers were stacked every-where, on the floor, on chairs, on the enormous coffee table. What a mess. He was a lawyer. Somehow she had expected something a little more . . . middle class.

"I was so tired from my chemotherapy," said a woman wistfully, "that I—"

"Could you turn that off!" shouted Ruth.

Stuart picked up the remote, and then there was silence.

"How can you stand to watch that?" said Ruth.

"It's CNN," said Stuart defensively. "It's important to keep up."

"With what? All the ways you can die? It's like listening to a—a hysterical mother." Ruth shifted the bags uncomfortably. "Worse. I brought you apples, bananas, orange juice, tea, honey, and four cans of chicken soup."

"Thank you," croaked Stuart.

"Where should I put it?"

"Here." Stuart gestured at the coffee table. "I'll have the orange juice in a minute."

She moved a stack of newspapers and set the bags down, then came closer and put her hand on Stuart's forehead. "You don't feel so feverish anymore. It's probably a twenty-four-hour virus. You just had one court appearance, and I canceled it."

"Did Victor Robles call, by any chance?"

"No."

"If he does, tell him to call me here."

Ruth nodded. "Want me to heat up some chicken soup before I go back to the office?"

"I just had a doughnut."

Ruth opened her mouth to say something about that, then remembered she wasn't his mother. Thank God. "Listen"—she moved another stack of newspapers and perched on a wing chair covered in frayed red damask—"Jackson called me last night. He was really upset. One of the inmates told him the Magician was murdered."

"We don't know that," Stuart protested. "We don't even know if he's dead, for God's sake."

"Jackson thinks the Magician knew something about Jenny's death," Ruth went on as if he hadn't spoken. "He told me the Magician came up to him and said Jenny's name. *Three times.*"

"He says everything three times," said Stuart. "It doesn't mean anything."

"But what if it *does*? Tell me everything you know about him."

"Why?" Stuart moaned. "I'm sick."

"You're better," said Ruth, "and it's important. The Magician. Doesn't he even have a name?"

"Ikan Danz."

"What?"

"I can dance, get it? Look," Stuart struggled to rise. "All I can tell you is he got arrested a couple of months ago for harassment 'cause some of the store owners thought he was scaring away the tourists, which was bullshit, and I represented him, pro bono. So they just automatically called me the second time. SEABHS did some kind of psychological workup the first time, and he's a D.S.M. something-or-other."

"A D.S.M. something-or-other what?"

"I can't remember. Actually, I didn't read it. But there must have been a diagnosis. What does it matter? Those psychology people, they just take a bunch of characteristics and squeeze them into a label. It makes them feel useful. They gave him some meds that seemed to help, but he quit taking them."

Ruth sighed. "There's something I need to tell you. It's about Jackson and me. We—"

The phone rang. Ruth jumped.

"Shit," said Stuart.

"Want me to get it?" offered Ruth.

But Stuart had already picked up. "Hello? Stuart Ross here. George. Where the hell have you been? No shit."

Waiting, Ruth gazed past the couch, through a dining room into a kitchen. Dishes were piled high in the sink. *I will not offer to do his dishes,* she thought. *I absolutely will not.*

"Norton," said Stuart.

Ruth looked over at him.

"So the fuck what. Sure . . . Yeah . . . When? Look, she's here right now. I'll ask her." He put his hand over the phone. "It's my investigator. He wants to set up an interview with you. Today, if possible."

"At the office?" asked Ruth.

"At your house. He wants it to be private. That means no Mara hanging around. It's okay, you can close up the office for a couple of hours. Why don't I tell him one o'clock."

"Fine," said Ruth.

"One. Yeah." He hung up. "You were saying?" he asked, but the phone rang again. He picked up. "Chloe. How— I did *not*. Jesus, Chloe, have a little faith. Who do you think I am? She must have done it on her own volition."

Chloe, thought Ruth. *And then there was Dakota, whoever she was. The hell with this.* She stood up. "Got to go," she mouthed to Stuart, and went out the door.

ALL MORNING, TWO uniformed officers had been searching the hills around the Magician's cave. Unseasonably cool winds from the north had scattered the clouds, leaving the sky a chilly blue. Frieda, wearing a thick brown and white sweater knit by tiny Peruvian children, had watched helplessly as Sergeant Jack Nelson, a bulky middle-aged man with a big mustache and sad eyes, lifted a sample of soil from the ground where the shoe had been and put it into an evidence bag.

Now he came up to her where she sat, disconsolate, on a rock a little way from the cave. The cave itself and the area around it were strung with yellow crime scene tape. In plain clothes—windbreaker, red plaid shirt, and jeans—he hunkered down on the ground, close to her.

"I don't know how to say it any better way." His voice was kind. "There's mine shafts all over these hills. Someone goes down one, well—they might never be found."

Frieda bit her lip. Then she shivered, pulling the sweater close around her.

"Are you going to be okay?"

She nodded.

"You the last person who saw him?"

She shook her head. "As far as I can tell, it was Mirabelle Hadley from SEABHS. She picked him up at the jail the day he was released. She said she left him off at the bottom of the Gulch."

"I'm familiar with Mirabelle," said the sergeant without enthusiasm. "No one's seen him since?"

For a second Frieda brightened. "I can ask around. If anyone did, I'll tell them to talk to you."

"That would be good. Now"—he paused—"I'm going to have one of my men stand guard over the cave. I got a fingerprint guy coming up here a little later. I don't want you or anyone else going in there, you understand? Come to think of it, you better go down to the station, get fingerprinted yourself."

Frieda looked at him in horror. "*Me?* Why? I'm not a criminal."

" 'Course you're not. But you've been in the cave, probably left some prints. It's for purposes of elimination is all."

She looked stricken. "Other people went in there, too, when we had the search party."

"Not smart." Sergeant Nelson's sad eyes got even sadder. "Damn it. Means we've got a contaminated crime scene."

"We didn't *know,*" said Frieda in anguish.

"Who went in? Everybody?"

"No." She paused. "I think actually just Ken. I know he did. And maybe Josh, but I'm not sure about that."

"Tell Ken to stop by, then, and Josh, too, if he went in."

"Oh, God." Frieda lowered her face into her hands and said in a muffled voice, "I can't believe this is happening." She gave a little sob. "That poor, poor man."

"Now, now." Instinctively, Sergeant Nelson stretched out a hand to pat her on the shoulder, then withdrew it. He hadn't had that much contact with people like her; she might take it wrong.

"Listen," he said, trying to make amends, "his leather bag and his hat? Hopefully there'll be something on them for a DNA match, so we can make sure the blood is Mr. Danz's."

Sergeant Nelson touched his mustache. DNA. He hadn't meant to say that; it just slipped out. DNA testing cost a fortune, and beside it probably was the old guy's blood. He suspected it was people just like this woman here who always voted against any additional funding for the department. "All that's way down the line, of course, takes forever, that DNA stuff, we got to send it to a lab in Phoenix. It's not like you see it on *C.S.I.*"

"*C.S.I.*? What's that?"

"*Crime Scene Investigation.* On TV." Sergeant Nelson stared at her with awe. "You've never seen it?"

"I don't watch TV," said Frieda. "I don't even own one. I don't read the newspapers, either. Even Ken's letters. He shows them to me before they're published."

"Then how the hell do you know what's going on?"

Frieda held out her arms and made a circle that seemed to encompass Sergeant Nelson, the cave, the mountains, the sky and the birds that flew in it. "This is what's going on," she said.

A BASKETBALL HOOP hung from the garage door at Ruth Norton's, the net frayed as if thousands of balls had swished through it. *Kids, she has kids,* thought George. He felt in his jacket pocket to make sure the voice-activated tape recorder was in place, then smoothed his hair back with his hands and walked up the path to the front door. He was a little nervous; the last couple of days had thrown him off balance. *You are a professional, Sam Elliot,* he told himself. He looked for a bell, but there wasn't one, so he knocked.

A woman about Sandy's age opened the door. She had a pleasant face, natural, not hidden behind a lot of makeup, and thick reddish-brown curly hair with a streak of white going back from her forehead. She wore a pale blue long-sleeved shirt and black pants.

Suddenly he felt awkward, even a little guilty. "I'm George Maynard," he said, forgetting to say "Hi there!" first. He fumbled in his pocket for his card and handed it to her.

"Well, I thought as much." She smiled. He noticed her teeth were an average off-white color. "And I'm Ruth. Come on in."

He stepped inside. "I'm sure pleased to meet you, Ruth. How do you like working for our boy Stuart?" Our boy? Where did that come from?

"Pretty intense."

He laughed, and she laughed, too. "I made coffee," she said. "We can talk in the kitchen." He followed her down a hall. "Sit," she said when they reached the kitchen.

George sat in a cluttered room with black ceramic tiles and stainless steel fixtures dimmed with use. On the black refrigerator were snapshots and children's drawings. He sat a little farther back in his chair, comfortable. "This is nice," he said, meaning it. "Homey."

"How do you take your coffee?" Ruth asked, by the coffeepot.

"Straight is good," he said.

Ruth set a thick white mug emblazoned with the University of Arizona basketball logo down in front of him, poured herself a mug, and sat down across the table. He took a sip of coffee, so strong it almost made him wince.

"Norton," he said suddenly. "Dan Norton. Played center for Buena a few years ago. He your boy?"

"Yes." Ruth smiled, gratified.

"Seemed like a really good kid. You must be proud of him."

She flushed with pleasure. "I am. He's my oldest—going to college in Seattle now, and Scott, the next one, is at UCLA."

This was Anita's evil temptress—the woman who supposedly was having a blatant affair with Jackson? George wanted to keep an open mind here, but what struck him about Ruth was that she was normal. Her kids were normal and she was normal. When was the last time he had met a woman who was normal? He couldn't remember.

"And Tyler, my youngest," Ruth went on, "was the one who saw Randy Gates going into Jenny's house all those times."

"Yeah?" said George. "Guess I should talk to Tyler at some point, too."

"He'd *love* that. But now," she said expectantly, "let's get started. Shoot. Give me the third degree."

"Aw," said George.

"The day Jenny was murdered," offered Ruth, "I was at an orientation for substitute teachers over at Buena High School, so I can't tell you much about what happened that day." She paused. "And now Sid Hamblin's dead, too. It's kind of"—she shivered—"scary. I mean, they said heart attack, but you don't think—?"

"Don't know. Have to wait for the autopsy. You knew Sid?"

She nodded. "Slightly. He was here in my house, at the memorial for Jenny. To be honest, I didn't like him. He sort of gave me the creeps. And then . . ." Her eyes shifted away. "He's dead. It doesn't matter."

"Heard a rumor that something was going on between him and Jenny. You know anything about that?"

"That's who Jenny was having the affair with? *Sid?*" She looked flabbergasted. "Oh, yuck, how could she?"

George bit his lip to keep from smiling. "It's just a rumor right now. How about Anita Selby, did you know her?"

"Jenny's friend. I met her once in passing, is all."

"Let's get back to you. You're pretty close to Jackson, huh? Been neighbors for years."

"Years," said Ruth. "My boys love him."

"And you?"

"And me what?"

"You love him, too?"

Ruth was silent for a moment, then finally said slowly, "When I was in college I took a philosophy class and we talked about the Greeks. They had different words for different kinds of love. *Agape* and *eros, philos.*" She frowned. "I can't remember them exactly. Eros is the sexual kind, but what I feel has to do with brotherly love. A warm feeling of camaraderie. That's what I feel for Jackson."

"You know," said George, feeling out of his league, "maybe I could use a little sugar in this coffee."

Ruth pushed over the sugar bowl. "Help yourself."

George spooned in sugar. "What about Jenny? You felt warm and camaraderie-like about her?"

"No. To be honest, I thought she was kind of a blight on Jackson's life, that he would have been happier without her."

George raised his eyebrows.

"Let me explain," said Ruth. "I loved my ex-husband very much." She closed her eyes for a moment. "He was so understanding and sensitive and *good*. He was the best father anyone could ever be; he got up nights with the kids, played with them, listened to them, *encouraged* them. My two oldest boys are strong, confident men now, because of him. Tyler, he's eleven, he didn't get all that as much because of the divorce."

"That's a shame," said George. "Poor little guy." He clicked his tongue. "Divorce. I'm divorced myself, can't blame my ex really, but it seems like nowadays a lot of people don't even try to stay married."

"In our case, it wasn't not trying. Owen is gay. I didn't know it when we got married, and I don't think he did, either, or at least he was trying not to know. Trying so hard." She blinked. "What were we talking about?"

"Uh," said George. "Jenny?"

"Jenny," said Ruth. "Of course. I was trying to explain about Jenny." She paused. "I never told anyone about this, because it hurt too much." She put her hand over her heart. "It *still* hurts. I liked her at first, then later not as much, but I kept trying to like her, you know, for Jackson's sake. Then one day, I guess it was the last straw, we were talking and she said wasn't I worried about sending the kids to see Owen in the summers because he was gay and he might molest them." Ruth's eyes filled with tears.

George fumbled awkwardly for a handkerchief, but he didn't have one. She grabbed a napkin from a napkin holder and wiped her eyes. "Sorry," she said.

"*No,*" said George with feeling. "That's cold. I can see how it would upset you."

"She did things like that," said Ruth. "Zapped you. I used to tell

Owen when things upset me, not that I would have ever told him that. But most things I did, because he knew me well enough to understand. Now there's no one." She sighed. "It's hard to be divorced. You lose so much of your past."

"You know," said George, "I never heard it put that way exactly, but it's true. All those memories you got of the two of you, well, they're kind of tainted."

Ruth smiled at him. "You seem like a nice person. Sympathetic. How long have you been divorced?"

"About a year," said George.

"A year." Ruth leaned toward him, eyes full of concern. "I guess it must still be pretty painful."

He nodded. She had a nice voice, he thought suddenly, *kind*. Bet she was one hell of a good mom. "Twenty years, I was married to Sandy. I thought we were okay. I mean, I had a drinking problem, but—aw—" He shrugged. "I got no excuses. No one to blame but myself, that's the real truth. But I've been sober now more than six months."

"Good for you," said Ruth.

"She calls me sometimes," George confided, "and asks me to do things for her, and for a long time I kept hoping it meant she still cared."

"Maybe she does and she's afraid."

He shook his head. "She doesn't. I looked at her the other day and I knew she didn't. She's changed—she isn't the same person anymore. I don't know who she is now." He shrugged, looking pained. "It's hard for me to even be around her."

"Hell is other people," said Ruth.

George looked at her with surprise and admiration. He ran his fingers through his hair. "That's deep."

There was a silence.

"You must be a very good investigator," said Ruth. "Just look at the stuff I've told you that I never told anyone before."

"I was a little talkative myself," said George. *"Damn!"*

"What?" said Ruth, startled.

"I got this voice-activated tape recorder." He patted his jacket pocket. "Right here." He took it out. "I've gone and taped this whole conversation."

"Ooh." Ruth shuddered. "If I'd realized that, I wouldn't have— You're not—" She giggled nervously. "You're not going to play it for Stuart, are you?"

George suddenly had the sense of a whole interview gone awry. "Are you kidding?" he said.

He opened the recorder and took out the little cassette. *You lost your grip, Sam Elliot,* he thought. He unwound the tape and crumpled the shiny ribbon. "I'm not going to play it for anyone," he said.

LATE IN THE afternoon, Stuart was stirring some of the chicken soup Ruth had brought when the phone rang. He went into the living room and answered it.

"Aha," said Victor. "Caught you at home."

"Had a little virus or something," said Stuart.

"Yeah? Then maybe this should wait."

"I'm fine now." From the kitchen he heard a hiss. Soup boiling over. "Hold on a second." He went back into the kitchen and turned the burner off. "What's up?"

"Got the autopsy report on Sid Hamblin."

"No shit. That was fast."

"Cause of death same as Jenny Williams."

Stuart sat down on a kitchen stool. "And?"

"Well," said Victor, "they seized those pills, the probiotics? Three months' supply. About two-thirds gone."

Jackson had been in jail less than a month. It was pretty simple math, but Stuart did it twice. "So what? Probably not even admissible," he said, tap-dancing. "I mean, where's the connection, really?"

"Couple of other things—sperm in Jenny's vagina? Looks like we got a tentative match, Sid Hamblin again. How's that for a connection?"

"DNA match?" said Stuart skeptically, to keep his hand in.

"Nope. But we'll go for that if we have to."

"What else?" said Stuart hollowly. "You said a couple of other things."

"This is nothing, really." Victor chuckled. "I mean, compared to the rest. Just a little e-mail your guy wrote to a friend. Dot-E-D-U, must be some kind of professor. Looks like in Chicago."

Stuart closed his eyes. He didn't feel as good as he had a few minutes ago, and he didn't want to hear this. "You don't have to fill me in on that. I'll pick up the disclosure first thing in the morning," he said, and hung up.

f i f t e e n

STUART SPENT A restless night, his dreams littered with former clients come back to blame others for their crimes and to blame him for their sentences. Toward morning he found himself in a courtroom with Jackson: Victor Robles was arguing in front of Judge Harrison. "Your Honor," he was saying, "it's either hanging or the guillotine."

Judge Harrison banged his gavel. "I've made my decision. It's the guillotine."

"That's barbaric, Your Honor!" shouted Stuart. "I'm taking this all the way to the—"

Stuart opened his eyes. *Supreme Court,* he thought. Murky light came through his bedroom window. It was morning. *Death penalty.* No way. Victor wouldn't seek the death penalty. The whole concept of the death penalty was in disarray anyway—they were bringing the old cases back because of Blakely where the Supreme Court had ruled that the sentencing phase of a death penalty case had to be decided by a jury. There was no way Victor would go through the hassle of being the first prosecutor in Cochise County to take the sentencing phase of a death penalty case to a jury.

Would he? Why the hell not?

RUTH WOKE UP that morning with old songs in her heart. *"You go to my head,"* she sang in her kitchen. *"Da da dum, da da da dum, da da da dum."*

"You're in such a good mood," said Mara. "What's that song?"

"Bowl in the *sink*," Ruth said to Tyler. "It's some old standard," she said to Mara. "It just popped into my head for some reason."

How Owen had loved those old songs. They used to dance around the living room to the music of Cole Porter, Owen bending her low, swooping her round in wide circles. She hadn't danced now in years. *Oh, wouldn't it be loverly.*

"I'm thinking about going to Tucson today," said Mara.

"Tucson?" said Ruth, distracted, still thinking of Owen. "What's in Tucson?"

"Malls," said Mara. "Lots of them."

"Tyler!" said Ruth. "Don't forget you're sleeping over at Buzzie's tonight. You got your p.j.'s and a toothbrush?"

"A sleepover?" said Mara. "On a school night?"

"They're doing a history project together." Ruth turned to Tyler. "And a change of clothes."

"Oh, Ma. I can wear the same ones tomorrow."

"No, you can't," said Ruth firmly.

Tyler left the room.

Ruth said to Mara, "There's a Tucson map in the right-hand kitchen drawer on the top. Why don't you take it?"

"I—Sure. Thank you."

Tyler came back into the room, carrying his backpack.

"It's seven forty-one," Ruth said to him. "You'll miss the bus if you don't get going right now."

"Then Mara can take me."

189

"She's not your slave. *Go on.*"

Tyler shrugged into his backpack. "You'll be here when I get home tomorrow, won't you?" he asked Mara a little anxiously on his way out the door.

Mara shrugged. "Probably."

"I'm running late, too," said Ruth when Tyler was gone. She was still wearing the Metallica T-shirt and sweatpants that she wore to sleep in. She ran her fingers through her damp hair, shaking it out. She'd washed it that morning. "The hair dryer conked out."

"Use mine," said Mara. "It's in the boys' bathroom. I'll finish cleaning up."

In the boys' bathroom, Ruth looked at herself in the toothpaste-flecked mirror. It seemed to her she looked better than usual. Younger, more animated. She hadn't had a hot flash in a while. Maybe they were gone. She hadn't thought about dancing with Owen for so long, it made her too sad, and now here it was in her mind again, and she wasn't sad at all anymore.

She turned on the dryer. *You go to my head*—what were the other lines? There was a mint julep in there somewhere, and champagne bubbles and sparkling burgundy brew. A whole lot of alcohol. George had said he used to be an alcoholic. Maybe that was what put the song in her head. She giggled. The hot air from the dryer whooshed through her hair, and her mind danced, her heart sang, thinking about what George had said as he left yesterday. *I'll have to stop by the office more often.*

Sergeant Jack Nelson took Frieda's hand and pressed her fingers on the ink pad in a rolling motion, then onto a piece of paper.

"See?" he said, releasing her hand. "That wasn't so bad, was it?"

"No." Frieda looked down at her inky fingers. "Not really."

She hadn't been able to sleep all night, worrying about being finger-printed, so to get it over with she'd gone to the police station first thing in the morning, and there was Sergeant Nelson.

He took her other hand and did the same thing. Then he handed her a moist towelette to wipe her fingers.

"I keep thinking," Frieda said, "maybe I could have done *something*."

"Now, now," Sergeant Nelson said. "It seems to me you did a lot for him, more than most people."

"People can be so *cruel*." She looked up at the sergeant, at his big mustache, his droopy eyes so sympathetic, not like a policeman's eyes at all. "I remember one time—do you know Sid? Sid Hamblin? He just died of a heart attack?"

Sergeant Nelson cleared his throat as if about to speak, but then just nodded as if he'd changed his mind.

"Maybe I shouldn't say this," said Frieda, "because Sid's dead, but I don't care. Ken Dooley and I went to Sid's house once, with the Magician? He was pretty hyper that day, the way he could be sometimes, and Sid got so annoyed at him that he took him by the collar and walked him out of the house." Her lip quivered. "His poor feet weren't even touching the ground."

The sergeant tsked-tsked.

"Sid's gone forever," said Frieda. "I can't get my mind around it. Death is so strange."

"That it is," said Jack Nelson. "I lost my wife, two years, five months ago. An aneurysm. A bubble burst in her brain and she was gone in seconds."

"Oh!" said Frieda.

"Couldn't think straight for a whole year afterward." He sighed. "Well, you've got to trust in the Lord, is all."

Frieda's eyes welled with tears.

AFTER RUTH LEFT, Mara finished the dishes and wiped off the table. Then she threw the sponge into the sink, went into Ruth's bedroom, and opened her closet. She flipped through the line of sedate longish tops until she found a knit polo in navy with a white collar.

She tried it on and found a full-length mirror on the back of the bedroom door. A demure Sunday-school blonde looked back at her. Perfect. Even though her jeans were low-riders, the top was long enough that she couldn't see any skin at all. Jenny's mother, Grace Dixon, would not like skin, she was sure of that.

Then she checked her purse to make sure the map she'd printed out from Mapquest was still there. Green Valley, where Mrs. Dixon lived, was close to Tucson, on the outskirts—one hour and forty-seven minutes driving time.

HEY THERE, CASEY. I was thinking—here we are, two professors and all we do is bitch about our wives. Jenny's mad at me and I know she wants me to ask her why, but actually I don't care. We haven't spoken for two days and you know what? I'm enjoying it, in a sadistic kind of way. I used to be a nice guy but you know what they say. Hell is other people. Maybe I'm just a coward but sometimes I even think about her being dead and all I feel is relief.

Inadmissible, thought Stuart automatically. Written eight months ago. Inadmissible, prejudicial, and irrelevant. He groaned inwardly. A plea, the only way out of this mess was to get Victor to offer a stipulated plea. Twenty years. But would he—?

The bell tinkled, and he heard humming from the outer office. Then Ruth appeared at his door, smiling, almost radiant. What did she have to be happy about?

"You're here early," she said.

"And you're late," said Stuart grimly.

"Sorry," said Ruth without remorse. "My hair dryer broke suddenly. Why are you so upset?"

"Upset? Why the hell would I be upset? Because I have a whole bunch of new disclosure on your friend Jackson? Really damning stuff? So what? It's all in a day's work, I'm a professional."

Ruth sank into the client's chair. "Jackson told me he gave you permission to discuss his case with me. Tell me about it."

And he did, the prescription bottle with the poison, under the bed; the sperm matchup; the probiotics and the cause of Sid's death—everything.

For a while afterward, Ruth just sat there, looking stunned. "Sid was murdered? Actually *murdered?* Well, it certainly wasn't Jackson who did it." She shuddered. "I should get better locks for my doors. Oh, dear, poor Jackson." She glanced at Stuart worriedly. "Have you told him all this yet?"

"Not about Sid. Tomorrow." Stuart's eyes shifted away. "I'm swamped today, and I'll need time to lay it all on him."

"You've lost your faith," Ruth said. "I *know* Jackson." She paused. "And you're forgetting something."

"Like what?"

"The Magician. *He knew about Jenny.* You said yourself he had moments of lucidity. He spoke to Jackson, and now something's happened to him, too, and Jackson couldn't have done that. Besides, isn't it true that the more things you throw at a jury, the less likely they are to convict?"

"Jeez," said Stuart. "You're a lawyer now?"

"You need to follow it up," Ruth said firmly.

"Okay, okay." Stuart rubbed his face. "I'll run over to Dudley P.D., get a copy of the file on the Magician. In the meantime, why don't you make copies of the new disclosure for George to pick up."

Ruth's face brightened again, and Stuart scowled. What did she have to be so happy about?

THE FUNNY THING was, George thought as he drove into the Sunset View Trailer Park where Rosie had said Randy Gates was staying, the car belching sooty gray smoke, he hadn't known precisely how he felt about Sandy until he'd said it out loud to Ruth. Saying it, he'd lost his focus, screwed up the interview. No, that was bullshit, it was already screwed up. But what the hell, he didn't see Ruth as a suspect. She'd never been much of one anyway.

Stuart had called him last night with news about the autopsy report and the results linking Sid to the sperm in Jenny's vagina. So what else was new? It fit nicely into a theory George already had: Jenny had been screwing Sid; Anita Selby found out and offed both of them. Poison—nine times out of ten, a woman's crime. That whole Ruth-Jackson affair a smoke screen created by Selby—George's hands tightened on the steering wheel—was doubly worse when you considered what a fine, *decent* person Ruth was.

From her reaction when he'd asked, he was pretty sure Anita knew Randy Gates; probably she'd scored a little grass from him, too. She could even have paid Randy to plant the aconite sometime after Jenny died—after all, the damn key was right there under a rock—and that would explain why Randy was running scared.

Naw—that would be stupid. Anita had plenty of access to the house. Anita could have gone over to Sid's later—to commiserate about Jenny or whatever—and spiked *his* pills then.

What about Sid's neighbors? One of them could have seen Anita, or her car. Check them out in case the police didn't—but they wouldn't, would they? They already had their chief suspect, sitting in a jail cell. And that guy Ken Dooley—he was a friend of Sid's, and he'd admitted to meeting Jenny. He might know something. Not only that, this all took the investigation to Old Dudley, where Ruth worked. He could pop in and say hello.

He drove on down to Lot Twelve, trailing smoke. The trailer park was small and more downscale than the one where Brianne lived, the double-wides older and not much in the way of landscaping around any of them. His junker fit right in. The trailer at Lot Twelve was a nondescript off-white. There was a weedy dirt yard, a wire fence, and no vehicles parked in its vicinity.

George stopped, got out, then reached in his jacket pocket and turned off his cell. Nothing like a cell going off at the wrong time. A TV blared from a trailer nearby. Grayish white curtains blocked the windows at Patsy O'Reilly's. He looked for signs of life, but Patsy, whoever she was, was too busy waitressing at Denny's to make a mark on where she lived, or maybe it was just a temporary shelter till she found something better. Or nobody lived there at all and Rosie had invented the whole thing.

He went up a couple of splintery wooden steps and knocked on the door. No one answered, no sounds inside. He knocked again. Still no one. He went back to the Olds, got in, and drove the whole trailer court, looking for any other entrances and exits, but there was only the one where he had come in. He exited the court and parked out on the street by the entrance, where he had a view of Lot Twelve.

While he waited, he smoked and sipped at the watery coffee he'd bought at the café up the street, so unlike the coffee he'd had yesterday— enough caffeine in that to keep a man awake for days—that coffee he'd had yesterday at Ruth's, at Ruth's, at Ruth's.

IN THE DISTANCE Mara could see a golf course, smack dab in the middle of the desert. It was bright green, dotted with the white of the sand traps and little retired people in golf carts were moving around on it. She turned down the very clean street where Jenny's mother lived. It was lined on both sides with pink stucco town houses with red tile roofs and decorative gravel yards scattered with well-tended desert plants whose names Mara did not know.

She parked Jackson's Volvo three doors down from the address because Jenny's mother might recognize the car and freak out—call the police, even: *My son-in-law the murderer has escaped from jail and come here to kill me.*

She checked her face and hair in the rearview mirror and dabbed at her lips with liquid color, Pearl Nude. She picked up the potted pink cyclamen plant she'd bought at a Safeway and got out. Birds, elderly and retired, too, maybe, chirped in the vegetation. It was at least ten degrees hotter here than it had been back in Cochise County. For a second she stood on the sidewalk, thinking of what her mother used to tell her to say whenever she felt uncertain.

I'm young, I'm beautiful, I can do anything. I'm not beautiful, Mom. *Of course you are.*

Mara touched the St. Christopher medal and marched down the street, opened a low wrought-iron gate, and went into the yard. In the center was a dangerous-looking plant with swordlike leaves, rimmed with thorns. The door was bright red. Before she could push the bell, the door opened.

A woman wearing an apple green tunic with matching pants stood in the opening. "Oh!" she said. "I'm just on my way out." She was maybe Ruth's age but stout, with round pink cheeks.

"Hello," said Mara, confused. "I'm sorry, I thought Mrs. Dixon lived here."

"Of course she does," the woman said heartily. "I'm Betty from home health, looking in on her. I'm new—that's why you don't recognize me. My, my, my, what pretty flowers. Are those for Grace?"

"Yes."

"She'll be thrilled. And she's having a good day today. Well, come in." Betty stood to one side and smiled knowingly. "I bet you're a granddaughter."

"I'm Mara."

"Well, Mara, you're a sweetie to come see your grannie. There's nothing like the sight of a young person to get the blood moving. I'll just take you to her in the living room, then I'll be on my way."

She followed Betty down a hall, the walls painted peach, the floor off-white tile, so clean Mara felt disheveled, sloppy.

"Grace!" Betty called cheerily. "You'll never guess who's here! Mara!"

"Who? Mara who?" said a woman's voice gruffly.

"Why, I don't know," said Betty. "She didn't say. I thought—"

Mara took a deep breath and turned the corner into a light-flooded room that was all white and peach, white wall-to-wall carpet, white couch and chairs, peach walls, and peach pillows everywhere. A white-haired old woman, wearing beige and masses of silver and turquoise Indian jewelry, was sitting in the center of the white couch resting both hands on a cane. Her eyes, behind pale blue tinted glasses, met Mara's.

"Harvey," Mara said awkwardly, clutching the cyclamen plant. "Mara Harvey."

"Never heard of you," said Mrs. Dixon abruptly.

"I thought—" said Betty again. "I'm sorry, Grace. Do you want me to stay?"

Mrs. Dixon paused for a moment, looking Mara up and down. "Well, she doesn't look like she's on drugs. Go, Betty, shoo, shoo. And you," she said to Mara, "sit down. There, where I can see you."

Still holding the plant, Mara sat where Mrs. Dixon pointed, on the chair closest to the couch. She heard the door close as Betty left and for a second longed for her to come back. "I brought you a plant," she said.

"Cyclamen. Very pretty. Well, don't just sit there with it. Put it on the coffee table where I can see it. The table's glass, it won't hurt it. Then you can tell me why you're here." Resting on her cane, Mrs. Dixon leaned toward Mara. "Not from a religious group, are you?"

"No." Mara set the plant on the table.

"Not that I would mind that much." She gave a bark of a laugh. "I've been converted three times already."

Mara looked over at Mrs. Dixon. It was hard to see her, beyond the silver and the turquoise and the blue glasses. "Jackson's my father," she said.

There was a silence, so deep Mara could hear the cars out on the street, birds chirping, and, as the silence lengthened, the whack of a club hitting a golf ball.

Then Mrs. Dixon said, "I didn't know Jackson had a daughter."

"I haven't seen him since I was three," said Mara. "I mean, until I came out here."

"And why," said Mrs. Dixon sternly, "would you want to see a father who abandoned you when you were three?"

"He didn't—" Mara flushed. "My mom told him to leave, then she married my dad and he adopted me."

Mrs. Dixon nodded. "It sounds to me like your mother was smart. What does she think about you seeing Jackson after all this time?"

Mara bit her lip. "She doesn't know. She—she died."

"I'm sorry," said Mrs. Dixon, her voice still stern but not unkind.

It gave Mara courage. "I was hoping you could write a letter saying it's okay if they let my father out of jail, lower the bail to something he can pay," she said in a rush. "I know Jenny was your daughter, but Jackson didn't kill her. I know he didn't."

"You're wrong," said Mrs. Dixon. "*Dead* wrong. He did kill her."

"No!" said Mara.

"Listen. Even if he didn't actually poison her, he still killed her. He ignored her and neglected her. He killed her spirit every day, day after day. I know that from what Jenny told me. *The memorial*—my God, I could hardly stand to be there in the same room with him. Mourning when he didn't love her."

"He loved my mother," cried Mara. "I'm sure he did."

"Your mother was probably just a fantasy to him," said Mrs. Dixon relentlessly, "because she left him. Some men, all they can love is fantasies. She left him and gave you a better life than he ever would have."

"That is so—so not *true*." Mara felt exhausted; her eyes watered from all the light in the white-and-peach room.

Mrs. Dixon's eyes were a blur of blue. "My little Jenny," she said sadly. "It's hard to lose a mother but harder to lose a child. I lost my little girl. I can't write that letter."

"It's okay," said Mara, giving up. "I understand. I do. And I upset you. I'm so sorry."

"I'm fine. I think you should go, though."

Mara stood up. She felt a little dizzy.

"Thank you for the flowers," said Mrs. Dixon. "They'll brighten my day."

Mara looked down at her. Beyond the glitter of the jewelry and the blue glasses, Mara saw how frail she was, tiny, the knuckles of her hands on the cane swollen and misshapen with arthritis.

"You'll be all right?" Mara asked anxiously.

"I'll be fine. I have a gentleman friend coming over soon. Henry." She paused. "I *have* friends. And of course, once in a blue moon, there's Kevin."

"Kevin?"

"You wouldn't have heard of him. Jenny never spoke of him to people. She more or less disowned him a while ago, acted like he never existed ever since. He's my son, Jenny's brother."

"Oh," said Mara.

"I don't know why she had to be like that. I know Kevin upset people sometimes, but he was her *brother*. And he's highly intelligent. He's traveled the world."

"Where is he now?" asked Mara.

"Alaska." Mrs. Dixon sighed, looking down at the floor. "He's been in Alaska for months." She looked up. "Time to shoo, shoo, little Mara," she said.

sixteen

As Stuart approached the Dudley police station, Ken Dooley was just coming out. Ken was back in sunny Mexico today in huaraches and a guayabera shirt.

"Hey there," said Stuart. "Shot any Border Patrol guards lately?"

"Not yet." Ken smiled genially. "But I'm loaded and ready. You gonna defend me?"

"You got the money," said Stuart, "then I got the time."

"What?" Ken said with mock surprise. "No pro bono for human rights?"

"I'm pro bono right now," said Stuart. "I'm here to see about the Magician."

"Great. But my guess is it's not going anywhere." Behind tinted wire-rimmed glasses, Ken's eyes gleamed a bright clear blue that implied some special knowledge. "Who cares about a homeless guy anyway, huh?"

Stuart thought there was a strong possibility there was some truth in this, but the last thing he wanted was to be drawn into a cop-bashing session with Ken Dooley. "I imagine they're doing their best with limited resources," he said.

"Isn't that what it's all about?" Ken went on as if Stuart hadn't spoken. "Impressions? Perception? Isn't that what lawyers do in front of a jury, create an impression and the truth be damned?"

"And what is it that *you* do, exactly?" said Stuart.

"Whatever I can," said Ken glibly. He held out his hands, palms up. His fingers were gray with ink. "Just got fingerprinted."

Stuart raised his eyebrows.

"For purposes of elimination," said Ken. "I went inside the Magician's cave when we were out there looking for him." He paused. "They mentioned DNA because of that blood on the sneaker. You really think they're going to spring for that?" His voice was sarcastic.

"No idea," said Stuart. "Excuse me." He turned away. "Got to run."

"DNA!" Ken shouted after him as Stuart went into the police station. "Ha!"

"Mr. Ross," said the young woman behind the glass. "Sergeant Nelson's waiting. You can go on back."

She buzzed him in.

Jack Nelson's door was open, and he sat behind a desk piled with folders, fiddling with his big mustache. "Come in," he said to Stuart. "Sit down. From what I hear you're pretty busy. Got yourself a first degree murder case, huh?"

"Yeah. Jackson Williams." Stuart sat on a rickety folding chair. The sergeant's desk was painted gray with metal showing through where it was scratched. It looked like the kind of desk you might buy at a government surplus auction. "You involved in the Hamblin investigation at all?"

"Nope. You said on the phone this was about the Magician. Got something for me?" Sergeant Nelson asked hopefully.

"Not really. What have *you* got?"

"Well, we talked to a bunch of people, names that Frieda gave us, but nobody knows anything, nobody saw him, etcetera, etcetera. What's your interest, anyway?"

"Well, he was my client," said Stuart. He debated mentioning Jackson, but what was there to tell? "*Is* my client, I hope."

Nelson looked skeptical. "So maybe he said something to you about someone being after him, having a grudge?"

"Are you kidding? He was barely coherent."

"Stuff on the sneaker *is* blood."

"It's his?"

"No way of knowing. Got nothing to compare it to."

"But you got DNA material."

Sergeant Nelson nodded. "So we find out it's his blood. So what? We might wait, just a bit, before we deal with that. And we still might, um, find him."

"What the hell is a budget for," Stuart said, "if not for that?"

"A budget is a budget, and money's something else."

"Why don't you give me copies of all the reports and maybe something in them will ring a bell."

"Anything," said Nelson dolefully. "Before that Dooley asshole starts writing letters. What I don't get is, Dooley being friends with Frieda."

Stuart shrugged. "Birds of a feather, I guess."

"I don't think so. She's a very special lady—*Christian.*"

"Christian!" Stuart guffawed.

"Sure she is," said Sergeant Jack Nelson. "Even if she don't know it."

GEORGE LIT ANOTHER cigarette. Nell's Café was right up the street—couldn't see the café itself from where he sat, just the red neon sign above it. He glanced at the sign longingly from time to time; he hadn't eaten since breakfast, and now it was dinnertime. Hours. He'd been parked here for hours. No one had gone in or come out of the trailer at Lot Twelve, no sign at all of Randy Gates. He reached into the glove compartment and fumbled around. He felt sunglasses, thick folded paper that was probably a map, a screwdriver, a plastic straw and plastic fork, and then his fingers closed over something small and round. He took it out and held it up to the light. A pack of wintergreen LifeSavers, two left. Ah.

He chewed the tiny LifeSavers greedily, studying the trailers in the park, again trying to imagine the lives of the people inside. Roomy lives compared to his life right now, stuck in a car. They could pee anytime they felt like it. One foot had gone to sleep, pins and needles. *I'm too old,* he thought. *Screw this.*

He got out and stamped his foot to bring back the circulation. He walked around a little bit, till he was moving easier. Then he headed up the street to Nell's Café. What the hell. He could take a seat by the window, keep an eye out.

He wasn't exactly thinking when he pushed open the door, more like sensing, sensing the warmth inside, sensing the smell and flavor of—What? Meat loaf. He loved meat loaf. There was a counter along one side and red vinyl booths along the other. The floor was beige linoleum. There were four or five people in the booths. He thought he would just sit at the counter near the door.

What appeared to be the only waitress was delivering an order at the back booth. George started for a scat at the counter. The waitress turned and dropped her order pad. She leaned down to pick it up. Now that she wasn't blocking the way, George could see the customer in the last booth, a youngish, handsome man with curly black hair and a strong chin.

Randy Gates.

JACKSON'S VOLVO WAS parked in front of the house when Ruth got home at five thirty, so Mara was safely back from Tucson. In her mind Ruth crossed that off her list of little worries. Her big worry right now was all the new stuff about Jackson that Stuart had told her. How much should she tell Mara?

Inside the house it was very quiet, too quiet. Where was Tyler? Then she remembered, he was sleeping over at Buzzie's to work on his history project. Hopefully it *was* a history project and they weren't experimenting with prescription medications from Buzzie's parents' medicine cabinet or building a bomb from a recipe they got off the Internet.

"Mara?" she called.

"In the kitchen."

Mara was sitting at the kitchen table where yesterday Ruth had sat with George Maynard drinking coffee. For a moment the thought warmed her.

"How were the malls?" Ruth asked brightly.

"I didn't go to any," said Mara.

"Well, I guess you saved yourself some money, then." Ruth sat down across the table. "I have a top just like the one you're wearing," she said.

Mara's face got pink. "This *is* yours. I borrowed it. I'm sorry. I should have asked."

"I don't mind at all," said Ruth.

"I—I borrowed it so I'd look extra presentable." Mara's mouth quivered. "So she'd like me, and now—" Her voice rose. "I feel terrible, like a jerk."

"So *who* would like you?"

"Mrs. Dixon. Jenny's mom."

"*What?*" said Ruth.

"I went to see her to ask if she'd write a letter to get Jackson released."

"For heaven's sake."

"I had to do something, and then when I talked to her, I realized that Jenny was a *person*, you know? An actual person, like you and me and my mother, and except for Mrs. Dixon nobody"—Mara looked at Ruth sadly—"nobody even cared that she was dead, including my father."

For a moment Ruth was shamed into silence, and the worst of it was that it was true. "Oh, Mara," she said finally. "I'm sorry."

"It's so, so not *fair*." Her voice rose again. "Mrs. Dixon isn't going to write the letter, and I don't blame her."

"Your father and Jenny weren't suited to each other," said Ruth gently. "I think he tried to love her, but he wasn't any good at it. We can't help how we feel, any of us."

"And there's something else Mrs. Dixon said," Mara went on. "I didn't realize Jenny had a brother."

"I only heard her mention him once. And that was—" Ruth shrugged. "I guess it was too painful."

"Mrs. Dixon told me Jenny disowned him," said Mara.

"Did she tell you how he died?" Ruth asked curiously.

"Died? He's not dead."

"Of course he is. Jenny told me."

"No, he's not," Mara insisted. "His name's Kevin, and he lives in Alaska."

Jenny's brother was alive? *Dead,* Jenny had said, *he's dead,* thought Ruth, and now he wasn't. How many times was she doomed to replay that scene in the kitchen with Jenny, a truly dead person? Every time she did, it seemed to get worse. Jenny had *lied*—she'd lied about her brother so Ruth would feel sorry for her and let her off the hook for saying such terrible things about Owen.

"You know what?" said Ruth. "Jenny deserved to die. She can rot in hell for all I care."

And Mara was a grown-up. Jackson was her father. She should be told what was going on in the case, Sid Hamblin, his affair with Jenny, the Magician, everything—she'd hear about it anyway, and who was there but Ruth to tell her kindly, gently.

IN BUZZIE'S BASEMENT, Tyler dipped a piece of sponge in green paint and put it on some cardboard to dry. A miniature kind-of-to-scale half-finished reproduction of an Indian village at Mesa Verde made with sticks and clay was spread out on a Ping-Pong table.

"Maybe we should do more brown bushes," said Buzzie worriedly. He was blond and small for his age, with round glasses that made his hazel eyes look owlish. "When I went to Mesa Verde with my folks it was really dry."

"This is during the monsoons," said Tyler.

"I don't think they had monsoons. My dad says they all starved to death 'cause there wasn't enough water to grow any crops."

"You know what *I* heard?" Tyler lowered his voice. "They got so hungry they *ate each other.*"

"*No shit.*" Buzzie giggled. "Like how? They just started gnawing on each other's arms and legs?"

"Naw. Probably they had a lot of big battles and the ones that were killed got eaten."

"They were probably thirsty, too," said Buzzie. "I bet before they ate them they *drank their blood.*" He giggled again, at a higher pitch. "*Bloodthirsty.* Get it?"

"You know what we should do?" Tyler said excitedly. "We should get red paint and put blood all over the village like they just had a battle."

Buzzie laughed, full out. "That would be—haw haw—so *cool.*"

Tyler laughed, too, which made Buzzie laugh harder. They rolled on the floor laughing. Buzzie's glasses fell off, and he let them lie.

"And there wouldn't be any bodies," Tyler gasped, "because they *all* got killed and they all ate each other."

"We could put in some leftover body parts!" said Buzzie wildly. "Some arms and legs! A *head*!"

Tyler laughed so hard his stomach hurt worse than ever. Tears streamed down his cheeks. He wanted to stop laughing, but he couldn't, and in the midst of his laughing, he was ambushed by what he'd been trying so long not to think about—that the man he'd seen going into Jackson's house at night wasn't the same man he'd seen go in the daytime. It wasn't Randy Gates.

He hadn't been able to tell exactly what he looked like, but he was pretty sure it wasn't anyone he'd ever seen before. It hadn't been all that dark; there was a big moon. *The man could have seen him. The man could come after him any day now, and Jackson wasn't home to protect him and Mara and his mom.* And his dad was faraway in Los Angeles.

o   o   o

GEORGE SLID INTO the booth. "I hear the meat loaf's pretty good here," he said.

"Detective Maynard," said Randy Gates, a cheeseburger halfway to his mouth. "Son of a *bitch*."

"No," George said. "My mother was a saintly woman, loved by one and all."

For a moment Randy glared at him, the muscles in his jaw working in a manly way. Had George cared about such things, he would have noted that the red in Randy's plaid flannel shirt set off his dark eyes perfectly. Like a lot of handsome men, his face when not animated resembled an ape's.

"I could walk out of here," said Randy. He pushed his plate away and half rose. "Who's going to stop me?"

"Not me." George raised his hands, palms up. "Don't have the authority. I'm not the cops anymore, I'm a private investigator, working for Stuart Ross, the attorney who's representing Jackson Williams. I just want to talk to you is all. Where's the harm in that?"

The waitress came back and set a glass of water in front of George. Heavyset, forties, with short blond hair and a name tag on her green uniform that said TANYA.

"I'll have the meat loaf, Tanya," George said, "when you get a chance. And coffee." He looked at Randy. "You can put his cheeseburger on my bill."

"Sure thing," said Tanya.

Randy sank back onto his seat. "I don't know what the hell there is to talk about anyway."

"Sure you do," said George. "Jenny Williams."

"Who's that?"

"Right," said George. "Except we got an eyewitness saw you go into her house the very day she died. Other times, too."

"Bullshit," said Randy.

George smiled and raised his eyebrows.

"God damn it." He sighed. "*Okay.* So I'd stop in and see her sometimes—she used to run past the construction site every day, and we struck up some conversations."

"Some conversations," said George. "And here you are, hiding out like you did something wrong. 'Course you were selling her dope on a regular basis, but big deal. I don't care about that."

"One meat loaf special," said Tanya. She plunked it down. "Anything else?"

"Not unless my friend Randy here wants some pie," said George.

Randy shook his head. Tanya put down the bill and left.

George grabbed his fork and stabbed a chunk of meat loaf with some mashed potatoes. The meat loaf was bland and not quite warm, but George was too hungry to care. Randy took another bite of his burger and set it down as if he'd had enough.

George swallowed. "You quit your job right after Jenny got killed. You've been running and hiding ever since. How come?"

"She got murdered is how come," said Randy through clenched teeth, "and I got a record. A bunch of phony trumped-up convictions that weren't even my fault." His voice deepened, full of self-pity. "Once you got those convictions, everything you do is wrong."

"Look," George said, leaning across the table. "I'm with you on that. We got clean-living prominent citizens in the community ripping people off every day and all they ever get is awards, but someone like you even looks the wrong way and bam."

"Damn shootin'," said Randy vehemently. He tossed his head like a girl, and a curl fell onto his forehead.

"I'll tell you what I think," George said. "You didn't kill Jenny. Okay?"

"Okay," said Randy.

"But," George went on, "I don't think her husband killed her, either. All we know is someone did. She ever ask to sample the goods, smoke a number with you?"

"Never," Randy said. "She was a clean liver, that lady."

"Then who was she buying it for?"

"You got me. Her husband maybe?"

"Sid Hamblin. She ever mention that name?"

Randy shook his head.

"How about"—George leaned across the table toward Randy—"Anita Selby?"

"*Anita,*" said Randy. "She's your so-called eyewitness saw me going into Jenny's house the day she got killed? That lying bitch," he went on, turning voluble, "thinks her shit don't smell. You tell Anita she wants to rat out me, I can rat out her big time."

"How's that?" George pounced.

"How'd that go over with her boss? A doper, out there selling fancy real estate."

"That all?"

"It ain't enough?"

"I heard," said George, "even though she and Jenny were supposed to be best friends, Anita didn't like Jenny all that much."

"Aw, who cares if she didn't?" Randy's mouth turned down. "Women. Always some weird shit going down between women." His voice turned falsetto. "*She said this, so I said that, then she said blah, blah, blah.* Take it from me, it don't pay to listen to 'em, get sucked into their bullshit."

"Help me out here," said George in exasperation. "We're talking Jenny was murdered. *Think.* She say anything to you strange or paranoid or whatever about Anita? Or anyone else, for that matter?"

"Only thing she ever said to me that was like strange was about a letter."

"A letter?"

"She said she was going to have someone write a letter." Randy scratched his head. "It was strange, you know, 'cause she looked like a lady who knew how to write."

"*Who?*" said George. "*Who* was she going to have write a letter?"

"Some guy." Randy's forehead wrinkled. "What was the name?" He snapped his fingers. "Ken. That's it, the guy's name was Ken. Ken Dooley."

o   o   o

STUART WALKED BRISKLY down Main Street, carrying a foam cup of Mocha Java from the Dudley Coffee Company. It was eight o'clock at night. It wasn't till he'd gone home and nuked and eaten some frozen stuffed peppers that he realized he'd left the reports on the Magician from the Dudley P.D. in a file on his desk at the office. Might as well go over them before he talked to Jackson tomorrow.

The Cornucopia restaurant had been closed for hours. A few die-hard tourists still wandered down the street looking into the windows of the shops that sold antiques and collectibles, and one of them was standing in front of Stuart's office, a middle-aged man in a baseball cap, a green-and-yellow-striped polo, and khaki pants, camera around his neck.

He smiled genially as Stuart approached. "Evening," he said. "Nice night."

"Yep." Stuart walked past him to the office and pulled out his keys.

"Say, do you know anything about the architecture of this building?" asked the man.

"Sorry," said Stuart. "Not a thing."

He turned away to forestall any more conversation and unlocked the door. The bell tinkled as he stepped inside, closing the door firmly against the tourist. The smell of charred coffee tickled his nose. The coffeepot was still on. He vaguely remembered Ruth saying cheerily as she left, "Don't forget to turn off the coffeepot!" He walked over and clicked it off. He promised himself guiltily that when it cooled he would clean it out. Ruth would never know.

He went in through the outer office and into his—there was the file right where he'd left it. He started to put on Dylan, then thought, *No, Mozart.* His mother had been a piano teacher. He slid in the CD, then sat at his desk and let the music calm him. It was so peaceful. It felt like years since he'd sat here alone at night. He tilted his chair back, put his feet up, and opened the file for Ikan Danz a.k.a the Magician. He yawned.

He was doing this—coming down here tonight when he could be comfortably at home watching TV or . . . well, he could be comfortably at home—more for Ruth and Jackson than he was for himself, so they would get off his back. It wasn't that he didn't care about the Magician, poor guy; but he wasn't *relevant.*

Stuart flipped through the reports; nothing new to add to what he'd been told by Frieda and then Jack Nelson. He paused at the inventory of evidence seized and read that more thoroughly.

Sleeping bag, three water jugs, paper sack, Baggie of dried apricots, Baggie of dried walnuts, three empty Baggies. One bologna sandwich. Stuart wrinkled his nose; imagine that sitting for years in an evidence room. One hat, red in color. Six tea bags, a bottle of echinacea. One large Mexican tin box. Contents of box: one dried mesquite pod; four stones, blue in color; two stones, pink in color; one button saying FRODO LIVES.

One paperback book, *Stranger in a Strange Land,* inscribed "from Frieda." One braided yarn bracelet, green and red in color. One bell, gold in color. One white handkerchief. One twenty-dollar bill, two tens, three fives, nine ones, and change. Two toothpicks; one woman's metal bracelet, silvertone in color; one card, STUART ROSS, ATTORNEY AT LAW. One card, KEN DOOLEY, AT LARGE IN THE UNIVERSE.

The guy had had nothing, absolutely nothing of any value except the cash. Nothing of any value except the cash unless you counted the two cards. His own and Ken Dooley's. Stuart smiled. His manager and his publicist. What the hell else did you need in this world? He yawned, closing the file.

"WILLIAMS!" ONE OF the guards, the short one with the macho attitude, was standing at the door to the pod. "Your lawyer's on the phone."

Jackson looked up, surprised. He hadn't talked to Stuart lately. *Why not?* He almost had the sense Stuart was avoiding him. No. That was just paranoia. You had to have faith. Probably there had been nothing new in the case to talk about and now there was. He stood up quickly and followed the guard to the bank of phones, thinking, hoping, *Maybe it's good news?* Maybe someone had confessed and Stuart couldn't wait till tomorrow morning to tell him.

"Hello?" Jackson said, his voice rising in anticipation. "Stuart?"

"Cool it, okay?" said an unfamiliar voice, smooth as silk. "This isn't Stuart, but I'd appreciate it if you'd act like it was."

"Why should I?" said Jackson, deflated.

"Hear me out, then you can decide."

Jackson turned so he couldn't see the guard at the end of the hall. "Sure, Mr. Ross," he said.

"My name's Ken Dooley."

"Sure," said Jackson. "I've read your letters in the weekly paper. I enjoy them." People didn't always like Ken, but to Jackson his talent overrode his flaws. "You have a compelling style."

"A scholarly remark," said Ken. "Thank you. I've kind of been interested in your case. Sid Hamblin, wasn't that something?"

"Yeah."

"Then there's the Magician," Ken went on. "Heard through the grapevine he was in your pod for a while. Even *spoke* to you."

"Not exactly," said Jackson, suddenly wary. "Mumbled something is all."

"Umm." Ken paused for a moment. "Good people on your side," he said. "Stuart's new secretary, for one. And her kid, what's his name?"

"Tyler."

"Yeah. Heard he saw someone suspicious sneaking around your house right before the murder."

"Who told you that?"

"Gosh, I don't remember. Maybe it was Anita. Jenny's friend."

No, thought Jackson. *No. Tyler doesn't get brought into this conversation. Especially by Anita.* "That's not true," he protested. Why was Ken calling him, anyway? Just to milk him for information. "Listen," he went on, "I really appreciate you taking an interest, but I can't talk about the case. You need to contact Stuart."

"Not a problem," said Ken. "I understand perfectly. I'll let you go, then."

SON OF A bitch. Stuart jerked awake and stared into the darkness. He'd fallen asleep on the couch again, shortly after returning home from his office, and entered a series of complex dreams—none of which he could remember, but he had the sense that each one opened into the next, like interlocking boxes, leading to a profound discovery. But what was it?

Stuart lay there letting his eyes adjust till he could see the outline of the window across from the couch, his bookcase with rows of books, trying hard to grasp hold of that last dream. Something to do with tonight, with his office—the last thing he'd done before leaving was to read the list of items seized in the Magician's bag. It must be something in the Magician's bag. But no, he had the sense it was something earlier. What?

Read the file again. Stuart sat up—it should be right there on his coffee table. No, *damn it,* he'd left it at the office again. What the hell. Do it in the morning. Before he went to talk to Jackson.

seventeen

"*DUDLEY WEEKLY!*" SAID a woman's voice, a little hoarse.

"Hi there," said George on his cell phone. "Ken Dooley around?"

"Ken's never *around*," said the woman. "He drops off his letters once a week and that's it."

"He's not listed in the phone book, is why I'm calling," said George. "He's an old friend. Maybe you got a phone number? Or an address?"

"I don't have a phone number at all, and the address I have is just a box," said the woman. "Sorry."

"Aw, shucks. Hate to be in town and miss him."

"Try the Dudley Coffee Company. He hangs out there a lot."

George punched off, drove down Main Street, and found a space to park close to the café. Outside were a couple of tables and some chairs where locals, judging from their shabby-chic dress, hairy faces, and unkempt hair, sat in good weather like today watching the tourists.

George ambled over, cowboy boots tap-tapping on the sidewalk, a study in contrast in stiff new jeans and a muted green-and-blue-plaid shirt with his best bolo tie, in anticipation of stopping by Stuart's office later, maybe around lunchtime, to see Ruth.

"Some car," one of them, a bearded man, said. "Nostalgic. What is it?"

George smiled, the thought of seeing Ruth later hovering over him pleasantly. " 'Fifty-six Coupe de Ville."

"Ah," said the bearded man.

"I'm looking for Ken Dooley," George said. "Seen him around?"

"He was here about an hour ago, with some flyers. Probably hanging them up around town."

"What's he driving?"

"*If* he's driving, old blue Dodge van."

George went back to the Caddy to think. He had an idea Jenny might have wanted to tell Ken some incriminating dirt about Anita and maybe Anita knew it. What kind of dirt? Certainly not her marijuana habit; this crowd wouldn't give two hoots about that. Real estate fraud, something like that? Jenny was basically unaccounted for for most of the afternoon before she died. With any luck she *had* talked to Ken. Well, he shouldn't be hard to find, and in the meantime George had other things to do.

MARA DROVE JACKSON'S Volvo slowly around the mining pit, an enormous hole in the ground, with crumbling terraces that led to the bottom, where toxic-looking water pooled. Why didn't they plant trees there or something? At the point where the pit reached its maximum depth was a sign saying SCENIC VIEW. Who did they think they were kidding?

Last night Ruth had told her everything about Jackson's case. Everything. Mara swallowed hard, remembering.

"But what can we *do*?" she'd cried.

"The Magician," Ruth had said. "Jackson thinks he might have known something about Jenny's murder." She hesitated. "We could talk to Frieda, she's his friend."

"I'll talk to her," said Mara. "Where—"

"I don't know. You could try the Co-op. She looks like a Co-op sort of person. They might know."

Just past the pit was another sign that said DUDLEY FOOD CO-OP with a big arrow pointing to the right. Mara turned and went by a stand of old brick buildings to a big building on the corner. She parked in front and got out.

Inside she saw rows and rows of herbs, bins of beans, nuts, and grains, and shelves of jars and canned goods, but no people except a blond guy in his twenties with a goatee and a pierced eyebrow, at the cash register reading a paperback book.

He looked up and smiled. "Hey there," he said. "What's up?"

"The sky," said Mara, from behind her sunglasses.

"You live in Dudley?" he asked. "Haven't seen you before."

"I'm just visiting."

"I'm Josh."

"Mara."

He set his book facedown on the counter and stroked his goatee. "Bet you're wondering how come a store like this that sells actual food to actual people is all the way out of town, while the stores that sell fake junk to fake people are right there on Main Street."

"*Yeah,*" said Mara.

"It's all about money. These investors came into town—"

"Excuse me?" A man stood in the door, wearing a red baseball cap, khaki shorts, and a bright blue polo, camera slung around his neck. He waved a map, coming closer. "I'm kind of lost here."

"Excuse me a minute," Josh said to Mara.

She moved away while he gave directions, drifting through the store like an actual shopper. There was a big freezer section, a little deli-restaurant, and, at the back, organic produce. Halfway to the back were the teas: for flu, colds, arthritis, menopause, menstrual irregularity, fatigue, anxiety, memory loss, sleeplessness—*everything.* After her mother was diagnosed, she had drunk lots of green tea, which was supposed to fight cancer; cup after cup all day long. *It's all lies,* Mara wanted to yell. *These don't work.*

For a moment she imagined sweeping her hands along the shelves, knocking all those teas to the floor. Then she drifted on, looking for something small to buy, and stopped suddenly, riveted in front of a bulletin board that she hadn't noticed when she walked in. In the middle was a sign, hand lettered:

HELP US FIND THE MAGICIAN!!

Under that was a fuzzy picture of a bearded man wearing a pointy cap and what looked to Mara like a bathrobe. *Our dear friend has vanished*, it said below. *If you have any information concerning his whereabouts, please leave a message here for Ken Dooley or Frieda.*

"Oh!" said Mara. She turned to the cashier. The tourist had gone, and he was back to his book. She pointed to the poster, about to ask where she could find Frieda, but he spoke first.

"Pretty sad, huh?" He set down the book happily and leaned across the counter toward her. "He was a great old guy, like a—a *saint*. He lived in a cave, and he almost never ate. And the worst part is there's lots of people probably glad to see him gone."

"*Really,*" said Mara. "Why?"

He stroked his goatee again. "Some people can't handle self-knowledge. A guy like that, living on nothing, gets to them, makes them question their priorities."

"I know what you mean."

"I was part of the original search party," said Josh eagerly. "With *Ken Dooley.*"

"Yeah, I see his name on the poster," said Mara. "Who is he?"

"He's, uh"—Josh waved a hand vaguely—"kind of this *activist.*" He lowered his voice. "Anyway, we're pretty sure the Magician was murdered."

"That's awful," said Mara, meaning it. "Um, Frieda. How can I find her?"

"You can't right now. She's the one that first found him missing." He lowered his voice. "She's so *traumatized,* she went on a retreat."

"Oh," said Mara, disappointed.

"We're making the cave a shrine," said Josh. "Everyone's been going up there, leaving flowers and shit."

"I could leave something, too," said Mara. "Where is it?"

"*You got me bushwhacked, baby, and now I'll do the same to you,
Whack your bush, baby, all day and all night too.*"

Pretty good voice, but George didn't think the lyrics would fly in prime time.

"*Thought I heard you say to me, oh, baby, baby, baby, ooh.*"

George knocked on the screen door. Through the rusty squares he could see a young man on a couch, hunched over a guitar. "*Oh, baby, baby, ba—*"

"Hello?" called George loudly.

The singer looked over, then got up and padded barefoot to the door, holding the guitar. His blond hair was braided into dreadlocks, and all he had on was ragged jeans. "Yeah?"

"Sorry to bother you while you're practicing," said George. He held up his card, and the young man squinted at it through the screen.

"Wow," he said. "An *investigator.*"

"You're—?" George began.

"Keoki." He smiled. "Stage name. This about Sid?"

George nodded. "Since you're his closest neighbor, I thought maybe you could help me out, answer a few questions."

Keoki scratched his bare chest. "I didn't even know the guy. I mean"—he gestured up the hill to Sid's—"he was kind of just up there. I'd say hi if I saw him on the street and that's about it."

"Maybe you noticed his visitors," said George. He opened a manila envelope, slid out a computer printout of a photograph of a brightly smiling Anita Selby, Woman of the Year in Sierra Vista two years ago, and held it up. "You ever see her go up there?"

"Jeez." He snorted. "Middle-class chick like that? Don't think so." He paused. "That doesn't mean she never went up there. It's not like I spy on my neighbors, you know? I'm gone a lot, play gigs in Tucson. There *was* one kind of middle-class lady went there a few times, but"—he looked at the picture skeptically—"it wasn't her."

"You're sure."

"Yeah, the one I saw had long hair, dark. Looked kind of . . . athletic, if you know what I mean."

Jenny. "So who did go up there?" George asked.

"Ken Dooley went there a lot." He tilted his head, considering. "Saw Frieda with him a couple of times."

"Who's Frieda?"

"Older lady, hangs out with Ken sometimes. You could show *her* the picture. She lives over on Wood Canyon—203-C. I went over to her place once to talk about playing a benefit for the Co-op." He paused. "One of the times I saw her going to Sid's she had the Magician with her, not that he'd be much— *Shit*."

"What?"

"Somebody offed the Magician, too, right?"

"*Offed* him?" George stared at the young man, suddenly alert. *Someone else was murdered, connected to Sid?* "Who's this Magician?"

"Old loony tunes guy, hangs at the post office? Pointed cap. Dressed in orange? You never saw him there?"

"No," said George. "I work out of Sierra Vista, mostly."

"Ask Frieda, she'll tell you all about him. *Man*." He hit his head with the heel of his hand. "What *is* this? Dudley's the murder capital of Cochise County now? I should move back to New York City, where it's *safe*."

JOSH OFFERED TO escort Mara to the Magician's cave, if she'd wait till he got off work at three. And after that, he could show her around town, all the cool places the tourists never got to see. And tomorrow, the day he worked the café, if she came back at noon, he would fix her a tofu and avocado whole-wheat wrap with radish sprouts, his personal best recipe.

Mara said no-but-thank-you-very-much-that's-so-sweet to all these things, left, and drove back to town, where she bought a big pink crepe paper rose made in Mexico from one of the tourist stores. Then she drove up the Gulch, past the vintage stores and the bars and the newly renovated bandshell for concerts and the little wood houses meandering up the hills, until finally the road stopped being paved and got so narrow there was room for only one car. She parked in a niche on the side and got out, holding the big pink rose.

A stand of weedy trees shed their yellow leaves onto the pitted dirt road. From behind a rusty wire fence, a tiny Chihuahua yapped with increasing desperation as she passed. In the next house a woman crooned a song in a language Mara recognized as Spanish, even though she didn't understand the words. Whatever they were, they were sad, glomming on to Mara's heart like a pang of impending tragedy.

Suddenly she missed her friends, Stacy in particular, who she'd only e-mailed once since she'd been here, but everyone else, too. They'd cushioned her, kept her safe.

Holding tight to the pink rose, she walked farther up to where the street ended in a little dirt path. Eyes down, watching for loose rocks, she followed the path as it wound upward around the waist-high bushes, some gray-green, some an explosion of white fluff, wishing she hadn't worn her cool pointy-toed espadrilles. Something prickly, a tiny cactus, snagged at one leg of her khaki pants, and she stopped to free it.

The sense of overwhelming sadness from the woman's singing was still with her. Up ahead now she could see the cave-shrine, obvious because of some bright flowers piled in front. She trudged up the rest of the way. At the cave entrance were lots of wilting flowers, chrysanthemums mostly, yellow and deep orange, daisies, some sprigs of rosemary. They seemed eerie, unnatural, in this faded desert landscape.

Mara put the pink crepe paper rose on top of the real but dying flowers, her hands a little shaky, *why?* Then, feeling off center, she sat down on a big rock on one side of the entrance to get her bearings.

Below her was the winding Gulch and the little wooden houses; above was more mountain, and higher still the blue sky where black crows swooped. *Where am I?* she thought. *Where the hell am I?* It felt like the end of the world here.

And right there at the end of the world, her mother's death roared over Mara full force, white hot, *searing;* as if no time had passed, as if it had just happened. The false hopes, the downturns—Mara began to cry, tears blurring her sunglasses—the smell, the horrible smell of the hospital where her mother went for chemo, her mother's face, how are you feeling, *better,* the Chinese herb doctor who lied, the hospice people at the end, the friends who stopped by with unneeded useless presents and food her mother couldn't eat. Mara cried and cried, shoulders hunched as she sat on the rock, riding it out.

Wood Canyon was just off Tombstone Canyon, and it wound around in a meandering kind of way. Big cottonwoods dropped their yellow leaves onto pitted asphalt that dissolved into dirt on the edges. Half the little wood and adobe houses didn't even have numbers, at least none that were visible. George found an adobe that said 200 at the curb, parked in the dirt, and got out. Overhead on a telephone pole a redheaded woodpecker pecked little staccato tat-tat-tats. Somewhere George heard the scrape of a rake, but he couldn't see anybody. A red-orange cat came out from under a gray van and slithered around George's legs, purring loudly.

"Hey, guy," he said, as the cat looked up at him with chilly eyes. George leaned down to give it a pat, and the cat bit him on the knuckle.

George recoiled. "Ow!"

Someone laughed. A gray-haired Mexican man in overalls stood by a wire fence, holding a rake. "That's one bad little kitty cat," he said. "But don't worry, she's had all her shots. She's just mean, like a lot of women I know. Even got a woman's name. Ruth."

"*What?*" said George.

"Ruby. 'Cause her fur's kind of red."

"You got any idea where 203-C is?" George asked, sucking his knuckle.

"That's Frieda's house," said the man. "You go down two houses, you'll see some steps on the left, go up the steps to the third house on the right."

"Thanks," said George, turning away.

"Hey, man, she's not a doper," the man called after him.

I'm that obvious? thought George as he climbed the steps. A pyracantha hedge blocked his view of the house across from 203-C, but 203-C was clearly visible, a wood house, painted silvery green, with a brick front yard and a big pot of red geraniums by the dark green front door. He opened a wooden gate.

"She's not home!" said a woman's voice behind him.

He turned—couldn't see anyone but sensed invisible people watching him everywhere, here on Wood Canyon. For a moment he had the feeling he was in one of those puzzle drawings where you had to find the hidden faces. He walked over to a spot where he could look into the yard across where the voice had come from.

A thin red-haired woman in her forties, wearing a long purple batik skirt, stood near a wooden porch painted a fading white. She was feeding a bright red-and-blue-patterned cloth into an ancient wringer washing machine.

"Son of a gun," said George. "I remember my grandmother used one of them machines out on the ranch forty years ago. You know what, I don't even think she did. What I remember is my grandmother telling me her mother used to have one."

"I'm a batik artist," said the woman. "This saves energy."

"I'll bet." George half smiled. "But maybe not time."

"What's time for?"

What's time for. For some reason the phrase struck George with some special significance. What *was* time for? To practice a guitar over and over, to make bright patterns on cloth? No. He drew himself up. To catch a murderer. "Got any idea when Frieda will be back?"

The woman stopped feeding the cloth into the wringer and brushed her hair out of her eyes. "Why?"

"Just want to talk to her."

"Are you a Realtor by any chance?" she asked suspiciously.

"No," said George, surprised.

"I hate Realtors." She looked disgusted. "They have no shame. They come around, trying to get you to sell your house for nothing, so they can turn around and sell it again for double. This guy was here earlier, I *know* he was a Realtor—he was actually taking pictures of her house."

"I swear to God"—George put his hand on his heart—"I'm not a Realtor. I wanted to ask her about the Magician."

"Oh." Her face brightened. "You can ask Frieda about the Magician anytime and she'll go on and on—but right now she's away on a retreat. She should be back tomorrow, though."

"You look like a local," said George. "One hundred percent. Maybe you can tell me where I might find Ken Dooley?"

"Everywhere." She gave the wringer a turn. "Ken Dooley is everywhere. At the Co-op maybe. Or the Coffee Company. The post office. One of the local galleries."

"He got a house?"

She smiled. "A school bus. Lives in an old school bus he's been caretaking for the owner. It's outside of town, on Highway Ninety-two. I can give you directions, but I think he's only ever there at night."

His lawyer pulled out page after page, showing Jackson reports, but after a while Jackson found he didn't even care. Worn out, overloaded with bad news, his mind drifted. He heard Stuart's words, one damning thing after another, but here in jail there was nothing he could do to fight back; it was like sinking in quicksand, the more you struggled against it, the deeper you sank, so after a while he stopped listening. He saw Stuart's mouth moving, saw the rows of books in the law library, the cinder-block walls. Then they blurred.

He had lived another life once where he had had everything; he reviewed it like a dream, some parts standing out vividly, others fading away. Absurdly, what stood out just then was the bicycle he had gotten for his birthday when he was ten. When he first saw it sitting in the driveway, it looked so beautiful, and he had wanted a bike more than anything in the world, though this one was cheap, prone to breaking down, an English-made racing bike, kind of metallic reddish purple with all metric parts that made it hard to work on but—

"Jackson?"

Jackson looked up, dazed. Stuart was standing up. The guard was coming into the room.

Stuart reached over and gave his shoulder a squeeze. "I know it looks bad for now," he said, "but I've got a *good* investigator working on it. Don't worry."

He had ridden that purple bicycle everywhere in the suburb where he'd grown up, gliding free in the fall, through yellow leaves of oaks, red leaves of maples, headed for—

Prison.

A poem. There was a true poem in there, Jackson was certain of it, though he hadn't written a poem in years. Words, phrases began to crowd into his mind. The guard took Jackson's arm.

"A notebook!" Jackson said urgently as the guard led him away. He looked back desperately at Stuart. "Could you get me a notebook? I need a notebook. And some *pencils.* Number-two automatic pencils."

THE SUN WINKED off the silver of the bolo on George's tie, set with a chunk of genuine malachite, as he ambled down Main Street headed for Stuart's office and Ruth. As he walked, a feeling came over him that felt like certainty and made up for everything—all the frustrations and wrong turns and backslidings. Everything would be okay. He was invincible.

'Course, the feeling was just temporary; it could be gone in a second. But what the hey, George thought, as he looked through the window of the Western Art Gallery at a painting of a bikini-clad Indian maiden with long black braids and enormous perky breasts, he might as well enjoy it while it lasted.

Up ahead the sun shone full on the big front window of Stuart's office, turning it into a sheet of light, but behind the light he could just make out Ruth sitting at Ellie's desk. He pushed open the door. The bell tinkled. In the second before Ruth looked up, he noted how ladylike she looked, with that silver streak in her thick hair and a dark red top that didn't fit too tight.

Then her face lit up. "George," she said.

"Ruth." He heard his voice ring in his ears, surprised, as if he hadn't known she would be there, even though he'd seen her before he walked in.

"I—" he began.

"You—" said Ruth simultaneously.

They both stopped. Ruth giggled.

"Uh," he said, "is the boss man in?" *The boss man.* Why had he said that? He'd been planning to ask her to lunch.

"No," she said, "but he should be back in a little while"—her voice lilted up hopefully—"if you want to wait."

"Sure," said George, suddenly gaining back his self-assurance. "What's time for." He sat on one of the chairs, tilted it back. "Maybe you can help me with something. Stuart's never mentioned it, but it might be relevant to the case. Tell me what you know about this guy, the Magician."

"Oh!" Ruth stared at him in admiration, her face luminous.

Beautiful, he thought. You might not notice it unless you knew her, but she was beautiful.

"The Magician," she said. "*Yes.*"

"The hell with Ross," said George. "Let's go have lunch."

225

e i g h t e e n

To the Editor:

A man sits in the Cochise County jail awaiting trial for the murder of his wife. Did he do it? The Cochise County attorney's office must think so or he wouldn't be in jail. His lawyer says he's innocent, but that's his job. And what do we think? We'll leave it to a jury.

Meanwhile our dear friend the Magician is still missing. Is there any hope we'll ever see him again? Our hearts persist in saying yes, but our brains fear otherwise. Our brains tell us he is likely dead, maybe even murdered. For what? Knowing too much? What could he know, a simple soul like our friend? The Dudley P.D., with their limited resources, say they are looking into it. But are they? They *look* pretty busy. They've fingerprinted some of us, questioned some of us, too. We have to ask, why us? We are his friends.

But what, you might ask, is that troublemaker, yours truly,

Ken Dooley, getting at? He starts off with a man in jail, then hops over to the Magician. Well, folks, the Magician and the accused murderer were once in the same pod in the jail. Not only that, they were seen conversing together. About what, no one knows— except the accused, of course.

Gas prices are rising everywhere (no reason for that except to make money for the big oil guys, our president's pals), so maybe Dudley P.D. with their limited resources can't afford the gas it would take to drive out to the jail to question the alleged murderer about his conversation with the Magician. Limited resources is the only reason I can think of. How about you?

Ken Dooley

IT WAS LATE afternoon when Stuart strode into his office, a copy of the *Dudley Weekly* under his arm. The office was full. Ruth was there with George and Mara, all of them drinking coffee and treating the place like a living room.

"This just came out," he said, holding up the newspaper. "Our friend Ken Dooley is at it again."

"What?" said Ruth.

Stuart flung the paper on Ruth's desk. "Read it," he said. "Page three, upper right."

George and Mara came around and read it, too, over Ruth's shoulder.

"How can he write that?" said Mara, looking sick. "It isn't fair. What a terrible man. What does he have against my father?"

"Conversed?" Ruth looked up at Stuart. "Jackson didn't say they *conversed*."

"Of course they didn't converse," said Stuart in exasperation. "Nobody conversed with the Magician. He'd pick up a word and say it over and over."

"Then what the hell is this all about?" said George.

"It's about nothing. It's about saying things to get yourself noticed.

The guy's a narcissist." Stuart sat down. "He should stick to shooting at the Border Patrol."

"I'm planning on going out to talk to Dooley tonight," said George.

"Why?" Stuart looked at George in amazement. "Because of this letter?"

"Because of a lot of things," said George, "but not this letter. Did you know he was friends with Sid Hamblin? You and I need to talk."

"It's libel," said Ruth. "You can sue Ken Dooley for libel."

Stuart shook his head. "It's not libel. He says accused, alleged, he covers himself. The guy isn't stupid. He just enjoys upsetting people."

"How could anyone enjoy that?" said Ruth in disgust.

"That's funny," said Mara suddenly.

"What?" Ruth asked.

"Just something somebody said. I wonder—" Mara stood up. "I'm going over to the Co-op."

Ruth looked over at her. "Why?"

Mara opened the door. "You said we needed some kind of vegetable for dinner. I'll get something there."

"I was going to pick up a chicken at the Safeway."

"I can still get a *vegetable.*"

Ruth tried not to look worried.

George put his hand on her shoulder. "Let her go," he said soothingly. "She's all grown up."

THE LETTER HAUNTED Mara, so nasty, insinuating. *The guy isn't stupid, he just enjoys upsetting people*, Stuart had said. *If I ever meet Ken Dooley,* she thought, *I'll kick him in the balls.* She mulled over the organic vegetables in the back of the Co-op and decided on green beans. She filled a plastic bag and took it up to the register.

Josh was ringing up an interminable purchase of mostly grains and vegetables for a young mother with a baby strapped to her front. His face reddened slightly when he saw Mara.

"There's mealybugs in the oats," said the mother.

"There's supposed to be." Josh glanced at Mara. "Cheap protein."

She giggled, but the mother didn't look amused.

"Sorry," Josh said to his customer. "I was just kidding." He pulled a big cardboard box from under the counter and began to fill it with the woman's purchases. "I'll make a note of it."

Mara plunked her beans onto the counter as the mother and baby left. "I went to the Magician's cave," she said. "I left a rose."

"You did?" Josh's face brightened.

"It's nice so many people care."

"Yeah." Josh weighed the beans, taking his time. He squinted at the scale. "That'll be two thirty-nine."

"I guess this person Ken Dooley cares a lot," said Mara, handing him a five. "I mean, his name's on the poster to call if you have any information. You said he was, like, this activist, but what does that mean? Who is he exactly?"

He put the change in her outstretched hand, not bothering to count it out, and shrugged. "He's Ken Dooley."

"Gee. That tells me a *lot*."

"I don't really know who he is," said Josh apologetically. "He hasn't been in town that long, but I heard he lived in Mexico before he came here. Puerto Vallarta. But then somebody else said Thailand, so who knows. He's a mysterious kind of guy, doesn't talk about his past." He lowered his voice. "I did hear this rumor—"

Mara waited. "What?" she said finally.

Josh glanced around the empty store. "Between you and me," he said.

"Of course."

"I heard Ken Dooley isn't his real name, that he changed it."

"Why?"

"Got in trouble with the feds. I told you he was an activist. Well, I guess he was really big time, offended a lot of people. Been running for his life ever since."

"Alaska," said Mara urgently. "Did he ever mention living in *Alaska*?"

"I— *Shit.*" Josh put his finger to his lips. "Here he comes now."

Mara stepped away from the register, holding her bag of green beans, as a man strode in, a sheaf of paper in his hand. His curly hair was tousled as if he'd been running, and he wore sunglasses, a Mexican guayabera shirt, jeans, and huaraches.

"Hey there, Josh," he said, but his sunglasses were aimed at Mara. "Got a bunch of flyers to post. Thought I'd leave you some."

"Sure thing," said Josh. "I read your latest letter, man."

"Yeah? What'd you think?" His sunglasses were still aimed at Mara.

Even though she couldn't see his eyes, she could feel his interest—he was the same age as her dad, as Jackson, maybe even older, but his attention didn't feel fatherly.

"Cool," said Josh.

Mara saw now that her resolve to kick Ken Dooley in the balls had been nothing but false courage. She moved around him in an arc, headed for the door, and opened it.

"Who was that?" she heard Ken Dooley saying as the door closed behind her.

Mara walked fast to her car, swinging the bag of beans. Across the width of the parking area she could see the high wire fence that surrounded the mining pit, a couple of tumbleweeds caught in the mesh. Parked next to Jackson's Volvo was a big old van, its once blue paint faded to off-gray. The windows were all open, and a God's Eye hung from the rearview mirror. As she reached the Volvo, someone called out to her.

"Hey, Mara!"

She turned.

Ken Dooley had come up so fast he was right there behind her. She could see a little chicken pox scar by his left eyebrow, a leather thong around his neck. She wanted to step back, but the Volvo was in her way; there was nowhere to go.

"What?" she said.

He smiled. "Josh says you're visiting. Just like to say hi to pretty ladies who are new here and maybe don't know a lot of people, make them feel at home. I think"—he lowered his voice—"you made quite an impression on him. He's a nice kid, if a little immature."

Mara put her hand on the handle and pulled, but she couldn't open the door far enough to get in because he was standing in her way. "Excuse me," she said. "I have to go."

"What's your hurry?" His voice was relaxed, leisurely. He rested the palm of his hand on the car. "You could at least tell me your name."

"You know my name."

"Your last name. Who you're visiting." He smiled again. "Might even be someone I know."

"Well, it isn't." Mara pulled on the door with all her strength and Ken Dooley stumbled, stepping backward.

Mara got inside fast and locked the door. Damn, she'd left the window open.

"I can find out, you silly cu—girl!" shouted Ken Dooley, his face red and venomous looking, as she wound the window up. *I know everybody in this town!*"

nineteen

GEORGE INSERTED THE magazine into his Colt Commander pistol and chambered a round. Then he shoved the pistol into its holster and shrugged on his tan corduroy jacket. He looked in the bathroom mirror. Not bad. If he was going to go clear out of town to the middle of nowhere in the desert to some school bus to see a guy who liked to shoot at the Border Patrol, it didn't hurt to be careful.

He remembered reading somewhere when he was a kid about famous people's last words. Errol Flynn's were "Hell, dying ain't so bad." For a while, he'd kind of been thinking living wasn't so great, but not lately.

Ruth had asked him to dinner and he'd had to say no, because of needing to check out Ken Dooley, but he'd given her a definite yes for tomorrow night. So now it seemed reasonable to be a little more careful—wouldn't want to get himself killed before he had a chance to have dinner at Ruth's.

Stuart drove slowly past the Quarter Moon Café, trying to see inside. Was Dakota working there tonight? He hadn't been back there since their disastrous date, but right now he had a craving for the Quarter Moon specialty, lamb and chickpea stew. Not worth it, though, if he had to see Dakota. Through the plate glass he could see her artwork on the walls, bright and ominous, but some other woman, a faded blonde, was working the tables.

Stuart parked, went inside, and ordered takeout. The blonde smiled, and when she smiled, she didn't look quite as faded.

"Dakota off tonight?" asked Stuart cautiously as she handed him his order.

"She's quit," said the blonde.

"Ah," said Stuart. Good. Now he could get something to eat here whenever he wanted to.

He drove back to his office. Ruth had washed the coffeepot before she left, and now he spooned in enough coffee for four cups, added water, and clicked it on. It felt good, being alone in his own office. It had been so crowded this afternoon, Mara, Ruth, and George. *Something was going on between George and Ruth.* Oh, surely not.

He wanted to think, go over some of his cases in peace and quiet. In particular, he wanted to read over the file on the Magician. Something in that file had wakened him in the middle of the night, and he couldn't for the life of him figure out what it was. He took the file out of his desk drawer and read through the inventory list again.

Sleeping bag, water jugs, paper sack, Baggie dried apricots, Baggie dried walnuts, three empty Baggies. Bologna sandwich. Hat, red in color. Six tea bags, bottle of echinacea. One large Mexican tin box. Contents of box: one dried mesquite pod; four stones, blue in color; two stones, pink in color; one button, FRODO LIVES.

One paperback book, *Stranger in a Strange Land,* inscribed "from Frieda." One braided yarn bracelet, green and red in color. One bell, gold in color. White handkerchief. One twenty-dollar bill, two tens, three fives, nine ones, and change. Two toothpicks; one woman's metal bracelet, silvertone in color; one card, STUART ROSS, ATTORNEY AT LAW. One card, KEN DOOLEY, AT LARGE IN THE UNIVERSE.

Nothing rang a bell. Could it have been something earlier that evening that had wakened him? Before the file? He had no clue.

He opened the takeout container and dug in with the plastic fork. The stew was a lot spicier than usual. Too spicy, really. Maybe Dakota had been there after all, seen him coming and ducked into the kitchen to spike his order with gross fucking gunk. He took a couple more bites and put down the plastic fork. Not as hungry as he'd thought.

At least he didn't feel as pessimistic about the Jackson Williams case as he had. *Was* something going on between George and Ruth? George was working several angles involving Anita Selby, and he'd said Jenny Williams might have told Ken Dooley something that might be helpful to the case. Maybe something would pan out.

Anyway, what could you do? You were dealt your cards and you just made the best of them. That was the beauty of the legal system, everything was known, debated, laid out on the table.

Then they brought in a jury and it was anyone's guess what would happen.

Music. That was what he needed.

He got up, turned on the CD player, then sat down again, tilting back his chair, closing his eyes, waiting for Mozart to kick in.

The noise of a heavy metal guitar, loud and dissonant, filled his office, backed by harsh screams. *What?* His whole body jerked, painfully alert. Oh, no, wasn't that—Stuart leapt up and pressed Stop twice to open it up. Guns N' Roses. *Appetite for Destruction.* Ruth must have done it, stuck in one of her kids' old CDs, and he'd almost had to listen to Axl Rose screaming, "Welcome to the Jungle."

Even home was better than this. Stuart turned off the lights and left, not remembering to turn off the coffeepot.

George drove south down Highway Ninety-two till he came to the bridge over the wash that Frieda's neighbor had told him to watch for, then slowed, looking for a dirt road just afterward on the right. It was close to seven, the purple sky deepening to indigo as the sun slipped down behind the mountains. Earlier a pickup truck had passed him, gunning its engine noisily, but now there were no cars behind him and none in front.

Jeez, he thought, it was so empty out here, that Dooley guy could shoot a border patrolman and bury him without anyone even noticing. He was driving the clunker for its inconspicuousness, but he realized now the Caddy would have been better—if he went missing, someone might remember the big yellow car.

George spotted the dirt road, and because it was dark he saw the school bus, a quarter of a mile down, its windows all lit up. Must be on a generator—and Dooley must be home. George killed his lights, made the turn, and stopped to debate his next move.

Back when he'd been a cop, this part of police work in a rural county was always a little tricky—going to people's houses in the middle of nowhere at night and knocking on their door. Unless you were some sort of SWAT team on a drug bust in your bulletproof vest, your best bet was to pull up in a police car, lights flashing, so the people inside knew who they were dealing with. A guy in an old gray Oldsmobile didn't have quite that authority.

Maybe reconsider the whole thing. Then George remembered Ruth's face when he'd told her he was going out to Ken Dooley's place to talk to him. Bright and soft at the same time, and so full of confidence in him. Well, what the hell.

He turned on the headlights, started the Olds, and headed down the road. You didn't want to sneak up on anyone out here in the desert. Soon he heard music, loud. Even with his windows up George could hear it—a kind of chanting, some of that New Age stuff. Enya. Maybe Enya. Sandy had played that for a while.

A shabby blue Dodge van was parked to the right of the bus at the driver's end. George pulled in behind it. The music was so loud, the guy probably didn't even know anyone was out here. The air was thick with the tangy smell of creosote and manzanita.

George got out of his car and the first gunshot blasted a few yards away from him, cutting through the air like fast-flying insects. The second round raised a cloud of dust close to his foot. He ducked down beside the Olds, but that didn't necessarily mean anything because of ricochet, *watch out for ricochet.*

Abruptly the music stopped.

Somewhere a woman screamed.

George felt something pierce his left arm as another round ripped through a mesquite tree near him. It felt like nothing much, a rock, then his arm began to burn. A fucking pellet from the shotgun blast— that goddamn son of a bitch had shot him. *You asshole,* he thought, *you blew it.*

RUTH WIPED HER hands on a kitchen towel and turned off the burner under the rice. "What was it you wanted to tell me?" she asked Mara.

"It's about Ken Dooley."

Tyler came into the kitchen. "I'm starving. How come we're eating so late?"

"I had to go to Safeway," said Ruth. "It's good that you're starving. You haven't been eating so well lately." She looked at Mara. "What about Ken Dooley?"

"What's for dinner?" asked Tyler.

"He came in the Co-op when I was there," Mara said, "and he followed me out. When I tried to leave he threatened me."

"What?" said Ruth. "How dare he!"

"What's for dinner?" said Tyler again.

"But that's not important," Mara said. "Remember what Stuart said about him, that he was smart but he liked to upset people?"

"Yes," said Ruth.

"Mom!"

236

"A roast chicken from Safeway," said Ruth, "rice, and green beans. Now hush for a minute."

"I hate green beans." Tyler looked like he might cry. "And besides, they're burning."

Hurriedly Mara took the beans off the stove and drained them. She put them in a bowl and added more butter than Ruth would have used in a week.

"That's exactly what Mrs. Dixon said about Kevin," she said to Ruth.

Ruth frowned. "Kevin?"

"Kevin Dixon, Jenny's *brother*. They didn't get along. And Mrs. Dixon looked like she had money. So if Jenny died, Kevin would probably get all their mother's money, not just half. And he could have planted that poison at Jackson's, so Jackson would be arrested and no one would think to come looking for him."

"But I don't see—" Ruth began, but Mara cut her off.

"Mrs. Dixon said Kevin was highly intelligent but he upset people, just like Ken Dooley. And she said he'd traveled the world." Mara's voice rose excitedly. "I asked about Ken Dooley at the Co-op, and he's traveled the world, too. And he hasn't been in town that long, he just showed up one day. *And he never talks about his past.*"

"Stop!" shouted Tyler. "Ken Dooley! Kevin Dixon! Who cares?"

"Oh, my God." Mara almost dropped the bowl. "Ken Dooley and Kevin Dixon. They have the same initials."

"That does it," said Ruth. "I'm calling George right now."

"*Mom!*" said Tyler again. "*Mara!* Listen to me." He began to cry in earnest.

"Tyler?" said Mara.

"Sweetie pie," said Ruth, "what's wrong?"

"Nobody ever listens to me anymore," Tyler blubbered. "I *saw* somebody and I think they saw me. They could come and kill me after school and nobody around here would even notice 'cause they'd all be gone."

"No one's going to kill you," said Ruth fiercely, "not unless they kill me first. Calm down, OK? And tell us what you're talking about from the beginning."

Dimly, George was aware of chimes. What—? His cell phone was ringing in his car. He'd forgotten to turn it off. The phone chimed. The shotgun clicked. *Out of ammo*, thought George, *wasted it shooting wildly, an amateur.* He stepped out from behind his car before the guy had a chance to reload.

Ken Dooley, naked except for tattered jeans, stood in a circle of light by the door of the school bus, holding a short-barreled shotgun with a hump receiver. A Browning Auto-5 shotgun. George's dad had had one just like it. But his dad had never played Enya.

The profound calm of total focus descended on George, and in some visceral way he remembered that this kind of thing was what he had liked about police work, all your worries and anxieties gone away, it was just you and the situation at that moment.

"Hi, Ken," said George, making sure the Colt Commander was in plain sight. His left arm felt strangely numb. "Could we get a little civilized here? Drop the gun, please."

Ken let the shotgun go, and it fell to the ground. On his forehead little beads of sweat glistened in the light. "Hey, don't I know you?" he asked suddenly.

"We met at Sid Hamblin's."

"Stuart's investigator. That's just great." Ken's voice turned snide. "Now he's hired you to terrorize innocent citizens?"

"Jesus Christ, man," George's voice rose in exasperation. "It's not like I had a choice. What do you expect, I drive down the road, an ordinary citizen, and you come out shooting?"

"I thought you were the goddamn Border Patrol. What are you doing here?"

"I just got a couple of questions for you." Something trickled down George's arm, sweat, probably. He ignored it.

From inside the bus, someone moaned, high pitched.

"Whoever's in there," said George loudly, "you better come out, hands up where I can see them."

A woman half tumbled down the steps of the school bus, hands held high. She had curly black hair and was wearing only a man's long striped shirt.

George looked at her in astonishment. "Dakota," he said.

"George." Dakota put her hands down and drew herself up defiantly. "I thought your voice sounded familiar. God damn it, I could hire an attorney and sue the pants off you." She turned to Ken. "I know why he's here. He found out about us and now he's pissed." She looked back at George. "What did you *expect*?" Her voice shrilled accusingly. "You were never home. I have a right to see anyone I want to."

"Of course you do," said George. "*That's* not why I'm here. Look, could everyone calm down here? I just have a couple of questions for Ken."

"Then ask away," said Ken. "The sooner you're out of here, the better." George glanced at Dakota.

Ken shrugged. "She can hear whatever you have to say. I've got nothing to hide."

"About Jenny Williams," said George.

Ken put his hands on his hips, cocky. "What about her?"

"I heard she came to see you," said George, "right before she died. Something about a letter she wanted you to write. Like to share that with me?"

Ken looked at him blankly. "Man, you are totally off the map here. I saw her at Sid's a couple of times—but she never came to see me about any letters."

George remembered then one time when he and Sandy went on a double date with another cop and the cop's new girlfriend. The cop had bragged to the woman all night. *We professionals can always tell when someone's lying,* he'd said. *It's a little knack you learn on the job.*

George had no idea whether Ken was lying or not. His left arm tingled; the adrenaline calm had worn off and he was very very tired.

"Now I got it!" said Ken triumphantly. "Payback time. This is really about the letter that was in the paper today, isn't it?"

"What kind of shit was that anyway?" said George in disgust.

"There's no connection between what happened to the Magician and Jackson Williams. Williams was in jail and you know it."

"The guy's a jerk," said Ken. "For all I know he killed Sid, too. Thought I'd sling a little mud and see if it stuck—for Sid and Jenny's sake."

"What? They were saints? Jenny screwing Sid behind her husband's back?"

"She was just trying to survive the best way she knew how. To make up for Jackson and his little affair."

"What affair?"

Ken looked self-righteous. "He never mentioned that, huh? Him and the woman next door."

"That's bull!" The blood rushed to George's head and he felt his face getting hot. His arm throbbed. "Anita Selby told you that, didn't she?"

"No, I—"

But George rushed on. "Anita came to see Sid after Jenny died, didn't she?"

"If she did I never knew about it," said Ken.

"Think, man. Anita wasn't exactly the friend to Jenny she pretended to—"

Dakota gave a little scream, interrupting him. She pointed to the ground. "What's that?"

George looked where she pointed, at some dark blotches on the ground.

"Look at your arm," said Dakota accusingly. "You're bleeding! *Gross.*"

The sleeve of his corduroy jacket was dark with blood. Seeing the blood made George feel light-headed. He felt himself sway a little. "Anita," he said doggedly. "What do you know about her?"

"Hey, man, I don't know *beans* about Anita," said Ken. "You better go to the emergency room, have someone look at that arm."

George thought maybe he was right, it was time to go. "You should have aimed," he said, needing the last word with Ken. "Then you wouldn't have hit me."

JACKSON SAT IN the pod with the notebook Stuart had sent over. It was a fine notebook, one of those old-fashioned-looking ones with black-and-white marbled covers. He opened it, smoothing the page down.

"Hey, Paco, heard your mother was selling it down across the line by the border."

"Yeah, man, five bucks a pop is what I heard."

The fluorescent lights shone on the white page with its faint blue lines. Jackson picked up the number-two automatic pencil.

"The egg of the sea turtle has been known to take a hundred years to hatch," said the television, which no one was watching.

"That's gin!"

"He palmed a card, I swear. I saw him."

Jackson began to write. He saw his arm, the orange sleeve of his prisoner's jumpsuit, moving across the page as the words flowed out, faster than he could write, image after image. He was swept along, not even sure where he was going, but he knew it was somewhere rich and strange.

"Look at that guy, writin' like a mothafucka."

"Hey, Jackson! You writin' a book? Are we in it?"

Jackson looked up, smiling. The faces of the other inmates, all of them benign, all falsely accused, seemed to glow with an inner light.

"Everything's in it," he said. "Everything in the whole world."

"Man!"

Jackson turned the page and the words kept coming. Here he was, a middle-aged man who'd basically given up, writing like a mothafucka. It was amazing, unbelievable. And he could do it anywhere, even in prison. *Better* in prison—no distractions. *Nuns fret not at their convent's narrow room. How did I get so lucky, so incredibly lucky?*

"Just give it to me straight, Doc," said George in the emergency room of the Sierra Vista Hospital. "Am I going to live?"

"I think so, now that I've given you the tetanus shot." The nice lady doctor smiled—God, how old was she, couldn't be more than twenty-something—then turned serious. "That barbed wire can be nasty stuff." She glanced at him. "Odd kind of wound for barbed wire."

George's eyes veered away to the white tiled wall. "Yeah." No way he was going to tell her it was a gunshot wound—she'd have to call the cops and they'd have to go through all that rigamarole.

"It's just a flesh wound, but you need to take all of those antibiotics, every single one. Change the dressing once a day, and don't get it wet. Showers but no baths."

"Sure thing," said George. He moved toward the door.

"Wait," said the doctor. "Let me give you some samples of Vicodin for pain, save you getting that prescription filled."

George took care of business at the front desk. His arm ached dully, so he stopped at a drinking fountain and took two of the Vicodin, then went out through the double glass doors to the parking lot. Since he hadn't eaten dinner, he'd planned to stop at a fast-food place, but it didn't seem worth the effort. He just drove on home.

Carrying the files he'd copied at Stuart's office and his tan corduroy jacket, he unlocked the door to his apartment and flicked on the light. The purple couch in the living room struck him as uglier than usual. He took the cell phone out of the jacket pocket, put it and the files on the oak veneer coffee table, and inspected the jacket. The bloodstained left arm had a jagged tear where the buckshot had grazed it.

Ruined. Not even good enough to donate to the Salvation Army. And he'd had it for what? Fifteen years at least. Sandy had given it to him for Christmas. A little memory rose in his mind; Sandy in red flannel pajamas, smiling, *Go ahead, open it.* Blocking the memory, he said to the jacket, "Well, at least you went out fighting." This struck him as exceptionally funny.

He began to laugh. Still laughing, he went to the kitchen and threw the jacket in the trash, which was probably illegal—that blood would make it a biohazard. That was pretty funny, too. He laughed so hard his knees felt like they might buckle under him. Oops. Pills were kicking in. He ought to eat something.

He opened the refrigerator door. There was nothing inside but a jar of salsa and a bottle of ketchup. Carefully, he went back to the living room, sat on the couch, and took a few deep breaths to reorient himself. "You're *fine*," he told himself out loud. To prove it, he got up again, found a pen, sat back down perfectly, and reached for the new disclosure on Jackson Williams he'd brought home with him.

He opened the file and began to read an e-mail, but the phone rang, the cordless one, not his cell. He looked at his watch; how did it get to be after eleven? He reached up for the phone on the shelf behind the couch.

"George Maynard here."

"Oh, good. It's Ruth." Her voice lilted up. "I know it's late, but I was worried. I've been calling your cell all evening."

"Yeah? Probably run down. I only heard it once." George leaned back on the couch to rest. "Too busy dodging buckshot to answer it."

"Dodging buckshot?" Ruth's voice was aghast.

"Ken Dooley thought I was a border patrolman and got me in the arm with a shotgun. Just got back from the emergency room, had it taped up. Just a scratch. Nothing to worry about."

"But—but—" Ruth sputtered, "Ken Dooley—is he in jail?"

"Un-uh. Make-my-day law. You go on someone's private property in Arizona, they got a right to shoot you." George rallied briefly. "Not that he isn't an asshole. Only thing that really pissed me off is I got nowhere with him."

"Maybe you didn't ask him the right questions."

George paused. He was tired, really tired. "What does that mean?"

"Tyler saw someone going to Jenny's at night. He doesn't know who it was, but it wasn't Randy Gates."

"Probably Sid," George said.

"No," said Ruth. "Tyler's met Sid. It wasn't him, either, but I think I know who it was. Mara and I—well, there's something we need to tell you. Did you know Jenny had a brother? Kevin Dixon?"

Anita had said something about a brother. What was it? His thinking was off. He couldn't seem to focus. Then he remembered. "Yeah. He died."

"No he didn't. It was one of Jenny's little lies. And now I'm scared for Tyler to be in the house alone. I think you should go see Jenny's mother right away. Here, let me give you her address. It's in Green Valley."

George scrawled the address on the front of the file, letters veering upward. "What am I seeing her about?"

"Ask her for a photograph of Kevin."

"Why?"

"Because—Mara found out a few things—it doesn't matter right now, I'll tell you later, but we think Ken Dooley might be Kevin Dixon."

"No kidding. Interesting," said George. It *was* interesting, but it didn't make sense. Maybe it would make sense tomorrow. He wanted to get off the phone while *he* still made sense. "I'll get on it first thing in the morning," he said. "Got to go now, okay?"

"George?"

George hung up. He closed his eyes and took some more deep breaths till he felt a little clearer. He pulled the disclosure file to him, opened it and started to read the e-mail again.

Hey there, Casey. I was thinking—here we are, two professors and all we do is bitch about our wives. Jenny's mad at me and I know she wants me to ask her why, but actually I don't care. We haven't spoken for two days and you know what? I'm enjoying it, in a sadistic kind of way. I used to be a nice guy but you know what they say. Hell is other people.

George stopped reading, stopped thinking. He pinched the bridge of his nose between two fingers. Then he read on.

Maybe I'm just a coward but sometimes I even think about her being dead and all I feel is relief.

George registered in a vague sort of way that this probably wasn't so good for the case, but that wasn't what bothered him. He went back to the line *Hell is other people.* Ruth had said those same words to him in her kitchen. *So Jackson said it to her and she said it to you,* he thought.

So fucking what.

He threw the file across the room, where it hit the TV. The e-mail fluttered out, like a big white butterfly. Ken Dooley had told him tonight that Ruth had been having an affair with Jackson—that made two people. Two people and he hadn't checked it out at all.

"So fucking what!" he said out loud.

twenty

THE NEXT DAY Ruth got to work earlier than usual. She'd seen Tyler
off with an extra hug since he'd be staying at Buzzie's, and Mara was
still sleeping in, so she'd figured she might as well go to work. She'd let
things slip a little, talking to George so much; she needed to catch up.
She hadn't been able to get to sleep the night before after that phone
call, worrying about George and worrying about Tyler—those stom-
achaches, she should have known something was wrong.

She didn't know why a murderer would show his hand by harming
any of them, when Jackson sat there in jail, but she couldn't take any
chances.

Finally she'd gotten up and straightened the three big drawers in the
kitchen. Tyler never put anything back where it belonged, and Mara
didn't know where things belonged, so it had gotten to the point where
she couldn't find anything.

Stuart must have come back to his office last night, because the coffeepot was on and she'd cleaned it before she left yesterday. A thick coffee syrup lined the bottom. She washed it out and made a fresh pot, then sat at her desk.

George had sounded funny last night—well, he'd been *shot*, but he'd said it was nothing, just a scratch. That wasn't what bothered her; what bothered her was that *he'd hung up on her.* She'd been about to remind him he was invited to dinner and he'd hung up on her. She was planning to have a pork roast with prunes and garlic, complicated, something she hadn't made in years. What if after all that he didn't come?

To stop herself from worrying, Ruth looked down at the court calendar to see if Stuart had any cases coming up she'd overlooked, but all she saw was a jumble of meaningless words. George had said he would go see Mrs. Dixon today. What if he did and because he'd been shot and wasn't alert he got into an accident on the freeway and was killed? What if Ken Dooley followed George to Tucson and shot him dead? Had she said the wrong thing last night and he'd suddenly realized she wasn't who he had thought she was and that was why he'd hung up on her?

The bell tinkled.

She looked up.

Ken Dooley stood in the doorway, eyes blanked out by imitation Ray-Ban sunglasses. He seemed to preen in a brightly striped shirt, the cloth made by Guatemalan peasants, a leather bag slung over his shoulder. "Open early," he said with a ragged, predatory smile.

NINE O'CLOCK IN the morning and the golf course was bright green, thousands of gallons of water wasted every year so people could go out and hit a ball with a stick. And they didn't even bother to walk, they rode around in little carts. Where was the sport in that? George turned down the street to Grace Dixon's house feeling not exactly chipper but at least clearheaded.

He'd virtually passed out on his couch the night before and slept heavily. That morning the first thing he did was to flush the rest of the

Vicodin down the toilet. Too powerful, too much like—*booze*. Look how it had screwed up his thinking.

If he'd known Jenny's brother was alive, he'd have checked him out no matter what, at least cursorily. He didn't know why Ruth thought Ken Dooley might be Kevin Dixon, but he liked the idea a lot, especially now that he saw where Grace Dixon lived. Definitely some money there, best motive there was. Under the dressing the doctor had put on, his arm ached, but not too bad. He focused on the street, checking the numbers on the pink stucco town houses till he found the one he was looking for.

He parked and got out. He wore jeans and a blue polo shirt, the only polo he owned. Sandy had given it to him to upgrade his image, but he'd only worn it once. It was hot—must be damn near a hundred degrees. At least he didn't need the ruined corduroy jacket. He took a deep breath. *Time to get lucky,* he thought.

Beyond the wrought-iron gate at Mrs. Dixon's, a big spiky yucca grew in the center of the gravel yard. He went up to a red door and knocked. He was about to knock again when the door opened. A skinny old man in pink walking shorts, a pink-and-blue-striped polo, and spotless white running shoes looked at him inquisitively.

No one had mentioned a husband. "Mr. Dixon?" asked George.

"Mr. Dixon died some time ago," said the man.

"I'm sorry," said George. "Actually I'm looking for Mrs. Dixon, Mrs. Grace Dixon."

"Grace is in the hospital, under observation," said the man. "Her heart's not too good, and she was having some chest pains yesterday." He peered out at George. "Who might you be?"

"George Maynard. I'm an investigator looking into the death of Mrs. Dixon's daughter." He produced his card. "I was hoping Mrs. Dixon could answer a few questions."

"My, my, my." The man took the card and put it in his polo pocket without looking at it. "It'd be good to put a few more nails in that Jackson Williams's coffin, hey?" His hand shot out. "I'm Henry Bradshaw.

Old friend of the Dixon family, known 'em forty years, no—I guess it must be forty-two years now."

George gripped his hand. The flesh felt like parchment paper. *Nails in Jackson Williams's coffin*—guy wasn't biased or anything.

"Me and my wife moved into this community same time Grace and Stanley did," Henry Bradshaw went on. "After my wife died and then Stanley, Grace and I have kind of kept each other company ever since. I come see Grace nearly every day, and since I have keys I'd thought I'd better look in, make sure everything was okay here. You come on in. Maybe I can answer some of your questions."

George followed him down a hall that looked like some kind of fancy bedroom into a living room that looked the same. All orangey pink and white; it didn't look like a normal person could sit anywhere without leaving a smudge. Henry sat down on a white couch, and George sat on the edge of the cushion on a white armchair.

"Hurt your arm, did you?" asked Henry.

George nodded. "I got shot."

"You don't say." Henry looked at him with admiration. "All you policemen, you deserve a medal, every one of you. I'm a big supporter of law enforcement. Watch *Law and Order*, faithfully. They have so many reruns on that show, you can watch it every night. What did you want to know?"

"Jenny's brother, Kevin?" George said. "Maybe they kept in touch, family members and all. She might have said something to him that could add a few more nails to that coffin you were talking about. How can I reach him?"

"Oh, my." Henry rubbed his jaw. "That's a hard one. Grace told me she spoke with him not too long ago, but there's times he won't call for months." He looked at George apologetically. "I don't think she has an exact address for him."

"Where is he?"

"Alaska. He's somewhere in Alaska."

"Alaska," said George blankly.

Henry laughed. "Makes sense if you know him. He's a real oddball, that Kevin, never could stay put, hold down a job. Every time he made a little money he was off to some godforsaken place, South America, India, Mexico, you name it."

"Alaska," said George again. "But he calls. Maybe you could find a number where he could be reached."

"I don't think Grace ever calls *him*. He calls her." He scratched his head. "Tell you the truth, I doubt if Kevin talked to his sister, 'cause they'd been estranged for quite some time."

"Oh?"

"Had the most on-again off-again relationship you've ever seen. Even when they were growing up, crazy about each other one week, hated each other the next. But I'll tell you one thing, Kevin loved his little sister to—well, he loved her. Even if she didn't always love him back, especially when he got . . . older."

"Look," said George, leaning toward Henry to make his point. "You never know. We'd really like to find him as soon as possible. It could make the difference. Maybe Grace has photographs lying around. We could"— George paused, then improvised—"post them on the Internet."

It sounded pretty lame, but Henry didn't miss a beat. "Photographs." He brightened. "Sure she's got photographs. Her bedroom's full of 'em."

"Maybe I could borrow a couple of the most recent."

"Grace wouldn't mind, I guess, if it will help pound in those nails!" He smiled, stood up and started out of the room, then turned. "As long as she gets 'em back."

"Of course."

George looked around as he waited for Henry. More pillows on the couch than anyone could ever use, and so clean. Maybe that was why Henry dressed the way he did, so he'd fit into this room. If George ever retired, he decided, he'd live in a log cabin, have brown leather furniture you could wipe down and it wouldn't show dirt anyway.

Henry came back holding a manila envelope. "Here you go, there's two pictures. I put 'em in here," he said, handing the envelope to George, "to keep 'em clean. They're not real current—maybe six or seven years old," he added apologetically.

George took the envelope, undid the clasp, and slid out the photographs. One was of a man with a neatly trimmed beard near a mountain, holding a pair of skis; the other a clean-shaven man on a couch in a living room. Not this couch or this living room and not Ken Dooley. George had never seen this man in his life.

MARA WOKE UP late to an empty house. Tyler was long gone off to school, and Ruth's car wasn't in the driveway, so she must be at work. They hadn't been able to reach George when Mara went to bed. She wondered if Ruth had gotten in touch with him later.

She showered and dressed and went into the kitchen. She didn't feel like cereal, so she ate what was left of the chicken from last night, tearing off pieces as she stood in front of the open refrigerator. She had had plans for last night, but Tyler had been so upset that they had all ended up playing Scrabble to comfort him.

Mara took the whole chicken out of the refrigerator, tore off the remaining wing, and threw the wrappings and the carcass into the trash. She nibbled at the wing, staring out the window at the bird feeder in the backyard.

A hummingbird flitted at the feeder. She tapped on the pane. "Tiny bird!" she called. It darted, flitted away, gone in an instant. Mara stared down at the wing she was eating. Yuck. She threw it in the trash with the rest of the carcass. At that moment she had a flash of insight, a little satori.

When this is all over, she thought, *I'm going to finish college and go to law school.*

Right now, however, she was going to do what she'd planned to do last night. She went into Tyler's room, turned on his computer, went online to Google, and typed in "Ken Dooley." Only eight hundred and twenty-one entries.

WHAT THE HELL *is going on?* George thought, driving back on I-10. Ruth sending him all the way to Green Valley for this—he glanced at the envelope containing the photos of a stranger on the passenger seat—this *nothing*. And he'd had other things to do—like check up on Frieda and the Magician. Maybe Ruth wasn't as straight-on wonderful as he'd thought. Aw. Maybe she was, but he needed to slow down with her, watch himself. Two people had told him she'd been having an affair with Jackson Williams. And Ruth herself had said, hadn't she, there in her kitchen, that Jenny was a blight on Jackson's life.

"YOU SHOT MY investigator," said Stuart, steely voiced.

"It was out-and-out intimidation!" Ken Dooley shouted. "I had a right to. He was on my property. There are statutes protecting a man on his own property in this state, and you know it!"

"Let's take a look at some of those statutes," Stuart sneered. "How about that?"

"Fine with me. You go right ahead."

There was a silence, maybe Stuart looking things up.

Ruth closed her eyes. It was late morning, close to twelve, and she'd sent Ken Dooley away once, he'd come back, and now he'd been in Stuart's office for the last twenty minutes arguing the same thing over and over. She hoped he wasn't carrying a gun in that leather bag. If he was, what if he got so mad he ended up pulling it out and shooting Stuart? Then he would come out and shoot her.

The bell tinkled. Ruth opened her eyes.

George walked in carrying a manila envelope. Ruth was so relieved, the blood rushed to her cheeks, turning them a healthy pink. She saw George's blue polo shirt first, because she'd never seen him wear anything like that, then the dressing on his arm before she looked at his face.

"George—?" she began tentatively, then stopped. His eyes were opaque, as blank as Ken Dooley's sunglasses. He *was* mad at her.

"I went to Grace Dixon's house," he said, looming over her desk.

"Oh!" she said. "And—"

He tossed the envelope onto her desk. "Have a look," he said.

She undid the clasp. Inside were two photographs. She slid them out and looked at a man with skis, a man on a couch. She looked up at George. She couldn't help noticing his polo shirt again, how good he looked in that particular shade of blue. "Why are you showing me these? Who is he?"

"Kevin Dixon," said George.

"Oh, *shoot.*" Her face fell. "Then he's not Ken Dooley after all."

"Kevin lives in *Alaska.* You sent me on a complete wild goose chase."

"What if I'd been right? I was only trying to—to help. And just because he's not Kevin Dixon doesn't mean he—" Her voice wavered. "Why are you so mad at me? You were mad at me last night, too."

"What do you mean, I was mad at you last night?"

He stared down at her with his blank eyes. She saw now how he could have been a cop, how he might look when questioning a suspect.

"You hung up on me," she said.

He blinked. Then the blankness went out of his eyes. "I did?"

"Yes."

"Look, Ruth—I wasn't in my right mind. I took some damn Vicodin for the pain, and my thought processes were just all fouled up."

There was a little silence. Ruth bit her lip.

"Aw, Ruth. I'm sorry." He ducked his head as if he were ashamed. "I'm just an asshole."

"You are *not,*" said Ruth firmly. "You're not an asshole at all. And look at your poor arm. Does it hurt? Are you all right? You know you need to change that dressing at least once a day."

"I'm fine."

"This Ken Dooley stuff, Mara and I really, really thought—we didn't mean—" She lowered her voice and glanced at the closed door to Stuart's office. "*He's in there now.*"

"Who?"

"Ken Dooley."

George looked disgusted. "Then I'm outta here." He turned away.

"George?"

"What?"

"Are you still coming to dinner tonight?"

"I'll be there."

GEORGE DROVE TO Wood Canyon, where the big cottonwoods were shedding their yellow leaves, thinking about Ruth as he walked down the pitted asphalt street that dissolved into dirt on the edges. There was no sign of the vicious orange cat. He'd thought angrily about Ruth all the way back from Green Valley, but seeing her there at her desk he couldn't stay angry; she didn't bear any resemblance to the Ruth he was mad at.

He trudged up the steps to Frieda's house, past the pyracantha hedge that blocked his view of the house across from her's. He opened the wooden gate and walked into the brick yard. A tin watering can stood by the big pot of red geraniums, and the green front door was wide open. He walked over and tapped on the wood frame.

"Anybody home?"

"Who is it?" a woman called.

"Uh," said George, "George Maynard, looking for Frieda."

"Oh." A woman in her fifties came to the door. A loose embroidered dress hung from her bony shoulders; her graying hair was pulled back tight, displaying long silver earrings dangling from her rather large ears. She looked at him suspiciously. "You're not the man who was here before taking pictures of my house, are you?"

"No, no," said George. "I'm an investigator. I thought you might be able—"

She interrupted. "I know. You were asking about the Magician. My neighbor told me." Her face turned welcoming. "You came at just the *best* time. Please come in. There's something I'd like to show you."

George stepped into a living room where Japanese paper shades filtered the sun. An empty cardboard box sat on an antique oak coffee table, and letters, bills, and catalogs were strewn over a futon couch covered in bright green and yellow batik.

"Excuse the mess," said Frieda gaily. "I've been on a retreat, and on my way back I picked up my mail. I don't pick it up for days sometimes and the post office saves it all for me in a box, which is really nice of them."

"Ah," said George.

She pirouetted in a half turn, limber for a woman her age, the embroidered dress fluttering around her legs. "Come on into the kitchen. I just made a pot of tea."

The kitchen was large, half the house, as if walls had been torn down to make way for it. There was an ancient gas stove and a white porcelain sink, and jars and bottles lined what was left of the walls. But the first thing George noticed was the flowers; the place was full of dead flowers, twisted into wreaths on the walls, hanging from rafters, sticking up from mason jars on the counters. Even the old-fashioned linoleum on the floor had big cabbage roses on it.

George sneezed. His arm hadn't been bothering him, but now it started up again. He sneezed a second time.

"Oh, dear." Frieda looked concerned. "It sounds like you've got some allergies."

George looked at all the flowers and sneezed again. "Good way to find out, I guess."

"Actually," Frieda said, "allergies are one of my specialties. I have something that might be good for that. And it looks like you hurt your arm. I have a really good salve—"

"I'm *fine*, thanks," George interrupted. He took out a handkerchief and blew his nose.

"Sit down, won't you." Frieda poured tea, put a big blue mug of it in front of George, and smiled at him. "You must know Sergeant Jack Nelson," she said.

"Who?"

"Aren't you with the Dudley police?"

"No. I'm a private investigator for Stuart Ross's office." He raised the mug to his lips. It smelled like flowers.

"Oh, *him*." Frieda made a little face. "I like his secretary, though. She's really nice. She came to my booth with her son when we had a festival in the Grassy Park this summer. Ruth. You must know Ruth."

"Great woman," said George heartily. "Great." He paused. "You were going to show me something."

"Yes. It's kind of embarrassing, but it's fabulous." She pulled open a kitchen drawer. "Really fabulous. Here." She handed him an envelope, a letter half sticking out. "It was with my mail, so I put it away for safekeeping."

"Embarrassing?" said George.

"Sergeant Nelson fingerprinted me and everything, and the letter was at the post office all along." Her eyes got soft. "Maybe it was worth it, though."

What was she talking about?

"Go ahead," she said. "Read it."

George took the letter out of the envelope and began to read.

Dear Freeda, me and a friend of yers are here at the halfway house and he asked me to write this for him. Yer friend had to leave fast becaws the soshul servish were comin to make him take his meds. He ran away and a pikup gave him a ride to Tuson. He's had a ruff time, but now he's got different meds better than there but he don't feel good enuf to write hisself but he feels a hole lot better. He still remembers the yo-yo you gave him that he left behin and the peecock feather. He still has the peecock feather and he's waving it right now to say hello and to thank you for all that you dun for him. I guess you know by now who I mean. It's yer old friend the Magishun.

That was it. George looked up. "Son of a bitch," he said. "Excuse me." He sneezed.

"I'm so *happy*," said Frieda. "I was about to go downtown to tell Jack when you showed up."

George blew his nose. He looked at the envelope. It was postmarked from Tucson a few days ago, with no return address. "But how do you know it's really from him?" he said.

"I can *sense* it. And besides, there's the peacock feather, he's the only one that would know that."

"Anita Selby," said George. "That name ring a bell? Thin woman, forties, short white hair. You might have met her at Sid's."

"No," said Frieda.

George stood up. His eyes were burning, and he was out of reasons to be there. "Guess I'll go, then," he said. "Leave you to your own devices."

"Look," said Frieda, "let me give you something for that allergy." She turned, scanning the wall with the jars and bottles. "Let's see."

George watched, wanting to go. He sneezed again and felt the ache in his arm. Then the jars and bottles came into focus, rows and rows of them with neat labels in tiny script, unreadable, except, near one end, several labeled clearly with a skull and crossbones. He went closer for a better look. "What are these?"

"They're poison," said Frieda. "I always label them that way as a precaution."

Curious, George took down a bottle. "Why even have them?"

"Some of them are only poison if the dosage is too high, and others are for teaching, like when I have my booth."

"What's the worst you got?" asked George. "Poison-wise."

"The worst, well, the very worst was the monkshood, but I don't have it anymore."

"Monkshood? What's that exactly?"

"A plant. It grows all over the U.S. Its scientific name is *Aconitum napellus*."

Aconitum napellus. George felt like he'd been hit with a brick. *Aconite. Aconite was what had killed Jenny, and Sid as well.* "You said you don't have it anymore? Why not?"

"Oh, one day I was going through my supplies and I noticed it was gone. It was so *annoying*."

"When?" asked George, his voice tense. He came closer to Frieda. "*When* did you notice it was gone?"

She stepped back. "I don't *know*."

"*Think*," he thundered.

Frieda flinched. "For heaven's sake, why are you being so *rude*?" She snatched the letter off the table. "Jack needs to see this. I have to go downtown right away."

George followed her out through the living room. She stood at the door, waiting for him to leave. "I need you to go now. I'm very busy."

"You said it was poison. Don't you feel any responsibility?" He raised his voice again, knowing it was the wrong thing to do, losing it a little. "Who had access to it?"

Frieda's face was pale. "Please won't you leave," she said plaintively.

He walked to the door, stepped out, and looked back in. "Tell me one thing," he said. "Just one. This summer, at your booth, when Ruth stopped by there with her son, *was it gone then*?"

"I don't think so." Her voice was defensive. "I can't say for sure. It's not like I keep track every single day. One day I looked and it wasn't there, that's all."

George turned and walked across the bricks to the wooden gate and down the stairs. Ruth had been at Frieda's booth. His arm ached like a son of a bitch. Halfway down he clutched the iron railing, seized with vertigo. Ruth, wonderful Ruth. She didn't like Jenny, a blight on Jackson's life. Ruth, always worrying, always trying to help, always trying to fix things. And Sid Hamblin, she didn't like him, either. He was at the memorial service at her house. He could have had the probiotics with him there.

But Anita—Anita had to have been at the memorial. Why not Anita? No. She hadn't had access to Frieda's aconite like Ruth had.

They'd found the bottle with the aconite under the bed. Why would Ruth leave it there to incriminate Jackson, her friend? Because all that rigmarole she'd given him about different kinds of love was bull and she *had been having an affair* and *it had turned sour*? Maybe she got rejected big time and wanted to get even. That nice woman—in her kitchen, they'd shared secrets. Were all her confidences just a ploy to get him to overlook anything incriminating against her he might turn up?

No. It couldn't be—it was just a paranoid fantasy. How did he *know*? Hell is other people.

twenty-one

MARA DROVE FAST over the Mule Mountain Pass in Jackson's Volvo. She went through the tunnel, down Tombstone Canyon, past the courthouse, and onto Main Street. Tourists were everywhere, moseying along the sidewalks and crossing right in the middle of the street, and their cars filled all the parking spaces. Mara circled and finally found a space two blocks from Stuart's office.

She grabbed a clutch of papers from the passenger seat and walked down Main Street past the galleries and the Cornucopia to Stuart's office. Through the window she could see Ruth at her desk and Stuart, standing, waving his arms. She giggled.

Stuart was talking when she walked in.

"Guys?" Mara said.

Ruth looked over at her. "My goodness," she said. "What's with you?"

"He was never any kind of activist," said Mara, all in a rush. "I went online and I found him. *I found Ken Dooley.*"

"You want a medal?" Stuart said. "We find him all the time."

"Hush," Ruth said to him.

"*Online,*" said Mara. "I printed it all out, the picture from the newspaper article and everything. I made two copies. *Here.*" She put half the papers on Ruth's desk, gave the other half to Stuart, and glanced at Ruth apologetically. "I don't see how he could be who we thought he was, but this is almost as good."

"A *certified public accountant,*" Stuart said after a moment, "for a firm in Pittsburgh."

"That's Ken in the picture, all right," said Ruth in wonder. "In a *suit.* Receiving a certificate for thirty-five years of service."

"A certified public accountant," Stuart said again, with glee. "His reputation will be *ruined.*"

"That doesn't mean he isn't dangerous," said Ruth darkly. "Maybe he's wanted for fraud somewhere and Jenny found out . . ." Her voice trailed off and she looked at Mara. "I already knew he wasn't Jenny's brother. I sent George all the way to Green Valley to check it out."

"What are you talking about?" said Stuart.

"Mara and I had this idea Ken might be Jenny's brother—"

"Jenny's brother?" Stuart cut in. "I didn't even know she had a brother."

"It's too hard to explain," said Ruth. She sounded tired. "I told George, and he went to Grace Dixon's and got pictures of her son, Jenny's brother. They're right here." She held up a manila envelope.

"George went all the way to Tucson 'cause you guys were playing amateur detective?" Stuart looked annoyed. "And for what? Damn it. Can't you leave him out of this? You're wasting his precious time."

Ruth waved the envelope at him. "Don't you want to see?"

"Why would I want to see? It's not even *relevant.*" Stuart grabbed the envelope from her hand and tossed it into the wastebasket.

GEORGE DROVE OUT to Tombstone Canyon and from there to the highway that bypassed town. From the highway he could see all the little wooden houses, the yellow trees. There was the courthouse, there was the Catholic church. He tried to think, but every time he had a thought, another thought would rise up to cancel it out. His arm throbbed. He shouldn't have thrown out that Vicodin.

At the other end of town, he got off the highway and drove back in, turned and went down the Gulch, past the bars and the local galleries, went clear to the end, turned around, and came back.

He drove up Main Street till he found a place to park. Then he sat in his car, trying to get hold of a thought. Maybe he was overreacting. There were other explanations for everything, for anything. It just fit so well into what George knew in his heart was his basically totally fucked-up goddamn pessimistic view of the world that he had from being a cop. There were two kinds of cops, your bullies and your world-savers, and God help you if you were the latter.

Okay. I am a professional. What would a professional do?

He had no idea. Just play it by fucking ear. What was the urgency, anyway? No one was going anywhere. He got out of his car and walked to the office.

Mara was sitting with her feet up on Ruth's desk when he came in. Ruth was probably at her desk, well, of course she had to be, but George didn't look. The door to Stuart's office was closed.

When she saw George, Mara took her feet down. "Guess what!" she said in an excited voice. "Ken Dooley was a certified public accountant for thirty-five years! In Pittsburgh!"

"Don't you think that's *amazing*?" Ruth chimed in eagerly. "Mara went online and found this picture of him in a suit, getting a certificate."

Ruth wasn't speaking especially loudly, but her voice hurt his ears.

"No kidding," he said without affect. "Stuart around?"

"He's in his office, *sulking*," Mara said. "Because you went—"

"Mara," said Ruth warningly. "What's going on, anyway?" she asked George.

"I need to see Stuart," George said, not meeting her eyes. "I don't want to talk right now."

"Ooh!" Mara said. "Maybe you can tell us at dinner tonight? Ruth is making pork roast with prunes!"

"Dinner." George banged the side of his head in a way that must have looked completely phony. He looked right at Ruth, but he didn't see her. "Can't make it," he said. "Something came up."

"That's all right," said Ruth quickly, as if she'd already known what he was going to say.

Suddenly the air was so charged with tension it felt as though it might ignite. *Tension, ha*, thought George, *just plain old bellyaching pain.*

"Excuse me." He edged past Mara to Stuart's office.

"I feel terrible," Ruth said to Mara. "Like I'm getting a migraine."

"You get migraines?" Mara said in surprise.

George knocked on the door.

"Who is it!" Stuart yelled.

"George."

"Come in!"

Ruth rose. "I think I'll take the rest of the day off."

RUTH LEFT THE office so suddenly, for a second Mara didn't even realize she was gone. She jumped up and went after her, trailing her down Main Street. Ruth was walking really fast, going out on the street to get by the tourists. Mara had to practically run to catch up to her.

"Ruth," she panted. "Slow down. Why are you going so fast?"

Ruth slowed. "Was I?" she said blankly.

"Yes. Is that good for a headache?"

"What do you mean, a headache?"

"You said . . ." Mara felt confused, then a little anxious. "Never mind."

"What are you doing here, anyway?" asked Ruth.

"You said you didn't feel well and I was worried. I wanted to walk you to your car."

"And here we are." Ruth stopped by the Honda Civic and rummaged in her purse for her keys. "I'm fine, actually."

"Are you sure?" Mara asked dubiously.

"Yes. I just needed to get out of that stuffy office." Ruth took her wallet out of her purse. "Damn. Where are my keys?"

"And George. He was acting really weird. What's wrong with *him*?"

Head bent, Ruth didn't respond as she rummaged some more in her purse.

"He wasn't even interested in *Ken Dooley*," Mara persisted.

"It's hopeless," Ruth said in frustration. "They're *nowhere*." She up-ended her purse and dumped the entire contents: grocery lists, pens, pencils, lipstick, pouch with coupons, pouch with makeup, sunglasses case, Kleenex, calculator, notepad, address book, *keys*, onto the ground and dropped her purse on top. Then she began to cry.

Mara felt giddy with déjà vu. Her mother had done things like that all the time when she was sick, all the time. Mara bent down, doing what she would have done had Ruth been her mother; she picked every-thing up and put it back in the purse, except for the keys and a Kleenex. She handed the Kleenex to Ruth.

Then she unlocked the doors, took Ruth by the arm, steered her to the passenger side, and opened the door.

"Get in," Mara said. "I'm driving you home. I can come back with you in the morning for my car."

Mara got in the driver's side and started the car. She touched her St. Christopher medal. You counted on grown-ups all your life and then they totally failed you. They turned out to be no different than kids, just bigger. One good thing, whatever was going on, at least Ruth wasn't go-ing to die of it.

"CLOSE THE DOOR," said Stuart as George sat in the client chair.

George stood up and walked back to the door. The outer office was empty, and Stuart's office was hot, stuffy. "You sure?"

"Yes, I'm sure." Stuart lowered his voice. "Don't want them to over-hear what I'm going to tell you."

"But there's no one out there."

"What do you mean, there's no one out there?"

"They both left. Ruth said she was taking the rest of the day off."

"Why?"

"She said—" George lost his train of thought. His arm still throbbed, and he felt too weary to talk. He sat down again. "A migraine or something."

"I got a little annoyed at her earlier," Stuart said. "It's probably my fault."

"I don't think so," said George.

"You don't look so good yourself." Stuart looked at George's arm. "That where Ken Dooley shot you?"

"Yep."

Stuart's mouth twitched. "They tell you?"

"What?"

"Ken Dooley was a *certified public accountant* for thirty-five years in Pittsburgh."

"Yeah," said George. He paused. "Yeah, they did." Both of them all excited, *happy* about it when he'd walked in. Well, he'd taken care of that.

"So I guess—" said Stuart. He began to laugh. "I guess—" He laughed some more, clutching his stomach.

George tried to laugh along, too. Ha. Ha. Ha.

"So I guess"—Stuart tried again—"all you got under that bandage is a—a—*paper cut.*"

"Ha." George arranged his facial muscles into a smile. "That's a good one."

Stuart looked at him with concern. "You're sure you're all right?"

"So," said George, not bothering to answer. "You know the poison that killed Jenny Williams?"

"Sure. Aconite."

"I found the probable source."

"You're kidding. Hot *damn.*" Stuart looked at George. "You don't look exactly joyous about it. Don't tell me." He frowned. "Bad for our case?"

A professional would tell right then and there. A professional would lay it out all neatly on the table. "It depends," George said.

"So what's the source?"

"Her name's Frieda. She—"

"Frieda?" Stuart interrupted. *"Frieda? Son of a bitch!"*

"And," George went on heavily, "that Magician guy everyone was so worried about? She got a letter from him. He's in some halfway house in Tucson."

"I wouldn't bet on that," said Stuart. "Listen—"

"Let me finish," George interrupted. "Frieda sets up a booth in the Grassy Park when they have these festivals." He sighed. "They had one this summer, and"—he paused significantly—"Ruth was there."

"Ruth," said Stuart guiltily. "I guess I was a little hard on her. But, God, I was pissed. Sending you off on these bullshit errands, wasting your time." He held up a manila envelope. "She gave me this and I threw it in the trash, then I fished it out again. Recognize it?"

"The photographs of Kevin Dixon I got from Jenny's mom's," said George sadly.

"Do they mean anything to you at all? Look carefully."

George took the envelope and slipped the photographs out again, the bearded man with skis, the man on the couch; the photographs that had taken five hours of his time, at Ruth's urging, to get. "Nothing," he said. "They don't mean anything. Smoke and mirrors. I guess that's the point."

"What point?" said Stuart. He paused. "But maybe you never saw him. I forget you've never spent much time in Dudley. I didn't realize it till today, but he came back. He was *here* one night, in front of my office."

"Who? Kevin Dixon?"

"Yes. Dressed like a tourist, camera and everything. He even asked me about goddamn *architecture.* I recognized his voice, you know, *subliminally,* but he looked so different I didn't make the connection."

"You already knew Kevin?" said George in surprise.

"Yes but I didn't know I knew him. It wasn't till later I had a sense of something screwy, but I thought it was something I'd read in his file."

twenty-two

THE SUN SHONE on the golfers in their bright microfiber clothing; it shone on their metal carts and sticks and on their little white dimpled balls lying on the green, wasteful grass. The man in the tangerine-colored polo shirt parked the red Volkswagen, a birthday present two years ago, on the street of pink stucco town houses and got out, smiling.

It was good he'd decided to stop taking the meds again. He was so clear today, remembering old friends, too many to remember them all, but they'd brought flowers and gifts to his grave, stacked them up, *he had pictures.* He had mingled with the tourists, just another wave in the sea, and also taken pictures of the lawyer's office and the Co-op and the post office and Frieda's house. Frieda. His best friend. In his polos and khakis, he'd passed her once going to the post office and she'd never blinked an eye.

He wished he could tell his mother the whole story, but he knew she wouldn't allow herself to understand, and besides, she'd just come home from the hospital. He would tend her like a good son. He would devote himself to her for as long as she lived; that would be something new, something good. The sun shone down on the pink stucco houses. It was a good day. A police car drove slowly down the street by him, patrolling the neighborhood, and he waved at the officer inside. The officer waved back at him. And why not? He was wearing his tangerine-colored polo shirt and khakis. People believed you or not because of clothes, that's all it took was clothes.

Down the way, a few houses past his mother's, a man got out of a big yellow old-fashioned Cadillac. He wore a blue-and-green-striped shirt, a bolo tie, jeans, and cowboy boots. He didn't quite fit in. Probably going to see *his* mother. The man in the cowboy boots walked toward him, limping a bit, a big smile on his face.

Another police car drove slowly by. Or maybe the same one as before. He couldn't remember which side the other one had been on, which direction it was going, though it was probably a pretty easy equation. *Equation?*

"Kevin Dixon?" said the man wearing the bolo tie.

He blinked. "Yes."

The man's hand came up; he felt it squeezing his shoulder.

"Name's George Maynard," said the man in a friendly way. "I'm an investigator for an attorney in Dudley, Stuart Ross. I think he was your lawyer once."

"Not mine," said Kevin Dixon.

"I just have a couple of questions." The man let go of his shoulder and took his arm. "Let's take a walk down to my car. Don't want to get your mom upset."

"Not mine," Kevin said again as the man took him down the street. "Mr. Ross is not my lawyer. He's the Magician's lawyer. I'm Kevin Dixon."

"Your lawyer says *you're* the Magician," said George Maynard. "He recognized you from some photographs, and I guess your voice, too. It doesn't pay to fool your lawyer. And Jenny Williams is your sister."

"I walked over the mountains to her house," said Kevin. "She never let me come around except at night when her husband wasn't home because she was ashamed of me. But deep down, she loved me from when we were kids, playing games."

"And you loved her?"

"I loved her," Kevin Dixon said, "every way you can love a person. I was thirteen and she was seven but I loved her like grown-ups love each other."

"Ah," said George.

"She said it was *wrong,* that she'd tell Ken Dooley all about me if I didn't take my meds, and he'd put it in the newspaper how much I loved her when we were kids," Kevin said. He looked at George confidingly. "I have my own kind of meds—if I really concentrate on thinking things *three times* it blocks all the bad stuff. But she said that was stupid. And she wanted me to go with her to a counselor to talk about everything."

"Ah," said George again.

"Counselors won't talk to you unless you're taking meds, but when I take them everything's so sad, it hurts. I wanted to just be me, my real self. But I started taking them, for her." He glanced at George. "But I still acted like my real self around my friends, so they would keep on liking me. *Frieda.*"

"And then what happened?"

"The meds made me understand what Jenny *really* wanted."

"What was that?"

"She wanted to die, of course. Jenny wanted to die so much."

Two days, two whole days George had spent staking out Grace Dixon's place, hoping Kevin would show. Two days of smoking too many cigarettes, peeing in a jar, drinking bad coffee, and eating takeout. His left hip felt permanently stiff.

Now he stared at Kevin Dixon. He hadn't thought it would be so easy. "Jenny wanted to die," he said cautiously. "Why is that?"

"He made her so unhappy her life wasn't any good anymore."

"Sure," said George. "I can see your point. But most folks, if they feel that way, they just get a divorce."

"No. She didn't have the strength."

"So why was it again she made you take the meds?"

"She said it was because of the counselor but she never even made an appointment so I knew that wasn't really why." Kevin's eyes jittered away from George. "I had to be clear to help. She couldn't do it on her own."

"Do what?"

"Die. She couldn't die. She cried all the time but she couldn't die. I took the poison stuff from—from—Fri—Frieda's." He stopped. "Just in case. And then—*she told Sid* about us when we were kids." His eyes jittered some more. "She said he wouldn't tell but he *threw me out of his house*. And I think he told see-bus about me. I heard someone walking on the path to my cave and it had to be that see-bus lady coming with my meds."

"So Sid had to go, too, huh?" said George.

"It was the meds." His voice rose. "They weren't good. They made me cold. Cold and—and *thoughtful*. And I really didn't need them—I had to put on an act instead of being myself. I dumped out Sid and Jenny's capsules and put some of that powder in. I put the rest of it in a bottle I found with her husband's name on it and put it under the bed so they would blame it on him. It was the right thing to do because he's the one who really killed her."

"Not exactly," said George. "Those meds, you taking them now?"

"Coming off," said Kevin. "She shouldn't have told Sid, and she was going to tell Ken Dooley, too, but Jackson was the one who killed her. I was just the *agent*." His voice rose, his eyes jittering wildly. "You ask my mother. She'll tell you the same thing. Jackson killed Jenny." He backed away. "I have to go now. My mother needs me. I'm wearing my best polo shirt just for her." He tugged at the front, stretching it out.

"Uh," said George, "I thought we could go for a little ride first, over to the police station."

"The police station?"

"Sure. It's comfortable there. You can tell your story again. It's a good story. Everybody will be interested."

"My best polo," said Kevin. "Polo, polo, polo."

twenty-three

"JENNY SAID HER brother was molested as a kid," said Ruth sadly, "when it was herself she was talking about. I think maybe she wasn't really so concerned about Owen and my boys—she just wanted to bring up the *topic*. But I was so mad I just turned off on her. She might have told me everything, if I'd let her talk."

"And if we had some apple pie, we could have pie à la mode, if we had some ice cream," said Stuart. "What's the point in beating yourself up about it?"

"At least Kevin confessed." She sighed. "Now it's simple."

"Simple!" said Stuart. "Ha! A confession means nothing. The guy was a babbling idiot by the time George got him to the police station."

"Maybe," said Ruth. "You never read the workup SEABHS did, did you?"

"Scanned it."

"Well, I *read* it. I've got it here. One of the things the psychologist said was" she read out loud, "'this guy is all over the map. I can't get a reading on him and I suspect possible *malingering*.'"

"*Possible* malingering," said Stuart. "His mom has money—for every shrink that finds possible malingering, there's another that will say there isn't."

"So what's going to happen?"

"His mom will get him some hotshot Tucson lawyer, and the first thing that lawyer's going to do is file a Rule Eleven."

"What's that?" asked Ruth.

"Motion to determine competency to stand trial," said Stuart. "The court will appoint an expert for the state and one for the defense to determine competency. If he's found not competent, they'll send him to a hospital, pump him full of pharmaceuticals. If and when he's restored to competency the case goes forward."

"How *stupid*," said Ruth.

"It's the law."

"I don't care, it's still stupid."

Stuart shrugged out of his jacket and hung it on a hook. He took off his tie and unbuttoned his shirt collar. "I'm taking the afternoon off," he said. "You can close up here if you want."

"Then I will," said Ruth. "I have a lot to do. Don't forget tonight," she called as he went out the door. "Jackson's welcome home party."

Stuart left his office and sauntered down Main Street, dodging tourists, headed for the Quarter Moon Café. It was late for lunch, so the place wouldn't be packed. He passed the Cornucopia, the post office, and the Mining Museum and reached the café. Aha. The not so faded blonde was working the tables. She had a nice smile, and she was well into her thirties, not *that* young. He wondered if she was married.

"Jackson's still sleeping," said Ruth, "and I'm making a list for the party. Mara and Tyler are going to the store."

"Steaks would be good," said George.

"Steaks?"

"Sure. Save you some work. I can grill a steak like nobody's business. Salt, pepper, a little Worcestershire. I'm partial to rib-eyes myself."

"I could do baked potatoes in the oven," said Ruth. "But maybe takeout potato salad would be better. I don't know. Do you think people would mind takeout stuff?"

"Naw. It's your party. People eat what you give them. Ruth?"

"What?"

"Your ex." George cleared his throat. "All those years you were married, you didn't know?"

Ruth sighed. "I think, every now and then, deep down, I did. We had friends, male friends, that Owen would get all bright and shiny around. But I never let it reach my consciousness. I guess I was selfish, just wanted to hang on to what I had."

"Selfish." George took her hand. "I don't think so."

"I had a boyfriend in high school," said Ruth, "and then Owen. There was someone a few years ago, but it wasn't much. I don't . . . I'm kind of . . . nervous."

"It's nice, holding hands," said George. "I can handle a lot of hand holding, at least for a couple of years."

Ruth giggled. "You were so *mad* at me," she said in a rush. "Like you didn't trust me. Like I'd done something wrong."

George sighed, looking out at Ruth's backyard, at the bird feeder and the apricot tree, at the half-built shed.

"You know," he said, "I got tools. I could finish that shed easy in a couple of weekends."

"You didn't answer my question."

"I guess it was more me," he said. "I didn't trust my own luck, that anything good could happen to me anymore."

A little breeze scattered the leaves around the apricot tree.

"What if the wind picks up?" Ruth said. "Won't it be hard to grill if it's windy?"

"You worry too much. Worry, worry, worry." He looked down at her fondly. "You could take a break sometime, Ruth, let me do your worrying for you."

An alcoholic, thought Ruth. He'd said he was an alcoholic. What if he started drinking again? What if . . .

THERE HAD BEEN a flurry of welcome when Stuart had brought Jackson home in the late afternoon yesterday. A banner had hung from his door, WE LOVE YOU, JACKSON. He hadn't touched another human being for a long time, and there were Ruth, Tyler, and Mara waiting by the front gate, all talking at once, all hugging him; Ruth, Tyler, Mara. His daughter. He'd imagined all kinds of conversations with her, but he'd felt shy. He didn't know her. What to do. What to say.

"There's Million Dollar Chicken in your refrigerator," said Ruth. "We're saving the official welcome home party for tomorrow. And I thought we could get hold of a cot, put it in the exercise room so Mara can move in with you after the party."

Tyler tugged on his arm. "*C'mon.* You have to play basketball."

Mara played basketball, too, the three of them outside in the driveway as the sun started to go down, until finally Jackson started to stumble, missing all his shots, and Ruth came out of the house.

"Go home," she said to him. "Get some sleep. We'll all be here in the morning."

He felt as though he hadn't slept in a hundred years. Exhausted, he'd gone home, walking blindly through the house to the bedroom, where he fell into bed. But the room with its oak bedside tables, its lamps with red-fringed shades, had seemed too crowded, the king-sized bed too large and too soft. He'd spent a restless, uncomfortable night. Near morning he'd finally slept, far into the day.

Now he stood in his living room, staring blankly at the beige couch, the decorative pillows in tan and terra-cotta, the terra-cotta-colored wing chair. There was the carved wooden screen that Jenny had bought at Cost Plus World Market. The screen was from some Far Eastern country, maybe Thailand or Indonesia, places Jackson had never been. On the coffee table were the round brass tray and the brass jar from India that Jenny had bought at Cost Plus, too.

I'll give it all away, he thought—*no, yard sale, then take the money and get different stuff. I'm pretty broke; it'll have to be from the Salvation Army, a couple of old couches. Get rid of the brass, but maybe keep the coffee table—we can put the board on it when Ruth and Tyler come over to play Scrabble.*

He left the living room, walking through his house from room to room, touching things. A thin layer of dust coated everything. He went to his office, picked up the marble-covered notebook Stuart had brought him in jail, and moved from there to the kitchen.

He had always liked writing in kitchens the best, even in this kitchen where the turquoise canisters too exactly matched the dish towels and the hand-painted tile of the counters. But whenever he'd tried writing here, Jenny would come in and interrupt. He opened the notebook, page after page scrawled with writing he'd rendered almost illegible in his haste to get it all down.

There was more, too, not yet written down. In Stuart's truck coming home, he'd thought a lot about Jenny, when he'd first met her, skiing down a hill like a butterfly floating, alighting right in front of him. He would save that Jenny, pin her down with words, make her live, if not forever then a little longer.

But it would have to wait a little while. He closed the book, stood, and went back to the living room and looked out the window. He could see Ruth's place from here, dear Ruth. Mara and Tyler must be back. Earlier he'd seen them drive off in Ruth's car, and now her car was parked in the driveway again, behind the yellow Cadillac that belonged to a man he'd never seen before. Ruth was with him now, coming around the side of the house. They were holding hands.

So much had changed already; different people lived next door now. They were all getting ready for his welcome home party. In a couple of hours he would shower, put on clean clothes, and walk over to Ruth's. Mara would be there, his daughter, the daughter he didn't know yet, but would. *I guess,* he thought, *we'll talk. And talk and talk and talk.*

o　　　o　　　o

UGLY CINDER-BLOCK WALLS, painted pale green. Bright fluorescent lights. A babble of voices. Men in orange jumpsuits sat in the row of chairs in front of the glass in the visiting room. All the jumpsuits weren't orange, he corrected himself. Some were orange and white stripes; a few were red. The Magician shuffled to an empty chair and sat down.

She sat behind the plate glass window, holding a phone, wearing a blouse covered with flowers. Her hair was braided into two circles around her ears where silver earrings dangled, but her lined face was plain and pure. *A nun,* he thought, as he picked up the phone, *a beautiful nun.*

"Hello, Frieda," he said.

She smiled. "Hello."

"Thank you for coming," he said.

"I brought you the yellow yo-yo," she said. Tears came to her eyes. "But they took it away from me."

"That's okay. It's good to have a visitor."

"You're so different now," said Frieda.

"I have to take my meds all the time. They watch to make sure." He paused. "Does that mean you don't like me?"

"I didn't mean it that way. I'll always like you," she said. "You're still you."

There was a silence. Frieda sniffed, produced a Kleenex, and blew her nose. "I'll come see you every week," she said. "I promise."

"They're going to take me away from here pretty soon," he said. "To a hospital in Tucson."

"Tucson." Her eyes got bright. "I have a friend now, Jack, who goes to Tucson all the time to see his grandchildren. I can easily come see you in Tucson."

He nodded. "That would be nice." He looked down at the floor, then looked up again. "I guess they probably told you. I'm not a good person. The things I did."

She smiled again. Frieda, Frieda, Frieda. There was nothing in her smile that was hidden, held back.

"We're all God's children," she said.